PASSION'S PRISONER

She hadn't really thought he would do it. The joke was on her. He twisted one arm behind her back and closed the metal cuff until the iron encircled her wrist, then did the same with the other. He turned her to face him again, this time more gently.

Every nerve in her body was taut. How dare he think he could still arouse her? She wanted to spit in his face but did nothing, waiting for his next move. Let him see what a miserable man he was. Let him be sorry for what he'd done to her.

He didn't seem sorry at all. He rested his palms on her shoulders, then slid them down her arms to the cuffs at her wrists. When his arms were around her, he pulled her forward, forcing her snugly against him.

"Some men wouldn't be bothered that you were handcuffed. In fact, seeing you bound would only add to the excitement." His gaze was hooded, his voice lowered. "You might like it too. Being helpless. Being able to do nothing while I ran my hands over your body, spread your legs."

She wanted to tell him she'd rather die than let him touch her again, but she was hanging on his every word. Her breath pushed hot and heavy through her nostrils.

He ran his hands back up to her shoulders, then gripped her hard enough to force a gasp. "The question is, am I that kind of man?"

CHERYL HOWE

AFTER THE ASHES

LEISURE BOOKS NEW YORK CITY

To Russ,
who believed in me before I believed in myself.

A LEISURE BOOK®

March 2003

Published by

Dorchester Publishing Co., Inc.
276 Fifth Avenue
New York, NY 10001

ISBN 0-8439-5173-7

The name "Leisure Books" and the stylized "L" with design are trademarks of Dorchester Publishing Co., Inc.

Printed in the United States of America.

Visit us on the web at www.dorchesterpub.com.

AFTER THE ASHES

Chapter One

New Mexico Territory, 1872

Christopher Braddock crept across the dilapidated porch, his pistol cocked. He wrapped himself around the bleached adobe as silently as his shadow. To kill the man inside was not his goal; he needed information more than another bounty.

The battered door jerked open.

Every muscle in Braddock's body tensed. It looked like he wasn't going to get his wish. As usual.

A woman poked her head out the narrow gap between wood and adobe. "Can I help you?" Her strained smile wobbled at the cocked .44 Smith & Wesson shoved in her face.

Braddock's heart thumped in his ears. He would beat the boy within an inch of his young life for sending a woman out to confront him. How quickly he could have shot her made his palms sweat. He eased his finger from the trigger, not trusting his wet grip, before he lowered his gun and straightened.

He nudged his hat back with his left hand. "Looking for Corey Sullivan."

1

The woman glanced again at his pistol and swallowed. "He's not here."

She lied badly. Must not be accustomed to the outlaw life yet. He glanced over the top of her head and tried to peer inside the adobe. She kept herself carefully squeezed between door and frame. He reholstered his gun, hoping to relax anyone inside. He didn't want a shoot-out with a woman in the middle. He didn't want a shoot-out at all.

"You might want to open those windows. Catch a breeze."

"I'm fine, thank you. I'm sensitive to the sun."

"You're a Southerner. Haven't been out here long."

"Two weeks. If there's nothing else, I'll say good-day. I have chores to attend."

"A Southerner with no hospitality? If I didn't know better, I might think you were hiding something."

"Well, I'm not." The woman slipped out past the door and shut it behind her. "I just don't have anything to offer. I haven't bought supplies yet."

She wore a faded gray dress that stretched tight across her chest and hung loose around her waist. Her pale skin and lush dark hair attested to a better life. She looked to be one of those women who wore a bonnet all the time, who didn't take to hard work, but the tired lines around her bright blue eyes told a different story. Still, she was a beauty. Way too good for an outlaw on the run. But who could figure women?

She shifted, growing more nervous under his scrutiny. He wasn't beyond using that to his advantage. "Well, ma'am, I'd say you've plenty to offer a man."

She played with the frayed lace on the high neckline of her gown, keeping her arm in front of herself in a protective gesture. Braddock didn't like how her hand trembled, nor being the cause of it. He glanced over at the water pump. "Me and my horse could use a drink."

She sagged in relief. "Of course." She released her breath in a nervous bubble of laughter that sounded as sweet as it was unexpected.

Braddock stopped himself from smiling. This wasn't a social call.

The woman veered around him to step off the low porch. Braddock hesitated. His path to the door cleared, but one quick glance at the woman let him know he wouldn't get far without her.

She rushed back the moment he didn't follow, gesturing for him to proceed her. "This way."

A bumbling outlaw and a determined woman were a bad combination. With Braddock's luck, both Sullivan and this woman would end up in a pool of their own blood. An imagined glimpse of red splattered across her white skin prompted him to step down into the yard.

He didn't let his back turn completely toward the adobe, but the precaution was unnecessary. The woman shadowed his movements, making herself a shield against any bullets foolish enough to fly his way. He picked up Lucky's reins and walked to the pump.

The woman glided across the red dirt of her barren front yard. She must have been something before the war. Unlike the rest of her people, she didn't act broken. She held her shoulders high. When his gaze strayed to her hips, Braddock forced his attention back to the wanted man inside the house. "You forgot your bonnet, ma'am. Sun's mighty strong this part of the day. If you want, I can go fetch it for you."

"No." She faltered in her step. "Please, I'm sure you're thirsty and I don't want to make you wait any longer."

She raced to the pump and urgently worked the handle. Braddock took over the job, though she appeared to know what she was doing. She might have been used to a better life, but she seemed to have adjusted to her new situation.

He sipped the cool water from a ladle while Lucky drank from a shallow trough.

"You married?"

She glanced away. "No."

He hadn't thought so. "How'd you hook up with a piss-poor outlaw like Sullivan?"

"I don't know who you're talking about."

"Thought you said he wasn't here."

3

She glanced at him for a moment, but she couldn't hold the eye contact. "I'm here by myself."

Her face paled. Braddock followed her eyes and saw a man's fresh boot print in the mud-splattered dirt, and faint signs of blood. Sullivan had been at this pump not long ago. He ducked his head to study the woman's downcast face.

"This is a bad place for you to be by yourself," he said. "I guess you know the folks who built this spread were murdered by Apaches."

"Those were bloodstains on the walls?"

"I imagine. What kind of man would let you stay in a place like this alone?"

She finally met his gaze, and Braddock glimpsed the spunk that had kept this woman's shoulders high despite the war. "You're the biggest danger I've encountered. You almost shot me when I stepped outside."

Braddock ran his hand over Lucky's muzzle. He didn't like being reminded. "You could go to jail for helping a murderer like Sullivan."

"That's not true!"

"It's true, all right. Maybe even hang." That wasn't true. Nobody was going to put a rope around this girl's pretty neck even if her lover had gotten himself tangled up with the lowest of outlaws.

"No. I mean Corey wouldn't murder anyone."

"Thought you said you didn't know him."

She folded her arms over her chest in a huff, working herself up again. "Well, I do. And he wouldn't hurt anyone."

"Sweetheart, men have a dark side, and I hope you don't find that out the hard way."

She didn't back down, not a lick. She jutted her chin out and her eyes sparked blue fire. "You might be talking about yourself, sir, but you aren't talking about Corey."

"Well, I just might be talking about myself. That doesn't change the fact your lover's a killer. He rides with killers and he's going to hang with them, too."

Her chin dropped a notch. "You're mistaken."

Braddock leaned on the pump and lowered his voice. "I

can help you get out of here. If you need money, I can buy you a ticket home. Just leave Sullivan before it costs you your life."

"I have no home. Corey is my life." She stared at Braddock dead-on. "You're wrong about him."

"They robbed a stagecoach carrying payroll for the railroad. Killed every last driver doing it. Some powerful men want to see them caught. They're going to be coming around after me, and they won't stop and talk. They'll burst through your door, guns blazing. Do you understand that?"

She blinked hard and turned her pretty face away from him. "Please leave now."

"Do you want to die, lady?"

She moved toward the adobe. "Just go, please. Corey's not here."

He grabbed her arm before she was out of reach. "What is it going to take to make you see you're helping a murderer?"

She stiffened. "All I see is that you've forgotten yourself, sir."

Braddock released his grip, jerking his hand back with the swiftness of a rattler's strike. Her tone was as good as a slap. He barely resisted the urge to check over his shoulder to see if anyone had caught him mishandling a woman. Then he clenched his jaw, reminding himself that being a gentleman only got you killed. He shook off her reprimand as he had his lessons from West Point. There were no rules to break out here. No social graces. She too would learn that soon enough. But he, for one, didn't have the time or the inclination to teach her. Why should he care if she destroyed her life by helping Corey Sullivan?

He took off his hat and slapped it against his leg. "He won't get away."

"This is all a big mistake. You've mixed Corey up with someone else." She stepped back up onto the porch, eager to escape once more into her house.

"Maybe you don't know the man like you thought."

The woman blocked the door with her body. If Braddock wanted to capture Sullivan, he would have to plow through her. He'd give the kid some breathing room instead. Once he backed off, Sullivan was sure to trip up and fall into his hands—or better yet, lead him exactly where he wanted to go.

"I'm not going away. I'll spend the night in Arriba, but I'll be back. I'll find Sullivan no matter where he tries to hide."

"Not if I can help it, you won't."

"What did he ever do to make you so damned loyal? Nothing as far as I can see."

"He's my brother. He doesn't have to do anything."

Surprise filled Braddock. The sensation hadn't touched him in so long, it took him a minute to figure it out. A jolt of dread followed, tightening his gut for this foolish woman who thought she could stand so tall and proud. One hard shove and she'd crumble like the regiments of her slain kinsmen buried beneath the South's fertile fields. For a moment he almost believed Sullivan was her brother, that she was acting out of familial loyalty. Then he remembered pure nobility existed only in theory. He sure as hell had never seen it.

He mounted his horse. "Tell your *brother* I'll be seeing him."

Riding away, he wasn't sure if he had just met the stupidest woman in the West, or the bravest.

Lorelei Sullivan waited for the stranger to vanish before she sagged against her door, unsure of how she'd found the courage to face him. The man was a big hulking omen of death if she'd ever seen one. Dressed in muted shades of black and brown, mounted atop his blood bay, he'd appeared carved from the desolate landscape. With the sun making a curtain of heat rise from the red earth, he'd seemed to melt back from where he came. At least he was gone. Unfortunately, she had no doubt she'd see him again.

She tried to push open the front door, but it didn't budge.

"Corey, let me in. He's gone." She banged her palm on the barrier's splintered surface. "Let me in, Corey Lochlain O'Sullivan."

Wood scraped against wood as he lifted the log blocking her entrance. Corey kept himself wedged in the shadows. "You sound like Ma."

She shoved the door wide, forcing him to step back. "I ought to whip you like Ma. What was that about? Did you hear the things that man was saying?"

Corey's gaze didn't meet hers. When he swayed, she noticed the blood pooling on the top of his bare foot. A dusty black boot covered the other. A second drip splattered onto the dirt floor. She followed the trail to the tip of his pinky. The wound on his arm must have opened. She stopped berating him long enough to guide him through the room to the knotted pine bed shoved in the corner.

"You shouldn't have tried to get dressed."

He sank onto the bed's tangled blankets. "I had to. I was afraid he was going to hurt you."

"He didn't."

Corey pushed himself up on his elbows, his eyes wide. "No, huh? I think he liked you, Lori."

"I wouldn't say that." She doubted the man liked anyone. His appearance certainly didn't invite getting acquainted. He looked like he should be the one on a wanted poster.

"I would say he liked you plenty. Didn't you notice?"

"I notice you've lost too much blood. You're delirious." She yanked off her brother's boot. "Who is he anyway? The sheriff?"

"Worse. He hunts down men with bounties on their heads. Doesn't care how he gets his man, either. He's been on my tail for days. Thought I gave him the slip." Corey sighed. "Guess not."

Lorelei covered him with a red-and-black Indian blanket. His eyes drifted shut as he settled deeper into the straw-stuffed mattress. But as much as he needed to rest and heal, she couldn't let him slip off yet.

"Why is he following you? You didn't really get thrown from your horse, did you?"

"That part's true." Her brother opened his eyes. "I did get thrown from my horse, but after I got shot."

Lorelei rubbed her temples. She'd thought the gash in Corey's arm looked too severe to have been caused by brushing a cactus. "Please tell me you didn't rob those people and kill—"

"No!" He sprang to a sitting position and gripped her shoulders. "I swear on Ma's grave I didn't kill anyone."

Lorelei pressed him back down. "So what did you do to get shot?"

He slung his forearm across his eyes. "You don't understand what it's like here, Lorelei. A man will shoot you for just looking at him cross-eyed."

"Then why did you let me come? You should have moved home instead." The nights she'd spent curled up with a kitchen knife, jumping at every howl and screech, had not been overreaction. This land was dangerous. "And what about the Indians killing the people who lived here. Is that true?"

Corey let his arm flop to his side. "They've taken care of the Apaches since then. Don't worry about that." He eased himself up until his back rested against the bed's rough headboard, pushed a shutter open, and stared out the window. "Sure, this land's dangerous, but it's beautiful and exciting, too. A man can make something of himself out here. Doesn't matter who you were before or who your father was."

Lorelei followed his gaze. Dirt, rocks, and knee-high shrubs that looked more dead than alive stretched farther than she could walk in a day. Only a distant mountain range, black and bare, broke up the sea of gray-green brush. This strange, barren place made her shudder. Still, she understood Corey's need to be free of Kentucky.

"Is this really your ranch, Corey?"

"It's our ranch. It's going to be great once we get some horses." He grabbed her hand and held it. "Hey, how was your trip out? I feel awful about not making Ma's funeral."

Lorelei squeezed his fingers. Her brother's shared grief gave her a moment's peace. After her mother's death, the hope of finding comfort with her only sibling had given her the strength to sell their family's possessions and secure a passage west. They'd had time to do little more than bandage his wound before that stranger had come riding out of the dust.

"First, I need to know what's going on. Why does that man think you did all those horrible things?"

Corey stared up at the beamed ceiling. "I wanted the ranch to be nice for you. You deserve to have it easy after taking care of Ma by yourself."

Lorelei recognized his stalling as an attempt to soften the blow that was sure to follow. She made her voice stern. "What did you do, Corey?"

He toyed with the fringe on the woven blanket. "I was with the men who robbed the stagecoach."

"Corey." She pinched the bridge of her nose. "What were you thinking?"

"I didn't know what they were going to do. I met this fella, Rowen Mulcahy, and he took a liking to me because I had an Irish name. I was kind of bragging about how I knew horses and how fast I can ride, and he said he needed a man like me." He reached for her hand. "I swear I didn't know they were going to kill anyone. I swear it."

She folded her arms over her chest, keeping herself out of his reach. "Who shot you?"

He stared out the window again, but it was clear he no longer enjoyed the view. "One of the men on the stagecoach. There was a lot of shooting going on."

Lorelei could tell by the way his soft brown eyes dulled that he spoke the truth. Whatever had happened shook him just to think of it.

"Where are the other men you were with? Were they caught?"

"I don't think so. I don't know for sure. I think Mulcahy was shot pretty bad. Might be dead. All I know is that when the shooting started, I took off. Hid for a night or two, thinking I was dead for sure. But after a while I had to find some food and water. That's when I first knew I was being trailed."

"I think we should go to the authorities and try to clear your name."

"No." He swung his legs over the bed's side. "No authorities. They'll just lynch me."

She gripped his shoulder to keep him from standing. "I don't believe that. Surely there is someone who will listen to you."

He brushed her hand aside and got to his feet. "The only thing I can do is hide till this blows over. There's lots of killing and robbing in New Mexico territory. Somebody will do something worse soon, and then they'll forget all about me."

"That man who came today won't forget."

Corey dropped a saddlebag he'd grabbed and sagged into a chair at the table. "I don't know how he figured out who I am. I was hoping it wasn't him, but after today I know it is. He won't let me get away."

Lorelei perched in the chair across from him. "You know him?"

"Know of him. His name's Braddock. Someone pointed him out to me once. You don't want to get on his bad side, the fella told me. He doesn't like Southerners, neither. He's all messed up from the war."

"But if we can convince him you're innocent—"

"If we can't, he'll take me straight to Santa Fe and they'll hang me for sure."

"I don't know how we're going to get you out of this one, Corey."

"Maybe you can talk to him for me."

Lorelei secured a pin in the heavy bun pulling at the back of her head. The thought of facing the man called Braddock again forced her heart to race. Even the beginnings of a beard couldn't hide his rugged good looks. His dark eyes had assessed her with a detached lust that both touched her physically and warned her she'd be no match for him. Which he knew.

"I already talked to him. He doesn't seem too fond of listening."

"You can go to his hotel room and talk to him. He might listen then."

Her fingers froze. "What are you asking, Corey Sullivan?"

"It worked on Berkley Ellard, didn't it?"

She slowly lowered her arms. The mere mention of Berkley's name popped the bubble of guilt she always carried in the center of her chest. "That was different. Berkley knew you. Besides, a crooked game of cards doesn't hold a candle to what you've been accused of. That Braddock fellow thinks you're a murderer."

Corey abandoned his chair to kneel beside her. "I saw the way he looked at you. And you don't even look that good right now. If you pretty yourself up like the old days, he'll listen to anything you have to say. I know it."

She tried to look indignant rather than shamefaced. She wasn't that same silly girl anymore. And Braddock could easily use her weakness against her. He had to have noted her nervous fluttering in his presence.

"What exactly are you asking me to do?"

"Nothing. Just stall for time. Sweet-talk him." Corey stood.

Lorelei ran her hand over the table's gouged surface. She held no power over men. Berkley had taught her that, and Braddock stirred her in a way that Berkley never had, even while he terrified her. But she had to do something.

"Do you know what he'll think if I show up at his hotel room dressed in some low-cut evening gown? He'll think I'm delivering myself to him on a silver platter."

Corey slid behind her and rubbed her shoulders, a sure sign he thought he might be getting his way. "You can handle him. I saw how you set him back when he grabbed your arm. He'll be the perfect gentleman in your hands, Lorelei."

She doubted Braddock even knew what a gentleman was. And even if he did, how could she expect him to behave like one if she wantonly showed up at his hotel room, alone, asking for a favor? "Corey, I can't do what you ask. It's not proper. Ma wouldn't approve, and she's not cold in her grave yet."

"If you don't stop him, he's going to hunt me down and they're going to hang me. Don't you think Ma would want you to save my life if you could?"

The only thing worse than having her only daughter turn into a harlot would be having her only surviving son, her baby, harmed. Lorelei braced her elbows on the table and covered her eyes with her fingers. "It's not going to work. I can't convince him to stop chasing you."

"Just keep him occupied. While you're talking to him I can sneak away. I know a place where I can heal up; then maybe we can figure out what to do. I just need to get him off my trail, Lorelei, or there's no hope at all."

She peeked through her fingers. Corey watched her, his brown eyes shining like sunlight on a sorrel's groomed coat, the color returning to his cheeks. She was the one who felt sick.

"I'll do it," she agreed.

When he opened his mouth to thank her, she stopped him. "I'm going to find out what he knows about those other men. I still think you should go to the authorities and tell them you weren't a part of the robbery."

A grin wobbled at the corners of his mouth, but when he limped back to the bed, her brother grimaced dramatically enough to assure Lorelei he wasn't as injured as he wanted her to believe.

"It's your arm that's hurt, Corey."

He cradled the arm she reminded him of as he sank onto the bed. "I'll clear my name with the law as soon as things calm down and folks aren't so hanging mad. I never wanted to be an outlaw, just a horse breeder."

Lorelei folded her arms over her chest, feeling duped. Their mother would claim being an outlaw and a horse breeder were one and the same; Lorelei didn't even want to think what she would say about the undertaking to which her daughter had just agreed.

Chapter Two

Braddock leaned against the cool iron headboard, and rubbed his hand over his freshly shaven face. He had forgotten how good it felt to be clean. The long, hot bath in itself had been worth the ride into Arriba. A sound night's sleep on a soft bed wouldn't hurt, either. He shifted his shoulders until his hard angles melted into the mattress beneath him, but the unknotting of his stiff back didn't do a thing for the nick in his pride left by that thorny flower of Southern womanhood.

The way she'd stood there—high and mighty, all the while he could tell she quaked in her boots—made him feel something he hadn't in a long time: like it was his duty to protect her. His honor-bound oath. But he had lost his taste for oaths and honor during the long war to preserve the Union. He'd done more hacking apart than preserving.

And as well as she put on the proper-lady act, he knew Sullivan wasn't her brother. No man would expect his sister to fight his battles. In Braddock's experience, family didn't work like that. They didn't help each other without something to gain. So what did this woman have to gain by protecting Sullivan? A wedding ring perhaps, or maybe part of the gold.

Braddock pushed himself off the bed. He pulled a clean shirt from his saddlebag and tugged its well-worn, black cotton over his shoulders, but left it unbuttoned. He hadn't done the woman a favor by letting her believe she'd succeeded in protecting Sullivan by standing up to him. She'd be in for a very unpleasant surprise if she tried to stand up to Mulcahy.

Caring what happened to a silly woman increased his strong desire to march to the saloon and get blind drunk. He hadn't given a damn about anything in a long time and he wanted to keep it that way. The sky turned purple outside, painting the wood-framed buildings that lined Arriba's one street deep blue. Braddock lay back on his bed. He wasn't going anywhere. Not tonight. He didn't feel like sitting outside Sullivan's place while the outlaw and the woman were inside doing things Braddock refused to imagine, but did every time he closed his eyes. He shifted, suddenly feeling all the lumps in the mattress.

A soft knock at the door brought Braddock swiftly to his feet. He grabbed his pistol from the holster hanging over the room's only chair. Silently he slid across the room.

He eased the door open.

The woman from Sullivan's ranch stood in the hallway, clutching a pink satin bag. A lantern spilled light over her glossy dark hair and the pale skin exposed by her off-the-shoulder gown. A satin vee highlighted a low neckline, revealing some deep, purposely tempting cleavage. His gaze dropped briefly to a skirt with a dozen pink bows, but quickly returned to the shimmering band of ribbon that framed the gown's best feature. This was a package too pretty to resist.

He opened the door wider. Her appearance didn't surprise him, though he almost wished it did. The high-and-mighty act she'd regaled him with at the ranch ran shallow.

"What do you want?"

He stuck his gun in the front of his wool pants, where she could see. It caught her attention. Then her glance strayed to the swatch of bare chest exposed by his open shirt. She actually looked more horrified by the latter. She averted her gaze, her perusal not reaching his face. Her grip on her purse tightened.

"I'd like a moment of your time, Mr. Braddock, if I may?"

He raised his eyebrows, resisting the urge to laugh. She'd showed up at his hotel room in this outfit and had the nerve to act a mannered lady? He had every intention of telling her to drop the pretense, but the way she held herself, stiff and proper, stopped him. Or maybe it was just the amusement of playing such a silly game. He bowed slightly from the waist.

"Please, come in, Miss . . . ?"

She seemed to relax at his tone. Her waltz past the threshold rustled her rose-colored skirts, and a soft sigh escaped her lips. "Sullivan. Lorelei Sullivan." She limply offered him her dainty, gloved hand.

"Sullivan. Of course. Corey's sister." He cradled her fingers in his palm and pressed his lips to the satin in a whisper of a kiss.

She withdrew her hand, then fluttered deeper into his den, looking for a place to land. Braddock removed the globe from the kerosene lamp mounted to the wall. He used the matches tucked into a metal pocket beside the base to light its wick. Gently he shut the door, then turned the key in the lock.

She spun at the sound, then backed toward the window as if she had walked into a trap.

He stalked her, no longer content to play her game. But her tempting bait hovered over a dark hole. Before he bit, he intended to find out what lay in wait. If she planned to entice him to step in front of the window so her lover could get off a good shot, she was going about it all wrong. She would be the one who wound up hurt.

"Step away from the window."

She slid sideways, her back pressed against the wall. "If you like, I can wait outside while you finish dressing."

"Why? We both know you came here to get me undressed."

He put his hands on his hips, letting his open shirt fall back. He fondled her with his gaze, blatantly enjoying the

15

way her gown pushed up her breasts and cinched her waist. She definitely possessed the figure for this job she was doing.

"I came here to talk about Corey."

The woman's cheeks flamed and she practically choked on her words. She might have agreed to seduce him, but she obviously didn't like it. Braddock found himself angry. "Why did you let a man like Sullivan put you up to this? You're no whore. Not yet, anyway."

She raised her chin, finally meeting his gaze. "You don't know what I am. And Corey didn't put me up to this. He's innocent, and I have to make you believe that."

"Fine. Let's see what you can make me do." Steeling himself against compassion, he shrugged out of his shirt and tossed it over the foot of the bed. "Come here."

She flattened herself against the wall. "I just want to talk to you."

"I don't feel like talking."

She edged along the wall as if she were making her way toward the door . . . or his gun belt. In two swift steps he blocked her path. He draped the belt over his shoulder.

"Why don't I spare you from wrinkling your pretty dress. I'll go gather up your 'brother.' What do you say, Lorelei?"

"I can't let you do that."

"How do you intend to stop me?"

His heart beat too rapidly to just be testing her. He wanted her to try to change his mind. She inched toward him, but teetered to an abrupt halt a good two feet from where he stood. Barely within arm's length, she gingerly placed her palms on his waist. He covered her hands lightly with his own. He'd give her the chance to move them only if they roamed in a direction he wanted them to go. Lower—not in the vicinity of the gun belt hanging over his shoulder. His body tightened at the thought.

She appeared clueless of what he wanted. With the invisible chasm still separating them, she turned her face up to his and puckered tightly closed lips.

He'd given Lucky more passionate caresses. "You're joking, right?"

Her eyes fluttered open, then narrowed at his obvious un-interest in her chaste offer. "I must be. I'm here with you, aren't I?"

She tried to yank her hands away, but he held her to him.

"That's more like it. Let's put that feistiness to good use." He gripped her waist and jerked her against him. She flattened her palms on his chest. Her efforts to push him away only succeeded in pressing her hips more firmly against his as she leaned back with her upper body.

He bent his knees to take full advantage of her squirming. If she wanted to play at coming to a man's hotel room to save her lover, he'd give her a good game of it.

"Let me go."

"You'd do anything for Sullivan, wouldn't you? Well, if you want to keep me from going out and hauling him in, you're going to have to offer a lot more than a closed-mouth kiss."

"I'll kiss you, all right. You won't even know your own name when I'm through with you, but not with your weapon digging into me."

He grinned. Her innocent charade was as weak as her high-and-mighty number. "That's the way we do it out here, sweetheart. We skip hand-holding and walks in the moonlight."

"What if it goes off?"

He swallowed hard, swelling at her words. God, any more talk like that and he just might. How long had it been since he'd had a woman?

"It won't go off until you want it to, I promise."

He rubbed his hips against her to make his point.

"Um, I don't want to get my foot shot off, and I'm sure you don't want to risk . . ." She glanced down between them, clarifying her point.

The weapon she spoke of was the .44 Smith & Wesson still in the waistband of his pants. How had he forgotten a weapon within her immediate reach? As he grappled with his stupidity, she jerked from his grasp.

Forcing himself to go slowly, he slid the gun belt from his

shoulder and reholstered the revolver. He took a deep breath in through his nose and out through his mouth.

Before he lost his senses altogether, he hung the belt over the black iron headboard of the bed. He wanted to keep his guns within reach just in case Sullivan planned to drop in when things heated up. Set-up or not, his body ached for this release so obviously being offered. If this woman wanted to seduce him to keep him from going after Sullivan, he'd let her—at least until dawn. He could easily catch up with her lover later.

He turned to face her again, but she had widened the distance between them. The atmosphere in the room had cooled. Braddock regained his composure, suddenly realizing the only one who had been on the verge of losing control was him. The little vixen actually performed her job perfectly.

He'd change that. The teasing portion of their game of dangle-the-cheese had come to an end. No longer would he be the hungry mouse. If she wanted to sacrifice herself for Sullivan, he intended to feast.

He met her gaze and slowly unbuttoned the top of his trousers. She visibly shrank at the challenge. He sank into the straight-backed chair and spread his knees. He slapped his thighs twice: a demand for her to sit in his lap.

She took a deep breath and talked to his feet. "This is what happened. Corey ran into this fellow who was interested in a good horse trainer."

"I know what happened," Braddock snapped.

"I don't think you do, because you're mistaken when you accuse Corey of being part of the robbery. He didn't know anything about it."

"Then why was he wearing a bandanna over his face?"

Her gaze jerked up. "What?"

"Christ, you actually believe that bull he's been feeding you. Not all the men died right away. An eyewitness saw your Corey. Seems he was running a wicked card game a couple of nights earlier in a saloon near Santa Fe. The witness remembered him because Sullivan lost big after someone hinted he was cheating."

"He wouldn't shoot anyone." The woman flattened her palms against her belly as if she were in danger of losing its contents.

He stood and buttoned his pants. Her queasiness was contagious. Suddenly he didn't have the stomach to take advantage of such a naive woman.

"All I know is that men died, and Corey was riding with those that did the shooting." He grabbed his shirt and punched his arms through the sleeves before he faced her. "The one I really want is Mulcahy. If you can get Corey to tell me where he is, maybe I'll put in a good word for him."

"Can you get him out of trouble?"

"No, but I might be able to keep him from hanging."

"Might?"

"Maybe, maybe not. At best he'll be spending a good part of his life in prison."

"I can't take that kind of chance."

"You don't have a choice."

"Why can't you just go after this Mulcahy and leave Corey alone?"

"It doesn't work like that." Braddock bent to retrieve his boots. He'd pack his gear and pick up Sullivan's trail. If she had any sense, this woman would go home once Corey was in custody. She was in too much danger out here. In too much danger in this room.

He glanced at her over his shoulder. The expression on Lorelei's face was one of deep thought; then she captured his gaze by unhooking the satin vee bordering the neckline of her gown. The dress parted not even an inch, but it was enough to reveal the soft, round tops of her breasts, and her corset's lace trim. She looked even more nervous than before.

Braddock straightened, unable to stop staring. "Don't start this again, Lorelei. Quit offering something you don't intend to give."

"I'm desperate."

He let his boots drop to the floor. She sauntered toward

19

him, stopping much closer than before. At some point she'd peeled off her gloves, and her smooth, pale hands fascinated him. With shaky fingers she unbuttoned the trouser button he'd hastily redone. He inhaled sharply when her warm knuckles grazed his stomach.

"My father died just before the war; my two older brothers were killed the year after that. I buried my mother not two months ago. I'm not going to lose Corey, too."

She took a breath that lifted her breasts, and unfastened another button of his trousers. Her hand brushed lower on his belly, making him feel light-headed as all his blood rushed to meet her slender fingers. She looked up at him.

He saw desperation and determination in her shiny blue eyes. They said she'd been through hell and back, and she'd get through this, too.

"You don't want to do this, Lorelei." He encircled her wrist with his fingers but didn't pull her hand away. "Even if he is your brother, he's not worth it."

His words tasted bitter. If Lorelei's claim was true, it proved his own statement: her actions were all the more pathetic and Corey's all the more despicable. Sullivan would destroy his sister in the process of destroying himself. Braddock's rusty conscience protested against being a part of it. His body disagreed.

Lorelei moved her hand, with him still holding her wrist, and unbuttoned the third button of his trousers. Two remained, but he knew she wouldn't have to go that far. His body already swelled in response to her touch. He closed his eyes to block out the sight of her pale hand against his darker skin, fought the strong desire to feel her small fingers fold around him. If he didn't do something soon, he wouldn't have to wait much longer.

He gripped her under her arms and tossed her onto his bed. Before she could untangle from her skirts, he came down on top of her, balancing his weight on his elbows and his knees.

"How many men are you willing to fuck to save your brother?" He reached between them and squeezed her leg above the knee, then slid his hand up her thigh. "I'm not the only man after Corey. There'll be more. Is that the kind of life you want, Lorelei? Is Corey worth spending your life on your back?"

She didn't push him away as he expected. Instead she remained motionless, letting him move his hand all the way up to the crotch of her thin cotton drawers. He came so close to cupping her between her legs, he could feel the moist heat.

Believing the damp cloth had anything to do with desire for him would be his ruin. Stopping might have been impossible if it weren't for the tears filling her eyes.

"I don't know what else to do."

Braddock eased his hand from underneath her skirts and discreetly pulled them back down to her ankles.

"I can't let him hang," she continued. "I promised I'd take care of him. I've always taken care of him."

He rolled away from her and got off the bed quickly, keeping his back to her. "It's not going to work this time. There's nothing you can do."

He refastened his pants. His heart knocked against his chest while the fire in his groin battled his good intentions. Knowing he was a bastard didn't stop his body from howling with unfulfilled lust. He increased the distance between them, retreating to the far corner of the room.

As much as he wanted to tear Sullivan apart for mistreating his sister, Braddock knew he himself wasn't any better. Maybe he was worse. While Sullivan used Lorelei to save his own hide, Braddock was only toying with her, trying to find out how far human beings would go for each other. He hated how far he'd sunk. So low he didn't even recognize himself anymore.

He hung his head, but a familiar tingling on the back of his neck brought him out of his self-recrimination. The sensation was one of danger. He slowly turned.

"Keep your hands away from your body."

Braddock raised his hands where she could see them.

She sat on the bed, her legs curled underneath her, pointing his pistol at him. The sure way she cocked the hammer warned him that she knew how to fire a gun.

"You want to be a murderer too, Lorelei? You want to hang next to your brother?"

"We're going to talk about this until you see reason. Sit in that chair," she ordered.

"You mean until he gets away. He won't get away, Lori."

More tears welled at his words. She swallowed hard to keep from letting them flow. "Don't call me that. Sit in that chair and be quiet."

Braddock sighed. He'd survived four years fighting a bloody war and six years chasing down the devils bred by it—all without a scratch. This little slip of a girl didn't have what it took to bring him down. He lowered his hands.

"Uncock the gun before you hurt yourself."

"I know how to shoot." Only the heightened pitch of her voice betrayed her panic. He doubted she had ever pointed a weapon at another human being.

"I imagine you do, but you won't." He eased toward her.

During the war, a rebel could jump out of the bushes and aim a rifle straight at his heart, but somehow the shot would go wild and some young recruit would take the slug, lose a leg. Once a ball whizzed by Braddock's ear and hit the regiment's drummer boy. After they buried him, Braddock learned he was only thirteen.

He took another step toward Lorelei. He'd suspected his fate before the war, of course. Back then he had thought he was just lucky. Now he knew it wasn't luck but a curse. Watching everyone around you die was a living hell.

He continued his advance, his muscles bunched, ready to lunge for her if she tried something stupid. He didn't want her to get hurt and bleed all over her pretty pink dress.

"Stay back." She brought her other hand to the gun. She focused all her energy on keeping a bead on him. All she had to do was contract one small muscle in her finger, and someone was going to die.

Unfortunately for her, Braddock knew it wouldn't be him. He stopped when the bed met his thighs.

She shoved the gun out in front of her. The barrel came within an inch of touching the center of his chest. He wrapped his fingers around steel warmed by her sweating palms. When he gently pulled the pistol from her, she didn't give the slightest resistance. In fact, she was careful to keep her finger away from the trigger. Poor Lorelei, she really did have a good heart. A fatal affliction out West.

He uncocked the pistol and slipped it back in its holster, then buckled the belt around his waist.

"Don't do that again. You point a gun at a man and he doesn't ask questions. It's a sure way to get killed."

She stared down at her empty hands.

He buttoned his shirt and tucked it in his pants. He retrieved his saddlebag and boots, then sat in the straight-backed chair to finish dressing. Lorelei remained eerily silent. After he pulled his pant legs over his boots and tied the rawhide thongs of his gun belt around his thighs, he could no longer avoid her.

"I'll take you back to the ranch."

"Please don't hurt Corey."

He ran his hand over the back of his neck. He had asked the barber to make sure not to trim his hair any shorter than the top of his collar—last time he'd had his hair cut, the back of his neck burned. It felt like the man did a good job. He glanced at Lorelei. *Damn.*

"All right," he said on a long sigh.

"All right, what?"

She hadn't budged from the bed, and it didn't look like she intended to unless he said what she wanted to hear.

"I'll try to keep that brother of yours in one piece while I find Mulcahy. If he helps me, maybe I can do something for him."

She crawled off the bed, smiling for the first time. "Thank you, Mr. Braddock."

He cringed at her gratitude. "But you have to do something for me."

"Anything. I'll do anything." As if she'd suddenly realized the implication of her pledge, a blush spread up her neck and

23

across her cheeks. She averted her gaze but didn't take back her words.

He gritted his teeth. "Not *that*. Don't ever again try to seduce me or any other man to save your brother."

"I won't. I promise." Her enthusiastic nod dislodged a dark curl that fell across her pale shoulder and over the top of her breast.

He had to glance away to keep from staring. "That's not all. You have to stay out of this. Don't try to help your brother. I'll do what I can for him, but this is his mess. You can't fix it."

"I can't promise that."

The firmness in her voice forced him to glance in her direction. He was thankful, she had straightened her clothes.

"You want me on your side or don't you?"

"I do, but—"

"But nothing. That's the way it is."

He gathered his gear. He wasn't going to get any sleep tonight in this room, not with her sweet scent all over the place. As soon as he took Lorelei home, he'd pick up the trail of her rotten brother.

"If he comes to me, I can't send him away," she said.

"You don't have to send him away; just don't defend him or talk to anyone for him." Braddock moved toward the door, saddlebag over his shoulder, rifle in his hand. He paused to turn down the lantern.

"I'm not going to hand him over if someone comes to the door asking for him, if that's what you mean."

He stomped down the hotel's narrow steps, not knowing what he'd meant. Or why he even cared. "Fine. Just don't go looking for trouble."

"You have my word, Mr. Braddock."

He could hear her small, light steps behind his. This country would eat her alive. And how that had become his problem was something he didn't want to consider.

A light burning inside the adobe signaled their approach to the ranch. Lorelei tugged on the old mule's reins. Was Corey still there? Unfazed by her efforts to slow him, the mule kept his pace, lurching the buckboard forward in painful jerks. The tail of Braddock's horse swished ahead like a beacon.

At least the dark saved her from having to look into Braddock's face and remember the way he had touched her—or the way she had exposed herself to him. She had felt a secret relish. She was thankful her mother's reprimanding voice had seeped past the yearning of her body to properly shame her into tears. Still, his nearness relieved her even if it reached out through the space between them, keeping her in a constant state of agitation.

Without his guidance, she'd never have found her way back to the ranch in the dark. She hoped the dangerous combination of gratitude and desperation wasn't all that urged her to trust him with her brother's life.

Lorelei yanked on the reins with all her weight, but the mule continued to plod forward. Her brother wasn't a killer. He'd never pointed a gun at another living thing. He didn't even hunt. Unfortunately, some of what Braddock had told her about the robbery, especially the cheating-at-cards part, sounded all too much like her mischievous brother. Unfortunately, his pranks were no longer boyish, but dangerous.

Braddock stilled his mount and waited for her to catch up. "I can make it the rest of the way on my own," she said.

"I'm sure you can. Take it nice and slow, Lorelei. I'll be right behind you."

The moment the buckboard rolled into the yard, Lorelei jumped down in a cloud of pink taffeta. She beat her rustling skirts into place, then listened for Corey. The call of crickets echoed across the empty landscape in rhythm to the beating of her heart, but there was no hint of her brother's presence. Silently Braddock dismounted beside her. He had a pistol in his hand.

"You won't need that."

He laid a finger across his lips and leaned over until his mouth was next to her ear. "Just in case it's not Corey."

She nodded, but her confidence evaporated with his words. The reminder that other men were looking for her brother chilled her more effectively than the idea of Corey waiting behind the weathered door with a Springfield rifle. If a lesser of two evils existed, Braddock was it.

She crept onto the rickety wooden porch, willing it not to creak. Braddock shadowed her movements, his pistol cocked.

The door stood slightly ajar. She pushed it open. What she saw made her stop and straighten. The place had been ransacked.

She rushed inside with Braddock on her heels. All the drawers of a pine wardrobe sagged open. Lorelei's few possessions spilled over the edges and onto the floor. The red-checked curtain beneath the dry sink hung askew, revealing that the few supplies she had bought were gone. She turned in a half circle to surmise the damage but stopped abruptly when she noticed her black beaded purse carelessly tossed on the bed.

The quick prayer she said was futile. If the ransacker had found the purse . . . She sank onto the bare, straw-stuffed mattress. He had even stripped the bed. A scribbled note lay next to the bag. *IOU, luv, C.* She checked the purse anyway. The silk lining gaped back at her, empty. The purse had held less than fifty dollars, but the money was all she had left in the world. Not enough to get Corey far. She didn't dare think of what the loss meant to her.

"What happened here?"

She crumpled the note in her fist and tried not to sound like her last shred of security had been severed. "Corey needed a few things."

"So nobody came and carried your brother off? *He* did this?" The slight sneer that tugged at Braddock's top lip as he surveyed the damage made her want to flinch.

"He was in a hurry." With as much dignity as she could muster, Lorelei drifted to the open drawers and started folding her collection of tailored gloves, suddenly finding her favorite things as worthless as they really were.

She rescued the lithograph, the only one ever taken of her entire family, from the dirt floor. She wiped the cherished picture with a wad of pink silk from her dress. What good did the tin do her if she couldn't eat or sell it?

"I'm taking you back into town."

She tucked the lithograph in a drawer, unable to gaze upon the faces that stared back at her.

Braddock touched her shoulder and she turned. She blinked, surprised at how dry her eyes felt. The hot wind that constantly blew across the yard seemed to have sneaked inside and snatched away her tears.

"I'll be fine here."

He took off his black felt hat and tossed it on the table. "Yeah. You look real fine." He braced his hands on his hips. "Let me put you up in the hotel in town."

"This is my home." She almost choked on the words. She was starting to despise this barren place. "This is where I'll stay."

He nodded and walked out the door.

Lorelei's chest hollowed as she watched him disappear. He took the air with him, and she could no longer breathe. How was she going to survive? At least back home she could forage for dandelion greens—even shoot squirrels at the toughest of times. Out here, dust and rock sprouted in place of the bluegrass she'd taken for granted. Lizards darted around the yard in abundance, but she couldn't see eating them even if she could catch one.

For the first time the fire to trudge on dimmed in Lorelei. She'd picked herself up too many times. Knowing Corey would need her had sustained her after her mother's death. But clearly she could do nothing for him. She gravitated to the table in the center of the room. She touched it to steady herself, though she yearned to sink to the cool dirt floor.

Braddock strode back through the door, a large wooden box in his arms. Without looking at her, he piled sacks of dry goods onto the table.

"I hope you like beans and rice, because you got a lot of them."

She watched him, unable to speak. He had woken the owner of the only store in town before they set out for here.

When he had loaded his purchases in the back of her wagon, she had been too preoccupied with worry for Corey to pay much attention. She swallowed her desperation, trying not to blatantly covet the food. She could live off of his supplies for a good six months. God knew she had survived on less.

"The shopkeeper must have charged you a fortune after you woke him and made him open the store just for you."

"He owes me a favor." Braddock headed for the door. "There's just a few more things."

"Don't bother. I can't pay for any of this. You'll have to take it back."

"I'm not taking it back. I got the supplies for you."

"Why did you do that?"

He shrugged. His usually penetrating gaze jumped, looking for a place to land. "I don't know. I needed things for myself and I thought you might need some things, too."

She laughed, but her eyes filled with tears. "I guess you could say I could use a few things."

"Good. Now you have them."

"Thank you, Mr. Braddock."

"Don't call me that. I feel like I'm back in school."

She folded into a chair, relief weakening her knees. "What's your name?"

"Just call me Braddock." He escaped out the door before she could question him further.

Lorelei sorted through sugar, flour, coffee, cornmeal, and a large quantity of dried beans and rice, but she didn't mind having so much of the same thing. In fact, she could kiss him. She instantly banished the thought and its appeal. Even Braddock's generosity would not make him the kind of man that she should let slip past her defenses, however weak they were.

He strode back through the door, a roll of blankets under his arm. The flannel bundle he tossed onto the bed appeared well worn but thick and comfortable.

"That's yours," she said, standing. "You'll need it."

"I never use a bedroll. Too hot." He walked over to the table. "Got everything you need?"

And then some. She looked up at him and found the courage to study his eyes for the first time. The darkness she'd first noted hid shards of green.

"Why all this? I can't possibly pay you back."

He held her gaze but said nothing. His stare smoldered with a hunger that made her want to blush, especially since she felt the same heat flare in her stomach. Then it occurred to her: maybe he had no intention of helping Corey, and this was his way of easing his conscience while he carted her brother off to jail.

"I can't accept any of this," she decided.

"You're too smart a woman to starve over principle."

She met his direct gaze, daring him not to be honest with her. "Do you still plan on helping Corey?"

He didn't blink. "I said I would, didn't I?"

"Then I guess I'm in your debt. I don't know what to say. Thank-you doesn't seem enough."

He crammed his hat on his head. "Just stay out of trouble and let me handle your brother."

And without even a nod of good-bye, he strode out the door.

Lorelei followed, lured by the strange pull he had on her. She paused on the porch and watched him mount his horse, afraid he would ride away without another word. "Next time I see you, I'll make you a nice dinner. I'm a pretty good cook."

He gathered up his horse's reins. "Sweetheart, next time we meet, I'm going to be looking for a lot more than a meal."

He shifted his weight, his horse bolted, and they disappeared into the night.

Chapter Three

Lorelei stood in her sleeveless chemise while the deputy marshal tore apart what she had spent most of the night putting back together. No longer was she relieved it had been the law that burst past her door and startled her from a heavy sleep. The faceless outlaws that Braddock had warned her about couldn't be any more threatening than the man who now pawed through her meager possessions.

"Can I get dressed?" she asked his hunched back, his head stuck in a trunk she had brought from Kentucky.

He glanced at her over his shoulder but quickly looked away. "Don't move. I won't shoot you if I don't have to. But you should know Mulcahy's gang's wanted dead or alive. So don't get any funny ideas."

"I'm not wanted for anything." She put her hands on her hips, despite the fact that the blush around his ears assured her that her chemise had grown transparent in the harsh morning light.

"You'll be singing a different tune when I find the gold." He dumped the contents of the trunk on the floor, then started beating its sides as if looking for a secret compartment.

"I don't have any gold. Please, those things are old and delicate."

Among the embroidered tablecloth and napkins tossed in the dirt sprawled her mother's wedding dress. The antique gown of gold silk and cream lace had always been treated with the utmost care. Lorelei clearly recalled the last time her mother had sewn fresh lavender and rose petals in the hem. She had so wanted Lorelei to wear the gown someday, and now the marshal's boot stood within inches of desecrating both the garment and her memory.

Lorelei reached for the dress. Before she could wrap her fingers around the delicate silk, the marshal swiveled in her direction, his gun drawn. "Get back."

She froze in midcrouch, then slowly straightened. "That belonged to my mother."

He leaned over and snatched up the dress. With the gun still pointed at her, he worked the material through his other hand. When his fist wrapped around the sachet lovingly placed in the bottom, he smiled.

"What's this, missy?"

"It's a sachet to keep it fresh."

The marshal draped the gown carefully over a chair back. Lorelei began to relax until he pulled handcuffs from his pocket.

He stepped toward her, his weapon trained on the center of her chest. "Don't like to get rough with a woman, but this is serious business." The blush that had stained his ears spread to his cheeks with renewed force. He dropped his gaze to her feet. "Turn around and put your hands behind your back."

Lorelei did as he ordered. Blush or not, he still held a gun. Touching her as little as possible, he clamped the handcuffs on her wrists.

When Lorelei turned to face him again, the marshal had reholstered his gun. Unfortunately he used his free hand to wad her mother's gown. She bit the inside of her lip to keep from screaming, or worse, crying. Her mother had worn gloves whenever she handled the delicate garment, not wanting to stain the silk with oil from her skin. This oaf had

31

probably snagged the fabric with his callused paws.

He glanced at her triumphantly as he fingered the gown's hem. "Feels like a bunch of banknotes to me." He pulled a knife from a holster hooked to his belt. "Reckon we better find out."

Lorelei tugged against the metal cuffs until they bit into her skin. "It's a sachet, like I told you. I'll show you if you let me out of these."

"Heard that one before." He inserted the tip of the knife into the seam. He might as well have inserted it between her ribs.

"No! Please stop."

Before she could think what more she could do, Braddock stormed into the adobe, pistols clutched in both fists. The marshal dropped the dress and knife, then put his hands over his head. Braddock's hard gaze slid to Lorelei. His eyes widened and, for the first time in their brief acquaintance, he appeared surprised, even scandalized, if he could feel such a thing. His gaze sliced back to the marshal.

"What the hell are you doing with her?"

"She's my prisoner, Braddock. And just so you know, I've been made a deputy U.S. marshal. That means you answer to me."

"The hell it does." Braddock stomped over to Lorelei. He scowled at the handcuffs. "Someone must have been pretty damned desperate to make you a deputy marshal. Where's the key for these?"

"Braddock," Lorelei sputtered when the marshal eased his hand toward his gun.

Braddock didn't flinch. "I'll shoot you dead, Langston. You know that."

Langston jerked his hands away from his pistols. "You've finally stepped over the line, *Captain*." The way he sneered the title let Lorelei know it was an insult rather than a show of respect. "The law wants Mulcahy. The U.S. marshal deputized a posse of good and honest men. We don't need the help of a bounty hunter."

"The law doesn't want *her*."

Langston nodded to the gown lying crumpled on the floor. "Just rip open that seam and I guarantee you'll find a wad of banknotes."

Braddock reholstered one of his pistols so he could scoop up the gown. He adjusted the dress to the crook of his arm, then picked up the knife. His scowl deepened as he examined the long, sharp blade.

Lorelei's gaze darted from the dress to Braddock. She said, "It's only a wedding gown. Those are sachets sewn in the bottom, not banknotes."

He tossed the knife on the table with a clank, then brought the fabric to his nose and sniffed. "Don't know of any banknotes that smell like flowers. Do you, Langston?"

Braddock held the hem of the gown to Langston's face. The man turned his head away. "We all can't be as smart as you, *Captain*. If you ask me, she seems awful attached to that dress."

Braddock laid the dress over his shoulder and reholstered his other pistol. "I'm not asking you, *Corporal*." Braddock removed Langston's guns and tucked them in his belt. He held out his hand. "The key."

Langston reached in his shirtfront pocket and dropped the small brass object into Braddock's palm.

"Knew it'd be only a matter of time before you went from straddling the line to full-fledged outlaw. What would your high-and-mighty papa think of you aiding and abetting thieves and murderers?"

Braddock stomped to Lorelei and unlocked her handcuffs. He cradled her wrists in his hands and rubbed his thumbs over the red splotches she had created by tugging against the metal. His brief glance told her he wanted to do more. Instead he carefully handed her back the dress and turned to Langston.

"I'm giving a lady back her wedding gown. I know you don't know much about women, but they tend to get upset when you take a knife to their pretty clothes."

"Especially if her husband is an outlaw and she's hiding his loot."

Braddock stepped toward Langston with his fists clenched. "Her husband's not an outlaw," he snapped.

Lorelei clutched her gown to her chest and willed Braddock not to say anything about Corey.

"I know you're looking for the kid that helped Mulcahy with the robbery. You're not half as smart as you think you are, Braddock. Look at her holding that dress. She's married to somebody. And don't tell me it's you, Braddock."

"You think that's funny, Langston?"

Langston took a step back and banged into the open door of the wardrobe. "You're not married."

"You keeping tabs on me, Langston? I don't like that either." Braddock pulled the man's pistols from his belt. "Lorelei, come hold these guns. Langston and I are going outside."

The perpetual blush that colored Langston's cheeks drained. Even the tufts of dark red hair sticking from beneath his hat seemed to pale. "I don't want to fight you, Braddock."

"Then you shouldn't have bothered Lorelei."

Lorelei juggled the pistols while Braddock unhooked his gun belt. He draped the thick leather over her shoulder. His gaze dropped to her thin chemise. His eyes flared slightly, but his voice remained controlled. "Get dressed, sweetheart."

She backed away, afraid that the moment she turned, Braddock would lunge for Langston. She wanted the deputy marshal out of her house, not beaten to a pulp. She didn't need any more trouble with the law.

"Honey," she said tentatively, "he didn't hurt me."

Langston's gaze landed on her, half disbelieving, half pleading. "She can't be your wife. She's too . . . small."

Braddock grabbed Langston by his brown vest and jerked him hard, sending his cream-colored hat tumbling to the floor. "Don't look at her. Don't even think about her."

Lorelei took an instinctive step in their direction, then hung back. Getting between them would be a mistake. They both towered over her, but Braddock handled the other man like a rag doll. He dragged him to the door and tossed him outside.

Lorelei laid the guns gently on the bed, picked up Langston's hat, and followed them out the door.

Braddock stood splay-legged on the porch while Langston sat in the dirt where he had landed.

"You'd better forget you ever saw her. And if you tell anyone anything to put her in danger, I'll hunt you down and make you one very sorry deputy marshal."

Langston stood and brushed off the red dirt that coated his clothes. "I'm not one for hurting women, but she's broken the law."

"Have you heard anything I've said?" Braddock took a menacing step off the porch.

"It's a little hard to believe, don't you think, Braddock." Langston backed up abruptly, tripped, then fell in the dirt again. "You? Married?"

"You can believe it and ride out of here in one piece, or I can beat you until you do."

Langston inched to his horse, then cautiously got to his feet. "Can I at least have my guns back?"

"Sweetheart, get his guns."

Lorelei scrambled into the house to retrieve Langston's weapons and hat before Braddock changed his mind and there was bloodshed. She hurried back, intending to hand Langston his pistols, not trusting the two men to be in swinging range. She had seen her brothers come to blows often enough to know one wrong move and Langston and Braddock would be rolling around in the dirt. Braddock's outstretched arm stopped her before she stepped off the porch.

He took the guns from her. Using his whole body, he reared his arm back and propelled one pistol then the other out into the barren landscape. Each landed with a fountain of dust, then disappeared.

Langston followed the metallic arcs before he turned back to Braddock. "How the hell am I supposed to find them?"

"You can use those keen lawman skills you've been bragging about." Braddock took the hat from Lorelei and sailed it at Langston, who fumbled to catch it as it hit him squarely in the chest. "You want your knife back, too?"

Langston settled his hat on his head, then turned his back on them. He mounted his horse and galloped away without another word. Just within shouting range, he abruptly circled.

"You won't get away with this. You interfered with the investigation of a deputy marshal. That's against the law. Even your buddies back in Washington can't change that."

"Let them know all about it," Braddock called. "Don't think harassing an innocent woman is going to get you a permanent position."

"Your family doesn't have any influence out here. If you're hiding something, I'm going to be the first to find out."

Langston redirected his horse and trotted to where his guns had landed. Together, Lorelei and Braddock watched him scour the brush for his weapons. He either found them or gave up, because eventually he spurred his horse off into the haze of heat rising in the distance.

Lorelei released a sigh of relief as she watched him ride away. Up until then, Braddock and she had both kept their gazes trained on Langston. Now she glanced at Braddock's hard profile. He stared at the place Langston had been as if even the dust from the man's horse posed a threat.

Though she had been glad to see Braddock, even grateful for his intervention with the deputy marshal, her relief evaporated. Now that the other threat had disappeared, she wondered what this one had in store for her. Heat flushed her cheeks and belly as she remembered his departing words at their last meeting. What he might demand besides a meal filled her with more anticipation than dread.

"Do you think he believed you?" she asked when he continued to stare at the horizon.

"No."

Lorelei gripped one of the porch's rough posts for support. Not only did she have to worry about Corey hanging, she was in trouble with the law herself. Her only ally was this man: a stranger, a bounty hunter, who stirred unwanted longings without so much as a glance in her direction. Still, she had no one else to trust.

"What are we going to do?" she asked. She openly studied

him. His long legs boasted heavily muscled thighs that tested the seams of his wool trousers. A black cotton shirt stretched across broad shoulders that made his hips look lean in comparison.

He turned abruptly and looked at her, forcing a quick prayer from Lorelei that he hadn't caught her inspecting that particular part of his anatomy. The way his gaze started at her bare feet and moved up her body gave her the distinct impression that he'd felt more than seen her ogling him, and his reason for returning to the ranch had nothing to do with Corey.

He stepped onto the porch. She resisted the urge to back away, telling herself she had nothing to fear except her sudden desire to be near him. When he rested his hands on her bare shoulders, her breath hitched at the skin-to-skin contact.

"We're going to play house to fool Langston. How real you want it to look depends on how fast you can get dressed."

Lorelei rushed for the shelter of the adobe. With the door secured behind her, she picked through the mess on the floor, trying to find a petticoat. She tugged on the first garments she found, a gray bodice and a brown calico skirt, not caring that they didn't match. Her immediate need to be dressed had as much to do with her rush of unladylike lust at his words as with his words themselves.

Despite her best efforts, he pushed open the door before she could finish buttoning her bodice. He didn't falter at her shocked expression but strode toward the bed and picked up his gun belt. He buckled the tooled leather around his hips and swaggered back out the door. Lorelei followed him as she pushed the last cloth-covered button through its hole.

Braddock had already unsaddled his horse.

"What are you doing?"

He turned briefly. "Can you make me something to eat?"

She tucked her hands under her folded arms, hugging herself protectively. A woman in her prime shouldn't be so vulnerable. She should have been safely married off years ago. Part of Lorelei desperately wanted him to leave so she could regain a sense of control over herself, but she'd promised him a home-cooked meal. Of course, what else he might expect was a concern.

"I'll be glad to make you breakfast or dinner, but—"

"Whatever you make is fine as long as it's quick. I need to mend the shed so it's sturdy enough to protect Lucky before this storm breaks." He studied a darkening sky. "Bound to be hail."

Lorelei followed his gaze. Tall, well-defined clouds crowded the horizon. They drifted closer with the force and authority of a slow-moving locomotive. Even the clouds out here in the West were threatening. She glanced back at Braddock.

"So you'll be staying until the storm passes?"

Braddock towel-dried his horse with powerful strokes. It stretched its long mahogany neck, apparently loving the attention. "I said I'm staying till your brother shows up or Langston believes you're not a suspect."

"I don't think for a moment he'll believe we're married."

"But I think he'll believe that we're . . . friendly."

He stared in a way that warned her he was thinking of her trip to his hotel room. She checked the buttons of her bodice to assure herself she was properly covered. That their relationship in truth swayed toward indecent rather than matrimonial didn't stop Lorelei from being insulted.

She folded her arms over her chest, hating the fact that being "friendly" with him wasn't as unappealing as it should be. "Couldn't you have thought of something else to tell him?"

He shrugged. "Sorry, Lorelei. He knows me."

She refused to turn away from his blunt clarification of his character. He was hiding his real intentions, and she wouldn't drop her gaze no matter how desperately she wanted to. "Why did you come back?"

He returned to drying his horse. "Someone followed our trail to the ranch. Thought it might be Mulcahy."

She sagged again at the reminder of the outlaw. She wasn't safe alone. Nor was she safe with him. "I'm sure you'd be more comfortable in town."

He dropped down to one knee and lifted his horse's right front hoof. "If I leave, Langston might haul you in to see if it brings back Corey." He picked out a pebble, then went on to the next hoof. "He needs a few notches in his belt to get a permanent deputy-marshal position." He examined the last of the four hooves, straightened, and brushed his hands off on his thighs. Reaching out, he grabbed Lorelei's wrist so casually that she didn't resist when he pulled her to him.

"Don't fight me. He's watching through field glasses."

Lorelei let him press her against the length of his body, but she kept her back straight. He wasn't going to see her swoon just because his hot breath teased her cheek or his chest brushed against hers. Despite her traitorous body and the things she'd been forced to do to protect her family, she still had a little pride left.

"If you don't believe me, you can see the sun reflecting off glass over my left shoulder."

A flash of light winked beside a distant clump of cactus, taunting her.

Braddock rocked her in his arms, nudging her closer against him. She jerked her gaze back to his. She felt the rumble of laughter in his chest as much as heard it.

His teeth were white and even; it was amazing that he didn't smile more with such nice teeth. "We need to make this look good. You're as stiff as . . ." He laughed again. "Never mind."

She gripped his biceps, fighting the urge to lean into him. His little joke about something being stiff didn't escape her, not when it pressed against her stomach. But she was sure another woman, a lady, would never acknowledge such a thing, even to herself.

"Why are you going to all this trouble to help me?"

At her question he seemed to withdraw, though he held her just as close. "I don't want Langston to get a jump on my bounty."

"You think you can use me to trap my brother." She tried to jerk away. Though his body responded readily enough, he had no trouble separating his cold intentions from any attraction he might have for her.

His grip tightened. "Hold on there. I want Mulcahy. Your brother is my only lead. If Langston gets him, he'll be out of commission. And so will you. You could be arrested for aiding your brother, you know?"

She hadn't known. Braddock had saved her and appeared to be Corey's only hope. Though his motivation served his own purposes more than she liked. She put her hands on his chest to push him away. His nearness flustered her, almost convinced her they were allies when in reality they were hardly on the same side.

"I guess I'd better make you something to eat. Looks like I have no choice but to keep you around."

"Before I let you go, I want you to kiss me."

"Excuse me?"

"Langston's watching. So far all he's seen is me grabbing you and you trying to get away."

Lorelei wanted to refuse, but she didn't want him to know such a minor request raised a cacophony of discordant emotions, desire being the most earsplitting. To reach his mouth, she was forced to stand on her toes. He was definitely making her work to hold up her part of their charade. Or was he testing his appeal? She'd kiss him quick and dry and be done with it.

She slipped her hand around the back of his neck and guided his head down to hers.

The smooth, warm texture of his lips surprised her, leaving her unguarded for the purely pleasant sensation that washed through her. She allowed the moment to languish longer than she intended while waiting for his restraint to crack. When he didn't try to force the kiss, just responded to her, she came down on her heels. His grip tightened before her feet landed firmly in the dirt.

"Not like in the hotel. A real kiss," he said against her lips.

His reminder of their shared intimacy convinced her beyond a doubt he was toying with her. He thought he could melt her with his masculine arrogance, but Lorelei knew she was a good kisser. She'd sent many a boy off to war with a dreamy smile on his face, promises of wedding bells on his lips. Braddock would be the one to swoon now.

With the tip of her tongue she traced the softly parted crease of his lips. When he responded by opening his mouth a little wider, she grew more daring and slid her tongue against his. He was warm and tasted of something sweet, like mint candy. His scent filled her, and she instantly recognized the smell from his bedroll. No wonder she had lain awake thinking of him. His sleeping bag smelled of sage and desert wind, too much like the man. Below the lighter scents was something dark and strong, like worn leather, but not that at all. It was uniquely him, uniquely male. Everything about him wrapped around her like the bedroll, and she couldn't resist slipping deeper into the lush comfort he offered.

By the time he worked his tongue into her mouth, she clung to him, kissing him as if her life depended on it. The realization of how far they had strayed from a pretend kiss stiffened her. She would have stumbled in her abrupt attempt to pull away had he not still cradled her close to his body.

She stared up at him and glimpsed the same wonder where she had expected a satisfied smirk. He was breathing as hard as she. She licked her lips, trying to wipe away what had happened, but even her own tongue against her tingling mouth sent sparks racing over her skin. He looked like he felt the same jolt, because his eyes widened. He appeared on the verge of swooping down and swallowing her whole.

She dislodged herself from his embrace, unnerved at how easily her plans went astray. "I need to get the stove lit before you have to settle for supper."

He nodded. When she turned, he stopped her by sliding his hands down her arm to gently hold her hand. The sweet gesture took her more off guard than if he had roughly pulled her back into his embrace.

"Lorelei." His voice sounded impossibly gruff. But Lorelei

found the sound pleasant rather than threatening. The deep timbre vibrated through her like a caress.

He brought their joined hands to his lips and kissed her knuckles in a touch so genteel he had to have learned it at a cotillion. "With me you always have a choice. You can say no at any time."

The sudden spark in his hazel eyes prompted her to jerk her hand out of his warm grip. "Fine time to tell me."

She did her best twirl, which didn't have the same punch when she wasn't wearing a hoop and taffeta petticoats. Even so, she managed to resurrect her old belle-of-the-ball haughtiness. Some things you never forgot, no matter how sad or silly they seemed later.

A hard slap on her rump ruined her exit.

She kept on marching, not daring to turn around lest he see the red burning her cheeks, a fiery combination of fury and humiliation. She wasn't the belle of anything anymore. Not even her own life.

"That's my girl," he called to her back.

She forced herself not to slam and bolt the door behind her. A quick glance around the room landed on the lone bed. If the display outside the adobe was any indication, it was going to be a long night.

Chapter Four

Braddock woke to the smell of sun-warmed rain. He propped himself up on one elbow and winced at the pain that shot through his side. Blistering daylight poured through the open windows.

His gaze wandered to Lorelei's empty bed. He punched his wadded, sheepskin jacket that served as his only cushion, then seriously contemplated crawling into the space Lorelei had left. The way his heart sped up at the idea made his mind up for him.

A good portion of the night he had listened to the sound of the heavy rain while cursing the fact that Corey's trail would be obliterated. In between, he damned the cold, hard floor he slept on. But mostly he held his breath to hear the soft intake of hers. He must be crazy. She asked him why he'd come back. After pondering the reasons all night, he'd found that insanity was his only explanation.

Braddock brought himself to his feet. His muscles screamed in protest. The hours of hard labor required to patch up the sorry excuse for a barn had taken its toll. Hunting men was easier. Maybe that's why he'd become a bounty hunter instead of buying himself a piece of land, as he'd intended when he'd first melted west.

Building a spread in this desolate place required vision, a dream. A man had to be able to carve something out of nothing. After the war Braddock had had neither. Still didn't. He saw things for what they were. And why he was wasting his time with a woman who was surely going to come to a bad end made no sense.

He found his boots and pulled them on. Checking on how Lucky fared through the storm kept him moving, though he wanted to collapse in one of the straight-backed chairs shoved under the table.

If he'd stayed with the sole intent of bedding Lorelei Sullivan, his actions would have bothered him less. There was no denying he wanted her. The kiss he'd insisted on for Langston's benefit confirmed her vulnerability. If he pushed it, he could easily breach her flimsy resistance. He rubbed his lower back. His long night on the floor proved he was just being a fool, gentlemanlike no less. He had to get out of here.

He staggered to the table in the center of the one-room adobe. Lorelei had set out a porcelain pitcher and basin with a towel neatly folded beside it. Braddock poured water in the basin, then splashed some on his face. Instead of the icy shards he had unconsciously braced himself for, warm water splashed him. His muscles untwisted a notch as the pleasant sensation registered. She must have heated the water.

Yet a dip in an ice-cold mountain stream was what he needed to get him thinking straight again. After he checked on Lucky, he'd see about doing just that—even if he had to ride all the way to Taos to do it.

He stumbled out the door and squinted against the blinding sun. Leftover rain steamed up from the red earth. The fresh smell of sage lingered in the heavy air, making the world seem like it had just had a perfumed bath. One look at the cracked earth and the cactus-choked yard assured him it was still the same old ugly world. He scanned the long stretch of desert grassland. Surely Langston had sought shelter in town.

He'd probably be asking questions about Lorelei. The folks

of Arriba weren't much on information, but this time it wouldn't hurt for Ivar to tell Langston about the supplies Braddock had purchased. Langston would never believe Braddock had bought those things out of the sheer goodness of his heart. Braddock himself didn't even want to believe it. But here he was with his back aching and his hands blistered from swinging a hammer.

His rational side assured him that capturing Corey Sullivan remained his single-minded purpose. Keeping a naive woman from getting in too much trouble happened to be a not-so-selfish result. Of course, if the first were true, he would have been better served following Sullivan's trail before the storm obliterated it. *Damn*. He needed to learn to lie to himself better.

Finding no sign of Langston, Braddock stepped off the porch and marched toward the barn to check on Lucky. Lorelei's soft grunt, followed by the crunching of dirt, forced him to veer around to the side of the adobe, almost against his will, to check up on her.

Standing a few feet from the adobe's east side, she smacked at the ungiving earth with a hoe. The fierce morning sun pummeled her with its full force. A large bonnet shadowed her face. Long sleeves covered her arms, and gloves protected her hands. He couldn't see an ounce of skin. Only a long strand of dark hair, curling toward the ground, betrayed that this was Lorelei.

He was close enough to grab her before she looked up. The lecture her inattention deserved died on his lips. She shot him a smile that left him dazed.

"Good morning. Sleep well?"

"The rain kept me up and the floor was hard."

Her beautiful smile wilted. It happened as slowly as a leaf fluttering to earth. He felt like he'd just smashed a butterfly under his boot heel.

"I'm sorry. I should have insisted you take the bed after all the hard work you did yesterday. The rain didn't bother me a bit. Made me feel like I was back home. Give me a minute to clean up and I'll get your breakfast."

45

Braddock broke up a clump of dirt with the toe of his boot. She actually was sorry he hadn't slept well. He couldn't remember the last time anyone had given a damn whether he lived or died, much less cared how he slept. And he'd thought he liked it that way.

"I'll just check on Lucky." He glanced at the hoe she had propped against the adobe. "Then I'll finish whatever you're trying to do here."

"Lucky's fine. I picketed him in the shade of the barn. Once the sun came up, the poor thing was sweltering."

He swung his gaze in the direction of the barn. Lucky had his head to the ground, scavenging for anything edible that popped up after the rain. "He doesn't like strangers. He could have hurt you."

She laughed and removed her green leather gloves. "He's a sweetheart."

He raised his eyebrows and she laughed again.

"If you know how to treat him. And I do. My family used to train horses."

Braddock nodded, unable to dispute the results. Another glance at Lucky proved she did know how to treat him. The big bay munched grass as leisurely as a cow chewing its cud. Braddock reached for the hoe, feeling as docile as his horse. Obviously Lorelei knew how to handle him, too, because it looked like he was going to do some farming.

"I guess you want me to plant something."

She pulled off her bonnet and he tried not to stare at the cascade of hair that tumbled down her back and over her breasts. The scent of something sweet drifted toward him. He tried to think of the name of the flower, but all he thought was Lorelei—as if she had her own genus.

She fanned herself with her wide-brimmed straw bonnet, fluttering her hair and making it impossible not to stare and even harder not to touch.

"If you could just till while I start the biscuits, I'd appreciate it. I was hoping the soil would be softer after the rain, but I'm afraid it's not."

Braddock raked the hoe over the crusted dirt. Even sagebrush would have trouble growing here. "What are you planting?"

She shrugged and looked away, as if she read his thoughts. "Just a kitchen garden. I brought our one at home to seed. Maybe a few flowers, too. Roses remind me of my mother."

He didn't bother to hide his disbelief. To his credit, he hadn't interrupted her to tell her she was crazy. He let her finish first.

"You might want to try some local crops first." *Like tumbleweed and dust devils.*

She must have noticed the tug at the corner of his lips, because she lifted her chin slightly. "Thank you for the advice, but I'm sure the seeds I brought from home will do fine. I'm known to have a green thumb."

He leaned on the hoe. Why bother stopping her? She was hopeless. Let her ruin her pretty hands and fry that milky white skin of hers trying to make the New Mexico desert the blue hills of Kentucky. She didn't have enough gloves for the job. He remembered the pink satin ones she'd worn to his hotel. The soft leather she now wore was a bit more practical, but not much.

"You got a lot of gloves, don't you?"

She neatly folded the items and tucked them in her pocket. Her sad smile made him hate the tone he'd used.

"I had a pair to match every outfit. I had to part with the gowns but my hands are too small. The gloves didn't fit anyone else."

He stared at her bare hands for a long while, not liking the turn of his thoughts one bit. There were a few things he'd like her to do with those small hands, and not one of them had anything to do with farming. He studied the horizon, wishing he'd never brought the subject up in the first place.

He straightened, then took off his shirt and handed it to her. "I guess I'd better get to work if I'm going to earn my breakfast. I'm starving."

"Oh." Her face flushed and, once she stopped staring, her

gaze fluttered everywhere but on him. "Aren't you going to burn?"

"This won't take that long."

"Oh," she said to the red dirt splattered on the cream stucco wall. "I'll call you when breakfast is ready."

She headed around the house, her skirts and the ribbons of her bonnet sailing behind her in a trail of lavender. Lavender was the fragrance she wore, but it smelled just like Lorelei on her.

Braddock propped the hoe's handle against his bare chest while he rubbed his hands on his thighs. A grin tugged at his face. He should probably quit thinking about the way she had watched him peel off his shirt. Still, imagining the flush on her cheeks spreading across her pale breasts made the job at hand a lot more palatable.

The first hard jolt into the soil reverberated up his arms and banished his lustful thoughts. He needed gloves but wasn't about to destroy his one good riding pair. He adjusted his grip on the hoe and tried again. He would need a shovel to till this ground. Not that he had ever really planted anything before. Growing up, he had played around at helping in the garden at his parents' country home, but he certainly didn't know what he was doing. And apparently neither did Lorelei.

He should tell Lorelei her project was hopeless. But she'd just break her back doing what he refused to. The look in her eyes when she talked about her mother's roses told him she wouldn't give up. Experience had already shown him she was blind to what she didn't want to see. Even when believing the impossible would be the death of her.

Braddock shielded his eyes with his palm and scanned the horizon. Still no sign of Langston. At least the man was smart enough to recognize a lost cause. Anyone who would break his back trying to hoe a desert must be either married or insane, or most likely both. Braddock had seen too many good men pour their souls into an indifferent, hostile earth with nothing to show for it but heartache and hungry mouths to feed. He'd be doing Lorelei a favor if he stopped acting like her plans had half a chance.

The rich smell of freshly brewed coffee drifted out to him. He turned but caught only a glimpse of Lorelei walking in front of an open window, then back again. A soft, breathless song followed her movements. He stood perfectly still, straining to hear what this misguided woman felt there was to sing about it. She wasn't singing; she was humming. Even worse. He didn't recognize the tune but it sounded like some sort of Irish jig.

He tossed down the hoe and walked to the barn to find a shovel.

Lorelei patted the soft earth around her mother's favorite rosebush. The sky blushed a peach-tinted sunset, and she could almost imagine how Corey's ranch would look when everything bloomed.

Keeping her mother's cherished shrub alive through the dusty trip west was worth the effort. With the rock border in place around her garden, she could picture the green, heavy stalks of a summer harvest. For the first time in a very long time, she looked forward to life instead of dreading death. Not wanting painful memories to spoil her perfect day, she let her gaze drift to Braddock.

He crawled on his knees, setting rocks in place to create a path to the adobe's front door. In the fading sun, the well-defined muscles in his shoulders glided under his tanned skin. She didn't care what he said; it wasn't hard to imagine him as some woman's husband. That he was a fine-looking man had never been in dispute. His gallantry had been the surprise.

The entire morning had slipped away before he finished turning the plot to her vegetable garden. To honor such a special patch of earth, she wrapped it in a ring of choice red rocks. With so much else to do, marking an empty patch of dirt seemed silly. But the special touch gave her a feeling of permanence, even if it was only an illusion. When Braddock followed her lead without having to be asked, her fantasy deepened.

Lorelei knew her contentment was based on make-believe. But reality hadn't been nearly as fulfilling. In her mother's last year, Lorelei's only hope had been her swift and quiet death.

Maybe that was why pretending Braddock was here for reasons other than taking her brother to jail came so easily. She let her gaze drift to his face, hoping something there would tell her he liked the fantasy as much as she. He stared back at her. She jerked her attention to the ground, wondering how long he'd watched her appreciating his heavily muscled physique.

With her eyes riveted to the task of patting down a mound of earth around the rosebush, she sensed him walking toward her as keenly as if she still studied him.

"What's that?" He knelt before her.

She raised her head and couldn't avoid glancing at his mouth. The memory of yesterday's kiss made her cheeks burn all over again. "A rosebush."

"It looks dead."

"Well, it's not. It's hibernating." Tenderly she picked at the end of one of the closely cropped limbs to assure herself it was still green in the middle. "It'll come back next spring."

He didn't say anything, just stood and stretched. The slight pull around his mouth told her he didn't believe her. The same way he hadn't believed that any of the seeds she brought from home had a chance of surviving, but he had helped her without complaint. He was a funny man, and she still knew so little about him. She wondered if he truly knew himself.

"What's your name?"

He studied the distant mountains. "Braddock."

"I mean your Christian name."

"Langston's back. Looks like he's getting ready for a long night."

Lorelei followed Braddock's gaze. The glow of a faraway fire gave her a surprising sense of comfort. Braddock wouldn't leave. With the deputy marshal keeping a watchful eye and Braddock under her roof, she couldn't feel alone. Lorelei didn't think she could bear another string of lonely nights with nothing but the howl of wind and coyotes to keep her company.

The sun sank deeper behind the dark mountains, turning the sky a violent red. Lorelei piled more dirt at the rosebush's base. Her efforts were unnecessary, but she didn't want to finish the first thing that felt right since she had stepped off the stage in Arriba. Planting her mother's rosebush was the only thing that had turned out as she had planned.

"What do your friends call you?"

With his back to the setting sun, his face was covered in shadows. "Braddock."

She couldn't tell if he was joking or just being obstinate. "Braddock Braddock?"

"Braddock, sir."

She picked up a clump of soft dirt and tossed it at him. "What's the big secret about having a first name?"

He ducked and she swore she heard him laugh. "I think you've been in the sun too long, Miss Lorelei. Better get your delicate little self inside."

"I don't sound like that."

"Pretty close." He reached out his hand.

She took off her muddy gardening gloves and accepted his offer to haul her up. He jerked her to the left before she set her foot down.

"Watch out. Tarantula."

A spider as big as a kitten reached a hairy arm out to her bare toe. She jumped and squealed at the same time. "Kill it!"

Braddock scooped the monster into his hand. The spider's body covered Braddock's palm and its legs stretched across his wrist and fingers. "Tarantulas are your friend. You want them in your garden."

Lorelei backed up until the adobe wall stopped her. She flung her arm out to ward him off. She wasn't the squeamish sort, but what he held was a freak of nature. Just when she

51

thought she had grown accustomed to this place, some new strange thing appeared worse than the thing before.

"That beast is not my friend."

Braddock held the spider up to her face. "He's harmless to you, but he does eat scorpions. You shouldn't be barefoot, by the way. A scorpion's sting will kill you." Braddock pointed near her left foot and jumped back. "There's one."

Lorelei involuntarily shrieked and hopped sideways. Braddock's deep-throated laughter stopped her from screeching a second time. The sound bubbled up from his throat like an ancient well that hadn't been tapped for centuries.

"Very funny."

He laughed harder and doubled over. He sank to his knees, hardly able to catch his breath.

She watched him with her hands on her hips, fighting her own smile. "It wasn't that funny, Braddock, sir."

He started laughing all over again. Finally, with tears seeping into the deep lines around his eyes, his outburst lessened to what sounded suspiciously like giggles.

"I guess that's the first prank you've pulled on anyone in a while."

He set the spider down and got to his feet. His prolonged amusement might have annoyed Lorelei, since she was the target, except for the fact that his whole face changed when he laughed.

"I don't think I've ever gotten anyone as good as I got you. Except for the time I put a snake in my sister's bed, but I was whipped for that, so it took some of the fun out of it."

"I hope that was when you were a child."

He cocked his head. "Maybe, maybe not—I'd check your bedroll tonight just in case. You might be sharing your bunk with my friend."

"Does *he* call you Braddock?"

Before she suspected his intentions, he swept her up into his arms.

"I wasn't kidding about the scorpions. They're deadly. Don't walk around barefoot."

She wrapped her arms around his neck as if being carried

by him were as natural as walking. The warmth from his bare skin sank into her as efficiently as the last rays of the setting sun. Stopping herself from leaning into him was useless. Tilting her head to smell his hair was avoided only by sheer will.

"What do scorpions look like?"

"They *look* deadly. They're a milky white, almost translucent, and they walk backward. You'll know one when you see it; that is, if you see it before it's too late."

"Are you purposely trying to scare me, Braddock?"

"Do you think I could? If I knew you were afraid of bugs I would have told you about tarantulas and scorpions on the first day we met. Would have saved me a lot of trouble if I could have convinced you to go back to Kentucky and leave your brother to me."

He walked toward the house. She pointed to her shoes near the front porch. "You can set me down here. I'll put my shoes on."

He shifted her in his arms and kept walking. "I'll carry you into the house. Langston's eyes will probably pop out of his head."

"You're enjoying this, aren't you? Tricking the deputy marshal."

He grinned. "Yep."

She tried not to notice that he carried her over the threshold. It made her fantasy too real, almost painful. No one would really carry her over the threshold of their home, not the way she dreamed, anyway. And she didn't like to think this was as close as she would ever get. "Aren't you afraid of anything, Braddock?"

He kicked the door shut on the encroaching purple night. "Just you, sweetheart."

Chapter Five

Lorelei filled the second bowl of stew to its glazed rim. Braddock slumped over the table, his head resting on top of his folded arms. A hot day spent mending the corral had left him too exhausted to even eat. For the past two nights he had done little more than gobble down a light supper, then collapse on the floor. Tonight she would make sure he slept in the bed. Where she would sleep churned dangerous ripples in the pit of her stomach.

After he'd carried her inside the night before, he'd done nothing but set her on her feet. She'd leaned against him longer than necessary, giving him ample opportunity to kiss her if he'd had a mind to. He hadn't. Her disappointment nagged her through a sleepless night and on into the next day. He was a fine man. But he wasn't hers. Even the fact that he worked like a mule just to please her wouldn't make it so. The gift of his labor surprised and delighted her, but after so many hard times she knew better than to question good fortune.

She set both crockery bowls on the table. He didn't move. Without thinking she brushed back his damp hair. He had bathed out by the pump before coming in. After throwing on a shirt and leaving his boots by the door, he'd collapsed into a chair and hadn't budged since. Maybe he'd fallen asleep. She stroked the length of his dark brown hair. Lighter streaks of burnished red and gold had appeared in the last couple of days.

"Are you hungry?" she said softly, careful not to startle him if he was sleeping.

He sat up slowly and winced. His alert gaze told her he hadn't been sleeping. "That felt good." He drew the bowl closer to him and started eating.

She slid into the chair next to him and concentrated on her stew, hiding her pleasure at his response. Her brothers had claimed she had the healing touch, though she suspected it was just so she'd rub out their kinks.

Her gaze shot to Braddock.

The least she could do to repay him for all his hard work was to rub liniment over his tired muscles. That was exactly what she would have done for her brothers. The idea of touching so much of him tightened her stomach and stole her appetite.

She pushed a cloth-covered ceramic bowl toward him. "Biscuit?"

"Thanks," he mumbled in between bites. He dipped his bread in his bowl and went back to focusing on his food.

She stirred her stew. Suddenly giving him a rubdown meant more to her than it ever could to him. She longed for the bits of closeness they'd shared, laughing in the garden, exchanging a satisfied grin when they had completed the rock border leading to the front porch. Those moments were as rare as Braddock's smiles. But the connection between them slipped away as quickly as it came, leaving Lorelei wondering if it had happened at all. She would wait, tense-muscled, trying to find the right thing to say or do to make the closeness return. Maybe she was so lonely that she imagined a bond that wasn't there.

"I'm going to rub you down with liniment."

He raised his bowed head, alert and wary, as though he had just smelled danger.

Lorelei returned to stirring her stew. She'd never get a bite past her tight throat. "It's going to smart a little, but you'll feel better tomorrow."

She felt his gaze on her but she didn't dare face him. She forced a sip of the stew's rich juice past her lips just to pretend everything was normal. If she acted as if rubbing her hands over his body were nothing to be flustered about, maybe he would believe it, too.

"All right," he said, as if accepting a challenge he'd been expecting.

Lorelei continued to lift her spoon to her lips, then return it to her bowl almost as full. She playacted her way through the rest of the meal. Everything had changed, and she was no longer sure how to behave, even how to hold her spoon. She kept up her part until he stood and took his bowl to the dry sink under the window.

She jumped when his arm brushed her sleeve.

"Finished?"

Though she had managed to swallow only a quarter of its contents, neither of them had the stomach to put off the rubdown any longer. He dumped the rest of her stew back into the pot on the stove.

She came up behind him and took the bowl from his grasp. "I'll just set these to soak. You can take off your shirt and lie on the bed."

He raised an eyebrow at her suggestion. "I'd rather sit at the table."

She shrugged, admitting only to herself that she was relieved. "Suit yourself."

She poured water into their dinner bowls, then dried her damp palms on a towel. The moisture sprang from nerves, not the dishwater. Finally, at the cupboard that held the liniment, she had to press her traitorous hands together to keep them from shaking.

The plain mason jar she'd seen earlier sat on the top shelf all by itself. The ointment seemed to be the only thing Corey never ran out of. It had been her father's recipe, and the men in her family swore by it. When she opened the cupboard, the greenish-white balm glinted back at her with a conspiratorial wink. She grabbed the jar, convincing herself she was being silly. It was just plain ointment. She'd made it herself a hundred times. Of course, she added extra eucalyptus and a touch of lavender. Luckily this jar wasn't made by her.

Even the thought of that smell tightened her throat. The scent had filled her mother's room those last months, but no matter how often she had gently tried to massage the congestion from her mother's chest, Lorelei couldn't reach her mother's broken heart.

She carried the jar, which seemed to radiate heat through her palms, to the table. Braddock had removed his shirt and straddled the chair backward. He buried his face in the folded arms he rested on the table.

She removed the lid and winced. Braddock lifted his head. The strong medicinal smell of camphor filled the room. He glanced at her over his shoulder.

"It might not smell good, but it works." Lorelei struggled to keep a nervous bubble of laughter contained. There was nothing unseemly about rubbing her hands over a good portion of his naked body, even if they weren't related. The pungent smell burning her nostrils proved there wasn't anything romantic going on. She just wished the idea of touching him didn't make her stomach flutter.

He laid his head back down. "Give me your worst."

She scooped out a large dollop of the ointment and smeared it on his shoulders. He jumped at her touch. "It's cold," he mumbled.

"Sorry." She scraped the liniment off his back and rubbed it between her hands, warming it and making it more pliable. Her hands coated with the thick ointment, she placed her palms flat on his back. His skin was hot. Though he looked golden brown in the lamplight, he must have burned from working much of the time with his shirt off.

He took a deep breath and released it, as if calming himself. She'd done little more than rub her palms lightly across his back, smearing the ointment over his skin.

"Come on, now. I haven't hurt you yet."

"Not yet," he said into the table.

The way he bent over the chair bunched the muscles along his back. Lorelei started with his shoulders, working around the prominent blades. He didn't moan or complain as she worked her fingers into his sore muscles. Her second-oldest brother, Donnan, would have been jumping at her every touch, screaming abuse, while Corey would have let her do anything to him as long as he was the center of attention. Braddock wasn't like either of them. If anything he was like Devine, her oldest brother: stoic while you did what needed to be done, but grateful you took the time.

She missed Donnan as much as she missed her parents, but sometimes she missed Devine the most. When he was alive, she'd always felt like the baby, the princess of the family. Even when he'd called her Her Highness Lorelei while pulling her hair, she'd felt like royalty visited upon the Sullivan clan. Oh, how the mighty had fallen.

She worked her hands back toward Braddock's bunched shoulders and up his neck. Tears burned behind her eyes and she sniffed to keep them from falling. Braddock tried to lift his head, but she pushed him back down.

"The camphor's burning my eyes."

He didn't question her.

She slid her hands around his rib cage, using her thumbs to work the muscles on either side of his spine. She could touch him forever. His skin radiated warmth all the way up her arms. The feel of him soothed her, letting her remember without the talons of pain that usually accompanied the images of her family.

She sighed. "Actually, I was thinking of my brothers. I used to rub out their kinks just like this. I miss them."

His long, uncomfortable silence made Lorelei regret sharing her inner self. What did he know about such things as longings?

Finally he said, "My sister would never do anything like this for me."

"Well, maybe if you let her call you by your first name and didn't put snakes in her bed she would have."

He chuckled low in his throat, and she felt his laughter through her fingertips. "She called me by my first name."

Lorelei dug her thumb into a knot tucked in between his ribs. "Which is?"

"Ow!" He squirmed, trying to get away from her probing, but she was relentless. "Christopher. Christopher Ellis Braddock."

She released the pressure of her thumb. "Christopher Ellis. Now that's a fine name. Don't know why you needed to make it such a big mystery."

He lifted his head and glanced at her over his shoulder. "Some Indians believe if you tell a man your name it gives him power over you."

She slipped her hands down to his waistband, working the tight muscles of his lower back. Occasionally her fingers would slip beneath his trousers, low enough for her to know he wore nothing else. She swallowed hard, keeping her voice light. "Well, I'm not a man, am I?"

He reached around with his right hand and grabbed her wrist, holding her in place while he turned to face her. "No, you're worse."

He nudged the chair aside. He sat on the edge of the table and brought her between his knees.

Lorelei followed his movements as willingly as a reflection in a mirror. She put her palms flat against his chest, spreading her fingers across the hard mounds of muscle. "I'm not finished yet."

His arms circled her waist and he drew her against him. "Any lower, Lorelei, and you'd have been finished, all right. I don't think you massaged your brothers like that." He leaned down and kissed her quick and hard on the mouth as if he couldn't help himself. "What were you thinking, girl?"

She let her head fall back, waiting for him to kiss her again. When he didn't, she raised up on her tiptoes and touched her lips to his. His mouth eased open but he let her do the kissing while he gripped her more tightly against him.

She darted her tongue into his mouth, relishing his heat, the feel of his skin under her hands and his mouth on hers. He was the sweetest thing she'd had in her life in a long time. And she wanted more of him. Maybe it was the play-acting of the last couple of days, but she wanted to know this man, to love him like a real husband. She glided her hands across his ribs, then up over the soft smattering of hair covering his chest, feeling the stampede of his heart. He was so alive and strong. She wanted his strength, and in return she would give him her softness, something she sensed he needed even if he never would admit it.

His hands drifted up her back and into her hair. His fingers entwined in her curls, guiding her head back. Sliding his tongue deeper into her mouth, he took over the kiss. He leaned into her as he tightened the arm wrapped around her waist. Rapidly he was becoming the aggressor, but she wasn't afraid. Not like she had been with Berkley. But Berkley had been a gentleman up until the time he had gotten her alone in his carriage on a deserted country road. From Braddock she'd expected nothing but fierceness and been moved by his kindness.

She pulled her mouth away from his and nipped his ear. "Is this what you were afraid of, Christopher?"

His hands slid down her back and cupped her bottom. He pulled her into the crook of his thighs. The heat radiating through his clothes rivaled the burn on his skin. "What are you doing, Lorelei?"

But he didn't give her a chance to answer. He nipped at the skin over her collarbone, then kissed her breast through the white cotton of her shirt.

The cloth between them intoxicated and frustrated her. She leaned her head back and closed her eyes, gripping his shoulders for support. She didn't know *what* she was doing. Her mind no longer had control over her body. From the moment he'd ridden onto Corey's desolate homestead, Braddock had summoned desire, unwanted and forgotten, within her even as her own arousal shamed her. But since then so much had happened, she didn't know why feeling so good should be wrong. What did it matter if they enjoyed each other? There was so little of it going around.

"I want to take you to bed," he said from somewhere in a dream.

"Yes." Her voice sounded different, deeper, like a stranger's.

He sucked at the cloth covering her breast until it was completely saturated. The wet cotton slowly gave way to the feel of his tongue as he flicked it over her nipple. The jolt left her wanting more. She fumbled for the top button of her blouse.

He encircled her wrist, halting her progress. He moved from the table and guided her near the bed. "I want to undress you."

The time to stop had come, warned a small voice in her head. The voice reminded her of the woman she had been, the proper lady she thought she was before her world had collapsed around her. She almost wanted to laugh at the old voice's weakness. She had no intention or inclination to stop. With arms limp at her sides, she stood like a dresser's doll, eager for him to do what he would. He hesitated at the first button, but she met his stare without blinking.

His gaze dropped to his fingers as he fumbled with the buttons. He had trouble pushing the small, cloth-covered balls through their tiny holes. She didn't feel the need to offer to help. He seemed fascinated with the task, as if undressing her were truly a wonder. Lorelei took a deep breath; her chest rose and fell against his warm hands. He brushed his knuckles down the thin chemise, the only thing left between him and her bare skin. After an eternity, he opened her white blouse and skimmed it off her shoulders, grazing her bare skin wherever possible. Instead of being chilled by her lack of layers, she felt heat rise from her skin in an anxious fever.

When he reached for her homespun calico skirt he stopped, looking for how the garment was attached. She took his hands in hers and guided him to the tape hidden in the folds. With one quick pull, the top skirt fell to the floor. Her knee-length chemise and one petticoat were all that remained of her modesty. She knew she should be embarrassed, but all she felt was urgency. Her usual layers would have made this process excruciating. Her skin already jumped with anticipation.

He rubbed his palms up her arms and over her shoulders, then back down again, pressing over her ribs and down her hips. Her body coiled into a knot of wanting at his touch. The secret place between her legs pulsed with a desire she had always been ashamed of until now. At this moment she wanted to follow that impulse wherever it led.

His hands returned to the waistband of her one petticoat, and he didn't hesitate this time but went right to the tie and pulled it. The white cotton undergarment pooled around the discarded skirt. He lifted her from the pile of her clothing and swung her nearer the bed. His heart hammered against her chest and his breath came warm and ragged against her neck. He dipped his head and kissed her deeply, with more intensity and hunger than ever before. She returned his onslaught with the same fervor.

He pulled away, breathing hard, then grabbed the hem of her chemise and pulled it over her head while she lifted her arms to help him. He absently dropped the garment to the floor, his gaze riveted to her naked body. He gripped her shoulders, holding her away from him so he could stare wherever he liked. Her cheeks flamed and she fought the urge to study her toes. Instead she watched his face, fascinated by his response. Looking at her seemed to excite him more than the kiss or even the touching. His pupils flared, giving him a dazed look.

She stood straight under his scrutiny, took a deep breath, and watched how the rise and fall of her chest drew him. She knew she was well formed, her breasts high and firm, her hips flared, her waist fairly small. But the way he looked at her, she felt rare and exquisite.

"Jesus," he rasped.

She hooked a finger in the top of his trousers. "Your turn." She unbuttoned the top button. While he watched her hands, his breathing quickened. His reaction to her touch made her feel powerful. If she didn't know better, she would have thought him the virgin.

Before she got halfway through the buttons, she brushed his hard, hot sex. She hesitated briefly, lost her nerve for an instant, but kept going. He didn't seem to notice. She glanced up at him. His eyes were closed. Each deep breath he took seemed to be the only thing sustaining him.

When she reached the last button she pulled his pants over his hips, and the rigid flesh she had touched sprang forth, straight and fierce. She knelt and pulled his pants all the way down his legs. She was glad he kept his eyes closed, because it gave her the chance to freely gaze at him.

She had seen a man naked before. You didn't live in a cramped house with three brothers and avoid that, but she had never seen a man ready to take a woman. She had grown up around horse breeding and knew the logistics. But seeing his male part thick and engorged, knowing he was like this for her, sent the strangest jolt of excitement through her, with just a touch of fear.

She dragged her hands back up his body. When horses mated, it wasn't uncommon for the animals to be hurt if the trainers weren't in control. Lorelei wasn't quite certain who was in control here. He kept his eyes closed and his hands by his sides as her palms roamed over his chest, back down his arms, and around his hips. She grazed him everywhere but where she knew he wanted her to touch him. The way he involuntarily jerked when her hands passed over the hollow of his hips gave his desire away.

She took a deep breath and wrapped her hand around his thickness. He inhaled sharply.

She squeezed, testing the hardness. It was such a strange thing, how ungiving it was, when she knew it would be pliant when he wasn't aroused. She ran her hand to the tip, feeling the smoothness of his skin in contrast to the hardness underneath.

"Lorelei." His voice sounded harsh, leaving her unsure whether he was encouraging her or asking her to stop. He wrapped one hand around hers; with the other he gripped her shoulder as if bracing himself. He guided her hand back down and up again; then he leaned down and kissed her gently on the cheek.

"Your touch is so sweet," he whispered into her ear.

He brought her hand up to his chest and pulled her into his arms. They stood toe-to-toe. Her breasts pressed against his lightly haired chest. Her head nestled under his chin. He just held her for a moment. She could hear his heart beat loud and strong. He rubbed his hands lightly up and then down her back. His gentle cradling was the nicest thing yet. She wrapped her arms around his waist and held him close. If she knew it would have been like this, she would have been eager the night in his hotel room.

When he cupped her bottom, molding her against him with a fierceness she sensed was only the beginning, she raised her face to his. He complied with her silent request and kissed her thoroughly. She had always liked kissing, but this was so much more. There was promise and hunger in this kiss.

By the time he stopped, her breath came in short gasps. Her stomach no longer fluttered with nerves but burned with an anxious need to continue. Wanting him inside her seemed as natural as gasping for breath. Before Christopher, she couldn't fathom yearning for a man as clearly as she did now.

Without a word he guided her onto the bed. She lay on her back on top of the bedroll, wanting to crawl underneath but awaiting his next move. He stretched out beside her instead of over her, as she'd imagined.

He raised himself on one elbow and kissed her while he explored her body with his other hand. He used sweeping strokes, focusing his attention from her shoulder to her hip. His breath quickened when he paused at her breasts to flick his thumb over her distended nipples. She shut her eyes and gasped at the sharp burst of pleasure, but he'd already slid his hand down her belly. Even with her eyes closed, she sensed his restless need. She shifted and watched him again, not sure what he expected or wanted from her.

Once he reached his destination, she understood exactly what he wanted. He smoothed his palm over her hip, around her thigh, then hitched her right leg at an angle, leaving her open for his probing fingers. At his first touch she almost jerked off the bed. He gently stroked her, then slid a finger easily inside. When he moved in and out, she couldn't help but match the rhythm with her hips. But almost as soon as she relaxed enough to let the exquisite sensation ooze through her body, he abruptly removed his hand.

He moved over her. "I can't wait any longer and you're ready for me. All right?"

She nodded, not sure what they would wait for anyway. Bracing his weight on his knees and one arm, he reached between them and guided himself to her opening.

"Spread your legs wider, sweetheart."

She did, raising her knees and tilting her pelvis.

His head remained bent, and he must have liked what he saw. "That's perfect. Open up for me."

The first touch was as nice as his finger had been, but when he continued to push forward with his hips, she tensed. He braced his forearm by her head, leaned down, and kissed her.

"Relax, sweetheart. I'm going to go nice and easy until you get used to me."

The pressure where they were joined grew increasingly uncomfortable, and for the first time Lorelei had second thoughts. She dug her fingers into his unyielding biceps.

He stilled his movements and kissed her, entwining his tongue with hers until the pleasure of their joined mouths coaxed her to relax. The pulsing fullness between her legs had begun to match the swirl of sensation in the rest of her body.

With more determination, he thrust forward again. This time she couldn't stop from trying to shove him away as she let out an involuntary yelp. He tensed above her. For a long minute his heavy breathing filled the room. His eyes were closed, and sweat beaded his forehead.

Finally he opened his eyes. They were greener than she'd ever seen them. His gaze skewered her, and she had the uncomfortable sensation that he was mad at her.

"Lorelei." His voice was harsh, like a parent scolding a child. "Are you a virgin?"

She wasn't angry at his question. It seemed everyone assumed she had lost her virtue, and it didn't bother her that he had to ask, but she had the distinct impression he felt she had cheated him somehow, lied to him about something very important.

"Yes." She stopped herself short of apologizing.

At that moment her body reminded them of their tentative connection by pulsing around him. The pain eased and the pleasure she had experienced earlier rushed back. She shifted, arching her back slightly. He closed his eyes, gritting his teeth.

"Lorelei." His struggle to control his apparent anger strained his voice and tightened his jaw. "Do you want me to stop?"

She ran her arms up his biceps. His muscles were tense and bunched, his skin wet from his strain. She didn't want it to end like this.

She took a deep breath and let it out. "No."

He kept his eyes closed, still not moving, and she wondered if he heard her. She wanted to ask if it would hurt again, but was afraid to speak. The closeness they had shared had shifted, teetering on a brink.

He opened his eyes and gazed down at her, studying her. He looked as if he were searching for a very important answer that could be found only in her face.

She touched his cheek. "I'm sorry," she said despite herself.

"That comes after." He lowered himself until his chest pressed against hers. He kissed her mouth and slid his forearms under her back, scooping her up against him.

Before she could ask him what he meant, he forcefully thrust his hips while he tightened his arms. The pain flashed like a lightning bolt, fading as quickly as it began. She sucked in her breath and dug her fingers into his arms.

He trailed kisses down her neck as she tried to catch her breath. She stiffened and squirmed but he held her tight, nuzzling the sensitive spot just under her earlobe in a way that tickled. She turned her head away and he stuck his tongue in her ear.

"Stop that." She laughed and realized the discomfort had ebbed away completely. Her body adjusted, sending pulses of pleasure out to her toes and the tips of her fingers. He raised back on his elbows and started to move.

First he rotated his hips in a gentle rocking. She arched against him, bringing her hips to meet his. As her eagerness grew, so did his aggression. His movements lost their gentle coaxing. He surged into her and she met him with a desperation she hadn't known existed. She was breathing so fast, the pleasure so acute, she felt light-headed. But neither of them could stop the maddening rhythm. She planted her feet on the bed and pushed up, wanting him to go harder, faster.

She existed on an eddy of pure sensation. She didn't know how long they went on, but abruptly he straightened his arms, pulling away from her.

"I have to pull out. Now," he said in between ragged breaths.

Their connection ended when he dropped his weight to his knees. He braced himself above her just as the first shudder ripped through him. A hoarse moan tore from deep in his chest. She tried to sit up, to see if he was all right, when hot liquid shot across her belly. He was spilling his seed. He'd pulled out to make sure she hadn't gotten pregnant. Lorelei felt chilled and relieved at the same time. She hadn't thought that far ahead.

She brushed her hands over his shoulders as spasms continued to rack him. She smoothed back his hair and said his name in soothing tones. He came back down into her arms, and some of the coolness of their abrupt separation ended.

He buried his face in the crook of her neck, and, with their heads on the same pillow, she listened to his breathing slow to normal. He slung an arm over her waist and a leg over her thigh. She nestled into him and he pulled her to his chest.

"I should have started off slower."

She kissed him lightly on the cheek, restless and too alert to be lying still in his arms. "I don't think I could have stood it if you did."

He brushed a lock of hair out of her face, hooking it around her ear. "Yeah, but you'd be feeling a whole lot more relaxed right now."

Lorelei shifted to her elbow. "What do you mean?"

"Lorelei," he started, then paused. "I guess I'm just trying to say I'm not the best of lovers."

"Oh." She thought about it a minute but didn't really understand what he was getting at. "I liked it. It felt good after the pain." Desire welled up in the pit of her stomach at the thought. In fact, she wanted to try it again, but could tell by the way he sank into the mattress that he barely had the energy to keep his eyes open. "You felt really good."

He grinned crookedly. "God, Lorelei. Don't look at me like that. You're going to be the death of me."

She laid her head on the pillow and scooted closer. "But you liked it, didn't you?"

He wrapped his arms around her and they shifted until they were both comfortable. "Of course I did, but that won't change who I am."

"I don't want you to change."

He sighed heavily, warning her she wasn't going to like what followed. "I'm glad to do the things you need done around here, but this isn't the kind of life I want."

She tried to pull away, but he held her close. He kissed the top of her head. "It's not you. I just don't want to be tied down to the land. I'm not a farmer."

"What are you then?"

"You know what I am."

She did, and the way he reminded her brought that reality back into the room. He had come to capture her brother. She hadn't forgotten, but she had in her own silly mind thought the past two days had changed him. Being in her arms had changed him. God knew it had changed her. How could she have trusted a total stranger so completely? She struggled out of his embrace to look into his face. Real pain tightened his gaze. He wasn't a total stranger. He was the first hope she'd had in a long time.

She traced his lips with her finger. "I wanted you to make love to me, Christopher. I don't expect anything from you because of what we did. I never expected you to stay."

Lorelei wouldn't let herself cry, though tears already constricted her throat. He would misunderstand. She wasn't sad because he wouldn't stay, or give her back her dreams of a life filled with love, a husband, a family. What hurt so badly was how easily she had come to accept the inevitable. No one stayed. There was nothing to count on. Not really. Not the love of a mother or a father, certainly not the love of a man she hardly knew.

He cradled her head in his palms, holding her while he searched her gaze. "I didn't mean to hurt you. I didn't intend for this to happen."

Lorelei was hurt despite herself. He had inadvertently reminded her of the things she no longer had, just when she had almost gotten used to the loss. "I know. You should leave tomorrow. Tell Langston we had a lovers' spat."

"Whatever you want." He nestled her against his side. "Let's go to sleep."

Lorelei closed her eyes and tried to match the rhythm of her breath to his. Just for tonight, she would pretend that whatever she wanted was still possible.

Chapter Six

Braddock woke with a start, then wondered if he had slept at all. The sting behind his eyelids and the bitter taste in his mouth left him with the sensation of having ridden through a sandstorm with both wide open. Through the window, night faded to charcoal gray. Lorelei slept evenly beside him, her warm skin pressed against his side. Dawn must be at least a half hour away. But that was still too soon.

He edged away from her so he could think clearly. He had no more answers about the trouble he'd gotten into than when he'd fallen asleep. Leaving Lorelei would be best, but he'd be damned if he would leave her at her brother's ranch by herself. Before, he could have ridden away—not liking the idea, but still, he could have done it. He'd figured out he couldn't save the world a long time ago. But after the way she had given herself to him with so much passion, so much heart, he could no more leave her drowning in quicksand than he could on this ranch.

The soft squeak of leather disintegrated Braddock's troubled thoughts. Suddenly he recognized the sound that woke him. He held his breath, keeping himself from tensing and waking Lorelei. A man's boot creaked, despite the owner's care to sneak up on the bed.

Braddock scrambled to recall where he'd left his guns. He couldn't remember—a first since the war. The noise sounded closer. The man was cautious. Langston was cautious, but Braddock hadn't thought him this stupid.

The shadow moved close enough to the bed for Braddock to see it wasn't Langston. Too short. It could be Corey or it could be Mulcahy, looking for Corey. If that was the case, they were in a lot of trouble.

The figure knelt by the bed. If it weren't for Lorelei, Braddock would have lunged at the intruder rather than wait to see what the man had in mind. But with Lorelei next to him, he couldn't risk that the shadow carried a loaded gun. Braddock knew who out of the two of them would be the one shot. His luck would have Lorelei taking the bullet.

"Lori, wake up."

The whispered words still held the squeak of youth. Corey. Lorelei stirred. "Christopher? What's wrong?"

Braddock didn't move a muscle. He was naked, in bed, with a wanted man's sister. A man who undoubtedly carried a gun. Never before had Braddock put himself in such a vulnerable position.

"Get dressed. We have to get out of here. Who's Christopher?"

Lorelei sat up, clutching the covers over her bare breasts. "Corey?"

The way Corey straightened, slow and easy, his body tightening, Braddock knew he'd just realized there was someone in bed with his sister. As the consequences of Braddock's lapse in judgment rained down on him, the fickle night deserted him, turning the room light blue. Not only could Braddock clearly make out the pistol Corey held, but he could see the weapon was trained on him.

"Who the hell is that?"

Lorelei glanced at Braddock as if she had temporarily forgotten. "The bounty hunter you sent me to town to talk to."

"That's right, talk. In town. I didn't say shack up with him."

"Didn't you? Well, that's what you meant."

"If you're blaming me for the fact that I've caught you bare-assed with a man in your bed, you can think again. My hide's the one that's on the line here, Lori—"

"Would you two keep it down," interrupted Braddock. Their voices had risen with the heat of their exchange.

"Sorry I disturbed your sleep, bounty hunter. Now get up with your hands in the air." Corey made a show of bringing his other hand to the pistol to steady his aim.

"Corey Lochlain O'Sullivan, you know better than to be pointing that gun at him."

Corey lowered the gun at his sister's reprimand, but quickly reaimed, as if remembering who was in charge. "Shut up, Lorelei. Get away from her, Braddock."

Braddock eased off the bed, his hands in the air. He didn't know what he hated worse, being undressed or unarmed.

Corey sneered at Braddock's nakedness. Unarmed, Braddock decided.

"I ought to shoot you for laying a hand on my sister. But I'm not a murderer like you think. Get some rope, Lorelei."

"Don't you dare threaten to shoot him for something you arranged. It's fine for him to do whatever he wants to me as long as it's to save your worthless hide." Lorelei wedged herself between Braddock and her brother, still holding the blanket in front of her. "If I want someone for myself, that's a different story."

"If that someone wants to take me to jail, then yeah, we got ourselves a problem. But you've always been selfish, Lorelei."

"You'd better watch your mouth, you little brat." Braddock lowered his hands.

"Shut up. This isn't about you." Corey raised the gun again, not seeming to be bothered that to get to Braddock he had to go through his sister.

While Corey and he glared at each other, Lorelei managed to find her discarded chemise and pull it over her head. "Put the gun away, Corey. I don't like them in the house."

"Don't you understand anything? He wants to see me hang."

"No, he doesn't. He wants Mulcahy. If you can help him then maybe he can help clear your name."

Corey laughed bitterly, and Braddock noted that he wasn't half as naive as his older sister. "That's the same thing, Lori. Mulcahy will kill me faster than the law if he finds out I double-crossed him."

"Braddock's your only hope."

"How many men are you going to let use you before you figure out we're all a bunch of liars? Now get dressed and let's get out of here before the man watching the house wakes up."

Corey glanced at Braddock, then turned away in obvious disgust. The gesture rattled Braddock better than a well-placed blow.

Half of him was fighting mad, but the other half felt immobilized with guilt. He hadn't lied to Lorelei exactly, but the idea that he was here to help Corey wasn't exactly the truth. And knowing that she never would have bedded him if she realized he still planned on taking her brother to jail further aggravated Braddock's bout of conscience.

Corey bent down and picked up his sister's clothes, then tossed them at her. The unwanted dawn revealed the shame flushing Lorelei's cheeks.

Braddock balled his right hand into a tight fist. "If it weren't for your sister, I would have hauled your butt to jail the first time I came here. Then you thank her by leaving her without any supplies or money. From what I see, you'd be dead right now if it weren't for her."

"You got what you wanted, Braddock—now just be glad I'm leaving you with your life."

Braddock took another step toward Corey. "Try it. You think you're a man. Try it."

Corey backed up. Still tugging on her blouse, Lorelei stepped between them. "Please stop."

Corey raised the pistol again. "You see, Lorelei. He got what he wanted. He's not going to help us."

Lorelei turned her gaze up to Braddock's. "Are you going to help us?"

Before he had to answer, the door swung open. Braddock reached for his guns before he remembered he was naked.

Langston swaggered inside with the harsh morning light. He gripped pistols in both hands. "Deputy marshal. Drop it, son."

Unable to do anything else, Braddock sidestepped Lorelei, putting himself between her and Langston.

Corey swung his gun in Langston's direction, his hand shaking visibly.

"Please, Corey. Put down the gun," cried Lorelei.

Braddock could see in his peripheral vision that she was moving toward her brother. The chances were good she'd get hit in the cross fire. Without thinking, Braddock reached out and wrenched the gun from Corey's grasp.

Corey yelped, then clutched his right hand with his left. "I think you broke my finger."

Langston turned his guns on Braddock. "Drop it, Braddock."

Braddock flipped the loading chamber open to find the rusty Colt empty. "I ought to break your head," he said to Corey, then, "Put your guns away, Langston, it's not loaded." Braddock tossed the gun on the bed behind him. "What the hell were you doing threatening me with an unloaded pistol, boy? Do you want to get yourself killed?"

"I told you I'm not a murderer. Besides, what were you going to do about it? You were too busy taking advantage of my sister."

Langston smiled, obviously amused with the situation. "Guess you're right, Braddock. Her husband's not an outlaw. Her brother is."

Corey pointed to Braddock. "He's the one you ought to arrest. Look at him. He molested my sister."

Braddock folded his arms over his bare chest. Corey would get the beating he should have gotten years ago before this was over. "That doesn't mean Lorelei has anything to do with the robbery. It's Corey you want. After I get the information I need from him, you can take him, but leave his sister alone."

"No!" Lorelei cried from behind him. Braddock didn't want to hurt her, but he knew the sooner he removed Corey from her life the better off she'd be. Then maybe he'd be able to convince her to return to Kentucky.

Corey turned to Lorelei. "I told you he's out to get me."

Lorelei marched to her brother's side. "He's done nothing wrong."

"The U.S. government says he has. Since they're the ones paying me, I'm going to bring you all in and let the courts decide." Langston turned to Braddock, not bothering to hide his smile of satisfaction. "You too, Captain."

"I know I didn't hear you right, Langston."

Langston motioned to Braddock's bare midsection with the barrel of his gun. "Looks like I got you at a bit of a disadvantage."

"None that I can see." He longed to punch something, and the sarcastic smile pulling up the doughy contours of Langston's face provided a perfect target.

Langston's grin deepened. "I'll be glad to haul you handcuffed and buck naked through Santa Fe, if that's what you want."

Braddock stalked toward Langston. Even if he pulled the trigger, Braddock knew the bullet would somehow pass smoothly through him without leaving a scratch. But Langston wouldn't pull the trigger. "How are you going to get me handcuffed?"

Langston cocked his guns. "These here are going to do it for me."

"I don't think so. You can't shoot me. How would you explain that to your boss? So I guess you're going to have to fight me."

"I'm not fighting you, Braddock. I'm arresting you. Stop right there."

Braddock took another step.

"Christopher, please stop."

He heard the terror in Lorelei's voice right before the gun fired.

Lorelei's scream tore through him with more force than the bullet. Suddenly Braddock felt vulnerable. He saw the foolishness in stalking an armed man without even a stitch of clothing for protection.

He glanced down. Blood welled from a long gash on his upper thigh. That hadn't happened before. The bullet had skimmed him, but a few inches to the right and there would have been real trouble.

The anger pumping blood to Braddock's temples drew his attention away from the gash on his leg. "You son of a bitch." He forgot his fear, ready to lunge at Langston.

"Stop! I mean it."

Lorelei's scream froze him in midcrouch.

Both he and Langston turned. Lorelei held a rifle aimed at Langston.

"I swear on my mother's grave, I'll shoot you. Lower your guns." She held the old Springfield rifle steady, leaving no doubt she'd follow through with her threat. Braddock had seen the rifle propped against the wall, but hadn't thought much of it. He didn't even know if the rifle fired, but the look on Langston's face as he lowered his pistols to his sides showed the deputy marshal believed it did.

Which meant Lorelei was in a hell of a lot of trouble. There was no longer a question of whether or not she had broken the law. Pointing a rifle at a deputy U.S. marshal was not taken lightly.

Braddock took Langston's guns from him. Langston always went by the book. He'd never give Lorelei the benefit of the doubt. He wouldn't stop until he took her to jail, and there'd be nothing Braddock could do about it.

Corey hid behind his sister and watched the proceedings like a bystander. This whole mess was the boy's fault, but that didn't stop Braddock from feeling like he himself was to blame. Why'd Lorelei try to protect him?

"Put down the rifle, Lorelei, and come here."

Corey reached around his sister and nudged the muzzle in Braddock's direction. "I don't think so. We're leaving."

Lorelei trained the gun on him for the briefest of seconds. Long enough for their gazes to meet and Braddock to feel the air forced from his lungs. Betrayal struck swift and hard.

As quickly as it came, the sensation ended when Lorelei lowered the weapon and walked toward him. But the weight of her trust staggered him. She asked something of him he was not sure he had the will to give.

He focused on aiming the pistols he held at Langston so he wouldn't have to meet Lorelei's gaze any longer. "Get the handcuffs from his belt and cuff him."

Lorelei set the gun on the far wall—away from Corey, he noted—and did as he asked.

After Langston's wrists were clamped together behind his back, Braddock found his discarded pants and pulled them on.

The deputy said, "You know, I really didn't believe it until now. You're an outlaw, aren't you, Braddock? What are you going to do—kill me in cold blood?"

Braddock snatched his shirt from the back of a chair. "I'm not going to kill you, Langston."

"It's too late to try to get on my good side. You're in a lot of trouble."

Braddock searched the room for his gun belt while he pulled on his shirt. When his gaze stopped on Lorelei, she pointed to a rack mounted on the door. She must have put his weapons there and he hadn't even noticed. He stomped over and lifted the heavy leather from the wooden peg. Once he had his pistols securely strapped to his hips, he added Langston's Colts to the belt.

"Lorelei and Corey, gather up some supplies."

Lorelei pulled a crate from underneath the sink. Her brother stayed planted on the other side of the room and glared.

Braddock grabbed Langston's arm and guided him to the bed. Langston didn't give any resistance. "You're not going to get away with this."

"I'm not trying to get away with anything. I'm just trying to get the gold back and stop Mulcahy."

At a shove from Braddock, Langston fell back on the bed. "You have a funny way of doing it."

"We're not going anywhere with him, Lorelei," Corey said in a hiss. He hovered over his sister and unpacked each item she packed.

Lorelei said something stern under her breath that Braddock couldn't decipher.

"Corey, get a rope," called Braddock, breaking up their secret discussion before Corey could talk his sister into something that would surely land her in more trouble.

Corey glared again, then reluctantly left the adobe.

"What the hell are you doing with those two, Braddock? Never known you to be so low-down before to use a woman, but there's no explanation—"

"Shut up, Langston, or I'll hang you instead of tying you up."

Lorelei focused on rearranging sacks in the bag she had packed. Her effort not to look in their direction made it apparent she had heard.

Corey returned with the rope and tossed it on the table without a word.

Braddock fumbled in Langston's front pockets until he retrieved the key to the man's handcuffs. He picked up the rope and placed the key on the table, then loosely tied Langston's legs to the bed. Langston eyed the dull metal lying out of reach. The deputy marshal would be able to get loose and retrieve the key, but it would take a while. It would leave Braddock enough time . . . for what?

"Even if she were your wife, that doesn't mean she's above the law. You either. You better stop and think about what you're doing. She threatened to shoot an officer of the law. Helping a couple of fugitives will ruin you."

Braddock untied the kerchief from around Langston's neck and poised himself to stuff it into his mouth the next time he opened it, which didn't take long. Braddock had the same things going through his head. He didn't need Langston to tell him he'd gone too far.

Langston spit out his gag. "You're going to be wanted, just like them."

Braddock forcibly stuffed the gag back in Langston's mouth and cut a length of rope to keep it secure. When he had tied the last knot, he turned his back on the deputy and the last of his sense. He strode toward Lorelei and picked up the bag she had packed with supplies. Staring at the floral, cloth-covered valise for a long moment, he wondered, what kind of fugitive loaded supplies in a flimsy bag printed with bright pink roses.

Lorelei touched his arm. "I don't like this. Maybe we should go to the authorities and tell them this was all just a big mistake."

Corey spoke up before Braddock could tear his gaze away from her trusting face. "Forget it, Lorelei. They'd throw us both in jail before we could even say 'boo.'"

Braddock knew Corey was right, and he wasn't going to let Lorelei spend one single moment in a jail cell. Nor was he himself. He'd already had trouble because he looked too much like a dead fugitive named Lincoln Knox. And he didn't think Langston would be too helpful if the law in Santa Fe got a little confused. Langston would love to see him rot in a jail cell, even if it meant Mulcahy would escape to Mexico.

"Trust me." The words left Braddock's lips before he knew what he was saying. Trusting him was the last thing she should do, the last thing he wanted her to do. But somehow he'd landed this misguided woman's life firmly in the palm of his hand, and he felt relieved when she nodded yes.

"Well, I'm not going to trust you," said Corey.

Braddock strode toward the door. "Good. 'Cause I don't give a damn about you, kid. Let's go, Lorelei."

He didn't stop and wait to see if she followed. Maybe she wouldn't. It would be better that way. He heard her soft steps across the wooden porch. He slowed, unable to help himself.

Corey stomped across the porch ahead of them. He went

around the house and returned leading a white pony splashed with various shades of brown. The animal was on the small side, a little too lean. Probably a wild horse, but the way it pranced behind Corey like a thoroughbred told Braddock the kid had at least one thing going for him: he knew how to handle a horse.

Langston's golden stallion shook its mane and backed away from them, testing the length of the reins looped around the water pump in the middle of the yard.

"Lorelei rides your horse," said Braddock as he stepped off the porch. "Corey, you ride Langston's."

"I'm not a horse thief," protested Corey with real indignation.

"Your sister's not riding a stolen horse. That's final. I don't have time to argue." Braddock strode to the barn to retrieve Lucky, knowing his reasoning was faulty. The only one Langston was going to blame for the theft of his horse was Braddock.

By the time he led a saddled Lucky from the barn, Lorelei sat atop Corey's horse while her brother soothed Langston's frightened animal with soft words and a scratch behind the ear. Once Braddock mounted, Corey quickly followed suit.

"I've got eyes in the back of my head, kid. So don't even think about it."

Corey cut his gaze across to the horizon, letting Braddock know he wasn't making any promises. Braddock contracted his thighs, sending Lucky into a trot.

Lorelei easily caught up with him. "Thank you."

"Don't thank me yet." Braddock used his heels to send the horse into a full gallop.

As they rode hard across the desert, he wondered how soon it would be until she was cursing him. He was already cursing himself.

Braddock had a long, hard ride to mull over his situation. Only one solution satisfied him: to beat the truth out of Corey Sullivan once and for all.

When they finally reached the tall red rocks that hid a

slowly fountaining underground spring, the sky was stained a bloody pink. The blue canopy of night closed quickly around them as they stopped to make camp for the night.

After Braddock dismounted, he helped Lorelei slide off the pinto's back. Her knees buckled, forcing her to grab his shoulders to stay on her feet. Once she regained her balance she made a show of straightening her wrinkled skirt. The way she tried to hide her obvious exhaustion fueled Braddock's volatile temper.

When Corey came trotting up behind them, Braddock wrapped his left hand around the palomino's reins and gripped Corey's shirtfront with his right. He dragged him to the ground before the kid could grunt a protest.

With feet braced, hands balled in fists, Braddock willed Corey to stand and take a swing at him. "You'd better start spilling your guts, kid. Where's Mulcahy?"

"Get away from me, you crazy bastard. I didn't ask for your help."

Braddock hauled him up by his leather vest. He gave Corey a teeth-jarring shake to let him know he was serious. "Where's Mulcahy?"

"I don't know." Corey remained limp. He didn't even try to fight back. He was smarter than Braddock gave him credit for.

Braddock reared back his fist.

Lorelei clutched his arm before he could follow through with the punch. "What are you doing?"

Braddock tried to gently shake her off. "Let go. He has it coming."

Corey closed his eyes tightly, preparing himself for the blow. For once he kept his smart mouth shut.

Lorelei wrapped both hands around the bend in Braddock's cocked arm and tugged with all her body weight. "I'm not going to let you hurt my brother, no matter what he's done."

Braddock dropped Corey to the ground. He could easily shake her off, of course, but he couldn't see slinging her into the dirt. As soon as Lorelei released him, he paced in the other direction. She would stick by Corey no matter what he'd done, nor how much it cost her. Braddock had to admit he admired her loyalty, even if it was stupid. Apparently his West Point lessons were harder to shake than he imagined.

Braddock took off his hat and ran his fingers through his hair. His schooled code of honor wasn't what had gotten him in this mess—running from the law, tied up with a bumbling outlaw and a vulnerable woman. His own personal code of ethics, tarnished as it was, had finally been forced out of retirement by his bad behavior. He had used Lorelei, and he didn't like his actions. She had filled a hole in him, if just for a little while, and he had opened up a wound in her she had just gotten closed. He would fix the mess in her life if it was the last thing he did. Then she was on her own. He couldn't save her from all the harsh realities of the world if she refused to let go of her worthless ideals. Ideals got you killed.

He stomped back over to Corey and Lorelei.

"You'd better tell me everything that happened from the moment you met Mulcahy."

Lorelei draped her arm around her brother's shoulders. "I told you what happened. Corey didn't know what they were going to do."

Braddock stared hard at Corey. "Not that load of shit. The truth."

"Why are you so angry?" Lorelei asked.

"Do you have any idea how much trouble you're in? You pointed a rifle at a U.S. marshal. As far as the law's concerned, you're as guilty as he is. And I stole a horse, for Pete's sake. You do know that's a hanging offense, don't you?"

She had the good sense to pale and drop her arm from around Corey. "I wouldn't have shot him. I just didn't want you to get hurt."

"From now on, don't worry about me or him." He jabbed a finger in Corey's direction, aching to do so much more. "Worry about yourself, Lorelei, 'cause right now we're all in the same boat, and it's sinking."

He clasped Corey's shoulder. "You will tell me what happened, or I'll beat you until you do." He glanced at Lorelei. "Even if I have to tie your sister up to do it."

Lorelei gazed at him as if she didn't know him. "Why are you doing this?"

"I have to get the truth out of him so I can figure out what to do next. I'm trying to save all our necks."

She glanced at Corey. He plastered a pleading expression on his face but remained silent.

She turned away from both of them and unstrapped her flowered valise from the pinto. "I'm going to get dinner started. Just don't break any bones."

Braddock gripped Corey's arm. "I'll take him far enough away so you can't hear him scream."

"Lori," the boy called before Braddock could drag him behind the tall rock shelter. "Don't leave me alone with him. He's crazy. Lori!"

When Braddock had him far enough from Lorelei so that she couldn't overhear their conversation, he shoved Corey, sending him sprawling. "Start talking."

"You're not getting me near Mulcahy. You can beat me all you want. Mulcahy will kill me." Corey pushed himself to a sitting position. He locked his hands protectively around his knees.

Braddock folded his arms over his chest. "So you were in on the robbery."

Corey stared into the night as if looking for help to ride up from the darkness. "I guess."

"Either you were or you weren't."

"You gonna tell Lori about this?"

"It depends. I doubt she'd believe me anyway."

Corey turned back to him and cocked his head. "She might. She's pretty trusting."

"So why'd you let her believe you're innocent?"

" 'Cause I care about her. I care about what she thinks."

"I don't care what she thinks as long as she stays safe. Thanks to you, she's far from that."

"You don't know anything about us. You're just like the others. You take what you can get while you can get it. You might fool Lorelei, but you're not fooling me."

Braddock had been grinding his teeth without realizing it. He had to unhinge his jaw to get his words out. "Tell me smart-ass, what the hell am I getting from being out here with you? Tying up a marshal and stealing his horse makes me a goddamned outlaw. So what's in it for me?"

Corey rocked, bringing his legs closer to his body. "Me. Mulcahy, whose bounty is triple mine. And Lori, when you've a mind to. I might have picked the wrong bunch to hook up with, but what I did, I did to myself. I didn't get some poor woman all twisted up in the process."

Braddock took three deep breaths through his nose. "Don't forget who sent her to me in the first place."

Corey pushed piles of soft sand around with his boot. "I met Mulcahy in a saloon outside Santa Fe. I'd been catching wild horses and selling them once I got them trained. It kept me fed, but it wasn't enough to send for Lorelei." He glanced up, checking for interest, seeing how his story was going over.

Braddock nodded. If he kept Corey talking long enough, he was bound to stumble onto some part of the truth. He nodded again for the boy to continue.

"Lorelei wrote to me when our ma died. She'd been taking care of her, and I promised Lori we'd be together after she passed on. Kentucky had too many bad memories. The war was —"

Braddock interrupted. "You can skip that part. I was there."

Corey picked up a rock and tossed it. "I didn't have enough to bring Lorelei out, so I took what I had and got in this poker game. I'm usually lucky with cards."

"Yeah. I heard you cheat."

Corey glared, but didn't deny it. "Anyway, I lost that night. This fella heard my name and decided to buy me a drink 'cause I was Irish. Or at least my parents were. I didn't bother telling him my pa dropped the O from O'Sullivan because he didn't have any use for Irish or Ireland. That man was Mulcahy, and he said he could use a hand like me for this job they had."

"So you knew you'd be robbing the stage."

Corey hesitantly nodded. Night had pushed out the last of the sunset, but the quarter moon and stars were as bright as white fire in the desert's black sky.

Braddock could see Corey's bottom lip jut out and tremble slightly. "I didn't know they were going to kill people. That I won't do. When the shooting started, I put my gun away. Mulcahy got hit, and he blames me. He said he was going to kill me, but I just ran away."

Braddock rubbed the stubble on his chin. It made sense. None of Mulcahy's jobs had ever gone so wrong. "Looks like you got a hell of a lot more trouble than the law. If Mulcahy said he was going to kill you, he will."

When Corey swallowed, his Adam's apple bobbed, his fear reminding Braddock that he really was just a kid.

"He was hit pretty bad. Maybe he died."

"I don't think you're that lucky, Corey."

"Nope. Guess not."

Braddock squatted to face him. "Seems to me you'd be better off in jail than running."

"They'll hang me."

"Not if we give them Mulcahy and the gold. I'd say it's your only chance, 'cause if the law won't get you, Mulcahy will. I know the man. You'd rather be hanged than have him get his hands on you."

Corey narrowed his gaze as if trying to see into Braddock's soul. "What do you want?"

Braddock didn't flinch under his scrutiny. There was nothing to see. "I want Lorelei someplace safe so I don't have to worry about her. I want Mulcahy to hang and the gold returned. Then I'll clear my name. In that order. If you get a lesser jail sentence in the process, that's fine, but it's not a priority."

"So why should I help you?"

"I'm the only chance you have to keep the skin on your neck."

"I could go it on my own." The boy lifted his chin, letting

Braddock know it was what he wanted him to believe he preferred.

"Or you could help me find Mulcahy in order to clear your sister's name. As long as he's free, you're going to have to sleep with one eye open."

"I don't trust you."

"And I don't trust you."

Corey shrugged. "I don't even know where Mulcahy is."

Braddock didn't believe him, but saying so wouldn't get him the information. Fortunately, he had something else in mind. "You know where he's been. We'll start there. I'm a pretty decent tracker."

Corey stood. "You stay away from Lorelei."

Braddock wished he could tell Corey the same thing. The girl would be better off without either one of them. "I'll leave that up to your sister," he said instead.

Corey walked back toward camp as if he hadn't heard.

Braddock rubbed the back of his neck, relieved Corey had dropped the subject. Unfortunately, he knew continuing his relationship with Lorelei was wrong. He also knew that wasn't going to stop him.

Corey turned back before he was out of earshot. "She'll hold you responsible if something happens to me. She won't forgive you."

Braddock folded his arms over his chest, glad it was too dark for the kid to see his arrow hit its mark. He regretted not slapping him around while he had had the chance.

Corey quickly turned away again, but not before Braddock saw he was smiling.

Braddock shifted his weight. His right thigh throbbed in protest, reminding him he needed to take a look at the graze Langston had given him. He reluctantly followed Corey back to camp.

A golden glow flared out from the dark outline of the rocks. Instead of moving toward the fire, Braddock veered into the darkness, longing for a drink. Just one good shot of strong whiskey to shake the feeling of unease he was carrying around. He walked farther into the distance, away from Lorelei and her brother, hoping the desolate landscape would seep into him, return him to his old self.

All these different emotions—compassion, guilt, longing—tightened his chest and throat. Even the small scratch on his thigh pulsed with the pain of being human. He couldn't say he liked being thrust back into the thick of things. After the war he had become numb. The only thing he felt was a dependable sense of indifference.

Once the war ended and civilization took hold again, he couldn't pretend that all those rules people set up for themselves and everyone else mattered. Couldn't be polite when he didn't feel like it. Couldn't act like he cared when he didn't. His parents had been horrified when their celebrated son came home and couldn't be shown off properly. Braddock had lost his ability to be respectable, or so he had thought.

Well, he couldn't say his intentions toward Lorelei were exactly respectable, not by most people's standards, but he did have a strong desire to please her. He wanted to show her how a man could make a woman feel if he had a mind to. For he had a mind to.

The night had turned sharply cool, but the day's heat still radiated from the ground. Thinking of the things he wanted to show Lorelei made the earth's warmth shoot through the soles of his boots and pool in his groin. The last woman he had made love to whom he hadn't paid was well before the war, a widow who enjoyed tutoring the boys from West Point in things other than academics. She had been his first real lover.

He hadn't thought of that time in years. Hadn't needed the widow's special instruction. Whores didn't care. They just wanted you to be quick or they charged extra.

On the long ride, knowing he'd have Lorelei close by tonight, he'd thought of the widow and what she had told him about women, what they liked. Hell, the damage was done. He had taken Lorelei's virginity. Not that it mattered much out here. Lorelei could have her pick of husbands and, with her beauty, they wouldn't care what she'd done in her past.

Braddock dropped the hand he'd been absently rubbing over his chest. Finding Lorelei a husband sounded too much like a good idea. What better way to appease his flickering sense of honor than to find her a husband?

He stared up at the stars, feeling betrayed by his own good sense.

He strolled back to the camp, sure of only one thing: his best chance of finding Mulcahy relied upon keeping the Sullivans close. But this opportunity to finally get Mulcahy came with a price: he'd be forced to live again. Meeting Lorelei, giving a damn, both made him as vulnerable as every other bastard out there. He shouldn't be surprised at the cost. Everything had one.

When he drew close enough to smell beans with a smoky hint of bacon cooking over an open flame, Braddock tried to squeeze back into his old shroud of indifference. It didn't work. When it came to Lorelei Sullivan, he was anything but indifferent.

Yet if he wanted to do the right thing by her, at the very least he had better adjust to being frustrated. Of all the emotions battling for control, frustration was his safest option. He should keep his hands and thoughts off her and deliver her to the first marriage-minded farmer he stumbled across. He ran his fingers through his hair and stomped the rest of the way back to the licking flames of the camp fire.

Lorelei knelt next to the fire, stirring a pot that hung on a tripod. When she saw him, she smiled. "Hungry?"

Against a rock, Corey silently spooned food into his mouth. His gaze spit heat when Braddock strode directly to Lorelei.

Braddock squatted beside her and winced.

"What's wrong?"

He shifted, taking the weight off his wounded leg. "The graze from Langston's bullet is starting to throb. Once I clean the wound it'll be fine."

"I'd forgotten in all the excitement. I'll take a look at it for you."

"Don't bother. It's nothing."

Corey sneered at the exchange. Braddock half expected the kid to stick his tongue out.

Lorelei ladled stew onto a tin plate, either purposely ignoring or not noticing her brother's imminent combustion. "I'll take a look at it after you eat. It might need a stitch or two."

"All right."

Braddock couldn't help but grin, forcing Corey to stare into the dented tin cup that served as his dinner plate. His satisfaction deepened when he noted he received the better utensils.

Braddock settled beside Lorelei, glad that he wasn't one to do the right thing.

Chapter Seven

Lorelei stared into the deep blue darkness that had swallowed Corey while Christopher eased his pants past his thighs. Her suggestion that Corey check the horses had earned her some time alone with Christopher. Her goal now accomplished, a bout of nerves threatened to swamp her purpose. She needed to be reassured that Christopher still intended to help clear Corey's name. Though Corey would never be convinced.

She set her pan of warmed water on the ground, then knelt in front of Christopher. When she dabbed a wet cloth around the blood-encrusted wound, he involuntarily tensed in a protesting jerk.

"Sorry." Her glance to his face stopped at his hips. His shirt tented with the beginning of arousal. She quickly returned her gaze to his wound. "I guess it doesn't hurt that bad."

"Guess not."

The laughter in his voice reassured her. His lighthearted tone belonged to the man who'd convinced her with his actions if not his words that he could never hurt her or her brother, one who differed greatly from the man who'd bested

Langston and ridden them hard into the middle of nowhere.

She cleaned the wound efficiently, touching him no more than necessary. The graze didn't even need a bandage, much less a stitch. Which was a good thing, because she didn't care for the longing that touching him brought. Her need to be reassured that he was the man she thought he was went far beyond her desire to help her brother. She wanted to keep Christopher for herself, if only for a little while longer.

She stood without looking at him. "You can pull your pants up. I'm done."

He did, then fell back into morose silence. Both he and Corey had been like two surly dogs since they returned from their discussion behind the rocks. Corey's cutting glares let her know he was furious; the only words he'd spoken were a hissed promise to leave at the first opportunity.

She rinsed the cloth she had used to clean Christophe_'s wound in the pan of water, then dumped it onto the dirt. The ground beaded, making the water look a solid thing. How quickly would it dry a person out if one got caught out here all alone? No matter what, she couldn't let Corey set out on his own.

"Did you get the information you needed from Corey?"

Braddock stared into the fire. "Enough."

The dull metal of his pistols caught the firelight, and Lorelei wondered if he wore them for protection from intruders or to keep her and Corey under his control. Corey was clear what he thought.

"What are you going to do?"

Braddock moved away from the ring of light cast by the fire and sat with his back against a boulder wedged in the sand. His face was masked in shadow.

"Find Mulcahy and bring him in. Corey's going to have to show me the places they've been so I can pick up his trail."

She settled beside him, not giving him the chance to melt away from her so thoroughly. She sat far enough away so they weren't touching, but close enough so he could reach out and take her hand. It was silly, but she wanted him to do just that.

"Corey still thinks you plan to turn him in."

"Aren't you worried about yourself? You're in trouble with the law, too."

She found it more convenient not to think about that. If she focused on helping Corey, she could ignore the fact that they were all fugitives or that she wanted this man to be more than just a bounty hunter whose main concern was catching his prey.

"Corey's in a lot more trouble than me."

He draped his arm around her shoulders, then pulled her against his side. He briskly rubbed her arm with his palm as if warming her. She scooted closer and laid her head on his shoulder. The warmth of his solid body seeping into hers had her feeling right again.

"If you keep trying to protect your brother, you're going to catch up with him."

"Corey doesn't believe you want to help us."

Braddock remained silent for so long, she feared he would say it was true. When he did speak, she could tell he chose his words carefully. "If Corey's bounty were my only concern, I would have let Langston have him. The price on Corey isn't worth the trouble I'm in."

"Then why didn't you turn him over to Langston?"

His gaze didn't falter from the entrancing dance of the fire. "I have my reasons."

"I'd like to know what kind of reasons would make you charge a man with a gun, unarmed, not to mention undressed."

"My facing down Langston might have looked pretty stupid, but I know the man." He turned to Lorelei and looked directly into her eyes. "Don't ever lift another finger in my defense. I know what I'm doing."

"I can't promise you that."

"But you want the world from me. You want me to tell you your brother's going to go free, when he's gotten himself into more trouble in his short life than it takes other men a lifetime to acheive."

"I just want your word you won't turn him in. That you'll do what you can to clear his name."

Braddock removed his arm from her shoulders. "Clear his name how? He's guilty."

Lorelei fought the desperate urge to draw him back against her. "He says he's innocent."

Braddock stood. "I'm not going to argue with you about this, Lorelei. If you can't see what's right in front of you, I'm not going to try to convince you."

She stood also, grabbing his arm when he tried to turn away. "This isn't only about Corey."

"Nothing's changed. I can't make you happy. I don't have it in me."

"I'm not asking you to make me happy."

"Then what are you asking?"

She sighed, wanting to ask him to make love to her again, to tell her he couldn't walk away from what they shared, but she kept her desires to herself. And not only out of obligation to Corey. Fear held her silent with a more powerful grip. She'd been walked away from before.

"I want what I've always wanted. I want you to try to help us clear Corey's name. He didn't kill anyone. And if he helps you find this Mulcahy and get the gold back, that should count for something."

He stared at her a long moment, and she imagined he could read her true thoughts.

"If Corey leads me to the gold, I guess it would count for something. But I can't promise you it will keep him out of jail."

"He'll help you. I'll make sure of that."

He brushed his thumb across her mouth. "That's all you want? To keep Corey safe?"

"That's already more than I have a right to ask you for."

"Jesus Christ, Lorelei," he exploded. "You have a right to a lot more than that. You deserve a husband who'll take care of you. You shouldn't be saddled with your rotten brother . . . or a bastard like me."

She touched his cheek. "Meeting you is the best thing that's happened to me in a long time."

He grabbed her wrist, pulling her hand away from his face. "Then you're worse off than I thought."

She tried to jerk her hand away.

He held her, but gentled his grip. "I'm sorry. I didn't say that to hurt you, but to warn you. I can't promise you anything, not even that I can keep your brother from hanging. I have no right to, but I want to make love to you again. And I don't have enough conscience to stop myself if you give me half a chance."

She rose on her tiptoes to touch his lips to hers. She wanted him, too. Any way she could have him.

"I told you to stay away from her, Braddock."

At the sound of Corey's voice, Lorelei came down hard on the balls of her feet. Braddock didn't budge a muscle.

"And you know what I told you, kid."

Corey braced himself with his feet apart, looking like he itched for a fight.

Braddock lowered his head, and Lorelei feared he was going to kiss her just to provoke her brother. She turned her head to avoid his mouth.

He said, "I'll do what I can for him, but only because of you. And I'll try to keep my hands off you. But if you want me, all you have to do is come to me. Whenever, wherever," he whispered next to her ear.

He straightened, then cut a bruising glance to Corey. Corey lowered his gaze and relaxed his stance. Apparently satisfied, Braddock turned his back on them. He picked up the rifle resting against his saddle.

"Get some sleep. I'm going to look around and see if we were followed."

As soon as Braddock melted into the darkness, Corey rushed to Lorelei's side. "We've got to get away from him."

She raised her hand and turned her face away from him. For the first time in her life she shut out her brother's plea. "I'm too tired to think about it tonight. You heard him. Let's get some sleep."

*   *   *

Lorelei thrashed, trying to escape from a disturbing dream. She was back home in her old house, the one where they had lived before her father lost everything. But she wasn't happy because she knew what could happen, what would happen, without knowing how or what. The smooth plaster walls of her home were slowly crumbling. She would no sooner patch one hole using mud, grass, and her favorite dresses, covering it all with whitewash, then the other walls would start to fall apart. Corey played cards with his horse in the living room. And even in the dream she knew everyone else was gone; she knew it with every part of herself, and every part of herself ached.

She blinked hard, trying to shake the effects of the dream. But its awful clarity left her with a sticky residue of pain. She opened her eyes wide, desperate for wakefulness. The open sky instantly brought her back to the present. Thousands upon thousands of stars stretched out into the velvet darkness. The vastness threatened to swallow her.

She propped herself on her elbows and searched for Christopher.

He sat on the other side of the fire, wide-awake, a tin cup in his hand. His steady gaze centered on her, as if he'd been watching her for hours.

She sat up and brushed her tangled hair away from her face. "Can't you sleep?"

"You're sleeping in my bedroll."

She touched the folds of the thick flannel, forgetting that it had been his. How had she come to think of it as hers so easily? "Sorry." She eased out of the cocoon of blankets.

"Stay. I want you to use it." He took a sip from the cup he held, then studied its contents.

She glanced at Corey, who slept a few feet away. They hadn't gone to bed angry with each other since before their mother took sick. There was no room for anger when there was so much sorrow.

She turned back to Christopher. His gaze had settled on her again but he pulled it away when their eyes met.

Lorelei stood and stretched. She'd slept fully dressed but he acted as though he had caught her in her underclothes. Which was silly, because they had gone way past that. Then she remembered what he had told her. If she wanted him, all she had to do was come to him. His eyes were hooded and she wondered if he was thinking of it too. Maybe he regretted making himself so available to her. Maybe he had thought about his pledge and realized Lorelei was too much to take on, even as a lover.

She sauntered toward him, only slightly surprised by her boldness. She felt free somehow. As if she were leaving behind everything she had ever known to be true. She realized she had nothing else to count on besides him, nothing else to believe in.

Last night had been different. Things had just happened between them without her having to make a conscious choice. Then she still had some of her illusions about her relationship with Christopher to sustain her. She could pretend there was a chance they could build a life together.

Tonight they were all fugitives. Nothing was certain. Not even that Christopher would help Corey.

For the first time in a long time, she was going to ask for what she wanted. She wanted to give herself to Christopher for no other reason than to be held in his arms.

Her courage faltered slightly when she reached him. He openly stared, his indifference gone. She sank next to him and avoided his bold gaze. He hadn't changed his mind about wanting her; that was obvious. Nor was he smiling. His jaw was tight, held with an intensity that reminded her of the man who had first stalked up to the adobe's door, his pistols drawn. This was the side of him she feared slightly.

She hugged her knees to her chest. Something in her wouldn't let her turn back, though the urge to slink back to her warm blankets tempted her.

"I had a bad dream."

His gaze returned to the fire. "What about?"

"I dreamed my world was falling apart, crumbling all around me."

"It is."

"I know." She touched his shoulder with the flat of her palm, letting it follow the contour of his arm. He was tense despite the way he leisurely stretched a leg out in front of him.

"I want . . ." She began but faltered, unable to say the words.

He turned to look at her. His hazel eyes burned light green with some inner struggle, but his jaw remained tight. He wasn't going to say it for her.

"You," she finished, her voice smoky and seductive. The word rubbed against her own skin like soft fabric after a warm bath.

He returned his gaze to the fire and tightened his grip on the tin cup. "Why?"

She studied his profile, unsure of what she was supposed to say. Braddock seemed coiled too tightly. Even she didn't know why she wanted to ignore propriety and give her body to him. The simple pleasure of being held seemed too shallow of a reason to turn against common sense. But the desire to feel his skin pressed against hers was stronger than anything she had experienced before. To be close to him, even for an hour, seemed worth whatever consequences might follow.

"I want you because you make me feel good."

He glanced at her sharply. Something in him had started to unwind. His breathing quickened.

"I want to make you feel better than you ever felt before."

He stood and offered her his hand. She placed her palm against his, and he brought her to her feet. Without a word he led her away from the fire, away from Corey. He paused to scoop up the discarded bedroll, then guided her behind the rocks.

In a nook where soft sand had been piled by desert winds, he spread the blankets. He turned to face her while pulling his shirt from his pants. As he freed the buttons, she started to do the same to her blouse.

He stilled her movements by gently touching her wrist. "I can't offer you anything but this. You know that."

"Yes."

He moved his hands and let her finish her task. His fascination with her progress urged her to slow the process. Capturing his attention so fully was a pleasure in itself.

His stare alone tightened her body, sending a rush of warmth to her breasts and belly.

"I want you to feel the same pleasure I do. Even if it takes all night," he said without taking his gaze from her hands as they worked to release the buttons of her blouse.

She peeled the cotton from her shoulders. "I do."

He grinned. "No, you don't. But you will."

He pulled her toward him as if he couldn't resist touching the skin she revealed. While he smoothed his hands down her back, he kissed her. In two quick motions he managed to relieve her of her outer garments and her underskirts.

His kisses drifted to her shoulder while he reached underneath her chemise to cup her bare bottom. "You're going to have to tell me what feels good and what doesn't."

The sensation of his rough hands gripping her so intimately forced a gasp of pleasure.

"That feels good."

When he pressed her more fully against him, the buckle of his gun belt dug into her stomach.

She braced her hands against his chest. "That doesn't. Aren't you going to take off your guns?"

He tensed and peeled her away from him.

She blinked, not believing what she saw in his expression: suspicion.

"What are you thinking?" She was more hurt than angry, which she wished weren't the case.

He unbuckled his belt. "I don't want a repeat of this morning. If I have to get caught with my pants down again, I don't want it to be without a gun."

He took one of the pistols out of the holster before he arranged the belt at the head of the bedroll. The single gun he laid on the center edge of the red-and-green-checked blanket, clearly within his reach. He wasn't taking any chances.

"Come here."

He guided her to her knees beside him. She responded to his gentle persuasion, not completely happy with his explanation of the guns. He shrugged out of his shirt. Before she could settle on the soft flannel, he gripped the hem of her chemise and pulled it over her head.

"God, you're beautiful."

His reverence went a long way toward helping her forget her doubts. She hadn't forgotten what it had felt like to be held at gunpoint by Langston, and if his precaution would prevent that, so much the better. He wouldn't think of hurting her brother while making love to her. He wasn't that callous.

By the time he yanked off his boots and shucked his pants, he was fiercely aroused.

She placed her hands flat on his chest, wanting to feel his strong pulse against her palms. Soon she'd be unable to think at all. The total absorption of joining their bodies, being consumed by him, was the only thing that let her truly forget the grief that had been her companion for so long she could hardly remember what if felt like not to carry its weight.

Her hands drifted down his rib cage. He stopped her before she went any lower.

"Lie on your back."

She complied immediately, ready as he was for their joining. Even the hard ground was a heady caress against her tingling body.

He moved over her, supporting his weight on his hands and knees. She spread her legs and arched up, unaware of how wanton, how eager that instinctual act was until he jerked his hips back, pulling away from her.

"Not yet, sweetheart. Though you tempt my resolve."

"Resolve for what?" She gripped his hips and tried to guide him between her spread legs.

"To make you come."

At first the word shocked her. She'd heard her brothers use it when they thought she wasn't within earshot. She hadn't thought a woman could do that, but the idea excited her just the same.

"Is that possible?"

With his weight lowered to his elbows, he dipped his head to cover her mouth. The wicked slide of his tongue against hers convinced her anything was possible.

"It's different from a man, but it's definitely possible," he said between openmouthed kisses that drifted across her collarbone. "But you're going to have to help me. Tell me what you like."

Her body arched everywhere he kissed, seeking more. When he swirled his tongue in a hollow at the base of her neck, her insides coiled with pleasure. Her desire for him seared straight to her sex, making her pulse with need. The sensation raged with an intensity that left her mindless with wanting. She couldn't help but rotate her hips, her whole body vibrating to urges that demanded a response.

He moved his attention to her breast, and when he sucked her nipple she cried out. He lifted his head briefly and laid his finger over his lips, reminding her of their need to be quiet. She nodded, then pressed her hand against the back of his neck to encourage him to continue.

She forced her eyes to remain open, to focus on the sea of blazing stars. She couldn't lose herself so completely that she was howling like a banshee. Corey slept just beyond the rocks. She couldn't let him find them like this. There was the loaded pistol beside her head.

She pushed thoughts of Corey away before they overrode the pleasure in her body. As Christopher's kisses trailed across her stomach, her hands drifted to her breasts, squeezing them, relieving the ache at his departure.

"Show me how to touch you like you like to touch yourself."

Her eyes opened, and, when she realized what she was doing, she immediately stopped, embarrassed by her neediness, her total lack of control.

She also became aware of how close his face was to her spread legs. She tensed, but his body blocked her from closing her knees. He guided her hands back to her breasts.

"I like to see you do that. It makes me crazy."

The huskiness in his voice encouraged her. Her fingers brushed over her straining nipples, and she felt a jolt all the way to her sex. She pinched the overly sensitized tips and had to swallow a moan.

"That's it; keep doing that." He wedged his shoulders under her knees and opened her fully to his gaze. With his fingers, he spread her inner folds. She jerked at the intimate contact.

"Relax, sweetheart. I want to taste you."

She lay back, reeling with the idea. Surely she'd be going straight to hell afterward, but she wanted the same thing.

When his tongue tentatively touched her, something in the pit of her stomach clenched into a fist. But one soft graze across her hungry flesh eased the shock, turning his caress into liquid pleasure that flowed across her skin like warm rain. She writhed under his insanely gentle assault. Christopher's soft kisses were almost torment.

"Have you ever touched yourself here, Lorelei?"

He eased a finger inside her slick passage, and she found it impossible to concentrate on his words.

"Show me how you like to be touched."

She wanted to tell him she never touched herself there and she didn't know, but she did know. She had touched herself, but had always been deeply ashamed. The experiences had left her tense and disturbed, and afterward she always vowed never to do such a wicked thing again.

He circled her opening with his tongue, then flicked the tip over her secret spot.

"Show me," he demanded.

"There," she whispered.

He spread her, exposing her in a way she could never imagine she'd allow. He gently licked the hidden pleasure point. She squirmed against him, wanting more. He took her between his lips and sucked. She jerked at the jolt of sensation.

He eased up instantly.

"Lick me there again, soft, like you were."

His eager compliance made her soon forget her horror at her own bold words.

She buried her hands in his hair and rotated her hips. The muscles of her sex pulsed. She needed to feel him inside her, but didn't want this new and wicked pleasure to end. She knew he needed more also, but he resisted just to please her. He laved her with his tongue as if she were all he wanted in the world.

The writhing urges of her body grew more demanding. "Put a finger inside me," she heard some other part of her command.

He did and she moaned, glad for her wantonness. Nothing had ever felt this good. He moved his finger to the rhythm of her hips, then slid his tongue around his finger. A groan from deep in his throat added his fire to her own.

Her whole being was centered between her legs. Her blood seemed to pump from her sex, pulsating spasms out to the rest of her body. She had to remind herself to breathe as her body closed in on itself, desperately grasping his finger.

"You're so close, sweetheart. Wait." He pulled away from her so abruptly the shock was like a hard shake. "I want to be inside you when you come."

He hooked his arm underneath her knee and thrust into her as he moved over her.

She gasped. His fullness forced jolts of pleasure to bite hard around the place where they connected. Waves of ecstasy tumbled through her.

He pulled back and pushed into her again, each movement slow and deep.

"Touch yourself, Lorelei. You're ready to explode."

She rubbed her secret spot while he slowly rocked in and out. She felt so raw it almost hurt, but something made her push harder. Her body wound tighter, she gasped, almost on the verge of tears.

He reached around her and cupped her bottom, spreading her as he pushed deeper into her. He was pushing past all her barriers. She couldn't let him touch her so intimately, open her so thoroughly.

"No," she whispered.

He eased out and in again. "Let go."

She didn't know what he meant. With the same sureness with which he had entered her, he eased a single finger into her as well.

Everything in her body clenched at this new, different invasion. She gasped, but no sound came out. Then she came undone. She bucked against him as a wave of concentrated pleasure raced through her.

He lowered her to the ground, keeping in connection with her. When the bone-shaking contractions had subsided, he kissed the corner of her eyes, her cheeks, around her mouth. Despite his gentle pecks he was still fully aroused inside her. His presence intensified each little spasm left over from the giant swell that had overtaken her.

With his weight on his elbows, he nuzzled her ear. "I think you did it."

She brushed his hair off his forehead. "You think?" Her limbs were deadweight. She dropped her hand back down, unable to do much else.

"I've never been with a woman like you before, Lorelei. So passionate."

Despite her exhaustion, she stiffened. Maybe she'd always known deep down she was wanton. Feared it. That was why she hadn't wanted to take her father's not-so-subtle hints to get herself in the family way with Berkley. It wasn't her pride. It was what she feared she might unleash.

He cradled her head with his palms, forcing her to look into his eyes. "That was a compliment. Your passion is honest. That's what makes you so rare."

She traced the outline of his mouth with her finger. "Thank you," she whispered. He made her feel cherished. That was why she'd risked so much for this intimacy.

She shifted her weight, the pressure on her spread legs becoming strained.

He closed his eyes as if he were in pain. A groan caught in his throat and he pulsed inside her.

"What about you?" she crooned, loving her power over him.

"I was hoping you'd help me out with that."

She gripped his hips, urging him to take his pleasure, but he hesitated.

He kissed the tip of her nose, then her forehead. "I want to try something different."

"All right." He'd given her so much pleasure, she readily agreed.

He trailed soft kisses around her mouth, his hesitation unnerving. What was he trying to soften her up for? His gentle coaxing stirred her body back to life. The lips of her sex pulsed lightly around his erection.

He must have felt the growing demands of her body as well, because he abruptly pulled away from her and sat back on his heels. "Roll over onto your hands and knees."

She stared at him a moment, unsure. But the intensity and plain desire on his face urged her over. She wanted him to lose control as she did, to be so vulnerable and pliable that he would let her do anything, touch him anywhere. But the places she wanted to touch couldn't be reached so easily.

Once she was planted on her hands and knees, she glanced at him over her shoulder. She didn't have to ask him if this was what he wanted, because she could tell it was. He stared at her in a way that made her desire flare all over again. He was breathing hard through his nose, his jaw tense.

He gripped her hips and wedged himself between her legs, pushing her knees farther apart with his.

She let her head roll between her shoulders. The position exposed her in a way she'd never been before. The desert night caressed her as much as his touch. Her sexuality dominated her with a primal power that surged through her. She arched her back in a catlike motion that released the tension building in her body.

There was a slight pressure as he entered her again, but the sensation quickly turned to pleasure. He grabbed her hips, steadying her for his powerful thrusts, pulling her to him as he surged forward.

She glanced at him over her shoulder again; his head was slightly back, his eyes closed.

"What are you doing to me?" he said on a moan.

She rotated her hips as he pushed into her. When that wasn't enough, she sat back on each of his forward strokes, maneuvering him to a place inside her she hadn't even known existed. As her pleasure increased, she laid her head on the bedroll, stretching her sex and deepening their connection.

"Yes." The increased fierceness of his strokes let her know he liked her shared passion as much as did his spoken word.

Unbelievably, she was heading toward the place where she would come apart again. She put her hand between her legs, touching the spot that had brought on an explosion of pleasure, and accidentally brushed him with her fingers. His gasp was audible. Drunk with her power, she stretched her reach and grazed him at each pass.

His breathing grew more ragged. His excitement burst like a blaze catching and roaring through her. This time she felt pulled up high, then dropped, the contractions coming so hard and fast it took her off guard. She arched her back, writhing with the pleasure.

She dropped her hand, her own touch too intense to take. He surged against her and she gripped him, pushing him as far as she could.

A guttural sound ripped from Christopher's throat as his hips slammed against hers. His whole body jerked as he spilled his hot seed deep within her. He gripped her hips almost painfully, and she knew there'd be marks there tomorrow.

He sagged to his hands, then eased himself to his side, taking her with him. She snuggled against him, her back fitting into the contours of his front.

"That wasn't good." His hot breath brushed her damp neck.

She wrapped his hand in hers, clutching it next to her chest. "I don't believe you."

He tightened his hold, obviously enjoying the closeness as

much as she. "Not that. That was incredible and you know it. My losing control is the problem. You could get pregnant."

She sighed. Their being together at all wasn't a good idea. No matter what men said, there was no guarantee to prevent pregnancy except abstinence: that was one thing both her mother and brothers made sure she knew. They had conveniently left out the other parts. The wonderful parts.

"The only way to guarantee I don't get pregnant is to stay away from each other."

Lorelei listened to his steady breathing behind her. They were playing a dangerous game, a game where she wasn't going to come out ahead. If she got pregnant, she didn't see him settling down no matter how much she wanted it. A child would be her problem. Not his. And then there was her heart. Despite herself, she was giving a little of it each time she let him into her body. Their union would end one day, and Lorelei could see no way to ease the pain of their inevitable separation.

He lifted a piece of her hair and wrapped it around his finger. "I'll stay away from you if you want."

She grabbed his hand and entwined her fingers in his. "That's not what I want. Do you?"

He pulled her tightly against him. "No."

A deep silence said what neither wanted to say.

Lorelei couldn't take the strain of emotions unspoken. "I don't expect you to be a different man than you are; all I ask is that you be honest with me. I'm taking a risk, and I want you to too. You have to let me know who you are, Christopher Braddock."

He remained silent.

"Do we have a deal?" she asked, not sure what she wanted from him or what she expected, but if they were to be lovers, she didn't want to be the only one exposing herself, risking her heart.

He buried his nose in her hair, then kissed the back of her neck. His growing erection nudged her bottom.

"Yes," he said fiercely, as if the word were yanked from him. "We have a deal."

Chapter Eight

Lorelei hummed an Irish lullaby while she cleared a circle for their night's camp.

" 'Sleep, oh, babe, for the red bee hums the silent twilight's fall,' " drifted to her lips like a warm memory she had forgotten existed.

When they were little, her mother had sung to them as she tucked them in at night. She'd start with Devine and Donnan, but Lorelei had heard her voice drift down the hall while she'd waited under her quilt of pink stars. Even when her mother had sung to the boys, Lorelei thought the song exclusively for her.

" 'My child, my joy, my love, my heart's desire, the crickets sing you a lullaby beside the dying fire,' " Lorelei sang as she picked up small pieces of wood for kindling.

After a climb through narrow red-walled canyons, they had reached a wooded area at a higher elevation. A hot meal over a roaring fire would cure the aches from two days of hard riding. Last night's dinner of canned beans had left everyone hungry, especially Corey.

Their mother had stopped singing by the time he was born.

As Lorelei strained to remember the rest of the words, they faded like the once brightly dyed cotton of her favorite royal blue gloves. She continued to hum, not letting anything sour her good mood. Soon she'd be in Christopher's arms. Like the coyotes that sang to the moon, she'd begun to live for the night.

She dropped her load of wood in the clearing's center. While she massaged a knot in her lower back, she tilted her head and marveled at the tallness of the pine trees. Their tented tops seemed to brush the amber-cast clouds that streaked across the sky. The vibrant green seemed a lush gift after so much sand. As she went to gather more wood, she caught herself waltzing.

"What the hell are you doing?"

She turned abruptly. Corey led his horse into the clearing. "Get him out of here. You're supposed to stake the horses away from the camp," she told him.

"This isn't our goddamned parlor, Lori. We're being held prisoner."

"What are you talking about?" She braced herself for her brother's anger. In her deliriously exhausted state, the long days of riding had given her plenty of opportunity to avoid him. And when the night came she didn't think of him at all. The realization of how thoroughly she had removed him from her mind prompted her to lower her gaze, weaken her stance.

He must have sensed her sudden shame, because he marched toward her with fire and brimstone in each step. "Don't think I haven't heard you when you think I'm asleep. You sound like a cat in heat. I can't believe you're my sister."

She tried to take deep, calming breaths, but all the sacrifices she had made for him surged up her throat, unwilling to stay swallowed.

"You could believe it well enough when you sent me to do the very thing you condemn me for."

"I didn't ask you to take up with him. Are you on his side?"

"We're all on the same side."

"If you believe that, you're a bigger fool than I thought. He's just taking what he wants and filling you with empty promises."

"Christopher hasn't promised me anything."

"Like I thought." He stalked past her. "Where's his saddle-bag? I'm getting my guns and heading out."

She stepped in front of her brother, blocking his path to Christopher's saddle and their supplies. Christopher had slipped away to shoot a rabbit for dinner. They'd have a stew with fresh meat tonight. Corey couldn't leave.

"Where do you think you can go?"

"Anywhere but here. Get out of my way."

She stood her ground. Her brothers had never been able to lay a finger on her. Her father gave them the spanking of a lifetime if they even raised their voices to her.

"You're doing no such thing. You just trot your horse back out to the field with Lucky and the palomino. We're staying with Braddock."

"Is that what he makes you call him—Braddock? Or is it Mr. Braddock?"

"He doesn't make me do anything."

Corey folded his arms over his chest. "So you've chosen to turn your back on me all on·your own."

"Turn my back . . . !" If he hadn't grown several inches taller than she, she would have followed through on the urge to whack him hard on his backside. "All I've done since I've gotten to New Mexico is clean up your mess. You're in a lot of trouble. *We're* in a lot of trouble because of you. You're not running out on your responsibilities this time."

"Didn't you learn anything from Berkley? Braddock's no different. He isn't going to help us. He just wants to get his axle greased."

Corey sidestepped her while she stood with her mouth open. When she recovered enough to use her voice, *You don't even know him* died in her throat. Those were the same words she had used when her mother warned her Berkley would never go against his father to marry her. She had been so sure then. Almost as sure as she was now.

She kept her distance while Corey pawed through Christopher's saddlebags.

"You shouldn't do that. Those are his things."

Corey raised a pistol in each hand. "These are mine."

After he stashed the weapons in his pockets, her brother went for the flowered valise that held their supplies.

She grabbed the bag out of his hand. "You're not taking our food."

"Our food?" Corey arched a brownish-red eyebrow. His cynical expression was that of a grown man. A hard man. She didn't know when or how the transformation had happened.

He lunged for the bag.

She twirled to the side, removing it from his reach. "Listen to me, Corey Sullivan. I'm just trying to keep you alive. I can't let you leave here by yourself."

He brushed past her. "What are you going to do, yell for your lover?"

She dropped the bag and grabbed his arm to keep him from reaching his horse. He shook her off and she stumbled back. He didn't even turn to see if she caught her balance.

"Corey, are you going to leave me?"

He dropped the foot he had raised to place in the stirrup. "I don't want to. I want us to be together, but you've chosen him over me."

"That's not true." She couldn't explain what Christopher meant to her. She didn't even know herself. "He's going to find Mulcahy and help you."

"Yeah, he's going to use me to find him, even though I told him Mulcahy wants to kill me for messing up the robbery. And then, if Mulcahy doesn't kill me, I get to go to jail for the rest of my life. No, thank you. I'd rather go live with the coyotes. At least they take care of their own."

"What do you think I've been doing?" Frustration broke her voice.

He must have seen her pain, because he turned back to his horse but didn't attempt to mount. "Don't cry, Lori. I'll find you after everything blows over."

Being wanted for murder wasn't going to blow over. He might look like a man, but he was still her little brother. She'd come all this way to be with him, and she couldn't let her own selfish desires separate them, or worse, cause Corey harm.

"If you have to go, I'll go with you."

He glanced at her over his shoulder. "He'll follow us."

"He'll follow you anyway." She knew it with a certainty she wished she didn't.

Corey turned. "You can stop him."

"I can't."

Corey gazed intently into her eyes, giving Lorelei the sinking feeling this was what he had planned all along. "Maybe if we work together we can get him handcuffed. There has to be a time when he has his guns off. A time when he isn't expecting it."

Lorelei took a step back, realizing what that direct gaze meant. "Oh, no! I won't use our relationship to hurt him."

"He'd do it to you."

"You might as well ride out of here, Corey. I won't do what you're asking."

She turned her back on him and walked toward the wood she had gathered for a fire. Her hands shook as she stacked the dried pieces of timber. Corey's boots crunched twigs and earth as he followed her. He hadn't planned on leaving at all, not without her cooperation. Christopher had good reason to worry about taking off his guns. Had he truly believed she would agree to such a thing using her body to trick him, ambush him?

Lorelei threw a heavy log on the fire with enough force to scatter the others. Of course he thought her capable of that kind of deception. Distracting him was exactly what she'd intended when she went to his hotel room on the first day they had met.

"Lori—"

"Go if you're going to go."

"Not without you."

She whirled around, a dried branch in her hand. "Right, then who will do your dirty work?"

"It's not like that."

She dropped the gnarled length of pine before she hit him with it. "Then how is it?"

"It's not like you didn't do the same thing to Berkley." He had the good grace to glance away.

The old pain in her chest flowered at the reminder of a time she'd rather forget. Her plan to meet with Berkley after his father had accused hers of cheating on a horse race had been the beginning of the end of her dreams. At the time, she'd believed Berkley's love was strong enough to weather his father's false allegations. She hadn't known her father would show up with witnesses, hoping to catch them in a compromising position. Perhaps she'd suspected, but she didn't know for sure.

Lorelei turned away, unable to face Corey. It hadn't mattered anyway. Berkley had let her reputation be ruined rather than go against his family to marry her.

Corey gently gripped her shoulder, bringing her back to the situation at hand.

In avoiding his persistence on a subject she wished to never speak of again, she spotted Braddock standing across the clearing. Christopher, her lover, the man whose gentle caresses made her feel safe, had remained in the woods. Braddock, cold and hard, a rifle clutched in his hand, surveyed the scene like a hungry animal. The muzzle of his rifle pointed toward the ground, but the way his body tensed warned he could swing the weapon up and fire at a moment's notice.

Their gazes met and held. Lorelei could tell by the black look in his eyes that he'd been there for a while. The tall trees that had embraced her earlier cast accusing shadows as the light drained from the sky.

"Who the hell's Berkley?" he said with the coldness of a stranger.

Corey turned, seeing him for the first time. Lorelei couldn't find the courage to fumble for an answer to his question.

Braddock strode toward them. Lorelei darted her gaze away, unable to meet the censure in his eyes.

"Going somewhere, kid?"

Lorelei forced herself to confront Braddock. She had no reason to feel guilty. In fact, she had refused to betray him even though the deepened lines around his mouth said otherwise.

"Corey wants to leave. He says you're holding him prisoner."

Braddock ignored the question in her statement, eyeing the pistols Corey had stuffed in his pockets instead. "You going to use those, kid?"

Corey kept his hands by his sides, too close to the guns for Lorelei's comfort. "I told you, I'm not a killer like you."

Braddock swung the rifle up and pointed it at Corey. "That's good to know, but since you're a lying little bastard, I'd feel a whole lot better if you'd toss them to the ground. Nice and slow."

Lorelei moved beside her brother but stopped when Braddock swung his rifle's nose in her direction. She gazed at Braddock over the barrel, not knowing him at all.

"She's unarmed. And these aren't even loaded. You took all the ammunition." Corey lifted his hands above his head. "Take them if you want."

Braddock strode toward them, and Lorelei backed away. He grabbed the pistols from Corey's pockets and tossed them to the ground.

"Turn around." He shoved the rifle into Corey's shoulder when he didn't comply fast enough.

Lorelei rushed to her brother's rescue, not sure what she intended to do. "Stop that. What are you doing to him?"

"Stay back, Lorelei. I have a tendency to shoot before I think when I'm irritable, and right now I'm pretty goddamned irritable."

She stopped, not wanting to believe he meant it but too unsure to discount his words.

Braddock shoved Corey toward his ransacked saddlebag. With the rifle in one hand, he fished out metal handcuffs with the other. He shifted the rifle under his arm and swiftly handcuffed Corey's hands behind his back.

"See, Lorelei? Do you see what I told you?" Corey cried. The sound of the cuffs clicking shut emphasized his point.

Lorelei tried to sound calm and in control no matter how laughable the idea was. Cold reason was all that worked with Braddock. "Are you turning him in?"

He didn't even glance at her before he shuffled Corey off to the base of a tree. "I'm going to find Mulcahy. Nothing's changed."

"Corey says Mulcahy will kill him."

"If he gets his hands on him, I imagine he will." He put a hand on Corey's shoulder and shoved him to the ground against the tree.

Braddock strode over to his scattered belongings then, inspecting what had been taken before he repacked the rest. Lorelei's gaze strayed to Corey. He looked like a pig trussed for market. With a motion of his head, he gestured toward Braddock in a silent plea for help. She stared at Braddock's broad back, not sure what she could do, but knowing she had to do something.

As she approached him, she noticed Braddock's rifle propped against a thick pine. She glanced back at Corey. The unguarded weapon hadn't gotten past him. He motioned again, the rifle clearly his intended target.

Braddock knelt between her and the weapon. She wasn't sure she could get to it, and was even less sure she could use it against him. Braddock wasn't a man who could be bluffed. Perhaps she could shoot him in the leg. The thought of hurting him at all sent her stomach to her knees. But if she didn't find her courage and something happened to her brother, she'd never forgive herself.

Helpless to make a decision, she maneuvered herself within reach of the gun, hoping it wouldn't come to that. "You can't let Mulcahy get his hands on Corey. Doesn't that prove to you he's innocent? The man he was supposed to be in cahoots with wants to kill him."

She noticed the rabbit then. He must have had it tucked

away during the confrontation with Corey. Braddock skinned the animal with quick, detached motions. His hands were covered with blood, his eyes filled with cold disgust. "He's not innocent."

His statement didn't leave room for argument. The rifle leaned directly behind her. Christopher remained turned away—purposely avoiding looking at her, she suspected. She could swivel on her heels and grab the weapon. Indecision mired her in what felt like knee-deep mud. The desire to trust him kept her feet firmly planted.

With great effort she took a step toward him, and one away from the rifle.

"What about me?"

He still didn't look at her. "What about you?"

"What do you intend to do with me?"

He glanced at her over his shoulder, then turned away. "I never intended anything, Lorelei."

She clasped her shaking hands behind her back. If she could get the rifle, what would riding out of here accomplish? Where would they go?

She glanced at Corey. His silent, anxious pleading unnerved her. What had justice ever done for any of them? Justice didn't rescue her father when he was accused of cheating in a horse race. They'd been turned out of their house to pay fines. And there was that awful month her father spent in jail. Supposedly the punishment had been lenient, but it had broken her father's spirit and his pride. He'd never been the same after that. Her mother's words haunted her. Corey was too much like her father.

Lorelei knew what she had to do. "After you catch Mulcahy, they'll send Corey to jail."

"Yep." Braddock stuck a sharpened spit through the poor rabbit's glistening body.

"There's nothing you'll do?"

He poured water from a canteen over his bloody hands, then shook them dry. "Nope."

"But you said—"

He stood and faced her, stopping anything else she might

115

have had to say. She backed up, suddenly afraid of him.

"I said I wanted to help you. Not him. He robbed a stage-coach. I said I might—*might*,"—his teeth shone white against his dark-stubbled beard as he ground out his words—"be able to keep him from hanging, but I never said anything about keeping him out of jail."

He turned away, but then abruptly whipped around as if he suspected her plan. "So you can stop looking at me like I have two heads. I'm not the one who had any other motives besides having a good time. Sorry I ruined your plans, sweet-heart."

He turned his back to her again and tossed wood into a pile to start a fire.

The urge to explain, to tell him he had overheard wrong, shriveled in the harsh light of his words. Shooting him in the leg—the thigh, better yet—became more and more appealing. She didn't deserve his cruel assessment. Even though there were never any promises made, and she should have known better, she thought there was more between them than "having a good time," as he so crudely put it.

She quietly and calmly picked up the rifle. He never once glanced her way. She had all the time in the world to fix her aim on his head while he crouched over the smoking wood.

Casually he raised his gaze to hers. His cold expression didn't waver in the least at the sight of her raised weapon. "It's not loaded, Lorelei."

The shaking started where she squeezed the rifle's long barrel and ran up her arm, blurring her vision. He knew what she had been up to. Had always had one eye on her. He'd never made himself vulnerable to her, as she had to him. His pistols were always right where he could reach them. Even when he was finding his pleasure inside her body, he was ready to shoot anything that threatened him, including her brother, maybe even her.

Lorelei cocked the gun, aimed at his arm, and pulled the trigger. The sound of the hammer hitting an empty cartridge widened his eyes. His startled look brought her little satis-faction, because his expression immediately changed to murderous. He shot to his feet and strode toward her, yanking the gun out of her hand.

For a moment she thought he would hit her. She willed him to, so she'd never doubt what kind of man he was again.

"You were never honest with me."

He ignored her and stalked back over to the fire, which crackled and popped as it caught the wood. With the sun having set and twilight taking over, the flame's glow flickered across the hard surfaces of his face. He nudged a piece of wood back into the roaring center with the toe of his boot, looking as if he had never smiled a day in his life.

"Aren't you going to handcuff me, too?" If she taunted him enough he would be pushed over the edge, be forced to give up this cruel act. Christopher could never treat her like this.

He picked up a long stick and used it to stir the fire. "Do I need to?"

She swallowed her fury, trying to match the coldness in his voice when she spoke. "If you want to keep me from slitting your throat while you sleep, then it might be a good idea."

She expected him to react. Wanted to scratch the indifference off his cool surface. How could he act like he didn't care when her heart was burning at his betrayal? At least if he would yell or scream or curse her, she would know she hadn't been such a fool. Hadn't been so wrong about him.

But his leisurely stroll to his saddlebags mocked her threat. When he turned to her, the firelight reflected off the dull metal handcuffs he held. He dangled them from one finger as if he were bringing her a pretty trinket.

"Lucky for me I keep a second set." His cocky smile faded when he reached her. "Turn around."

She lifted her chin, refusing to budge.

He grabbed her by the shoulder and roughly spun her so her back faced him. She almost wanted to laugh. She really hadn't thought he would do it. Still didn't. The joke was on her. He twisted one arm behind her back and closed the metal cuff until the iron encircled her wrist, then did the same with the other.

He turned her to face him again, this time more gently.

With her arms behind her back, her chest thrust against her white blouse.

He lowered his gaze, making a show at perusing what the position revealed. Her nipples stretched the worn fabric to bursting.

Every nerve in her body was taut. How dared he think he could still arouse her? She wanted to spit in his face, but did nothing, waiting for his next move. Let him see what a miserable man he was. Let him be sorry for what he'd done to her.

He didn't seem sorry at all. He rested his palms on her shoulders, then slid them down her arms to the cuffs at her wrists. When his arms were around her he pulled her forward, forcing her snugly against him.

"Some men wouldn't be bothered that you were handcuffed. In fact, seeing you bound would only add to the excitement." His gaze was hooded, his voice lowered. "You might like it too. Being helpless. Being able to do nothing while I ran my hands over your body, spread your legs . . ."

She wanted to tell him she'd rather die than let him touch her again, but she was hanging on his every word. Her breath pushed hot and heavy through her nostrils.

He ran his hands back up to her shoulders, then gripped her hard enough to force a gasp. "But I'm not that kind of man."

He dragged her by a bound arm to where Corey sat, then lowered her to the ground next to her brother. She hated herself for noting that he handled her with more care than he had Corey. It didn't mean anything, because he didn't care.

He stood above them and gazed down at her. "Look at me."

She didn't want to look. Her cheeks burned, half with embarrassment and half with the desire he had ignited at his simple touch. He had even turned her body against her, using his sexuality as another thing with which to taunt her. Shamefully, she ached for what he had described.

"Look at me, Lorelei." His words were a harsh command.

She glared up at him just to show him she could; she wasn't afraid of him, and this wasn't over.

Shadows cut across his face but she doubted the lack of light made his expression any darker. He showed no compassion at all—and there was no hint that he had ever had any. "*This* is who I am. Is this the man you wanted to know?"

He walked away before she could answer.

Chapter Nine

Coyote Pass's tallest building peeked over the next dusty rise, but sighting his destination didn't tempt Braddock to increase the pace. He'd gotten past caring if they ever reached the outlaw town. Numbness had slipped over him like a hood. Each day was just something to survive. Riding with a morosely silent Corey and Lorelei, both handcuffed to their saddles, marked the exclamation point of the last ten years of his life. It was the hell he'd been working up to without even knowing it.

He should be happy to have his worldview restored so powerfully. He'd slithered back into his old self like a snake returning to its discarded skin, a very unpleasant sensation made worse by his moments of freedom. The emotions he'd experienced with Lorelei—not just the lust, but the tenderness, the laughing—had rubbed parts of him raw. His suit of indifference no longer fit. It scratched to the point where he was sure real blood dripped down his rib cage.

He glanced over his shoulder. Despite her best efforts, Lorelei looked tired and dirty. The faded white flowers that dotted her brown cotton bodice and skirt had vanished in the coat of dust that covered them all. In two short days he'd accomplished what the four-year war and the slow loss of her family hadn't done: he'd broken Lorelei's spirit. He quickly returned his gaze to the dilapidated town that grew in size as they topped the hill. The time had passed to let the urge to release her win.

If he had wanted to be decent, he should have done it the first night. Actually, he never should have lost his temper at all. For the tenth time in the last hour, he mulled over the things he had overheard.

With a cool head, he could convince himself that Corey had been trying to talk Lorelei into something she wanted no part of. But at the time all he saw was her betrayal. And that he wasn't the first man she'd tricked.

He gripped his reins and spurred his horse over the rolling landscape, bringing the town's deserted main street into full view. Braddock had almost believed that he could trust her. But he wasn't the kind of man who trusted or wanted trust from anyone else. He was a cold bastard all the way down to the granite that rested where his heart should be. Maybe that was the reason he survived what killed other men. He didn't have the organ to stop that the others had.

"That's Coyote Pass," yelled Corey from behind him.

Braddock was grateful for the distraction from his turbulent thoughts. "Glad your memory's coming back."

Corey managed to stop Langston's horse without the use of the reins. "I'm not going there."

"I wasn't asking you."

Lorelei tossed her head, trying to shake away a lock of hair that had come loose from her bonnet. The pinto she rode continued to trot forward. "What's so bad about Coyote Pass?"

Braddock tried not to cringe when he noticed how she struggled without the use of her hands. He grabbed the horse's bridle before she passed him.

"Mulcahy runs that town. He'll be there," answered Corey.

Lorelei blew her wayward curl, but it fell back into her

eyes. "Fine. Let Braddock arrest him so we can get this over with."

"Unfortunately, it's not that simple. Mulcahy's bounty has tripled. And this is the first time he's left any witnesses. He won't be bold enough to hang around where he can be caught." Braddock gauged Corey's reaction, which happily saved him from watching Lorelei.

Corey yanked on his bonds, causing his horse to nervously dance sideways. "He'll have men there. Everyone answers to him."

"If you tell me where Mulcahy's hiding out, then maybe we won't have to go to Coyote Pass."

"You've got a death wish, Braddock. 'Cause they'll kill you, too. You're a bounty hunter. Half the men in that town are wanted for something."

"Maybe I do have a death wish. Let's go."

Braddock headed Lucky toward town. He didn't want to notice the way Lorelei frowned when he talked so carelessly about his life.

"What about my sister?" called Corey. "What's going to happen to her if we both get killed?"

Braddock brought Lucky to a halt. He knew the kid was more worried about himself than Lorelei, but he had a point.

"I'll look out for her. You're on your own."

"I'm handcuffed. I'll be a sitting duck."

Lorelei turned to her brother. "Maybe you should just tell him what he wants to know."

Braddock watched the exchange between the two, wondering if Lorelei knew more than he'd thought. Maybe she had been in on Corey's scheme from the beginning. Part of him wanted to believe that. Then maybe the last flicker of compassion would die out and he could truly be himself again.

"I don't know what he wants to know. Can't you see he's crazy?"

She glanced at Braddock. Their gazes held. Painful emotion welled up in him like a fountaining wound, and he had to bite the inside of his bottom lip to keep from blurting out that he was sorry.

"He's not crazy," she said, looking away first.

Braddock shifted in his saddle to keep his exhalation of relief from being noticed.

She studied the barren town. "I must be the crazy one to be out here with either of you."

The grin creeping up on him felt too good to stop. "I told you that from the start."

Braddock guided his mount beside Lorelei. He fished out the key to her handcuffs before he fully realized what he was about to do. Just as well. Thinking always got him into trouble. He unlocked the cuffs.

"Thank you." She rubbed her freed wrists.

He reached into his saddlebag and retrieved one of Corey's pistols. If he watched her much longer he'd have to take her hands in his to examine the damage he'd done to her soft skin. Instead he loaded the pistol, then handed it to her.

"You can thank me by not shooting me in the back."

"I wouldn't do that."

He cocked an eyebrow, silently reminding her of her promise to slit his throat. She dropped her gaze to examine the gun more closely. He shouldn't be so satisfied at the proof that she'd never intended to carry out her threat, but he was.

"You do know how to use it?"

She cocked the hammer, then released it. "I'm better with a rifle."

"What about me?" asked Corey. "Those are my guns."

Braddock feigned surprise. "I just took your advice and made sure your sister had protection. I figured since she was your main concern you wouldn't mind her using your gun."

"If you'd let me go, I could protect her myself."

Braddock chose to ignore him. There was too much he had to say about the boy's ability to protect his sister. He turned to her. "Keep the pistol hidden. Use it only if you absolutely have to. And that doesn't include saving him or me. Got it?"

"She isn't going to lift a finger to save you, Braddock. She's got you all figured out. Right, Lori?"

Lorelei gazed at Braddock, her face open, her eyes bright.

"Understand me?"

"Tell him, Lori. Tell him what you think of him," Corey pleaded.

She held Braddock's gaze. "I think I understand."

"Good."

This time he looked away first, sure the pounding of his own heart gave away how much her words meant to him. What did she understand—why he'd handcuffed her or why he was such a bastard? Well, she didn't understand either.

"Follow me," he called without looking behind him. The sound of Corey's whining assured him they complied.

"Lori, can't you see what he's doing? He's going to get me killed."

"Seems to me you've been doing a pretty good job of that on your own, Corey Lochlain O'Sullivan."

"Don't tell me you're on his side."

"I'm on the side that gets me out of this blasted saddle the fastest."

"Mulcahy's going to kill me!"

Braddock swung Lucky around and trotted toward Corey. "Do you have any idea how to keep quiet?"

"What?"

Braddock retrieved the key to the boy's handcuffs and unlocked him. "Maybe if you could keep your mouth shut, we could leave here without alerting the whole town that you're the one who screwed up the stagecoach robbery."

"I didn't screw it up. Mulcahy didn't plan right. He didn't know there'd be so many guards."

"What did you say?" Lorelei turned in her saddle.

Corey glanced out over the cactus-covered hills surrounding the town, realizing his mistake. "It's just what I heard. It wasn't my fault. That's all I'm saying, but Mulcahy won't see it that way."

Lorelei stared at her brother, and Braddock knew she didn't believe him. She'd never known anything about the robbery. Not that he'd really doubted it, but even his cynical side couldn't deny the shock she tried to blink out of her wide blue eyes. For her sake, Braddock almost wished the kid's story were true.

"Let's just ride into town like we're passing through and see what we find out."

"Can I have a gun?" asked Corey.

Braddock reached out and tugged the brim of Corey's brown slouch hat down on his head. "No. Now keep your mouth shut, and I'm sure no one will recognize you."

He urged Lucky to pick his way down the rock-covered slope.

"I might have helped myself to a few extra cards here and there, but I wasn't the only one," said Corey.

"Shut up, kid." Braddock would be a lot more amused by Corey's fall from grace—not that he'd had far to fall—if it weren't for Lorelei's silence.

He turned to her. "You're my wife and your brother's a hired hand. We're on our way back from selling a herd of cattle in Santa Fe. We have a spread northwest of here. But don't say anything unless you have to. Let me do the talking."

"I don't want to be the hired hand."

"Shut up, Corey," said Lorelei before Braddock had the chance.

At their approach, the weathered row of false-front buildings remained still and silent. Before they reached the first structure, a planked two-story with an overhang, Braddock made sure the nose of Lorelei's horse could be hit by a swish of Lucky's tail.

Coyote Pass had been built by a group of settlers who didn't last. Run out by Indians, outlaws, and the sheer desolation of the location, the settlers had left their hard work to be taken over by anyone who didn't want to be found. A store remained open where one could actually buy or trade things, if they didn't mind stolen goods. Next door, a livery stable worked on the same philosophy, but the main attraction was the saloon and brothel that had once been intended as a fine hotel. Ending the street was a church with intact stained-glass windows and a steeple whose crowning iron cross Braddock was always surprised to see had not yet been hit by lightning.

His palms itched to rest on the butt of his gun, but that would be a mistake. He was supposed to be a rancher. He slipped off Lucky's back and grabbed the pinto's bridle.

"Get on her other side, kid."

For once Corey didn't argue, and he did as Braddock asked. The stallions stood taller than the young pinto and since Lorelei didn't sit exactly tall in the saddle, they were able to shelter her.

Braddock studied the quiet street. Nobody was going to die today. He'd make sure of that.

They walked all the way to the saloon without seeing another soul. Mulcahy wasn't the only one lying low. Civilization was pushing west with the railroad, and outlaws were becoming as hunted as buffalo.

Braddock tied Lucky to the rail at the far side of the once-whitewashed building. Paint peeled in layers, making the grand facade look as though it were melting. The horse trough in front held a green film of algae in the bottom, and he didn't want Lucky to test the slime for water. He tied the pinto next to Lucky, then helped Lorelei out of the saddle.

"Thank you," she said a little too breathlessly.

He looked away before he saw the shy smile he heard in her voice. Corey dismounted and Braddock grabbed the pinto's reins.

"I'll water the horses." Corey hunched behind Lucky's tall, thick back.

"I don't think so." Braddock found a place on the splintered boardwalk that seemed solid, and held his hand out to Lorelei.

She didn't hesitate to place her gloved palm in his. He tucked her hand in the crook of his arm, then unsnapped the metal thong holding his pistols in their holsters. Lorelei's grip on his arm tensed.

"Come on, kid." He nodded toward the saloon.

Corey's mouth pursed into a white line.

Braddock stopped him before he said something stupid and gave them away. "The time to argue is over."

Then he moved forward and peeked into the dark cavern of the saloon. The door hung off its hinges. He guided Lorelei inside, keeping her close. Dusty windows filtered out the bright daylight. Two men sat at a table by the back wall, playing cards by the glow of a lantern. Another man hunched over a table near the bar and cradled a bottle of whiskey, his right eye swollen shut, his lip split. He stood at their approach.

The card players in the back stopped and stared.

Braddock fought the urge to shove Lorelei behind him. If he didn't panic, Lorelei would be the perfect cover. No one in their right mind would bring a woman here if they knew the sort of lowlifes who made this place their home.

"Are you open for business? Like to get a drink for my wife. She needs to get out of the sun," he said, effecting a Southern drawl to make himself sound friendly.

"Absolutely," said the man with the black eye. He grinned, then winced when the effort tugged at his cracked lip. " 'Scuse me." He giggled. "Forgot about my face. I must look a sight."

The man was stinking drunk. He stumbled behind the bar. "What can I get you folks?"

Braddock set Lorelei in a chair near the door. Corey stuck by his sister, keeping his head down and discreetly turned away from the man who appeared to be the bartender.

Luckily, the drunk was far from observant. Braddock approached the marble slab that served as a bar, the card players at the far table in his peripheral vision.

"Regular beer for me and the kid. Ginger beer for my wife, if you've got it." Braddock leaned his back on the bar and surveyed the room like a tenderfoot. "This place must have been something in its day. Didn't expect to find anything so fancy out here in the middle of nowhere."

Red wallpaper with a swirled gold-leaf pattern peeled from the walls. The floor matched the pink marble of the bar, but which held more dirt was debatable. Braddock swore he saw hoofprints in the drifts of dust and sand that had accumulated here. A chandelier hung askew from the half-painted ceiling, dripping crystals like a waterfall.

The bartender giggled from behind him and set three dusty bottles on the counter. "I don't even know what ginger beer is."

Braddock picked up one of the green bottles, examined the murky liquid inside, then turned the bottle upside down. The contents had congealed into a sludge that had trouble sliding to the corked top.

"How about if we just stick with whiskey?"

"That we have. For all three of you?" He pushed a bottle and two large shot glasses across the bar. They made trails in the dust that allowed the rose-grained marble to peek through.

"The missus had better stay away from the whiskey. She's a delicate thing," Braddock said, as if he were confiding in the man.

The bartender glanced in Lorelei's direction. "She's a mighty pretty one." His gaze jumped to the card players, and he frowned. He leaned forward and whispered, "Don't want to seem inhospitable, but this isn't the best place to bring a lady of quality, or your son, if you know what I mean."

Braddock lessened the distance between them. He nodded to the two men who were watching the exchange. "Had trouble here, have you?"

"You don't know the trouble." The bartender gingerly fingered his swollen eye.

A chair scraping against the marble floor drew their attention to the table in the back. One of the cardplayers stood. His belt sagged with the weight of two navy revolvers. "Who's your friend, Archie?"

Archie grabbed a soiled cloth from under the counter and wiped the bar, leaving as much grime as he mopped up. "A stranger passing through."

The man strode toward them, both his hands resting on his guns. "What's your business, stranger?"

Braddock spread his hands on the bar. "I don't want any

trouble. I've got my wife and son with me. We're on our way back from selling our herd in Santa Fe."

The young gunslinger studied Lorelei and Corey. "If you're from around here, you should know better than to wind up in Coyote Pass."

"Come on, Buster. He just wanted a drink for his wife and boy. You don't want to go shooting up women and children, do you?" Archie put another bottle of whiskey on the counter. "Have a drink on me and finish your cards."

The gunslinger strolled in Corey and Lorelei's direction.

"If you had a few less drinks on the house, Archie, maybe you'd learn how to pick your friends better. How old's this kid?"

"Thirteen," said Lorelei before Braddock could answer.

"Almost fourteen," Braddock followed up, wondering if the gunslinger were blind enough to believe Corey was his son. He should have stuck with the hired-hand story.

Behind him he could hear a bottle being uncorked, a drink being poured.

"I told you that Sullivan fella wasn't my friend. He just wanted a game, had his own cards. I didn't introduce him to Mulcahy. I didn't have anything to do with it," Archie said.

The gunslinger—Buster, the bartender called him—stared hard at Corey, then turned back to Lorelei. "You look much too young to have a child that old, ma'am. You're a girl yourself."

Lorelei returned his flirtatious smile. "Thank you."

Braddock marveled at the acting ability of both brother and sister. They hadn't even flinched when Archie had mentioned Corey's name. Luckily, Buster had his back to him and Archie was too busy drinking to notice Braddock tense.

"Son, take your mother outside. This is no place for her."

"Yes, Pa." Corey's voice sounded higher than usual. Whether the change was intentional or just a result of plain terror, Braddock didn't know. But it sounded good.

"Proper or not, I'll just faint if I get back into that heat." Lorelei removed her bonnet and fanned herself with it. "I'm fine here, sugar."

He'd warned her not to do this. "What about the corrupting influence on our son, dear? He's too young to be in a saloon with gambling and spirits and God knows what else." Braddock laid on the Southern drawl so thick he almost choked on it.

Archie poured himself another drink. "There's no whores here. Not anymore. All the girls left after Mulcahy's men tore up the place looking for that Sullivan. I don't care if a gambler offers to give me half the pot, I'm not trusting any more slick-talking—" The bartender stopped in midsentence, then glanced across to Corey.

Braddock turned back to the bar. This was a bad time for Archie to sober up. "I need a drink."

Archie's attention returned to the bottle of whiskey. "Me too." He filled both glasses to the rim. "Here's to your health." He gulped the whiskey without pause.

Braddock rolled his glass between his fingers as he turned back to Buster.

He had placed his booted foot in a chair and leaned over to leer at Lorelei. "I've got a room in the back. It's on the shady side and catches a nice breeze. You're welcome to put your feet up, if you've a mind to."

Braddock slammed his glass down on the bar and reached for his guns before he could think clearly. "Over my dead body."

"That can be—" The gunslinger swallowed his words and stopped himself in midreach when he turned to find Braddock already had both guns drawn.

He slowly raised his hands to his ears. "You don't draw like no rancher."

The back of Braddock's neck itched. He had momentarily forgotten about the third man, the one at the table. The one who, judging by the sound of the click, was now pointing a Springfield rifle at his back.

"He ain't no rancher," said the third man.

Buster lowered his hands. "Good, then he won't mind if I take his wife for a little ride." He grabbed Lorelei's wrist and hauled her to her feet.

Braddock squeezed out a single shot, striking Buster in the shoulder.

"Son of a bitch! The bastard shot me." Buster clutched his shoulder with his opposite hand, momentarily forgetting about Lorelei.

She scooted back against the wall, blocking Corey with her body.

Boots alternately crunched then dragged in the dirt, marking the rifleman's approach. The sound and the fact that Braddock hadn't already been shot in the back confirmed his suspicions. Braddock knew the Springfield well. The old confederate weapon had only one shot and was cumbersome to reload. It was known for its accuracy, but only if the shooter had a steady hand. The man with the rifle didn't. He was wounded. That was why he'd let his younger, more inexperienced friend confront the newcomers. When they'd walked in, the way that he had held his cards close to his body gave him away. The rifle's weight would soon be unbearable to lift.

The closer the rifleman came, the better his chances. Braddock contemplated swinging around and firing before he got close.

"Shoot him," cried Buster. "I'm bleeding bad." He wilted into the chair Lorelei had abandoned.

"No more shooting, Larry. I mean it. Let these folks go on their way. Buster had no business messing with his woman. No business." Archie sounded on the verge of tears.

"Have another drink, Archie," said Larry, the third man. " 'Cause there just might be some shooting. But that's up to you, Fast-draw. You think you can swing around and pop one off before I can shoot you?"

Braddock let his center of balance sink to his knees. "I know I can."

"I know you can, too." The shuffle of his boots stopped and a chair scraped as Larry sank into it. "But can you get me before I get her?"

Braddock shifted his weight and swung his aim to Larry. The man had fallen into a barrel-backed chair. His rifle leaned on the armrest and the sight was centered on Lorelei. Braddock tensed short of pulling the trigger. His hand ached from the strain of stopping the motion.

Larry laughed, but it quickly turned into a racking cough. "Better get out of the way, Buster," he said when he caught his breath.

"I'm hurt," cried the younger man.

"Move!" yelled Larry.

Buster slipped to the floor like molasses oozing from a split tin.

"I can't watch you shoot a woman. I've seen too much bloodshed. I can't see this. Don't shoot her." Archie sounded desperate, but Braddock didn't have the luxury of paying him any attention.

Neither did Larry. "Let's see that son of yours. Get out from behind the woman's skirt and take your hat off."

"Don't shoot the boy. That's worse than the woman." Archie had started to cry in earnest. "Don't shoot the kid."

"Shut up, Archie," growled Larry. "If that boy's thirteen then I'm twenty-five. Let's see your face, son."

Corey moved away from Lorelei without Braddock having to tell him to do so.

"I'm a bounty hunter," Braddock said, trying to draw the attention back to himself. "The name's Braddock. Heard of me?"

Larry glanced his way, but unfortunately it didn't seem to alter his aim. "Matter of fact, I have. I'll have to make sure I kill you before I'm done."

Lorelei shoved Corey farther away from her in a flurry of motion that raised dust. "But he's the one you want, isn't he?"

Corey stumbled. "Lori!"

Braddock's gaze swung to Lorelei. What in the hell was she doing now?

"Go ahead, shoot him," she cried. "He's not my son. I can't fool you."

Larry kept his aim on Lorelei. "You never did, lady. I'm not going to shoot him. Not until we settle something between us. We understand each other, don't we, Corey?"

"I don't know what you're talking about."

"You can tell me, or you can talk to Mulcahy, and he's real mad. He'd love nothing more than to strip the skin off your back."

"I don't know anything, Larry. I swear."

Buster propped himself up with the help of his left elbow. "Is that the little son of a bitch we've been looking for?"

"Yep," said Larry.

"That's not Corey Sullivan," said Archie. "He's not thirteen."

"Neither is this one. Talk to me, Sullivan, and I'll see you get out of here alive. That's better than you deserve. If it weren't for you, we'd all be drinking it up instead of crawling into holes to die."

"You're not going to die. You look healthy to me," said Corey.

"Let's just even up now, and I won't take a potshot at your mother over here." Somehow Larry found the strength to lift his gun to eye level, his aim clearly targeted at Lorelei.

Before Braddock could decide to take the risk and pull the trigger, a bullet whizzed by his right ear. He heard the explosion at the same time the shot knocked Larry back, forcing the rifle to slip from his grip.

"I couldn't let you shoot a woman, Larry. Not after Lila. She was just a girl. You shouldn't have treated her like that," whined Archie. "Shouldn't have done it."

Braddock pivoted on the balls of his feet and shot Buster in the center of the chest as he fumbled for his pistol with his left hand. Obviously he was right-handed and hadn't learned to use his other hand; he never even cleared the gun from the holster.

Braddock turned back to Archie, not sure of the man's state of mind, but the bartender had disappeared.

"Get his guns," Braddock directed Corey, pointing his pistol at Buster.

He leaned over the bar to make sure Archie wasn't reloading in order to pick them all off. Archie had slid to the floor, the shotgun beside him, and was sobbing into the hands that covered his face.

"Lorelei, see to him."

Braddock knelt beside Larry, who lay flat on his back, gasping for breath. His hat had fallen, and his long silver hair slithered across the dirty floor like a dozen grass snakes.

"I was already dead," he said through half-opened eyes.

"Where's Mulcahy?"

Larry grinned despite the film of blood over his yellow teeth. "Ask your son."

"He says he doesn't know."

"You're a dead man when you ride with that one. They're going to get him."

"Why didn't you shoot him when you had the chance?"

"Greed dies hard, I guess."

"Where's Mulcahy?" Braddock tried again.

Larry coughed. Braddock rolled him on his side to keep him from choking on his own blood.

Corey leaned over Braddock's shoulder. "I didn't want anyone to get hurt, Larry. I told you I wasn't signing up to kill people."

Larry opened his eyes. "But you're fine with gold, aren't you lad—bloodstained or no."

"I didn't want anyone to get killed. I wouldn't have signed up if I knew."

"Well, do yourself a favor, O'Sullivan. Give it back afore it's too late." Larry's slight brogue deepened as his voice grew more faint. "Wait. It *is* too late. I'll be seeing you soon. Aye, lad."

"Tell me what you know, Larry." Braddock tried one more time.

"I need a drink," mumbled the outlaw.

"I'll get you one as soon as you tell me where Mulcahy is."

"Get me a drink, you bastard. I'm dying," he rasped.

Corey brought a glass of whiskey to Larry's lips. "I'm sorry, Larry. I really am."

Larry choked on the drink and coughed up more blood than liquor. "You're all right, O'Sullivan. To tell you the truth, I'm glad it's over. I'm going to sleep good tonight."

Then Larry laid his cheek against the dirty marble and closed his eyes.

Braddock turned to Corey. "You've got some explaining to do, kid, and you're giving back your share of the gold."

Corey's eyes widened. "I didn't get a share. I ran. I don't know what Mulcahy's telling them."

Braddock shook his head. "If that's true, if Mulcahy's using you to cut the rest out, you're a dead man. I can't protect you."

Lorelei suddenly loomed over them. "The other one's dead, too. Archie says there are more coming and we should get out of here."

Braddock reholstered his gun. Larry curled in on himself as he clutched his midsection. Whether he was dead or not, they couldn't wait around.

"Let's go."

Corey set the bottle of whiskey within Larry's reach before he got to his feet. Braddock couldn't help but notice that the kid looked to be on the verge of tears himself. He gave Corey a shove and wished someone had beaten him at an early age.

Lorelei blocked their path to the door. "We have to take Archie with us."

Braddock strode toward the door, dragging her with him, pretending he didn't hear.

She yanked from his grasp with a surprising amount of strength. "He helped us, and they'll kill him when they find out. He's already been beaten up."

"No one's going to tell who killed who."

"We have to take him. He saved my life."

"He can't ride. He's too drunk."

"He can ride with me," Corey spoke up.

Braddock ground his teeth. Corey Sullivan, do-gooder by day, stagecoach robber and card cheat by night. Not a good combination. "No."

"He has his own horse," argued Corey.

135

"Where?" Braddock could use this information. He wanted Lorelei on a better mount.

Lorelei spoke up. "There's a stable behind the saloon. You get the horses, and I'll get Archie."

Braddock opened his mouth to argue, but decided not to waste his breath. "Corey, gather up our horses and meet me in the stable."

He strode toward the door, then stopped, turned back to Corey. "Don't try to run. Mulcahy's men are near, and you can't cover your tracks worth a damn."

"He won't run," said Lorelei. "Just hurry."

Corey's sick pallor convinced him, rather than Lorelei's pledge. One thing the kid had said was true: he didn't like bloodshed.

Braddock sprinted to the stables, wondering how such a solitary man had gotten stuck with such a needy group of misfits.

Chapter Ten

The sun dipped behind the rock strewn horizon. Soon darkness would overwhelm them, but Lorelei had no desire for rest. She couldn't put enough distance between her and Coyote Pass. Gentle splashing as they waded against a shallow stream covered the desperate huffs of the horses, but did little to soothe her jangled nerves. Her heart still thudded to the beat of hooves as they rode for their lives.

She shifted but, like the borrowed gelding she rode, the saddle was several sizes too big. Every jar of the horse seared up her spine. At least her attempts to focus on the bouncing red landscape that rushed by saved her from recalling the vivid horror that had taken place at Coyote Pass. But there was one thing she refused to forget.

Corey hadn't been telling her the truth. His story about innocently being sucked into the outlaws' scheme fell away in shreds. Coyote Pass wasn't a place you stumbled upon, and those awful men knew her brother.

Shoving Corey to distract the man with the rifle had been too easy. Fury had floated over Lorelei like a red, gauzy veil. She hoped Corey had believed she meant it when she told Larry to shoot him.

But she had known Larry couldn't shoot Corey. She had seen his arm shake with his effort to hold the gun on her. Moving the heavy weapon in Corey's direction would have taken the last of his strength. She could have retrieved her weapon and fired before Larry had a chance to aim accurately at Corey. But none of her efforts had been necessary.

Lorelei stiffened her back, ignoring the pain in every muscle of her body. None of the horror at Coyote Pass had needed to occur.

Corey would finally tell her the truth if it was the last thing he did.

They left the stream without Lorelei's notice; the taste of dust alerted her to the change in terrain. Smoky blue twilight draped around her like a cool silk cloak. In the distance, a dark silhouette of trees guarded the top of the mesa. Luckily the horse she rode picked his way up the rock incline, guiding her to their destination without assistance.

Braddock glanced over his shoulder, silently checking her progress. She stared through him, unable to muster up enough energy for a reassuring smile or a nod of her head. His frown deepened before he sat forward in his saddle again. She was tired of pretending everything was fine when it wasn't. Things hadn't been fine for a long time.

Under the shelter of trees, her mount dutifully halted beside Braddock's horse. She tried to swing her leg up and over her saddle horn, but her leg wouldn't cooperate. She checked to see if her foot was stuck.

Christopher gripped her waist and pulled her effortlessly into his arms. "This gelding's a little big for you."

She sank against him, not trusting her own feet to hold her. "I need to switch with Archie. We'll just have to tell his mare I bite back."

A muffled thud drew their attention. Corey had tried to help Archie dismount, but the pair had landed in a tangled pile instead.

"Can somebody help me?" Corey grunted.

Braddock steadied Lorelei, then rolled Archie off her brother. Unable to face Corey just yet, Lorelei forced her feet to move and hunted for a place to set up camp.

What had she accomplished by trying to protect her brother from Braddock? He had every right to handcuff Corey. What would have become of them if they had met those men from Coyote Pass without Christopher?

For the first time, she truly wished she had stayed back in Kentucky. This was no life for her.

That was what she would do. She would leave here and let Braddock do what he wanted with Corey. She'd ask to borrow the money for the fare. Then maybe she could erase the images of red rock, dust, and blood from her mind forever.

When she heard her name called from far away, she realized she had wandered deep into the shelter of trees. Not wanting to be found, she ducked under the bent shadow of a twisted juniper. Each time Corey shouted her name, he sounded more desperate. She slid down the tree, too tired to stand.

Then Christopher's voice rang through the night like a sudden thunderclap. Lorelei waited, listening to the sound of their footsteps veering away from her. She feared he wouldn't call her name again.

"Over here," she yelled. Suddenly she wanted to be found. Wanted to have Christopher hold her so she could again pretend that everything was all right.

They discovered her quickly, and walked directly to her.

"Lori, are you all right?" Corey rushed forward. He stopped a foot or so from her. He couldn't have seen her expression in the shadows, but she knew her anger was a weighty thing.

Christopher had no such hesitation. He knelt beside her, touching her face. "Are you hurt?"

She wanted to wrap her arms around him and bury her face in his neck, but now that he was so close, she was afraid—afraid of everything that had come between them and all that would. No matter how much she wanted to be free of Corey, he was still her brother. She doubted she would ever have the strength to turn completely away from him.

She cupped the hand Christopher held against her face. "I want to go home."

"You can go home if you want. I'll buy your ticket. But we have to clear your name first. You understand, don't you, sweetheart?"

A sob caught in her throat, stealing her breath. "I want to go home tomorrow. I can't stand this place anymore."

He smoothed back her tangled hair. Never had he been so gentle, not even when they made love. "I'll take you myself once the gold is returned. You might be arrested if I send you off alone."

"What about me, Lori?"

The comfort that flooded her at Christopher's touch was jerked away by the sound of her brother's rude question. "What about you? You lied to me, Corey."

Corey stared into the shadowed recesses of the night. "You wouldn't have understood."

She tried to stand, but Christopher held her down with a firm grip on her shoulder. "You need some food in you."

"I understand you put our lives at risk." All her anger pounded into a single vein at her temple. Yelling at Corey seemed the only way to relieve the pressure.

"You don't know how it's been for me. You always had it so easy. You were always everyone's favorite."

She pushed Christopher's restraining hand away. He supported her waist and elbow when she insisted on struggling to her feet. She took a step toward Corey, not sure if her shaking came from the long day's ride or his audacity.

"Ma and I did everything for you. Everything! I gave you all I had so you could come out here and make something of yourself."

Corey glared at her as if he were the one who had been wronged. "But whatever I did was never good enough."

She closed in on Corey, ready to pull him over her knee and give him the whipping he should have gotten fifteen years ago.

Braddock slipped his arm fully around her waist, stopping her. "This isn't doing either of you any good."

She jerked out of his grip. He could have held her if he'd wanted to. Instead he hovered nearby, as if he thought she might collapse at any minute. But suddenly she felt stronger than she ever had in her life.

"How could you do this? How could you get yourself in so much trouble?"

"I guess you wish it was me instead of Devine that was killed. Or even Donnan. Both you and Ma wished I wasn't the brother that was spared."

Lorelei didn't answer for a moment. The part of her that didn't flinch at his accusation shamed her. Even in the darkness she could see how her hesitation hurt him. "You were just a child when they died. You didn't understand."

"I understood well enough that I was too much trouble."

"If that were true, why did we hide you during the war, go without so you could have enough to eat?"

"I tried, Lori. But I wasn't as strong as Devine. I couldn't even make you laugh like Donnan. Don't think I don't know that Ma used to say I was just like our pa."

Lorelei's anger faded, leaving her with an unbearable throbbing behind her eyes. She massaged her forehead with the tips of her fingers. "He was a good man, Corey."

Corey's bitter laugh sounded stuck in his throat. "That's why he was the dirty joke of Louisville. That's why he went to jail for cheating in a horse race. That's why we lost our home, even our chance to hold our heads up."

"We held our heads up."

"*You* did, Lorelei. 'Cause everyone liked you. They said, 'That poor Lorelei, such a pretty thing, such a shame.' Me, they said, 'The apple doesn't fall far from the tree. Watch out for that little Sullivan boy.' "

Lorelei gazed up at the sky, looking for an answer as to how things had gone so wrong. The first star of the night winked at her foolish request. "Does it matter now, Corey? All those people who used to look down on us, most of them lost everything in the war. They were begging and scratching for food just like us. But you had the chance to leave. Make a new home for us. What happened? Why didn't you just stick to training horses?"

"I wanted to. But I wanted things to be nicer for you."

She shook her head. "You have to take responsibility for your own actions."

"It's the truth. I wanted to show you I was as good as Devine. I know you missed him the most. But I'm not as good as him." Corey swallowed his shaky words and remained silent, his face averted.

Lorelei stepped toward her brother and took him in her arms. He hugged her so fiercely in return she knew what her anger had done to him.

"I'm sorry, Lori," he whispered, his voice husky with unshed tears.

Lorelei rubbed his back. She stopped herself from saying it was all right, because it was far from all right. "You have to tell me everything, Corey. No more lies."

"Just don't be mad at me anymore."

She pulled away from him and held him at arm's length. His hair had gotten redder since he'd been out west, like Donnan's. But he wasn't Donnan or Devine; he was Corey. He was all she had. "I can't stay mad at you, though I should."

"I didn't mean to put you in danger. I should have known better. Braddock should have known better." His jaw was set and his eyes glittered with anger instead of tears as he glanced over her shoulder.

Lorelei took a deep breath, not willing to put herself between Christopher and her brother again. "You're not going to blame what happened in Coyote Pass on him. You could have told us you knew those men. I haven't forgotten you were involved in the robbery, if that's what you're thinking."

"I know. I'm just afraid he's going to get us killed if he keeps on looking for Mulcahy."

"If he doesn't find Mulcahy first, Mulcahy will hunt you down anyway. But you don't have to trust him, Corey. Trust me. I want him to help us. We need him."

Corey folded his arms over his chest. "You need him."

"I need him," she agreed, still unsure of what that meant. She just knew Christopher would do what he could to keep them all safe. Somehow she had known that from the beginning. Even when she had ventured to his hotel room, she had sensed he could be trusted with her body. It was her heart that concerned her.

"What do you want me to do?"

Her gaze darted in search of Christopher. Braddock now leaned against the juniper's slick trunk, tucked in the shadows. The fact that he had moved away, given them some privacy, said he trusted her.

She turned back to Corey. "Do you know where to find Mulcahy?"

He let out his breath. "Yeah."

Lorelei paused to keep herself from shouting at him for withholding the information. "You have to tell Braddock. You have to tell him everything you know about Mulcahy and the robbery."

"You won't like it."

"I already don't like it. I don't like any of this."

"I'm not going with him to Mulcahy's hideout, and neither are you. You'd better make sure that's clear before I talk."

"Fine," she said, not sure she could talk Braddock out of anything once he made his mind up, but she knew she had no one else to turn to. "Let's go talk to him together."

Corey put his hand on her shoulder to stop her. "What do you expect to get from him?"

"Nothing," she answered. In the same instant, her daydream from the adobe reared up to tell her she lied. A life as husband and wife didn't seem possible for them, but the knowledge didn't stop her from wanting it.

"You aren't really sweet on him, are you?"

Lorelei felt herself blush. Denying it would be pointless.

"I know you have needs." Corey cleared his throat. "I mean, just because you scratched an itch doesn't mean you have to be sweet on him."

Lorelei opened her mouth to tell him her relationship with Christopher was much more than an "itch," but she stopped before she gave herself so pitifully away. "He's been good to me, Corey." She tugged on Corey's arm. "Come on, I'm hungry."

Christopher straightened from his relaxed position and stretched. "Think you two can stop fighting long enough to get some food in your bellies?"

"Corey knows where you can find Mulcahy."

Christopher looked bored rather than surprised by the revelation. "Is he going to tell me?"

"Only if you swear not to put my sister in danger again." Corey shrugged off Lorelei's grip and stepped closer to Braddock.

Lorelei tried to drag him back.

Christopher stuck out his right hand to Corey. "You have my word."

Corey seemed as surprised as Lorelei by the gesture; he hesitated, then gave Braddock his hand.

Christopher yanked him forward. "But don't lie to me, kid. I can't protect your sister when I don't know what you have up your sleeve."

Corey tried to pull his hand away. Lorelei touched Christopher's shoulder in a gentle suggestion. "He's going to tell you everything he knows. Right, Corey?"

"Yes."

Christopher released Corey. "Good. See to the horses. We'll talk after we eat."

When she nodded that it was all right to leave them alone, Corey followed Christopher's less-than-subtle request.

They watched Corey disappear; then Christopher squeezed her shoulder with his free hand. "You gonna make it?"

She shrugged. "I don't have a choice. Though I don't think I can take many more afternoons like that."

Christopher dropped his hand from her shoulder and moved away, instead of pulling her into his arms as she would have liked. "You won't have to. I never should have taken you to Coyote Pass."

"Corey should have told you the truth," she blurted.

She could see Christopher mentally closing himself off. "I

knew better," was all he said, and she feared he meant so much more than their excursion to Coyote Pass.

She didn't want him to dismiss all that they had shared as a mistake. "I never should have said I'd slit your throat. I was angry and hurt, but you were right."

He kept his hands by his sides, his body stiff. He left no opening for her to push into. "No matter what you said, I shouldn't have handcuffed you. But I guess we both learned what kind of man I am."

"No." She tried to embrace him. "I don't believe that's who you are."

He caught her arms and gently lowered them to her sides. "Don't. It's better this way."

"Not for me." She hated the pleading tone in her voice. To keep from touching him again, she folded her arms in front of her and squeezed. "I'm sorry I pointed the rifle at you. I never would have hit you."

He actually smiled at that. "I'm not so sure."

She returned his smile, but it was a weak effort. She wasn't so sure, either. "I wouldn't have killed you. I can't change the fact Corey is my brother."

"I don't want you to."

"I don't know what you overheard, but I wasn't going to trick you. Corey doesn't know anything about what happened between Berkley and I. Berkley—"

"I don't want to know."

"Won't you let me explain?"

"There's nothing to explain."

Lorelei wished she could just keep her mouth shut, but Christopher Braddock meant too much to her to let her pride stand in her way. "What about us? Don't you feel anything for me at all?"

His jaw clenched, his expression pained. "There isn't any 'us'. Staying with me will only get you killed."

She clutched his sleeve. "I'm willing to take that risk."

He jerked out of her reach. "Goddammit, Lorelei. Don't do this to me. I've seen too many people die. I don't want to care about anyone. I don't want to care about you."

The emotion in his voice forced her a step back. "It doesn't have to be that way."

He laughed, a dry, hysterical snort. "Were you at Coyote Pass? Do you realize what could have happened to you? What would have happened if a drunk hadn't gotten off a lucky shot? It wouldn't have been pleasant. You would have begged to die long before you did."

Her throat went dry. She refused to think about that. It hadn't happened, and she had plenty else to worry about. "But you saved me."

"No. I dragged you there. I don't save people."

She needed to say something to erase the look of misery from his tight features. "You bought the supplies. You kept me from getting arrested. How can you say you didn't save me?"

When he finally faced her, she could tell by the harsh line of his jaw that her words had succeeded only in triggering his anger. "This is the way it's going to be. I've got my own ass to save, thanks to you and your brother. And that's what I'm going to do. All he has to do is tell me where I can find Mulcahy, and I'll act like neither one of you ever existed."

She clutched the threadbare muslin that covered her knotted stomach. "What do you mean?"

"I mean I won't turn Corey in. That's what you want, isn't it?"

"But what about . . ." She stopped. It was obvious his plans included no future for them. No contact. "What about . . ." she started again, but could only stare at him, disbelieving.

"I'm going to take you and Corey to a friend's place. He'll protect you both while I find Mulcahy. He can use the help on his farm. I expect your brother to work off the favor. Can you see to that?"

She nodded, unable to speak.

"You'll be fine. Better than fine. Lots of single men have settled in the area, because the land's cheap. They need wives—"

She was grateful when he stopped. Even in the darkness he must be able to read the horror on her face.

"Corey will have to change his name. You too, I guess, unless you marry." He had the good grace to hesitate on the last word. He looked away for a moment. "Don't worry about Langston. I'll handle him. It's the best thing. Corey will like it."

She joined her hands in front or her. An unnatural calm, like the eye of a hurricane, settled over her. "Yes, he will."

"It's what you wanted from the start, isn't it? For me to let Corey go," he said again, as if testing the words out. Making sure they still sounded good. He gave her a wan smile, so she guessed he thought so.

He remained silent, staring at her. She supposed he actually expected her to respond.

"Yes, that's exactly what I wanted. How can I ever thank you?" Her voice sounded as hollow as her heart.

"It's for the best."

Why did those words always follow a painful experience, an unbearable loss? What utter nonsense.

"Corey will be pleased," was all she could think to say.

His features sagged with his shoulders. At least he'd stopped acting as if this were pleasant, that their parting was for the best.

With a nod of his head, he gestured toward the glow of a small fire burning in the distance. "We should go back."

She gazed at the flickering blaze longer than necessary. Corey surprised her. It wasn't like him to take the initiative in anything, much less go to the trouble to start a campfire.

Christopher waited for her to move toward the camp. She did, but made certain not even the breeze of her movement brushed him. She would survive this. Her heart still beat. Her limbs still moved on command. Losing Christopher really wasn't that bad in comparison to the other things that had been snatched from her. She had never had any real hope with him anyway, and she had gained Corey's freedom.

Still, this fresh blow seemed especially cruel. Maybe she thought Christopher was some prize for her endurance. But there was no prize, only more to endure.

She lifted her skirt and increased her pace. A rock dug

through the thin soles of her worn shoes, toppling her fragile balance. Her breath whistled through her teeth at the sharp jolt of pain.

Christopher was instantly at her side to steady her. "Are you all right?"

His touch hurt more than the rock. Not because his concern wasn't real, but because it was. He did care for her. Unfortunately, he decided how it would be between them, and her opinion didn't even count. He did what he thought was best. Men always did, and look how terribly things turned out.

She shook off his grip. "I'm fine, thank you," she said, and strode toward the camp ahead of him, alone.

Braddock couldn't stop gazing at Lorelei across the campfire, watching her blink back her tears before they could spill onto her cheeks. If it weren't for Archie and his antics, keeping semicomposed would have been that much harder for her. The tension hanging over the campfire still had the potential to ignite at any moment.

He swirled the coffee in his mug. Maybe he should have taken a shot of Archie's whiskey after all. The liquor seemed to work well for everyone else. He couldn't believe he was actually grateful for Archie's presence, but the unbearable silence that surely would have surrounded them had the man not been present might have broken him. He still didn't know if he could walk away from Lorelei forever.

All he had do to was summon back the vision of Lorelei being dragged to her feet by the outlaw, and Braddock knew he could do whatever it took to keep her safe. The safest place for anyone he cared about remained as far away from him as possible. Time had proven that again and again.

Lorelei tossed her head back suddenly and genuinely laughed at something Archie said. Probably something outlandish. Corey laughed too, and Archie, who laughed at just about everything. Braddock had missed the joke. His own miserable thoughts barred him from the others' joy like a wall of cold, wet stone.

He tore his gaze away from the warm light in Lorelei's eye and the way her dark curls danced around her shoulders as she continued to giggle. There was no need to pretend he was anything but an outsider, their jailer.

Archie leaned over and refilled Corey's cup with whiskey. Lorelei put her hand over her cup and shook her head.

Archie raised his glass. "You're a lovely lady, Miss Lori May. Corey, why didn't you tell me your mother was so pretty? Would have liked to have heard about that. That's what I miss most about St. Louis, the pretty girls."

Corey laughed too loud. The kid couldn't hold his liquor. Braddock should have put a stop to the drinking before it started. But when he and Lorelei had returned to camp, Archie had already made a fire and started a decent stew of beans and salted meat. And, of course, a shot of whiskey for flavor. Braddock had been in no condition to take charge of anything. By the time he was able to draw a steady breath, Archie had already passed out the stew and the booze. He must have stuffed his saddlebags with whiskey before they left.

"Is your husband from Kentucky, too?" Archie asked.

"He's not her husband. I told you, he's a bounty hunter who wants to find Mulcahy." Corey took another gulp of whiskey.

Archie finished the bottle at the mention of Mulcahy's name. Lorelei stared at the fire, unblinking. Her face had turned a chalky white. She didn't look as if she could hold down her liquor or her meal. She set her half-eaten bowl of beans away from her. Braddock couldn't help but notice that her illness coincided with the mention of their ruse as husband and wife.

Archie, who didn't bother to eat at all, tipped over as he grabbed for another bottle. "Don't want to know nothing about Rowen Mulcahy." He half reached for, half crawled to his saddlebag, righting himself only after he retrieved his prize. "No, sir. Don't know nothing about that red-haired Irishman."

"He expects me to tell him where to find Mulcahy," Corey said with a glare in Braddock's direction.

Archie froze with the bottle in his hand. For a moment he looked stone-cold sober. "Don't tell me. I don't want to know."

"Well, you're going to know, because that's where he's taking us."

"Not me." Archie's face flushed. "Lori May, talk to your husband. He must be crazy." Archie grabbed the cork with his teeth and pulled it out. He spit it past the circle of light thrown by the fire, then took a long draw from the bottle.

Lorelei watched him, her round blue eyes pulling down at the corners. "You'll be sick, Archie. Don't drink any more."

"Not me, missy. I don't get sick anymore. Except when I don't have my tonic." He toasted her with the bottle.

"That's because it's killing you."

"Let him be, Lori. You can't save him either," Corey snapped.

Braddock looked between brother and sister. She bowed her head as if the weight on her shoulders had gotten too heavy. He wanted to put his arm around her. She had had too much in her life for such a small woman to bear. Braddock forced himself to look away before he was caught staring like a doe-eyed suitor. He was doing the best thing for her, even if it killed him. His chest ached with each breath, and he wondered if he were truly, physically wounded in some way. He had to force himself to relax just to get air in his lungs.

"That'd be something. To die by drink. I'd like that."

The campfire danced in the sheen coating Lorelei's eyes. "You won't like it. It's a horrible way to die. My father drank himself to death."

Archie shook his head in an exaggerated motion. "Not as bad as being caught by Apaches. They peel the skin right off you and let the flies nibble on your juicy innards."

"Or being hanged," piped in Corey. "I saw three men hanged in Santa Fe my first week in New Mexico. I won't forget that soon. They didn't even put hoods over their heads.

You could see their eyes pop out and their faces turn red as fire."

"Or"—Archie took a big gulp from the bottle—"or being dragged through town by a horse when you got a broken arm and a couple of broken ribs. It takes a long time to die like that."

Even Corey blanched. "Who did that?"

Archie looked around as if to see if someone might be eavesdropping. He leaned toward Corey and whispered loudly, "You know who."

Lorelei placed one hand over her mouth and the other over her stomach. Braddock stood. He should have never let this start.

"That's enough." He took Corey's tin cup and dumped out the contents.

"I was wondering when you'd stop the fun." Corey thrust his hands behind his back and leaned forward. "Go ahead. Lock me up for the night."

Lorelei dumped her cup of whiskey without being asked.

Archie hugged the bottle to his chest. "I need this for medicinal purposes."

Braddock was in no mood to wrestle the bottle from him. "We're riding out of here early tomorrow, and I have no problem leaving you behind if you can't keep up."

"I'll keep up . . . with a smile on my face and a song on my lips." Archie gave his bottle a loving kiss.

"Just keep up." Braddock turned to Corey. "You ready to tell me what you know about Mulcahy?"

Corey glanced at Lorelei. "I've got some conditions first."

Lorelei stared into the fire. "He's going to leave us at a friend's house while he finds Mulcahy by himself."

Archie took a gulp from his bottle. "That'll kill you faster than this ever will."

Corey snorted. "What friend? Does he have bars for a front door?"

Lorelei sighed. "I don't know."

Braddock went to his saddlebag and pulled out a map to keep from snapping at Lorelei. She knew he wasn't taking her to jail. He returned with the map and squeezed between

Corey and Archie, avoiding the larger space between brother and sister.

He unfolded the map and laid it on the ground in front of him. "My friend's farm is a couple of days from here. You and Lorelei can stay there, but you have to help out."

"I don't like farm work," complained Corey.

"I like it. Always did. I like to get my hands dirty. Lila likes farms too."

Braddock glanced at Archie. "We'll have to find someplace else for you to go. My friend's got his hands full."

"He can take my place," said Corey.

"If you don't want to work for your keep, kid, you can go to my other friend's house, the one with bars for a front door."

Corey picked up a twig and tossed it into the fire. "What's the difference? That's where I'm going to end up anyway."

"Do you think you could drop me off in San Francisco? I always wanted to go there." Archie stared into the distance, lost in another conversation.

"No." Braddock didn't bother telling him how far San Francisco was from the New Mexico territory. Archie might as well have asked to be dropped off on the moon.

"Heard they had gold streets there. I know it's not true, but that's what I heard," said the man to no one in particular. "Good place to start fresh."

Lorelei lifted her head and snared Braddock's gaze. It was all he could do not to flinch under her direct scrutiny. "Braddock's letting us go. He won't come back for us. Isn't that right?"

"Yes." He didn't make promises lightly. He wanted her to know that about him.

"He won't come back because he's going to be dead," mumbled Archie. "What about Helena, up Montana way? A man could make something of himself there."

"Yeah, he's letting me go, and I've got some land to sell smack-dab in the middle of Apache country. They don't mind neighbors."

"It's true, Corey. We'll have to change our names, but we can start over."

Archie stood on wobbly legs and crouched in front of the fire. "There's a bird that burns itself, then rises from its own ashes. Flies away better than before. That's what I'm going to do."

Braddock got to his feet and grabbed a fistful of Archie's shirt. "You fall in that fire and you'll just be ashes." He yanked Archie a little too hard, because the momentum sent him sprawling in the dirt.

Lorelei sprang to his rescue. "Do you have to be so mean to him? At least he wants a better life."

Braddock stood back as she helped Archie to his feet, then guided him next to her, away from the fire.

"There's fire; then there's ashes. There's nothing else." Braddock sank to the ground and forced himself to remember Coyote Pass all over again. Wherever he went, he'd leave a scorched trail in his wake. It was better for Lorelei to hate him.

"Even if I did believe you'd let me go, what about the deputy marshal who came to the ranch?"

For once, Braddock was glad Corey thought only of himself.

"I'll tell him you died. Once I bring Mulcahy in with the gold, they'll forget about Lorelei. Especially if she marries." Braddock watched Lorelei tense. He knew his words would upset her, but it was best for her to marry. He needed to start accepting the idea himself.

Corey made a face. "Marry? Marry who?"

"New Orleans, that's the city for me. People know how to have a good time there," said Archie.

Braddock swallowed. He suddenly felt hot and cold at the same time, as if he had drunk too much bad whiskey. "Anyone would want to marry your sister. She needs a man to take care of her."

"Anyone but you, huh, Braddock?"

"Please, Corey." Lorelei clasped her hand to her forehead as if she were trying to compress a raging fever.

Braddock balled his hand into a fist, barely restraining the urge to punch the sneer off her brother's face. "Lorelei deserves better than me. She can have a home and a family of her own, a safe place to live, if you don't screw it up for her."

"I'm not the one who took her to Coyote Pass. I don't believe this story about your friend's farm. You just want me to spill the beans about Mulcahy."

"I don't know anything about Mulcahy, and I don't want to know," recited Archie on cue, like a parrot repeating his favorite line.

"Stop it. Both of you." Lorelei moved her hands to clutch her stomach. "Braddock is giving us what we wanted from the beginning. The least you can do is tell him where he can find Mulcahy."

"You won't be safe while he's still free. You don't have a choice, kid," Braddock said.

"You believe him?" Corey asked his sister.

"Yes, I do."

Corey studied Braddock. "Something's funny here. What's in it for you if you let me go? I already told you I'd tell you where Mulcahy is. It's not like I have a choice."

"I want Lorelei to be safe. And if I don't let you go, she's going to keep getting into trouble to save you."

Lorelei bent her head while she massaged her temples. She appeared to be unable to decide which hurt worse, her stomach or her head. Maybe they'd all drunk from an alkali runoff without realizing it.

Corey glanced at his sister, then back to Braddock. "This is about something else. What did you do to her, Braddock?"

Lorelei lifted her head. "Nothing. He didn't do anything to me. He's just trying to help, which is more than we deserve."

"You deserve a lot more than I can give you, Lorelei." Braddock was unable to control the emotion in his voice any more than he could stop the words spilling from his mouth. "A lot more."

"I don't want more." She rapidly blinked, but a tear still

managed to slide down her cheek. She fiercely brushed it away.

"Hold on one second." Corey stood. "I know what's going on here."

Braddock dropped his head to massage his brow as Lorelei had done. Splitting headaches were catching, and he knew it wasn't from bad water. He said, "I can't risk it, Lorelei. I just can't."

God, how he wanted to. He'd never thought he would want to take a chance on a normal life. Settling down with one woman, having children, and pretending you could have a nice, quiet life seemed as substantial as a daydream when one knew the thousands of things that could befall you. The world waited to explode with violence. It was too easy to die, or worse. But the desire to keep Lorelei safe made Braddock's decision, though the pain in his chest almost talked him into saying anything to hold on to her.

The crackle of the fire punctuated the abrupt lull in the conversation. A sudden clap of thunder couldn't be any louder than the quiet tension. Something had to break, and Braddock was sure it would be him.

"You're knocked up," Corey blurted.

Archie stirred from his slumped position. "I love babies. Who's having a baby? That's what's wrong with the New Mexico territory: not enough babies. Who's having the baby?"

Braddock lifted his gaze to Lorelei, sure lightning had just ripped through the top of his head and surged out the heels of his boots.

She shook her head. "I'm not with child."

Braddock's horror at Corey's accusation must have shown on his face, because Lorelei's eyes narrowed in anger. "You'll have no tie to me. You don't need to worry."

"That's not it," Braddock began, but stopped himself before he hurt her more. There was nothing he could say to make the situation any better.

"Don't you worry, little lady. You're a young thing. All you and your husband need to do is spend a little more time together. You'll be in the pink in no time. A little less horse riding though," Archie said in a loud whisper, presumably for Lorelei alone.

"Oh, no. He's staying away from my sister if he wants me to tell him where to find Mulcahy."

To Braddock's relief, Lorelei swung her angry gaze to her brother. "Just stay out of this, Corey. You'll tell Braddock about Mulcahy so we can be done with this mess."

Archie desperately gulped whiskey as if he wanted to pass out again as soon as possible. "I don't know anything about Mulcahy, and I don't want to know."

"I'm not telling him anything until we see this friend of his." Corey folded his arms over his chest and cocked his hip in a determined stance.

Braddock stood. "Fine. Once we get to Jay's farm, you can tell me about Mulcahy."

"And if I don't like him, we'll just have to make other arrangements."

Braddock picked up his rifle. He would check the perimeter of the camp to make sure they weren't followed from Coyote Pass. Sleep certainly wasn't an option. "You'll like him. He and his wife are good people."

Corey snorted. "Then why are they friends with you?"

Braddock paused to glance at Lorelei, who packed away the dishes they had used for dinner. She stilled when his gaze touched her. The way her shoulders stiffened told him she was still angry. Better angry than hurt, though—which didn't make him feel any better.

"Guess their luck isn't any better than yours," he answered at last. Then he walked away, half fearing he would finally see a hint of forgiveness in Lorelei's eyes, and half fearing that he wouldn't.

Chapter Eleven

Braddock rode Lucky onto the neat dirt perimeter that marked Jay Hartman's front yard and braced himself. The sea of milky-topped cotton that threatened to swallow the small homestead lulled him into such a false sense of ease, he thought he'd arrived at the wrong farm. But as he drew closer, he recognized the single-story ranch house.

Despite everything, Jay appeared to be getting on all right. The house's planked front had a fresh coat of white paint, and an adobe addition peeked from the back. A swing creaked on the porch, and beds of flowers bloomed in the surrounding shadows. The last and only other time Braddock had visited his friend's place, he hadn't counted on Jay's lasting a year. If it weren't for the occasional letters that reached him, he would have assumed the Hartmans had moved back east to live with Jay's folks.

Braddock glanced to his companions, who followed at a wary distance. Compared to the night he had sworn to let Lorelei and her brother go, their journey had been uneventful. Even Archie had behaved. Though not quite sober, he wasn't painting-the-town-red drunk. Braddock suspected he was rationing his supply of booze. He didn't doubt Archie needed the stuff for medicinal purposes. Archie was so hooked on it, he probably wouldn't have survived the two days of hard riding without it.

He swung off Lucky and draped the reins around the porch's rail; then Braddock climbed the steps to the front door. His actions felt exaggerated, as if he had to put on a show to keep from helping Lorelei dismount. But if he didn't keep his distance during the day, he'd never make it through the nights. The camp loomed silent then, and he could hear her heavy sighs. To keep from touching her, holding her one last time, required all his strength. More than that, he at least wanted to tell her he was sorry. But that would make their inevitable parting that much harder. And that he must leave her and never see her again was the one thing he was sure of.

He knocked on Jay's door. His stomach clenched with the unreasonable and unwanted hope that they had moved. He stepped back and waited. A restless wind that ruffled the yard's lone tree was his only answer.

He scanned the grounds for signs of life. His prisoners had dismounted and stared at him expectantly. Lorelei wiped dust and sweat from her eyes. She was clearly exhausted.

Braddock knocked again, louder. There was still no answer, no movement behind the door. "Hello," he called loudly. "Jay, Beth. Anybody home?"

"Don't give away it's you. They might not answer," said Corey.

Braddock took off his hat, avoiding looking over. The little smart-ass was right. Braddock himself wouldn't answer the door if it were him. He stepped down from the porch, intending to go around back. A high-pitched squeal followed by a woman's surprised shriek stopped him in midstep.

He swiveled in the direction of the noise, adjusted his weight to his knees, and reached for his guns.

A child's scream melted into a peal of laughter.

Braddock barely had time to reholster his pistols before a dripping, naked child ran full-speed around the corner.

"I'm gonna get you, Rachel. Ma's going to whip your behind."

The taunt that followed her kept the little girl running past the haggard strangers in her front yard. The boy chasing her, however, stopped in his tracks. His eyes rounded into blue saucers.

"Rachel, get over here," he commanded with real concern in his voice.

His sister continued to giggle while she careened around Archie, then Corey. Her pursuer's sudden desperation seemed to make the game that much more fun. The two men held their hands up in the air and jumped to avoid the child the way they might have if a sea of rattlers were winding through their path.

The naked little girl bounded straight for Lorelei, wrapped her fists in her skirt, and hid behind her.

Beth waddled around the corner. "Did you catch her, Chris?" she called. The white apron she wore over her blouse and skirt was soaked up the front, and she was even more pregnant than the last time Braddock had seen her.

She stopped, apparently not recognizing him, and wiped her wet hands on her drenched apron. "Hello. I didn't know we had visitors."

Archie stepped forward. "You're with child. How wonderful. Eight months, looks to be. You'll be having the baby a little earlier, from the way you're carrying."

Her smile seemed strained until she spotted Lorelei standing behind Archie. Lorelei had coaxed the little girl in front of her and wrapped her skirt around the child. "You must have a lot of children. Is this your wife?" She sidestepped Archie to check on her daughter. "Rachel Hartman, get your fanny over here. You're getting that nice lady all wet. I'm so sorry."

Lorelei smiled. "She's fine."

The girl burrowed more deeply into Lorelei's skirts. "I'm hiding, Mommy."

"Lori May is *his* wife," said Archie, pointing to Braddock.

Braddock stepped forward, hoping to cut the ex-bartender off. "I'm sorry to drop in like this, Beth."

She turned to him for the first time. "Christopher Braddock, I didn't even recognize you in all the excitement. Is this your wife?"

Braddock forced himself not to cringe. Nor did he have the courage to deny it.

"We're not married," Lorelei spoke up. She kept her gaze on the little girl. "She's so cute. How old?"

"Three." Beth shot Braddock a curious glance. She wanted an explanation, and if he didn't hurry she was going to concoct one of her own.

"These are . . ." He stopped, not knowing what to politely call the ragtag assortment. "These are some people who need help. I was hoping as a favor to me you could put them up for a while. They can help around the farm, of course."

Beth Hartman pulled her gaze away to examine the others. Her face showed she didn't believe him completely, but she respected him too much to say so. "You know Jay would do anything you asked. He'll be thrilled you finally asked." She appeared to suspend her silent investigation and smiled warmly. "Are you all hungry?"

"Starved," Corey spoke up.

"Let's get you all something to eat, then."

Beth's son, who'd been sticking to his mother's side, finally moved toward them. "I'll show you where you can put your horses. Is that an Indian pony?" he asked Corey.

"Hope not. I caught him wild and don't want to get scalped for doing it."

"We have wild horses on our land, but my ma won't let me get near them."

Corey winked. "She's a smart woman. Better listen to her. This one about kicked my teeth in before we became friends."

"Can I be his friend?" asked the boy.

"I don't know." Corey rubbed his chin. "Sugarfoot's pretty selective. Why don't you come over here and let her give you a sniff?"

The boy turned to Beth with pleading blue eyes.

"As long as you don't touch her without permission. But first I want you meet your namesake." She touched the boy's shoulder and angled him in Braddock's direction. "Christopher Braddock Hartman, meet Christopher Braddock."

Braddock stared at the child. He should have known Jay would follow through with his threat to name his unborn child after him. His only hope had been that the child Beth had carried would have been a girl. *Poor kid.*

"Both names, huh?" was all he could think to say. The kid looked too old to change his name now.

The boy returned Braddock's stare with none of the eagerness he'd shown toward Corey. Beth urged her son forward with a gentle shove.

"Do you think Jay could be persuaded to do any less? I guess you're just lucky he didn't name him Captain Christopher Braddock Hartman."

"I'm not a captain anymore," said Braddock, not because it needed to be said, but because he was at a loss. Something was expected of him but he didn't know what.

The child inched toward him reluctantly.

Braddock could feel Lorelei's gaze on him. She would see just how truly incompetent he was with anyone who wasn't a criminal or an enemy, and she'd be glad to be rid of him. Still, he didn't want to scar the child for life. He already had his plate full, with the cross of a name he'd been given.

Braddock hunched down, trying to bring himself to the boy's level, and reached out.

The boy placed his small hand in Braddock's. "Nice to meet you. My dad says you're a hero."

Braddock shook with a gentle grip, but he couldn't find the smile he wanted to give. "No, your dad's the hero."

Christopher Braddock Hartman grinned from ear to ear. "Really? What'd he do?"

Braddock rested one knee on the ground. "He had you. And your brother and sisters. That's pretty brave, if you ask me."

Braddock hadn't said it as a joke but the child laughed anyway. "That's what my ma says when we try to teach her to ride. She says having so many kids is all the excitement she can stand."

"It is. I don't need to go racing around on the backs of those big animals when I have plenty to do with chasing after you and your sister."

Christopher Braddock Hartman looked to the sky while a silly, upside-down grin tugged at his mouth. Braddock recognized the gesture as his father's. He hadn't seen Jay make that face since before his injury, and he wondered if it had been passed down like his blond hair and blue eyes. Braddock got a funny feeling in his chest. To his horror he felt like he was going to cry. He hadn't cried since the first year of the war. But the emotion, being as overwhelming as it was, he recognized instantly.

"My mama's afraid of horses," little Christopher whispered loudly.

Braddock swallowed hard and forcibly got himself under control.

"I'm not!" yelled the boy's sister. She escaped from Lorelei and ran in their direction. She stopped in front of Braddock and stuck her fingers in her belly button. "I'm not afraid of horses," she said as she swayed from side to side.

Braddock stood mute, totally unsure of the proper etiquette with naked female children. He glanced at Beth, who seemed amused over his discomfort. A glance to Lorelei garnered the same response.

"She can't ride yet. She's too little," said Chris. "Is that your horse?"

Braddock's gaze strayed to where Chris pointed, knowing Lucky was the horse in question. Now that the little girl was taking inventory of her body parts, Braddock needed something to do with his eyes.

"Yep. That's Lucky."

"Can I ride him?"

"Christopher," reprimanded Beth. "How many times have I told you not to ask people if you can ride their horses? Now, go take your sister around back and finish her bath so I can get our guests something to eat."

"I want to help with the horses," the boy pleaded.

"I'll be glad to finish her bath." Lorelei extended her hand to Beth. "Lorelei Sullivan." The two women shook hands. "And this is my brother, Corey."

Corey whipped off his hat and bowed.

"Sorry, I guess I should have . . ." Braddock didn't finish his sentence. His lack of social graces spoke for itself. He hadn't used to be so inept, he reminded his hurt pride.

"And this is Archie." Lorelei gestured with a twist of her wrist. "But we just met and I didn't catch his last name."

Archie followed Corey's lead and bowed gallantly. "Dr. Archibald Banks the Fourth, of the Virginia Bankses."

Lorelei's gaze widened, unsure as Braddock was as to the validity of his statement. Doctor of what was something they all probably didn't want to know.

"Yes, and you know . . ." Lorelei hesitated. ". . . Christopher."

The way she said his name, as if she never really knew him, unreasonably irritated Braddock. He finally found his voice. "Is Jay around?"

"He'll be along shortly. Come on inside so I can fix you all something to eat. Rachel, would you like Miss Lorelei to finish your bath?"

Little Rachel finally pulled her curious and penetrating gaze away from Braddock, who sighed with relief. He'd rather be watched by an Apache scout.

The little girl's stare targeted Lorelei. "You have pretty hair."

Lorelei squatted. "Thank you, Rachel. If you let me give you a bath, I'll let you return the favor. I bet I need a bath more than you."

Rachel grasped Lorelei's hand. She led her across the yard without a word to anyone, Braddock and everyone else forgotten.

"Corey, can you bring my bag? I think I'm going to need a change of clothes," Lorelei called over her shoulder.

Beth, the only one brave enough to tangle with her naked daughter, put her palm on Rachel's forehead, halting the girl's abduction of Lorelei. "Hold on there, little miss. You mind Miss Lorelei. And if you don't keep yourself in the tub this time, I'll swat your bare behind."

"But she wants a bath." The little girl tilted her head almost off her neck to look up at her mother.

"Maybe she does, but you're still going to mind her. You understand?"

Rachel held on to Lorelei's hand as she would a favorite blanket. "Yes, ma'am."

Beth's gaze rose to Lorelei. "Thank you. I can't keep up with her anymore." She rubbed her swollen belly. "You're already a blessing. I didn't know how I was going to make it until the baby was born."

Lorelei smiled, but it came out lopsided. "Wait until you hear our story. You might not want to keep us around."

"I'll want to."

Little Christopher turned to Corey. "Let's take the horses to the barn. We have lots of oats. Your horse will like that." He swaggered toward the structure, not waiting to see if Corey followed.

Braddock watched with a painful swelling in his throat. The little boy had an exaggerated adult gait. He was big for his age, already a little husky, but long-limbed. He walked like his father had. Braddock swallowed hard, hoping that if he had to cry he would be able to do it in private. His stomach started to burn in his effort to hold back the emotion.

"He's Jay's son, isn't he?"

Braddock's gaze was drawn to Beth's. Shameless tears pooled in her eyes. Braddock set his jaw, ruthlessly grinding his teeth. He blinked, and was grateful his eyes were as dry as dirt. He looked away from Beth before that could change. He almost said, *Jay's a lucky man,* but stopped himself. Jay's luck was rotten. He just said, "Yep," instead.

The sound of a horse galloping in their direction drew everyone's attention. Braddock had to blink to make sure it was Jay who sat atop the big draft horse. He'd never expected to see his friend riding again.

Jay slowed the horse when he reached the clearing and

trotted right up to Braddock. He sat back, his hands resting on the saddle horn. "Thought I'd been out in the sun too long, but it is you."

Braddock looked up at his friend's face and shielded his eyes with the flat of his hand, half to block the sun and half to hide his expression. He purposely avoided looking at the empty stirrups. "It's me. I've come to ask for a favor."

Jay grinned. "It's about time."

"Pappy!" squealed Rachel as she broke from Lorelei and ran toward her father. She stopped in front of him and lifted her hands. "I want a ride."

He didn't pause at her state of undress. "You bet, sunshine." He reached down, scooped up his daughter, and set her in front of him.

"Hey, Pa, my friend Corey's got an Indian horse," said Chris as he appeared and ran to his father's side.

A shrill whistle, followed by the thud of more galloping hooves, caught their attention a second time. Two mules stirred the settling dust all over again. Both riders dismounted before the young mules stopped moving. A girl, Alice—the oldest, if Braddock remembered correctly—smiled at her younger brother, Jason. "Beat you."

The boy glared at his sister. "You cheated. I didn't know we were racing until you took off after Pa. That doesn't count, does it, Pa?"

Jay rolled his eyes and flashed his crooked, upside-down grin at Braddock. "It's worse than the war." He turned back to his brood. "Would you all start acting like you've seen company before? They're going to think we're a bunch of wild savages." He set his naked daughter on the ground. "Beth, you need to keep clothes on this child."

Braddock balled his hands in fists to keep from pressing them over his heart. Jay was back to his old self, almost. He finally had the courage to glance past Jay's thighs, and he could see where his pants fell over the wooden prostheses— that's what they called them at the hospital they'd finally gotten Jay to. Braddock swallowed and looked away. Jay might have finally accepted the inevitable, but Braddock had spent big hunks of time forgetting. He wasn't ready for any of this. It was a mistake to come here.

"I was going to give her a bath." Lorelei walked from the corner of the house. As she spoke, her gaze wasn't on Jay. It was on Braddock. He feared she could see his weakness. See him crumbling around himself.

Beth swept her hand at his ragtag group. "These are Christopher's friends. They need a place to stay."

"Well, they're welcome here," Jay said, as if there were no question about it.

"Before you make up your mind, we need to talk." Braddock leaned forward. "In private."

"If you want, Chris, but my mind's made up. Beth, why don't you take our guests inside and get them something to eat?"

His wife put her hands on her hips. "That's what I've been trying to do."

Jay made the face again. Luckily he didn't recognize Braddock's discomfort and laughed at his wife's aggravation. "I've learned not to argue with a pregnant woman."

"I would hope you've learned something, as many times as you've had to deal with one." Beth turned and marched toward the house. Archie rushed to her side to help her up the steps.

"I'm going to help Corey with the horses," said little Chris.

"I'll help him," said Alice.

Little Chris's face fell, and Braddock figured the boy was usually showed up by his older siblings. He unwrapped Lucky's reins from the house's railing. "I think you'd better handle Lucky, Chris. I bet he'd take to you, since we have the same name."

The little boy swelled a couple of extra inches as he swaggered over with his father's old walk to take Lucky's reins. Braddock felt he had finally done something right.

The child smiled at Braddock, then at Lucky. "Don't worry, Lucky. It's just me, Chris," he said as he led the giant horse away.

"Alice, you can take Malicah." Jay shifted in his saddle.

The moment Braddock had been dreading was finally at hand. He moved forward swiftly, but not fast enough. Jay had already swung one thigh over the saddle horn. He lowered himself to the ground by gripping the saddle. His horse must have been well trained, because he didn't even budge while Jay hung on to him for balance.

Braddock stopped, not knowing what to do. No one else moved to Jay's aid. His daughter absently held his horse's reins, unconcerned with her father's struggle. Jay's older son and wife had already disappeared with Archie, and little Chris seemed more concerned with Lucky than anything else in the world.

Braddock's gaze strayed to Lorelei. Her brow furrowed, but her concern was directed at Braddock, not Jay. She must see his panic, the sweat beading above his lip.

Jay regained his balance, then lurched toward the house without so much as the use of a cane. Braddock could do little more than watch him in fascinated horror. Half of him was thrilled to see Jay on his feet; the other half howled for the loss of the man's healthy swagger.

Jay's oldest daughter led their draft horse to the barn without giving her father a second look. They all must be used to his painfully jerky stride. Every move Jay made twisted a rusted length of barbed wire running the length of Braddock's body—a length of barbed wire laid the day Braddock led his friend into a field full of buried shells. A length of barbed wire that festered every time he thought of Jay and the accident.

Lorelei finally let Rachel pull her around the house for what was probably to be the drenching of her life.

Only Braddock stayed planted where he was, more unsure than he'd ever been in his life.

Jay stopped and glanced over his shoulder. "You want to talk on the porch?"

Braddock took a deep breath, then dragged himself after his friend. As Jay maneuvered the steps by clutching the rail, Braddock took his time wiping his boots on the dirt. Jay finally settled into a rocking chair at the end of the porch.

Braddock took the swing beside him. He sat forward, his forearms on his knees. Gazing into Jay's clear blue eyes, he remembered all the times he had confided in him.

His friend appeared strong and healthy, as he had when he was first assigned to Braddock's unit. Braddock hung his head, unable to look at him. This wasn't the same man who had been assigned to his unit.

"I'm in a lot of trouble," he said.

Jay shoved Braddock's shoulder, sending him and the swing off balance. Braddock looked up to find Jay grinning the way he did when he had a winning poker hand. "I've been waiting to hear you admit that. Now, tell me what I can do."

"Corey was involved in a stagecoach robbery near Santa Fe. He's not a killer, though. He's just . . ." Braddock never expected to find himself defending the kid. "Stupid," was all he could think of to explain Corey's behavior.

Jay rocked back, and Braddock tried not to notice how his wooden legs bent. He was unsuccessful.

Jay rubbed his thighs. "You'd never bring anyone here I'd have to worry about. I trust you, Chris."

Braddock leaned forward, squeezing his hands together. Jay never missed a chance to reassure him that the injury wasn't his fault. Of course, there was no disputing who had led him into the booby-trapped field and who had walked away without a scratch.

"Well, don't trust me, Jay. Because if the law doesn't get Corey, Rowen Mulcahy will. That is, if I don't find him first."

"Mulcahy again. I told you, he's not worth your trouble."

"Corey knows where to find him. He'll tell me. He has his sister to worry about."

Jay rubbed his brow as if putting all the pieces together. "The woman's this Corey's sister. Who's the other fella?"

"He's someone we picked up in Coyote Pass. I won't leave him here."

"Coyote Pass?"

"Do you have anything to drink?" It was a long story, and Braddock didn't really want to tell it. But Jay wasn't one of those people he could skirt the facts with—nor did Braddock have the right to.

"Lift up that plank to your right."

Braddock found the loose plank in the porch and liberated a bottle of whiskey. "You don't tell Beth about this?"

Jay shrugged. "We've got liquor in the house, but sometimes a man wants to have a drink by himself."

"Are you in pain a lot?" He pulled out the cork and handed the bottle over.

Jay motioned for Braddock to drink first. "Let's hear about Coyote Pass and the sister."

Braddock took a long swig, knowing Jay would dig right down to the meat of his problem. He gulped enough to burn all the way down to his toes, then set the half-full bottle away from himself. The temptation to get rip-roaring drunk was too strong.

"I met up with Lorelei when I tracked Corey to his homestead after the robbery. She tried to hide her brother." Braddock stopped himself. He wouldn't tell how Lorelei came to his hotel room, or what had happened between them back at the ranch, though he knew Jay would understand. "Then Langston showed up. Remember him?"

Jay nodded with a grimace.

The look on Jay's face reminded him that Jay was the one who'd gotten stuck begging for supplies after Braddock lost his temper with Langston's ridiculous need for proper protocol. The fact that Langston had broken his leg during a training exercise and spent the entire war shuffling papers was something he never let anyone forget.

"He wanted to arrest Lorelei as Corey's accomplice. I stopped him, but how I did it wasn't exactly legal. Since Langston's now a deputy marshal, I guess that makes me an outlaw."

Jay raised his eyebrows. "I guess it does."

"And Lorelei aimed a rifle at Langston because he had his guns on me. You know Langston. He isn't going to ignore that."

Jay sat forward. "Langston outdrew you?"

"Hell, no." Braddock flinched at the insult. "I didn't have my guns."

Jay's surprised expression had Braddock rocking back in the swing and averting his gaze. Braddock wasn't about to admit he had been buck naked at the time.

But he didn't have to; Jay's clear blue eyes had already assessed the situation. He rapidly concluded the only circumstance in which Braddock would be caught without his guns.

"So you brought them here to protect the woman."

Braddock met Jay's penetrating gaze. "Yes."

"What about the brother? What are you going to do with him?"

"I'm going to let him go. I don't think he'll try anything like the stagecoach robbery again."

"Let him go? Why in hell would you do that? The man's a thief."

"He's not a man. He's a kid who got caught up with the wrong bunch."

"You're in love with his sister."

Braddock gazed out over the yard. Oh, he wanted to deny it. Vehemently.

"Maybe."

Jay laughed. "I never thought I'd see the day."

Braddock gave Jay his fiercest scowl, which was pretty damned fierce. "Are you going to help me or not?"

His anger didn't seem to lessen Jay's amusement. "Of course, I'm going to help you."

"I'd like to see Lorelei married to a good man. Someone who can take care of her and make sure she doesn't let her brother talk her into anything that's bad for her."

Jay finally did lose his humor with the situation. He frowned. "I thought you said you loved her?"

"What does that have to do with anything? You know I can't be tied down to a woman. I'd only get her killed. I was the one who dragged her into Coyote Pass. I was so determined to find Mulcahy, I didn't stop and think."

"But you came out of it all right."

"I care about Lorelei more than I have a right to. I'm going to do the right thing by her. I want your help with that."

"How does she feel about you?"

"It doesn't matter. This is the favor I want. The one you've been wanting to give."

"If it's what you want, I'm not going to argue about it."

Braddock grabbed the whiskey bottle and took another swig. "Thanks."

He handed it to Jay, who sipped instead of guzzled, then wedged the bottle between his thighs. "Do you want to help pick out her husband?"

Braddock's fingers itched to grip the bottle. "No. Do it after I'm gone. When I leave here to find Mulcahy, I won't be coming back."

"You going after him by yourself?"

"Yeah."

"You looking to commit suicide?"

"If I bring a posse up there it will give too much warning. Mulcahy will get away like he's done in the past. I'll have to take him by surprise. If I can get him, his gang won't last."

"One of these days it's all going to catch up with you, Chris. You're not invincible, like you think."

Braddock gave in to his weakness and snatched the bottle back from Jay. If only he could be so lucky.

Chapter Twelve

"Tell us how Mr. Braddock saved your life, Pa," said little Chris through a mouthful of food.

Lorelei rearranged Rachel on her lap so she could glimpse across the table. There Christopher was studying Beth's blue-and-white china, which still held a large hunk of untouched corn bread. As if the question asked didn't concern him, he stabbed a piece of pork from some pinto beans and chewed on it as if he were being forced to eat Lucky.

"Christopher saved your life?" Lorelei asked. "He must make a habit of doing that." She flashed Braddock a teasing grin, but her effort didn't erase his frown.

Little Chris stood on the rawhide seat of his pine chair. "That's why he's a hero and I'm named after him."

"Sit down and finish your beans." Beth cocked her head and studied Lorelei in a way that made her shift. "You know, my dear, Chris doesn't tell many people his first name. He only told Jay because he thought he was dying."

Christopher's gaze lifted, but he didn't comment.

Jay set down his fork. "He had everyone in the regiment guessing at what went in between 'Captain' and 'Braddock.' "

Lorelei smiled. "He tried that on me, but I got it out of him."

Corey made a mulelike noise through closed lips. "Lucky you."

Alice's gaze strayed to Corey, and she smiled slyly. Lorelei noticed that the girl couldn't keep her eyes off her brother.

Beth's stare darted from Corey to Lorelei to Christopher. She didn't miss a thing. "How did you get it out of him, Lorelei?"

Lorelei forced down a piece of corn bread that had suddenly swelled in her throat, wishing she'd kept her big mouth shut.

"She twisted my arm," Christopher said flatly, closing the subject.

"So how'd he save your life, Jay?" asked Corey.

Lorelei suspected Corey asked to annoy Braddock more than out of any curiosity.

Alice raised her gaze to Corey. "My pa was crossing a field to get to a farmhouse where some farmers were hiding."

"They weren't farmers, Ali! Let me tell it," exploded little Chris.

Beth brushed back her youngest son's blond hair. "Your sister was talking, sweetheart."

Alice's cheeks rivaled the apple-red background of the calico tablecloth. She stared down at her plate, looking like she wanted to crawl under it.

Corey encouraged her with a coaxing smile. "Then what happened, Alice?"

She blushed even harder but grinned from ear to ear when he said her name. "They weren't farmers, they were—"

"Bounty jumpers!" Little Chris practically leaped out of his seat.

Alice shook her head, but her giddy grin remained. "Chris's heard this story a thousand times. He can tell it better than I can. He's always wanting to hear stories about his namesake." She nervously darted her gaze to Braddock, as if the mere mention of him might get her into trouble.

Christopher managed a tight grin for the shy girl, but Lorelei could tell the effort pained him.

"Maybe little Chris should hear the story from big Chris." Corey slung an arm over the back of his chair and smirked triumphantly.

Christopher met her brother's challenge with a look that promised it wasn't too late for him to follow through with some of his earlier threats.

"I'll tell the story," said Jay from the other end of the long table. He leaned forward, capturing everyone's attention. "It was just a few of us, not the whole regiment. We were looking for some bounty jumpers." He turned to Lorelei. "Those are men that sign on for an enlistment bonus. It was up to three hundred dollars in 'sixty-four. That kind of money makes some men greedy, and we had quite a few who signed up, then deserted first chance they got. The fellas we were looking for had taken off two days before, right at the start of the Cold Harbor mess. Stole some ammunition to boot. Cap'n Braddock was spitting mad." Jay chuckled.

Braddock hooded his eyes and played with a spoon, flipping it faceup, then facedown.

Jay's humor faded. He looked directly at Lorelei. "One of those fellas was Rowen Mulcahy."

Lorelei's gaze whipped to Corey, her mouth already open in accusation.

"I didn't know," he said.

Jay's smile held more sympathy for Corey than Lorelei thought her brother deserved. "Don't feel bad, Corey. He fooled us, too."

"He didn't fool me," mumbled Braddock to the tablecloth.

Jay snorted. "Well, he sure fooled me. I was the one who was supposed to be keeping an eye on the new recruits."

"It was my responsibility. It was my regiment." Braddock glanced up.

Jay shrugged, then dismissed Christopher as if they had had this argument before. "Back to the real story. We were sneaking up on the farmhouse around early evening. After three days of fighting, it was the first chance we had to go after deserters. Usually we just let them go, but not this time. Braddock was too damned riled."

Beth's brow wrinkled. "Jay."

Jay nodded at his wife's reprimand. "I'll try to keep it clean. Anyway, we were all spread out, walking through this field that looked like it had just been turned for planting. At the time I remember thinking, this farmer's seeds are going to be trampled by all the troops. That was the last thing I thought before I was flying through the air."

Lorelei gasped. "What happened?"

"They buried shells. Step on one and you're done. I think Jay must have set one off by kicking a clod of dirt. I never expected it." Christopher's voice was so flat and unemotional, he gave himself away: his pain was unbearable. Lorelei hugged Rachel to keep from grabbing his hand.

"How could you have known they meant to kill us? Bounty jumpers usually just ran." Jay took a swig of his coffee. "Thought I was dead for sure."

Beth stood. "I hate this part. Alice, help me clear the table, please."

Lorelei stood, a sleepy Rachel in her arms. "Let me help you."

Beth urged her back down with a hand on her shoulder. "Oh, no, you haven't had the pleasure of hearing Jay's war stories."

"Sit down, Beth. I'm not going to tell it in detail."

"All right. But the first word about blood loss and I'm leaving the room."

"Here's the short version, Lorelei. Chris ran over, picked me up, and lugged me back to camp. I remember lying there knowing everyone was afraid to move, 'cause no one knew what else was in that field. The others were yelling at Chris to stay put, but he didn't even hesitate. But that's not all he did. That was the easy part. The hard part was not giving up on me when I cussed at him for not leaving me there to die."

Jay glanced to Christopher, who just stared past the flagstone fireplace mounted with elk horns and a mantel lined with porcelain figurines.

"Getting better took a long time. The sawbones didn't think I was going to make it. Didn't want to bother with me at all. Chris changed his mind real quick."

Beth smiled at Braddock. "We're all grateful to him for it, too."

"He wouldn't have been there in the first place if it weren't for me." Christopher sneaked a guilty glimpse at the woman praising him.

"But I wanted Mulcahy, too." Jay winked at Lorelei. "Don't think it was easy telling Chris the new recruits slipped away with ammunition. Shoot, I think it was worse than getting my feet blown off."

Beth and Christopher stood at the same time, the latter nearly toppling his chair.

"I need some air." He headed for the door without a backward glance to anyone.

They all held their breath until he was gone. After the door slammed shut, Beth turned to Lorelei and her child. "Let me take her from you. She should have been in bed an hour ago."

"I'm not sleepy," Rachel said. She was passed to her mother without ever opening her eyes.

Lorelei rubbed her arms, not realizing how heavy the child had become until her deadweight was lifted away.

"I'll take her, Ma," offered Alice.

"You kids clear the table and start on the kitchen. And make a plate for Archie. He'll probably be hungry when he wakes up."

Lorelei reached across the table and picked up Christopher's empty plate, stacking it on top of hers.

"I'm supposed to help with the horses," complained Jason.

"Me too," mumbled little Chris, who had already laid his head on the table, his eyes half-shut.

Corey stood. He took a stack of dishes from Alice's hands. "How 'bout if we all do it together? Then we'll see to the horses."

Alice blushed. "Thank you, Corey."

Jason followed the pair, grumbling. Little Chris lost the

battle to keep his eyes open and fell asleep, slumped over the table with butter and bits of corn bread stuck in his blond hair.

Jay and Lorelei watched the older children file into the kitchen at the far end of the house. Corey had never volunteered to do dishes before. Obviously Alice's affection didn't go unappreciated. The adjoining room was partially open, but the clank of dishes and buzz of chatter meant the others were occupied—leaving Jay and Lorelei alone for the first time.

"Sit down, Lorelei. I'd like to talk to you."

She sat in the chair vacated by Beth, having known he had something on his mind even before he made his request. "I'll speak with Corey about Alice."

Jay dismissed her concern with a wave of his hand. "She acts like that around any unrelated male between the ages of twelve and twenty-five. Beth says not to worry about it."

"I don't know what Christopher told you, but Corey's not a bad person. He just looks for the easy way to do things. He wouldn't do anything to hurt your girl."

"Chris said the same thing."

Lorelei blinked. "He did?"

Jay's grin was slow and easy. "Yeah, he did. I think you have a greater influence on him than you know."

Lorelei looked down at her folded hands, wishing it were true. "Christopher doesn't seem to listen to anyone."

"He listens. He just does what he thinks is best."

"Yes." She didn't dare look up at Jay. The man's eyes were too kind, and she was sure she would cry.

"But you don't think what he thinks is best, is best."

"I know it's not."

"So I guess I don't need to ask if you're interested in marrying one of my neighbors."

"He asked you to marry me off?" Lorelei didn't know which emotion tightened her chest—horror, anger, or a hurt so deep she didn't dare contemplate it. Better to be angry. "He had no right to do that."

Jay raised his hand as if to fend her off. "Guess I shouldn't have told you that. It wasn't easy for him, you know."

"And marrying a stranger would be easy for me? Christopher's trying to convince himself there is nothing between us, but that doesn't mean it's true. He doesn't even want to take a chance."

"He's not thinking of himself, Lorelei."

She turned her chin up to Jay. "I think he is. I think he's afraid."

"Afraid for you."

Lorelei wanted to argue, to call Christopher every name in the book, including *coward*, but she knew it wasn't exactly true. He'd lay down his life for her. She dropped her gaze to hide the rawness she knew was reflected in her eyes. He'd give his life, but he wouldn't share it.

"What should I do—marry some man I don't love? Do you think that will make him happy?" Lorelei glanced up.

Jay frowned. He appeared almost as sad as she felt. "I wish I knew. If you haven't changed him, I don't know who can." Jay took her hand. "I was hoping he'd meet a woman he was crazy about. One who made him go against everything he ever thought he was. Beth did that for me. She's the real reason I survived. Her, Alice, and Jason." He laughed. "Never expected there'd be three more."

He winked, but then his smile faded. "I was scared I wasn't good enough for them anymore, all hacked up the way I was. Guess I thought I wasn't a whole man. But the thing was, I realized I'm the piece they need. And it's a special fit."

"Do you think I'm the piece Christopher needs?"

Jay's frown deepened. "I don't know if there is such a thing for him. He's got something missing on the inside. A hole maybe nobody can fix. He's more wounded than me, really. I healed; I don't think Braddock will be satisfied until he gets himself killed."

Lorelei hated Jay's words, because they confirmed what she already suspected. "Why? Why is he like that?"

"He never said it to me, but I could see. Every soldier who served under him who lost his life, Braddock feels like he owes. He tried hard to get himself killed during the war. But instead he was called a hero. His daddy wanted to parade him around after the fighting was said and done, but he wouldn't have it. He came west and turned his back on the lot of them. Said he wouldn't profit for what he'd done."

"It was a horrible war. Everyone suffered."

"But he'd gone to West Point and was trained to be a leader. Once he got in the thick of things, he didn't like what he saw. Said honor was something for men who didn't have to wade in the mud or stand on the front line. He was mad as fire once he figured out what war was really like. Since then, he doesn't believe in much."

"He's honorable. I know from experience. He didn't have to do what he's done for Corey and me."

"You don't have to convince me."

"Maybe he'll feel different after he arrests Mulcahy. I'd wait for him as long as it takes."

Jay patted her hand, and Lorelei stared down at his thick fingers to keep from meeting the pity in his gaze.

"There're a hundred Mulcahys. And there will be a hundred more after that. Sometimes you've got to turn away from the Mulcahys and into the arms of a pretty woman." He lifted her chin. "I haven't given up on him."

"I think you're right." She stood. "I'm going to talk to Christopher."

Jay stopped her with a light touch on her arm. "He's got to *choose* life. You can't make him or convince him. I don't want you to get hurt."

"I just want to let him know he has options." She smiled at Jay. "At least for a little while. Christopher and I are both survivors. We just go about it differently. I plan to have a family again, no matter what he does."

Then Lorelei turned and walked to the door.

"Give him hell, Lorelei."

Jay's words propelled her out the door and onto the porch. She wandered into the dark night with no light to guide her, looking for the one man more lost than she.

* * *

She found him standing in the moon-cast shadow of a small tree, several yards from the barn. He stood with his hands in his pockets. When she reached his side, she saw that he was facing a fenced-in square.

"Jay's done a lot with this place."

She smiled to herself. It was Christopher, the man she knew how to talk to. She touched his arm. "He seems happy."

He didn't pull away, but he didn't reach out to her either. "He wouldn't let me know if he wasn't." He fell silent for a moment. "I don't know how the hell he does it."

"He has a lot to live for."

Christopher nodded. For once, he didn't seem to be in the arguing mood. "He's practical, though. Left plenty of room in the graveyard."

Lorelei suddenly noticed white crosses dotting the space in the center of the fence. She stepped back, her breath in her throat. "Who?"

Christopher encircled her waist and brought her against his side. "They're just graves of birds, squirrels, and a colt that was stillborn. Chris showed me them this afternoon."

Lorelei relaxed against his side, unsure why she was so shaken. She'd seen plenty of graveyards in her life. She'd buried two parents. Her brothers lay under a battlefield in southern Kentucky. But these little crosses seemed worse stuck in the middle of so much life.

"Why did they bury them so close to the house?"

Christopher glanced behind him as if to check the distance. "It's not so close. They planted this white oak when they first moved here. It's doubled in size, and it's the only shade for miles. This is a good place to be buried, I think."

"Is that where you want to be buried? Under the shade of a tree?"

"No, I just want to be left where I fall. I want to turn into dust. Blow back into the desert."

Lorelei tried to pull away from him. This was not the conversation she had planned to have. "That's awful. I can't bear to think of you dying alone."

He held her to him. "No. Don't think about that."

"How do you want me to remember you?"

"As a man who tried to help you." He tightened his hold.

"Should I tell my husband about you?"

He swallowed, then turned his attention back to the little graveyard. "No."

Arguing with him didn't work, so she'd give him a taste of his good idea. "Don't you think he deserves to know? Some might say I'm soiled goods."

He turned to face her, gripping her shoulders. "Don't say that. It's not true."

She traced the line of his cheekbone. "I said somebody else might think that. I don't think that."

He closed his hand around hers and brought her fingers to his lips. "Good."

She forced herself to keep her breathing steady. "How will you remember me?"

He flattened her palm against his mouth and licked the sensitive center. "As the woman—" He cut himself off.

Lorelei clamped her lips shut to contain her sudden burst of hope. He meant to say something he didn't want to say. She waited but didn't prod. If he felt too vulnerable, he'd close up and their conversation would be over.

He dropped her hand. "Hell, I won't have to remember you. I'll never be able to stop thinking about you."

Difficult as it was, she kept up her game. "It must be hard to give me up, then."

He wrapped his other arm around her waist and pulled her to him. He stared at her mouth for a long time, then kissed her hard, forcing his tongue past her lips as he pulled her tightly against him.

Lorelei leaned into him, gave herself over to the kiss in knee-sagging relief. His familiar taste carried her past all the things that had torn them apart.

But he broke the kiss too soon. "Walking away is easy. Thinking there could ever be anything else between us is hard."

"I don't believe you. The way you kissed me tells a different story."

He shrugged, casually disengaging himself from their embrace. "Kissing you isn't something I have a problem with. I would gladly lay you down right here, in plain view of the house, and make love to you until the sun comes up. It's what comes after that's a problem."

"Being stuck with me?" She heard the hurt in her own voice; surely he would hear it too.

He shoved his hands in his trouser pockets. "Being stuck with you is the good part. Your life expectancy would be the problem."

She planted her hands on her waist to keep from swinging at him. "Jay doesn't blame you for what happened."

His defeated calm rippled ever so slightly. "You don't know about that."

"What's there to know?"

"I don't want to talk about Jay."

"I'm involved in this, too. You're shutting me out. I gave myself to you."

"I never asked you to."

The anger in his voice won his argument and silenced Lorelei. She clamped her mouth shut, but the effort couldn't keep back her words. "I can't help but care about you."

"I told you from the start, I'm not the kind of man you want. I can't do what Jay's done. I can't build a life out of dust and desert, keep working on it year after year, knowing the desert's going to win. I couldn't build a graveyard with room enough for my family and keep on going."

She moved in front of him and smoothed her hands over his chest. Through his cotton shirt, she could feel the heat of his body and the rapid thud of his heart. "What else is there to do? I've buried my share of family, but I'm still here. I still love you."

He touched his forehead to hers. "Don't say that."

She rested her palm on his cheek. "It's true."

As if unable to stop himself, he gripped her forearms and pressed his mouth to hers. Gently he slid his tongue against hers, slowing his pace as if memorizing her shape.

"I can't do it, Lorelei. I can't." His lips hovered so near hers his words spilled into her mouth.

Their bitter taste told her what her heart didn't want to accept. He wouldn't change. He wouldn't give them a chance. He seemed utterly incapable of it.

She pulled out of his embrace and stared at the black horizon. "When will you go?"

He moved behind her and rested his hands on her shoulders. "I know I should see how happy Jay is. But all I can see is the man he used to be. The man he should be now. I don't know why he stepped on the shell instead of me."

She wanted to turn to him. To tell him he was spared so he could save her, but his grip held her in place.

"Being with you is more than I expected. But if I tried to hold on to it, I'd crush it. Capturing Mulcahy is all I can think about right now."

"I'll wait for you."

He kissed the top of her head. "Don't. I won't come back."

Lorelei closed her eyes. How could she get through to him? If he wouldn't choose life, she would. She stepped out of his grip and turned to face him. "If I can't change your mind, I have no choice but to move on." She forced a smile. "Jay already has a husband in mind. A good man who's desperate for a wife."

When his mouth and eyes simultaneously tugged down at the corners, she didn't find the satisfaction she had expected from her well-placed blow. "I want to thank you for all you've done for Corey and me."

He gazed at his boots. "You're welcome." When he glanced up at her, his jaw was stiff. "If I can get the information I need from your brother, I'll be out of here by sundown tomorrow."

She laced her hands in front of her, trying to appear calm. *Tomorrow.* How would she ever survive watching him ride out of her life?

"I'll make sure he cooperates. He'll be glad to see you go."

Lorelei let out her breath. If he thought he could walk away from what they shared, then she would let him know she could too. "Well, good-bye, Christopher."

"I'll see you tomorrow."

"I know, but we probably won't be alone again. I want you to know how much you've meant to me."

His jaw went slack. He appeared beyond speech.

The tears were thick in her throat, but she wouldn't let them fall. She'd already cried too many tears in her life. "You've made me realize that I still have hope, even if you don't. I want a life with a family to love. I didn't survive just to give up. Thank you for giving me back my dreams."

He nodded, but remained silent.

"Good-bye, then." She strode past without looking at him again.

Chapter Thirteen

Braddock lay angled across the nailed planks Chris and Jason used for a bed. Though his feet still hung over the side, the straw-stuffed mattress was comfortable enough and the soft cotton sheets smelled like sun-soaked wind. But that didn't matter. He couldn't sleep. He couldn't stop thinking about Lorelei. The tips of his fingers still tingled when he relived watching her walk away. At least the rest of him hadn't betrayed him and run after her. But he just hadn't been able to stop himself from reaching for her as she walked out of his life.

He deserved to be left. That went without question. Though he hadn't expected their parting to be so destructive. He felt like he'd been tied and beaten, utterly helpless. Then again, he was supposed to be the one looking forward with her at his back, not the other way around.

He tried to calm his racing thoughts long enough to listen to the silence of the house. A steady wind blew, rattling a window, calling a hollow tune. But not as hollow as he felt inside.

Lorelei slept with Alice next door. He strained to hear

her, to feel her presence, but she might as well have been back in Kentucky. She had slammed the door on him.

He would have preferred to sleep in the barn, but Chris had run out and excitedly told him he was going to get to sleep with the horses like Corey and Jason. Braddock didn't want to break the kid's heart. Nor did he have any desire to sleep close to Corey.

He hadn't returned to the house until well after the last light went out. He had stayed on the fringe of Jay's yard, feeling like a ghost haunting the place. He could have slept outside. He was more at home on the cold ground than in a quilt-covered bed. But something drove Braddock to a bed that didn't quite fit. Had he secretly hoped sleeping in the room next to Lorelei would accomplish something? Give him another chance?

He slung his arm over his eyes, knowing he had. He'd thought he could steal a glimpse of her, soak up her essence through the walls. That wouldn't be fair, though. He had already taken more than he deserved, and there would be a high price for his thievery.

Tonight during dinner, he'd watched her with the little girl on her lap and knew that was what she was made for: cradling a child in her arms with that dreamy look on her face. But even if he wanted to be the man at her side, he didn't fit in the picture.

He was the outsider at Jay's table. He had no right to be there. Didn't they know that if it weren't for him Jay would be whole? But they all went on ignoring the obvious. Smiling. Laughing. Braddock couldn't do that. He couldn't have Lorelei or a normal life because he knew what waited. The darkness that followed him was just a breath away, and it was never him whom it hit. He was just left to pick up the pieces.

Braddock turned onto his stomach and buried his face in his pillow. He wouldn't go to Lorelei. No matter how badly he wanted to be something else, he wasn't.

When the door creaked open, Braddock didn't move. Too many times during the long night he'd imagined Lorelei coming through that door. He wouldn't turn just to find the room empty, the door shut tight. But this time her presence was unmistakable. He waited, still thinking his imagination was sending out its heavy artillery. Not another sound penetrated the heady silence, but he knew she was there. His heart started to beat more rapidly. She was *here*.

He twisted abruptly.

She stopped a foot from the bed. Her breath whistled through her teeth in an audible hiss.

He stared at her in the darkness. She wore a white nightgown that reached her ankles. Her hair spilled over her shoulders. He said nothing, fearing that if he did she would evaporate.

"I thought you were sleeping."

He adjusted his weight onto his elbow. "I couldn't."

"I couldn't either." She crept toward him until the bed pressed against her thighs.

He kept his best poker face. Even in the dark, emotions rolled high. An imaginary lamp had been turned up, leaving them both exposed in the sudden glaring light. Every muscle Braddock had was tensed and bunched.

She glanced to the hooks where the boys hung their clothes. His gun belt was draped on the closest one to the bed. A lone pistol curled around a fallen group of toy soldiers scattered on the roughly made nightstand. He hadn't even thought about it, but the slight pull at the corners of Lorelei's mouth showed him what a strange thing it was to arm yourself for an attack in your closest friend's home. Not strange to him. That other voice, the one that couldn't sleep without a loaded gun in reach, told him he should send Lorelei out of the room right now. He didn't belong around someone like her.

"Who were you planning to shoot?"

She had no idea what was out there. What was lurking. She'd seen it, but still she could forget. Coyote Pass wasn't that far away. He had to be ready for anything, but he was glad she could forget. He let out his breath and licked his lips, readying himself to say the hardest words he would ever have to say, to tell Lorelei to go back to bed.

But instead he pushed himself to a sitting position and reached his traitorous hand out to her.

She didn't hesitate; she took his hand and crawled onto the bed.

He wrapped his arms around her and there was no longer any part of him that wanted to resist. Even the nagging voice of doom, his constant companion, was swept away by the wave of pleasure Lorelei's nearness brought.

She laid her head on his shoulder. "I couldn't leave things the way they were. I'm sorry for how I acted. Hurting you wasn't my intention when I came outside to find you."

Braddock gripped her shoulders and pulled her away to look into her face. "Don't apologize. I deserved it."

She sat back on her heels. "I know how hard it is for you to see Jay. I just want you to know that I do understand. I even understand why you won't give us a chance."

He held on to her hand. How could she be so brave? This conversation was making him ill.

"Lorelei," was all he could get past his suddenly thick lips.

She picked up his other hand so both their hands were joined. "I wanted to tell you again that I love you."

He felt pinned by her gaze, slugged by her words.

"I'll wait for you."

"No," he managed to squeeze past his tight throat.

"Yes. I'm going to. At least for a while. And if you don't come back, I'll have to accept your decision. I can't say I'll marry. I can't say I won't. I can't say what I'll do, but I'll go on. But if you feel half of what I do, Christopher, you'll come back."

He bowed his head and stared at their joined hands. "You have too much faith in me, Lorelei. You have too much faith in everything."

She turned his hands over and rubbed her thumbs across his callused palms. "I have enough for both of us, if you'd only give me a chance."

He gazed at her, unable to say anything. What he wanted

to say was *yes*, to put himself in her hands, to give up trying to know everything—but he couldn't. So instead he pulled her against him. He brushed her long hair with his palm, the sensation flowing up his arm like a warm river.

The heat of her body teased him through her nightgown. The arousal he'd struggled with since she walked in the room became uncontrollable, but the urge to make love to her was wrapped up with so many tangled emotions, he felt tied. He feared making a move would strangle him.

She snuggled against him until she lay across his lap; if she moved one knee, she'd be straddling him. If he had any doubt, the way she arched her hips into his sang a blatant invitation.

"Lorelei, I want to make love to you," he finally said.

She slid her palms up his bare chest to cup his face. She kissed him softly, her mouth pliant and parted. "I want that too."

He greedily kissed her again, opening his mouth wider to taste her before he said what he had to say. She responded so eagerly. Her body would be just as open, just as sweet. He pulled his mouth away from hers and swallowed hard.

"I can't promise you anything. This doesn't mean I've changed my mind."

She smiled as if he had said something amusing. "I didn't come here for a promise. I came here to feel you, if only for one last time. If this is the only way you can let me get close to you, then I'll take it." She slid her hand between them and gripped him through his wool trousers. "This is why I came into your room into the middle of the night, silly."

The feel of her fingers circling him, teasing his rigid flesh with the rough cloth, made him buck slightly. Much more of that and he'd never make it inside her. He pulled her against him fiercely, forcing her to straddle him. He'd never been so glad to be called silly. In fact, that was something he'd never been called, but, God, he liked it.

He slid his hands up her thighs, bunching her gown past her hips and cupping her bare bottom as he arched against her.

She unbuttoned his pants, then eased the flaps aside. Eagerly she slid against his length. Her warmth seared away all conscious thoughts except one. He pulled his mind away from surging into her. They were going too fast and he wanted his time with Lorelei to last.

When he grabbed the hem of her gown and drew it over her head, she lifted her arms to help him. Shadows wrapped around her feminine curves, but he saw every one with a second sight. Her high, full breasts, the dip of her waist, the flare of her hips, and most especially the secret cleft between her thighs, all burned into his senses. He gripped her hips and nudged her against him in a rocking motion. His eyes grew heavy, but he kept them open. Watching her was as pleasurable as the feel of her warm, wet opening riding him, tempting him beyond endurance.

She looked so perfect, as if she were created for him. Her dark hair flowed over her shoulders. A single lock fell over one breast, emphasizing the red, aroused nipple peeking through. He brushed her hair aside, sitting up to take that teasing flesh into his mouth.

She writhed as he sucked her, keeping the rocking connection of their bodies a spiraling pleasure and a constant torture. The taste of her skin intoxicated him to the point of dizziness. She gripped his shoulders and leaned her head back while she arched her hips forward.

The urge to shift her, to penetrate her, was too strong. He slid from beneath her to halt his body's imminent insubordination. She made a soft sound in the back of her throat, letting him know she didn't like the change. He maneuvered her to her back and got off the bed to work his pants the rest of the way off. She propped herself up on her elbows and watched him.

Liking her gaze on him, he slowed his movements. After he shucked his pants, he straightened. He stood before her, his chest heaving, his breath coming fast. A smile curled her lips. He smiled too. He'd never get tired of that bold stare.

He crawled onto the bed, feeling more intimidated by her

blatant appraisal than he'd like to admit. "Like what you see?"

"Very much," she said. "Is it all for me?" She wrapped her hand around his jutting arousal in a tight, confident grip.

He jerked back. "Yes, ma'am." She held on, stroking him to the tip, then sliding her hand back to the root. He gasped and grabbed her wrist. "Slow down."

She hooked her hands behind his neck and tried to pull him closer. When he didn't comply, she squirmed under him, brushing the tips of her strained nipples against his chest. "Why? It seems like forever since we were together."

Braddock stilled, his smile fading. This would have to last them forever, because there would be no next time. She must have seen his shift in mood, because she dropped her hands from his neck; her body sagged against the mattress. Braced on his hands and knees, he hovered above her, trying to memorize her features, but now she was the one frowning.

He forced a slight smile and kissed the tip of her nose. All the things he thought to say would only make her frown deepen. He wanted to tell her good-bye the best way he could. Wanted her to remember him by this night. But even he didn't think he could stand to hear to those words spoken aloud.

He eased down to his elbows and kissed her on the mouth, swirling his tongue against hers for endless moments. The sensation sent urgent sparks to his straining sex. He pulled away, then kissed her neck, their joined mouths causing too much sensation.

He blew on her ear and she turned her head, laughing.

"I've been thinking about you, Lorelei. Every night. I want to show you what I've been thinking."

That put the smile back on her face. He had definitely created a monster with a sexual appetite to rival any man's. The bastard who got to be her husband would be one lucky son of a gun. Braddock pushed the thought away.

When she drew her knees up and arched her back, he forgot to think anything.

"Show me," she crooned.

Why wait? Why resist? The question rang like a command. He leaned back on his heels, hooked his hands under her thighs, and spread her wider. "Are you ready for me?"

She didn't stop him, just laid her head back and opened for him. "Yes," she drawled with her eyes closed.

"Let's see."

He inhaled her desire before he tasted her. It was a heady experience, almost too much. He licked her, then slipped a finger inside, and that was enough. Her heat seared him. The sound of her soft moan ignited all his other senses. Enough was enough.

He positioned himself over her and drove in with one long thrust, lifting her with its intensity.

She opened her eyes in surprise, then gripped his shoulders, steadying herself after his demanding entry.

They were nose-to-nose. "This is what I've been thinking about."

"I see. I've been thinking about you, too." She wrapped her arms around his neck and her legs around his hips as if it were going to be a rough ride and she were holding on for dear life.

Smart girl, he thought before his body took the luxury away. He moved his hips, arching up with each thrust. Going slowly, making love to her as he'd been taught wasn't going to happen. Each alluring thrust dragged him deeper into a world of pure physical lust. He was lost in the need of his body. All he could do was move, desperately grabbing her with each stroke.

Her breath came warm and heavy on his neck. She was straining as hard as he. He could hear her pleasure and desperation on each rhythmic exhalation.

He slid his hands under her back, wrapping one arm around her, pulling her to him tightly, while he cradled her skull with the other. He held her head so his mouth could take her breath as he took her body.

Urgency piled on top of itself until he was desperate for release. He went harder and deeper, his grip tightening. He couldn't stop this. Couldn't control it.

He had a vague sense of her stiffening in his arms. He tried to clear his mind enough to loosen his hold, fearing he was seriously hurting her. Her slick passage clenched around him and all hope of releasing her was lost. Acute pleasure squeezed the breath from his lungs. He thought he yelled but it came out as something deeply silent, like the quaking of the earth under a rumbling thunder. He came hard and slow. All his pent-up lust and emotion ripped from him in wrenching spasms. He peaked a second time, sure his heart had burst.

He collapsed, his head dropping into the crook of her neck and shoulder. He angled himself so his hip sank into the lumpy mattress, sparing her his full weight. The sweat from his body seared them together. He could feel the throbbing of his own heart through her.

Lorelei rubbed his back in large, calming swirls, then brushed back his wet hair. The sound of his breathing filled the room. He jerked involuntarily as a lingering spasm gripped him.

"Are you all right?" she asked with a smile in her voice. She knew what she'd done to him.

He lifted his head just enough to gaze at her. She had a contented grin on her face, and he didn't think her satisfaction came from his performance as a lover.

He laid his head back down. "Sorry." He wasn't sure that he was sorry he'd lost control, but he wasn't ready to think that hard yet.

She rolled over, easily overpowering him. He was too limp to do anything but follow her movements. She arranged them both on their sides, face-to-face. Her fingers brushed his lips. "How could you be sorry? For what?"

"I lost control."

"I know. I liked it."

"You could get pregnant."

She dropped her gaze. "I can't say I'd be sorry if I did."

He stiffened and tried to sit up. "Lorelei—"

"Don't say it." She braced her hand on his chest. "I know you won't stay. I don't care. I'd still love your child."

He caught his breath, and his heartbeat steadied enough for him to see her clearly. If she did wind up carrying his child, there was no other place he'd rather have her than with Jay and his family. But he didn't want to think about that now. He was still too sated from their encounter to have room for regret. He'd have the rest of his life for that.

She relaxed against him, looking pretty satisfied herself. Her lips were redder than normal, and a flush spread over her cheeks and across her breasts. He remembered the gripping pleasure of her body that had sent him over the edge. A grin spread across his face, and, unbelievably, that wasn't the only part of him to stir. "So you, ah . . ."

"Yes." She playfully pinched his nipple. "As if you didn't know."

"I knew," he crowed in a whisper.

The silence settled between them. He reached out and stroked her cheek, gazed in her eyes, and almost made a terrible mistake. She didn't seem to notice, only closed her eyes and snuggled against him.

He held her tighter instead of telling her he loved her. That was something he dared not say. Not now. It would be too cruel to give her false hope. He was too much of a coward to reveal himself like that, so the thief in him held on to what he could grab in the moment. And yet he still wanted more.

Lorelei sauntered down the kitchen's side steps, two sweating glasses in her hand, just as Braddock poised to backhand Corey. He let go of the kid's collar and stepped away. He pretended to study the distant cotton fields so he could compose himself before he had to face Lorelei. He hadn't been going to hit the kid hard, only shake him up enough to get him talking.

He turned back to see her hand a jar half-full of murky water to her brother. Corey greedily gulped the contents instead of saying anything.

Lorelei turned to Braddock and handed him the second jar, her smile as sweet as a kiss.

"Thanks, sweetheart," he said, unable to stop himself.

"I'm going to puke," grumbled Corey.

Braddock cut his gaze to the kid. With Lorelei between them, Corey didn't intimidate as easily. He was a royal pain in the ass any way Braddock saw it.

"I'm tired of the crap, kid. Are you going to tell me what I want to know or not?"

Lorelei put her finger to her lips. "Little Chris and Rachel are still around. Do you want them to hear you?"

"Sorry." Braddock brought the rim of the jar to his lips and hesitated. One quick glance at Lorelei told him he had better not sniff the cloudy mixture first. She smiled in anticipation, as if she had just handed him some kind of special gift. He braced himself and took a gulp. Lemonade! The tartly sweet tang puckered his mouth and showered him with a flood of memories. Summertime and careless days washed over him. He stared at Lorelei. How he wished he'd known her then.

"Can you believe Beth had lemons? A neighbor has a tree. I haven't had lemonade since before the war."

Neither had he, but he couldn't seem to do anything except stare at the glow in Lorelei's eyes. Every time he looked at her he felt all soft inside and lost his whole taste for Mulcahy and the gold. He'd rather drink lemonade with Lorelei.

He locked his gaze on Corey, a safer target. The boy's smug expression reminded Braddock that Mulcahy wouldn't disappear just because he had lost interest. He grabbed the other dining room chair Beth had insisted they take out behind the house for their talk. He'd tried to refuse, but didn't want her to know he planned to beat the information out of Corey rather than have a civil conversation.

Placing the chair in front of Corey, he sat down. He gulped the rest of his lemonade in one long swallow. No sense in lingering over something he couldn't have. He took Corey's half-full glass and handed both to Lorelei.

"I'm not finished," complained the kid.

"You are now." Braddock made his gaze threat enough.

"I can see this isn't going well." Lorelei's slight smile belied her words. She practically levitated with happiness, which made Braddock smile in return.

She had left him well before dawn. He'd hated letting her go a moment before he had to, but farmers rose early. If Beth or the kids caught her in his room, they'd have a wedding on their hands by sunset.

Corey glanced to Braddock and then back to his sister. He frowned, but withheld any comments on the obvious change in his sister's mood.

"Go inside, Lori. This is between me and Braddock."

Braddock rubbed his hand over his mouth and studied Corey. If Corey could use his sister for subterfuge, he usually did. The kid glared back at him, a glint of accusation in his narrowed eyes. *Damn.* Suddenly Braddock felt like a criminal slated for interrogation.

Lorelei put her hands on her hips, confronting Corey with none of Braddock's reluctance. "I'll go in once you promise to give Christopher the information he needs."

Corey sneered. "I'll tell him what he needs to know."

The side door slammed, saving Braddock the effort of appearing calm. Archie staggered out toward them, prompting Lorelei to rush to his aid. Corey stood and watched them, turning his back on Braddock.

Braddock raked his palm over his face, grateful for the distraction. Corey had the upper hand and Braddock didn't like it. That he deserved Corey's disdain he liked even less. Making love to Lorelei last night had been selfish and irresponsible. His leaving would be that much harder for both of them. He wouldn't be able to wipe the indignant look off Corey's face with any satisfaction.

"Are you all right, Archie?" Lorelei's worried voice brought Braddock back to the present.

Archie looked like hell. Sweat slicked his hair to his head and beaded on his face. His clothes hung in awkward angles. He appeared to have been wadded up in a saddlebag and ridden across the country. When you hadn't been sober in weeks—or in Archie's case, maybe years,—the hangover had to be brutal.

"I just need some air, Miss Lorelei." Archie swayed toward her before staggering past.

She caught his arm. "Let me help you, Archie. Beth told me of a spring a few yards from the house. Let's see if we can find it."

"I'd be ever so grateful." Without his slur, it was obvious Archie was a Southerner and a gentleman, or had been once.

He paused in front of Braddock's chair. "I implore you one more time, sir. Take me to a town. Any town."

Braddock gazed up at him. "What about Beth and the baby?"

Archie covered his bleary eyes. They were so red it was a wonder he could see from them. "I'd be no good to her."

Braddock shrugged. "You shouldn't have told her you were a doctor. She has her heart set on you delivering her baby."

"I used to be a doctor." Archie dropped his hand. "Why did you listen to me, anyway?"

"You never shut up. How could we not listen to you?"

Lorelei gave him a harsh look and shook her head. "You said you liked to deliver babies, Archie. Please stay. Beth said the midwife who lived near here moved away. If you don't do it, I'll have to. And I know you can do a better job than me."

Archie tried to disengage himself from Lorelei's grip. "Thank you for your consideration, Miss Lorelei. You shouldn't see me like this."

"We've seen you worse, Archie," said Corey. "But we still like you. Do me a favor and let Lori take care of you so I can talk to Braddock about Mulcahy."

If it were possible, Archie's pallor turned a few shades lighter. He suddenly clamped his hand over his mouth. Braddock sprang from his chair just in case Archie lost his breakfast. After a moment, the man took a big shuddering breath that returned a touch of yellow to his colorless cheeks.

He let Lorelei guide him toward the spring without any resistance.

"You'd better talk to him, Corey," she called over her shoulder. "You'll be talking to me if you don't."

They both stood until Lorelei wandered out of earshot.

Corey sat down first. "I think she wants to get rid of you."

Braddock sank into the chair's rawhide seat. He hoped the kid didn't notice how the idea jolted him. "Why would she?"

The way Corey cocked his head said he'd noticed how he rattled Braddock, but that the kid wasn't nearly satisfied. "Why wouldn't she? You're no good for her."

A muscle worked in Braddock's jaw. He didn't like hearing his own thoughts out of Corey's mouth. "Let's talk about Mulcahy."

"All right. He's going to kill you. How's that?"

The topic of his death at Mulcahy's hands was preferable to a discussion of his treatment of Lorelei. "That's my problem."

Corey glared. "No, that's mine. Who in the hell do you think you are, using my sister like you have? She's not some whore just hanging around for your convenience. How do you think she's going to feel when you leave? You owe her, you son of a bitch."

Braddock could do little more than stare at Corey, hating the fact that the boy was right. The argument that Corey had sent her to him in the first place was played out. Braddock had to take responsibility for what he'd done after that.

"I'm not good enough for her."

"You got that right. But you're going to ask her to marry you just the same. It's her choice if she turns you down."

"Since when do you want me in the family?"

Corey stood up, knocking back his chair. "You're not going to ride out of here making my sister feel like she's not good enough for you."

Braddock stood too. He grabbed fistfuls of Corey's leather vest and jerked him hard.

The boy didn't flinch. "Go ahead, big man. Take a swing. You'd just better make it a good one, 'cause I'm not going to back down. I'm not going to let you break my sister's heart."

Braddock shoved Corey away from him. The boy quickly righted himself, his stance ready, his fists clenched.

Braddock ran his fingers through his tangled hair. "Sit

down. I'm not going to fight you. Believe it or not, I do care about your sister."

Corey righted his chair and sat in it, arms folded over his chest. "Yeah. That's why you're going to ride out of here, leaving her to fend for herself with your baby in her belly."

Braddock gripped the back of his chair. "She's not," is all he could get past the rock wedged in his throat.

"Yet. You might think we're some white-trash Southerners, no better than we ought to be—"

"I don't think that." Braddock released his hold of the chair's thin wooden slat before he snapped it in two. "I'd kill anyone who said that about Lorelei."

"Yeah, but you'd leave her to explain when her stomach starts to swell."

Braddock shook his head, refusing to look at the kid. *I'm supposed to be doing the questioning*, he told himself—but his thought rang hollow.

"Don't tell me you weren't doing what you shouldn't with my sister. I see she didn't get much sleep last night. And that grin on her face. What the hell did you promise her?"

Braddock glared at Corey. "Nothing. I didn't promise her anything."

The boy glared back with righteous anger that made Braddock want to hang his head. "Yeah, that's what I thought. But don't think you're anything special. Lorelei would love a three-legged dog. She's just like that. She's got a big heart."

Braddock stared at the dust covering his boots. "Yeah," was the only retort he could come up with.

"Yeah. And Lorelei gets hurt. Again. I'm sick of it."

Braddock raised his head. Corey's face was red. His eyes looked damp. How dared he look so damned wronged?

"I'm sick of it, too. So why don't you stop acting like a spoiled brat and let your sister live her life?"

Corey stuck out his chin. "I plan to. But I'm going to get you, Braddock. You can't treat Lorelei like you have and get away with it." The soft fuzz that covered his jaw in sparse dark patches didn't diminish his threat.

"Let me tell you something; if it weren't for Lorelei you'd

be swinging from a noose right about now. I'm taking care of her the best way I know how."

Corey stared through him, calling him a liar without saying a word.

Braddock paced as he'd seen Lucky do in the corral beside the barn. They both wanted to run. Facing Corey was harder than he'd ever imagined. What had he been thinking last night? He couldn't leave Lorelei to handle the consequences of his lust alone or expect some other man to take responsibility for a family Braddock had created. He thought he had left honor at West Point. But that was the kind of honor men made up. This was flesh-and-blood real. How in the hell did he think he could walk away from a child or a pregnant woman?

His thoughts pounded in his head. He had to grit his teeth to think about something else. "Where's Mulcahy?"

"Specter Canyon," Corey answered. He didn't blink an eye.

Braddock was forced to sit down. He knew the canyon. It was in the middle of Apache country, narrow and unpassable. Outlaws had hid there before, but were rumored never to come out.

Corey must have read his expression because he grinned. "Know it?"

"How do you get there?"

Corey shrugged. "Never been there myself, but if you got a map, I can show you."

"Then how do you know of it?"

Corey looked him straight in the eye. "They showed me. It's where we were all supposed to meet up."

Braddock studied him. Corey was either telling the truth or was an excellent liar. Braddock already knew the latter to be true.

Corey picked at a callus on his palm. "You won't get out alive. If the Apache don't get you, the rattlers will. There's only one path through the canyon. You have to dismount and lead your horse through blindfolded. Horses know better than to go through something so steep and narrow."

"I'll manage."

Corey nodded and smiled. "Yeah."

Braddock stood. "I'll get a map."

He wrenched open the side door, eager to escape Lorelei's brother, if only for a few seconds. He rubbed his forehead as he strode through the Hartman kitchen and into the living area. Guilt gave him a headache. A tingling on the back of his neck stopped him cold. He turned slowly, his hand poised to grab the Smith & Wesson strapped to his hip.

Beth sat in a rocking chair beside the front window, a sleeping Rachel draped over her lap while she sewed a torn patch on the sleeve of one of Jay's work shirts. Her gaze knifed him.

"I'm getting a map," he said.

"I know. Voices carry out here." Her gaze dropped to her mending. The way she stabbed the blue cambric with the needle let him know she was still thinking of him.

Braddock watched her, willing her features to soften. He'd never seen sweet Beth look so vicious. Even the soft swelling of her belly and the sleeping child in her lap could not alter the chilling effect of her judgment. If she had a gun, he was sure she'd shoot him.

He held out his hand, took a breath to explain, then let it out. Instead he escaped into the boys' bedroom to get a map from his saddlebag. Anything he tried to say to Beth would sound like an excuse. His reasons for leaving Lorelei had already begun to stack up short in his own mind.

He never should have made love to Lorelei under Beth's roof. If he didn't get out of here today, she'd be bending Jay's ear until he was forced to marry Lorelei at gunpoint. Braddock sat back on his heels, map in hand, and felt a rush of relief wash over him like a waterfall. That was what he wanted. Why fight it?

He strode back into the living room and stopped in front of Beth. She didn't glance up, but her pinched lips let him know she wasn't unaware of his presence. He opened his mouth to tell her he'd do the honorable thing; he'd marry Lorelei. But his voice seized in his lungs. Dark, cold fear gripped him. Jay's old wheelchair loomed in the corner of the room, just past Beth's shoulder. A half-finished quilt was draped over the back, and a pile of mending filled the seat, but the big ugly wheels were in plain view. Why hadn't he seen the hated chair before?

All too clearly he remembered the first time Jay had been in that chair—they'd forced him to leave his bed and plopped him in it against his will. He hadn't met Braddock's gaze at the hospital when Braddock came to prepare him for his wife's visit. Jay had even cussed when Beth and the kids had come. But he'd been dying a little every day, and Braddock had known it was all his fault. He'd had to bring them.

To escape the sobering reminder of Jay's wheelchair, Braddock stumbled through the kitchen. He had to leave here and never see Lorelei again. It was the only way. He couldn't go through what he'd gone through with Jay. What he'd gone through hundreds of times during the war. Bad things happened when he was around. Lorelei would have hurt feelings when he left, but at least she would be in one piece. And if there were to be a child between them, any man would gladly take it with Lorelei. Jay would make sure he was a good man. A better man than Braddock.

With his hands braced on the door frame, Braddock paused to steel himself against facing Corey. He forced himself to remember who he was. What he was. During the war he had gone off alone each night to let himself be overwhelmed by his grief and horror, then hardened himself again for the next day. He could do that again. Eventually there would be nothing left to fight against. He would be numb.

Willing himself to feel nothing, he strode out the kitchen door. His efforts might have worked if the first thing he saw wasn't Lorelei.

She gazed up at him and a well-placed hammer came down to shatter his glass resistance. But he didn't return her smile. What was there to smile about?

He thrust the map at Corey. "Show me." He made a special point not to look at Lorelei again.

Archie sat in the chair Braddock had vacated. Lorelei must

have found the spring, because the man had washed his face and hair. Sober, he appeared younger. He was probably around Braddock's age. Coherence sharpened his clear blue eyes. And in those eyes was pain, a frozen pain that had just started to wake after a long hibernation.

Braddock didn't wonder what had happened to Archie. He could guess a hundred different scenarios. He turned away before he recognized too much, but not before he noticed Lorelei rest her hand on Archie's shoulder.

Braddock looked at her. She didn't even glance his way. Her dark eyelashes fanned her cheeks while she watched Archie clench the wool trousers covering his thighs. She knew what had happened to Archie. They had shared something at the spring. She'd found a new three-legged dog to rescue.

Archie wasn't good enough for her either. She didn't need to take on his ghosts.

Corey pointed to the map he had unfolded and smoothed across his lap. "Here."

Archie abruptly stood. He clutched the loose shirt covering his stomach and swayed. "Excuse me."

Lorelei worried her bottom lip as she watched him stagger behind the barn. She finally turned her gaze to Braddock. "He was in the war."

"Weren't we all." Braddock knelt beside Corey's chair so he could get a better look at the map. Finding Mulcahy's location was what he'd been wanting for years. Unfortunately, having the map right in front of his face didn't help him focus. The image of Lorelei spending her days tending a drunk blurred the map's faded script and worn lines.

Corey used his finger to trace a path. "You come in here. Follow this creek bed. If it floods, you're dead."

"Is there any other access?"

"Nope."

Lorelei sat in the chair across from them. She leaned forward to touch Braddock's arm. "Why do you have to go alone?"

Corey answered when all Braddock could do was stare at the map and try to make sense of it. "Not that I think he's going to make it, but the more people you bring the less likely you'll be able to get in unnoticed."

He had to recommit to his mission. Mulcahy deserved to be brought down, and Braddock knew he was the man to do it. Violence was all he was good for. Braddock shifted to his other knee, knocking away Lorelei's grip as casually as possible.

"What good will it do if he gets killed?"

"I won't get killed." He would survive. That was the one certainty. The sky could fall, the seas could rise, and the sun could burst, but he wouldn't get killed. For some reason his destiny was to survive.

Corey folded the map and handed it back to Braddock. "What else do you want to know?"

"Where are the guards?"

"The canyon narrows until you're sure you won't get through. You will, and it widens after that. The first set of guards is stationed on top of the narrowest part."

"How many men do they have?"

"Hard to say. Some died in the robbery, probably a few more from their wounds. But Mulcahy isn't the only outlaw who uses the hideout. There are others who are just as bad. There could be fifteen to fifty."

"Against one?" Lorelei pleaded.

Braddock finally glanced at her, and he was once again her favorite stray. The sheen coating her dark blue eyes made them look even brighter in the sunlight.

"The more there are, the better it will work to my advantage. They'll have their guard down, thinking they're safe. But men like Mulcahy breed chaos. The more there are, the more chaos—the easier it will be for me to slip in unnoticed."

"Are we through?" Corey stood.

"Sure." Braddock kept his gaze on Lorelei. She stared into the folds of her faded gray dress. The glow she had started the day with had been blotted out by a dark cloud. As usual, he was responsible.

Corey glanced at his sister, then glared at Braddock before he turned and walked away.

Braddock eased into Corey's vacated chair. He thought of all the things Corey had said, of Beth's stabbing stare, and knew he had to think of something to give Lorelei. And it wasn't just because he was desperate to see her smile again. He owed her more than just a good-bye.

He waited for her to look up at him. She didn't.

Finally he lightly squeezed her knee. "I'm going to be all right."

"You're not indestructible, Christopher."

He wished. How much easier his life would be if that were true. "This won't be the death of me, but breaking your heart might."

Her chest rose and fell with her uneven breathing. "Then don't."

Braddock rested his forearms on his thighs and hung his head. "It's not that easy."

"Yes, it is," she pleaded. "Give us a chance."

"Lorelei," he said, not knowing what went after that. Finally he glanced at her. "What would I have to do?"

She blinked, opened her mouth to speak, then closed it. His question took her as much by surprise as it did him. "I don't know exactly. Come back, for starters."

He clasped his hands together. "I'm not a farmer."

Her face lightened with her growing hope. "I never asked you to be."

Braddock stared past the barn, trying to glimpse the white crosses in the graveyard. But the sun beamed in his eyes and the lone shade tree ruffled its leaves, refracting light like a thousand tiny mirrors. What was he doing? All he knew was that he couldn't let her go. But he shouldn't give her false hope.

"Is your brother being straight with me?"

"I think . . ." She paused, apparently startled by the change of subject. "Yes, he'd better be. He knows I'll never speak to him again if he wasn't."

He took her hands in his before he came to his senses. "Give me a month."

"For what?"

Some part of him was commanding the rest of him. His rational mind screamed for him to stop, to shut up, but he couldn't. "Wait for me a month."

"After that?"

"Hopefully you'll smarten up and won't even care after that."

"Does this mean you're coming back?" She scooted to the edge of her seat.

He rubbed his brow. "I can't leave things like this." He dropped his hand and told her the only thing he could decipher in all his warring thoughts. "I can't leave you. I want to take care of you, but I'm afraid."

She laughed. "I can take care of myself."

"What's so funny?"

"I didn't think you were afraid of anything."

He smiled. "I didn't think I was either, until I met you."

She grabbed both his hands. "I'll wait for you as long as it takes."

"No." He pulled his hands away. "This is all new to me. I don't want a forever kind of promise. Just give me a month."

Her smile widened. "A month is what you have."

He stood, not knowing what to do now, not even sure what he had promised. But his headache faded with the knowledge that he had a little more time to think of Lorelei as his.

She faced him, grinning from ear to ear. Suddenly she leaped toward him, throwing her arms around his neck. "I love you."

He eased his arms around her waist and took the biggest risk in his very dangerous life. "I love you, too."

Chapter Fourteen

Lorelei stepped off the empty porch and into the arms of the starless night. Christopher hadn't said good-bye. He'd left a little before dark while she was occupied preparing dinner with Beth. Lorelei understood. Not even Beth's sympathetic gaze when Jay delivered the news of Christopher's departure could spoil her optimism. Christopher loved her, had said he was coming back in a month. His promise was more than she had dared to even hope for.

Corey on the other hand, instead of being thrilled by news of Christopher's departure, seemed to have sunk into a funk. He barely ate his dinner, and even Alice's glowing admiration couldn't bring a smile to his face. After he excused himself with a mumble, he'd disappeared. Everyone had gone to bed and he hadn't even returned to say good-night.

Lorelei navigated the path to the barn in the pitch-black night, expecting to find Corey fussing over Sugarfoot. Whenever he was upset, he turned to a horse. No matter how many times she told herself she wasn't the cause of his troubles, she still felt guilty for being so happy because of them. If Corey hadn't garnered a warrant for his arrest, she never would have met Christopher.

As she neared the barn, she could see the light seeping underneath the wide door. She doused the grin she'd been sporting ever since Christopher had told her he loved her, and swung the door open.

Corey sprang away from Jay's horse, which occupied the first stall lining the barn's long wall. When his gaze collided with hers, he sagged in relief. "It's you."

"What are you doing?"

The plowhorse nickered and lifted its head, urging Corey to pat its long black nose. Green leaves crusted the horse's upper lip.

She stepped over to the chest-high gate to peek into the trough. "What did you give him?"

Corey strode to the far side of the barn, then turned to face her while he kicked something with his heel. She kept her gaze on him, only briefly pulling it away to pick out the small leaves dusting the hay. The plant had been rolled in sugar. She brought it to her nose and recognized the scent immediately. Even coated with sweetener, the minty smell of skullcap evoked powerful memories. The plant grew in abundance back home, but still she had to hunt for it daily. Her mother required large doses of the brewed leaves to take the pain away. It usually lulled her into a deep, dead sleep.

"Where did you get this?"

"Had some. Found some along the way."

She checked the stalls of the other animals and found more of the sugar-crusted leaves spread over the hay. She marched over to Corey, the evidence piled in both her hands. "Why were you drugging the horses?"

"It wouldn't have hurt them. I wouldn't do that."

"They just won't be able to work tomorrow. Really, Corey, are you so lazy that you would undermine Jay's livelihood just to get out of a day's work?"

"You don't know anything about me, Lorelei, or you wouldn't ask me that."

"Explain it to me."

He stared at her a long moment, then retrieved the bedroll and knapsack that he'd been trying to hide under the hay.

"I'm leaving. I don't want to hang around and wait for Mulcahy to find me."

"He won't. Christopher said . . ."

Corey shook his head. "Braddock's not going to make it. Didn't you hear anything I said to him? He's not going to get past the first checkpoint."

"What did you do?"

He dropped his bag. "You know what? It would have been a lot easier for me to give the horses locoweed. There's plenty of it around here, and that way Jay couldn't come after me ever. But I didn't."

She stuffed the evidence of Corey's deceit into the deep pocket of her skirt. "If you think I'm going to pat you on the back for this kind of behavior, you're mistaken. I don't know what you've become, Corey, but I don't like it. You're not the brother I grew up with."

"No, the brother you knew would have given them so much locoweed the animals would have had to be destroyed. That's what happened back in Louisville, you know. Pa went to jail because Mr. Ellard's horse had to be shot after our old man got through with it."

"Pa didn't do anything wrong. Mr. Ellard was angry with me."

"You actually believe that? Pa did it. And it wasn't the first horse race he fixed either. He did every last thing he was accused of. I know. I was with him. He was proud of himself for poisoning Mr. Ellard's horse. Thought he'd show him and win a bunch of his money to boot. Well, guess who showed who?"

Lorelei turned her back to her brother. The truth in his words swirled around her ankles like a cold fog. She burst into motion, pacing to one side of the barn, then back. She opened her mouth to deny his words but no sound came out.

"Why then . . ." She finally pushed words past her dry lips. "Why did Pa rave that Mr. Ellard had him arrested to keep me and Berkley apart when he really did poison that horse?" She took a deep, cleansing breath, but it didn't dissipate the awful clarity her words evoked. Unfortunately, she would never be able to swallow the lie again. "Why did he let me believe it was all my fault our family was ruined?"

Corey shrugged. "He was drunk most of the time. Probably forgot."

She strode to Corey. "But you knew. Why didn't you tell me?"

Corey tilted his head. His wet brown eyes pulled down at the corners. "I thought you knew. I thought we all knew Pa was a no-good cheat."

She shook her head. "I didn't know." But what she should have said was, *I didn't want to know*. And she didn't want to know now.

Corey picked up his gear. "Not like it was the first time Pa pulled a fast one."

She followed Corey, her hands balled into fists. "Nor you."

Corey glanced at her over his shoulder. "I do what I have to. I don't like to hurt anybody."

She put her hand over her mouth to stop the scream that grew in her chest. She moved her hand to her throat, closing off the wall of pain. "Christopher. You lied to Christopher."

His shoulders squared under his worn, wool jacket. He secured his gear to his horse's saddle with stiff movements.

Everything Lorelei had ever believed in slid off her and lay in a black puddle at her feet. Her whole life had been a lie. Maybe she had known in some dark recess of her mind, but what kept the lie alive, gave it power and strength, flavored the illusion so it could be swallowed whole, was family. They had all conspired to protect the family at all costs, even if it meant embracing a lie. And now even family loyalty was a lie. Corey had betrayed her.

"Tell me. Did you lie to Christopher?"

Corey closed the distance between them with a menacing step. "Why do you care about him so much, anyway? He used you, then left you high and dry. He doesn't care about you any more than Berkley did."

"He's coming back for me."

Corey took off his hat and brushed his fingers through his rumpled hair. "He's not coming back, Lori."

"I swear to God, if you did something to get him killed you won't be my brother anymore."

Corey crammed the slouch hat back on his head. The brim covered his eyes, but the hurt was as clear as the anger flushing Lorelei's cheeks.

"Did he say he was going to marry you?"

"He said he loved me."

"That's not the same, and you know it."

Lorelei hugged herself, refusing to look at him. No, Christopher hadn't said anything about marriage, but there was a chance for them. A chance for Lorelei to be happy.

Corey squeezed her shoulders. "Come with me. We'll start over. I'll build a nice house. Buy you pretty clothes like you used to have before Pa lost everything. Soon enough you'll forget Braddock ever existed. You'll have beaux beating down the door."

She jerked away from Corey. "That's what you said when you left Kentucky with my life savings. Did you know Ma and I had to go without sugar that whole next year? But we were glad to do it for our little Corey. If this is the dream, Corey, I want to wake up."

"You don't know anything. You don't know what I've done for us."

"Tell me. Make me believe you're something more than a criminal, that all those things Christopher said about you weren't true."

"I can't talk to you." He strode to his horse.

Lorelei rushed past him to grab the paint's bridle. "You're not going anywhere."

The horse whinnied and shied sideways. Archie's mare stomped in her stall, growing nervous at the commotion. Corey yanked Lorelei away from his horse.

She tried to kick him in the shin, but he managed to avoid her blows as he wrestled her into a soft pile of hay. Anger blurred her senses. She thrashed, desperate for a way to hurt him as he had hurt her. He straddled her stomach and stretched out her arms.

He squeezed her wrists in a painful grip. "What the hell

do you think you're doing? You can't keep me here."

She bucked her body in an effort to throw him off. Too soon she grew breathless. He was too strong. But that didn't stop her from using her sternest older-sister voice "You're not leaving until you tell me what you told Christopher."

At last Corey's face flushed an angry shade of red, and he panted from trying to hold her down. "All I told him was how to find Mulcahy. That's what's going to get him killed. But you told me to tell him. You can't blame me for that."

"What else? What did you leave out?"

Corey rolled off of her and sat in the straw.

She crawled from the hay and stood. "You lied to me. Used me since the day I arrived. Even before that."

He hung his head and picked at the golden dried grass. "I never meant to hurt you."

"Then please, please, tell me the truth. Were you honest with Christopher?"

He lifted his gaze. "There's a lookout on the mesa approaching the canyon entrance. But that's not the entrance everyone who knows the place uses. If you're one of them, you use a back way. I didn't tell Braddock about the back way."

Though she suspected the truth, had begged to hear it, his words forced the air from her lungs. "How could you?"

"In case you've forgotten, 'cause I sure as hell haven't, he's a bounty hunter who came after my head."

"Things have changed. He said he was going to let you go."

"And you said he was coming back."

"For me."

"What about me?"

"What about you, Corey? Everything doesn't revolve around you. Christopher's in love with me. He doesn't care about you."

"Let's say he makes it back from his trek to find Mulcahy and comes away empty-handed. Because if he survives at all, he won't get Mulcahy or the gold. Then what? You think he's going to settle down with you, empty-handed? No. He's going to turn to me, because something is better than nothing."

"He's not like that."

"He's a bounty hunter, Lorelei. Most of the time the reward is dead or alive. It's not the kind of job that attracts the forgive-and-forget type."

Lorelei stared at her brother, trying to find the lie in his words so she could tell him he was wrong. But she couldn't. Her desire to have Christopher return put her brother in danger. Still, she wouldn't let him leave without righting what he'd wronged.

"You have to tell me how to get to Specter Canyon so I can warn Christopher."

Corey's eyes widened. "Not on your life. He'd really have my ass if I told you where it was. It's too dangerous, Lori."

"Fine." She turned on her heel. "I'm going to wake up Jay. You can tell him."

"No." He stopped her by grabbing the hem of her gown. "He'll turn me in. Jay won't give me a second chance after I lied to Braddock."

She jerked her dress out of his grasp. "You don't deserve a second chance."

"They'll hang me."

She stopped before she reached the open door. They weren't talking about sending Corey to his room without supper. He would go to jail at best, and at worst—most likely . . . She couldn't even think about her brother hanging. Turning Corey over to the marshal wasn't an option.

"Tell me where to find Christopher."

He pushed himself to his feet and straightened his jacket. "I did him a favor. A sharpshooter will take him out long before he ever gets to Mulcahy. Mulcahy wouldn't have killed him quickly."

"I'm begging. I've done so much for you and all I ask is this one little thing."

Corey led his horse to the barn door. For a brief second she thought he'd mount and slip into the night. She knew there was nothing she could do, would do, to stop him.

He paused in front of her. "Follow the Tewa River until it runs dry. It's marked on most maps. The canyon's not. In the distance you'll spot two rocks standing side by side, one half as tall as the other. That's where I told Braddock to go. Don't go any farther than the tail end of the riverbed. They'll see you, but they won't come after you unless you get close to the entrance. You'd better find Braddock before that."

She touched Corey's cheek. "Thank you."

He grabbed her hand and squeezed it hard. "I mean it. Don't go into the canyon."

Lorelei wasn't about to make such a promise. Instead she stepped back so Corey could mount his horse. She slid the barn door open wider, giving him a clear path to freedom. There was nothing else she could say to her brother. Anger and sorrow battled within her. She still loved her brother, but she doubted she'd ever forgive him.

"I'm sorry," he said before he rode off into the night.

Chapter Fifteen

Maneuvering the narrow cliff Corey had warned him about proved even more treacherous with Braddock's hands tied behind his back. He centered his sights on the scuffed toes of his black leather boots, not daring to glance at the chunks of rust-colored rocks that tumbled over the edge with the brush of his steps. Funny, he had never been afraid of heights before. The guard at his back poked him with the tip of his rifle, and Braddock bent his knees to keep from plummeting with the shower of dust. Maybe his plan wasn't going to work after all.

He had had too much time to think on his way to Specter Canyon. Thoughts of Lorelei plagued him, kept him awake at night, and then invaded his dreams. Once he got used to her constant presence, he'd liked it. And then he had needed it. He needed to get back to her, and that changed everything.

The guard prodded him again.

"Watch it," Braddock called over his shoulder. "I'm gonna get untied once we get to camp, and then I'll be looking for you."

The guard tucked his rifle closer to his body. "I'm just doing my job. If you are who you say, you know we can't be too careful. I don't want to go to jail any more than you want to go back."

"I just ain't forgetting how you're treating me, is all." Braddock laid on the Southern accent. He wasn't sure if Lincoln Knox was a Southerner, but with a name like Lincoln, he had better do something to unite himself with Mulcahy. Hopefully being a killer and a rapist would be enough.

"How'd you break out of Tombstone's jail anyway?"

"Let's just say I had some help from a lady friend."

Braddock kept his gaze on the next turn in the trail. A hunchbacked juniper clung to the side with grasping roots. It required all his concentration to maintain his balance while picking his way around the base of the tangled tree. Just as well. Better to keep his mouth shut. He didn't know a whole hell of a lot about Lincoln Knox except that his wanted poster looked too much like Braddock. He'd had to go after him just to keep himself from being hunted down.

When he'd found the town where Knox had been killed, several people thought they'd seen a ghost. Knox had been buried in an unmarked grave, having died under an alias while hiding out. Braddock didn't want to give the lowlife any more notoriety than he deserved. He figured dying anonymously did Knox more justice than the big trial in Santa Fe that had been waiting for him before he escaped jail.

For once, Braddock's morose sense of justice worked in his favor. Being escorted into Mulcahy's camp, even at gunpoint, should have suited him fine. Unfortunately, now that he had something to live for, the insanity of the situation rocked him. Like all the other forgotten emotions Lorelei had unlocked, a healthy dose of fear was making an appearance.

After the sharp turn, followed by a climb over a cascade of rocks, he and his captor started down a slope leading to a flat mesa tucked into the canyon's side. The formation of the red-rock walls protected the bandits from view until you were right on them. Corey had actually done him a favor by keeping his mouth closed about the first set of guards. Better to be brought in as one of their own seeking refuge than to get caught sneaking up on the camp. That had been Braddock's plan in the beginning, anyway. He'd already used Knox's name once or twice in places like Coyote Pass, where being a bounty hunter would be instant death. Actually, it wasn't too popular a profession anywhere, a fact that had never bothered Braddock before.

Mulcahy's refuge consisted of several tents and a few wooden structures, all in various stages of completion or dilapidation. Wooden walls had tarps strewn across their top, and adobe bricks lay scattered about, rotting under the sun and wind. No one seemed in a hurry to finish any of their half-assed efforts at shelter. A few men glanced his way; others didn't even notice. Several congregated in the shade of a scrub pine. Another picked at the hoof of his horse's foreleg. The canyon must have a second entrance. Before the steep climb, he'd been forced to leave Lucky in a natural corral created by a deep groove in the rock wall. You couldn't force a horse the way he'd come, not even blindfolded.

Braddock made a casual sweep with his gaze, looking for Mulcahy. Once the excitement of the hunt kicked in, he forgot his fear. He mentally noted his surroundings and calculated what could be used to his advantage. As he grew closer, he noticed the men under the trees were playing cards, except for one who had slumped to the side in an awkward pile, a whiskey bottle still clutched in his hand. Though the men were fewer in number than he'd expected, none of them had their guard up. The mood was glum. They certainly didn't act like a group that had just stolen a fortune in gold. The robbery must have taken its toll, as Corey had said. But Braddock knew not to place too much stock in anything Corey claimed.

The guard guided him to a wood-framed shack that had recently been fixed to create a decent shelter. A blanket hung as a door. The sunken roof consisted of juniper branches with the needlelike leaves and berry-sized blue cones still attached. A man with a rifle across his lap and a hat pulled over his eyes sat on the ground with his back against the weathered plank wall.

The guard stopped a few feet short of the resting man. "Ricochet?"

"Your time's not up yet, Cole."

Cole shifted. Even in Ricochet's relaxed position, he forced the hair on the back of Braddock's neck to rise.

After glancing around the camp either for help or someone else to take his prisoner to, Cole finally gave up and cleared his throat. "This one says he's Lincoln Knox."

Ricochet pushed the stiff leather hat off his face and gazed at Braddock. "What entrance did he come in?"

"South. The one you told me to guard."

"Why didn't you shoot him?"

Braddock steeled himself against a rush of anger. Corey had failed to mention a second entrance. Either the kid purposely lied to him, or Mulcahy was planning on getting rid of Corey from the beginning. Both excuses seemed plausible.

"He broke out of the Tombstone jail. Wants a place to hide."

Ricochet didn't alter his bored expression. "I don't give a shit. Take him out and shoot him. Your orders are to shoot anyone who gets near the south entrance. Now do it, boy."

Cole lowered his rifle. Luckily for Braddock, Cole wasn't taken with the idea. "But he's an outlaw. He wants a place—"

"He's seen the hideout. Now, that don't make it a hideout anymore." Ricochet eased his finger around the rifle's trigger and maneuvered the barrel to point at Cole. "If you don't want me to take you with him, you'll take him out and shoot him. Away from the camp, Cole. Mulcahy's trying to sleep."

Cole stood as if his feet had sunk into the dry sand. He let out his breath. "Come on," he finally mumbled to Braddock.

Braddock held his ground. "Listen here, mister, I've been four days in the desert to get here. I'm not going to let you shoot me."

"What the hell you going to do about it?" Ricochet must

have sensed something dangerous in Braddock, because he sat up and steadied his rifle with his other hand.

Braddock tugged at his bindings one more time. They had come loose, but not enough to get his hands free. Even if he could, he had let Cole take his guns, and his rifle remained strapped to Lucky's saddle. He had made it through worse situations, he reminded himself, though he couldn't recall how.

"Let's just say I know things. And they're going to die with me if you shoot me."

Ricochet got to his feet as fluidly as a snake slithering up a tree. His sneer assured Braddock that he'd be glad to do what Cole hesitated to. "There ain't nothing I need to know."

"Not even how to find Corey Sullivan?"

Ricochet's sneer drooped. "He send you here?"

Braddock smiled. "You want to find out, you better untie me and give me back my guns."

Ricochet grabbed his shirt and tried to shake him, but Braddock towered over the little weasel. Overpowering Braddock with brute force wasn't going to happen, even if his arms were tied behind his back.

Realizing the same thing, Ricochet gave Braddock a hard shove, which he absorbed easily. Ricochet's face turned as red as the dirt at their feet. He jabbed his finger in Braddock's face.

"You're going to tell me everything you know about Sullivan, boy, even if I have to peel the skin off your hide to get the information out of you."

If he hadn't sensed it already, the way Cole inched away warned Braddock that Ricochet wasn't known for idle threats. Braddock didn't flinch under the outlaw's furious stare.

"Cole! Get your ass over here and take this smart ass and tie him down. We'll see how fast we can wipe that smug look off his face."

One quick, stabbing glance from Ricochet convinced Cole to grip Braddock's arm.

Braddock easily jerked from Cole's grasp. Though he was younger and good-sized, Cole had no enthusiasm for the job. Braddock noted that other gazes had turned to the confrontation, but no one moved to do anything about it.

Cole made another weak attempt to restrain Braddock, who swung away from him.

"Stay out of this, Cole, or I'll have to kill you too," warned Braddock.

"It don't matter. Either you're gonna do it or he's gonna do it." Cole approached one more time but jumped out of the way when Braddock tried to stab him with his elbow.

From the corner of his eye, Braddock caught Ricochet lunging for him. He twisted a quarter turn, then planted the sole of his boot firmly in the center of the man's chest. He pushed out, sending Ricochet flying into the wooden shack. True to his name, the outlaw bounced off the wall and landed hard on his knees.

"You're going to die, boy." Eyes bulging and practically foaming at the mouth, Ricochet retrieved his rifle without ever taking his rabid glare off Braddock.

"You'll never find Sullivan if you kill me," Braddock snapped. It was his best defense.

"To hell with Sullivan." Ricochet brought the rifle to his shoulder and took aim squarely at the center of Braddock's chest.

With a desperate tug that felt like it took most of the skin from his wrists, Braddock yanked at his bonds. Unfortunately, it didn't do him a damn bit of good. He could do nothing but stare down the barrel of Ricochet's rifle.

A smile curved the outlaw's lips.

"Ricochet. Stop."

Braddock tore his gaze away from the weapon's deadly snout to find the owner of the commanding voice. A redhaired man leaned on the shack's door frame. To hold back the blanket that served as a door required all his effort. Sweat beaded his forehead. A torn and bloody shirt was draped over his shoulders; his pants were pulled over his hips but were only partially buttoned. A dirty bandage wound around his chest, and his arm was in a sling. The two words he had spoken must have worn him out, because all he could do was pant.

Cole rushed to his side. "Are you all right, Rowen? You feeling better?" His voice was hopeful despite the obvious.

Braddock glanced back to Ricochet. He had lowered the rifle, but he still looked mad enough to kill.

"Didn't you hear me yelling at you to stop?" Mulcahy wheezed between his words.

"I didn't hear nothing," said Cole.

"He's a smart-ass," answered Ricochet reluctantly, his seething glare trained on Braddock.

Mulcahy gripped the door frame. Cole wrapped a supportive arm around his waist. Despite his weakness, Mulcahy brushed him away. "Just get me a chair."

Cole disappeared into the shelter while Mulcahy studied Braddock.

Braddock met his gaze straight-on. The steely blue eyes Braddock remembered had dimmed. Even the vibrant red of his hair had faded. Braddock looked him over, noticing the swollen red fingers sticking from the sling. They were infected. He'd lose the arm, if he survived at all. Corey hadn't lied about that.

"I know you from somewhere," said Mulcahy.

Cole returned with an army-issue folding chair. He popped the collapsible legs open and helped Mulcahy ease onto the canvas seat.

Braddock maintained an outward calm while his mind scrambled for his next lie. He had never expected Mulcahy to recognize him. His hair was longer, the color altered by the sun. He had let his beard grow, and the wrinkles around his eyes and mouth caused by a permanent frown were deep enough to make even his parents not know him. He wasn't the same man Mulcahy had briefly served under. Braddock barely recognized himself as that man.

"He escaped from Tombstone jail. I read it in the papers," supplied Cole.

Ricochet hovered to the left of Mulcahy's chair, breathing fire through his flared nostrils.

Mulcahy let Cole wipe the sweat from his brow with a red bandanna he'd untied from around his neck.

"No. It was during the war. Whose side were you on?"

Braddock shrugged. "Both, when it suited me."

Mulcahy grinned. "I hear you. Damn stupid war that solved nothing."

Braddock nodded, not having to lie about his agreement. He picked at the frayed ropes still wound around his right hand, then deliberately dropped his broken bonds to the ground.

Mulcahy's sharp gaze showed he didn't miss the significance. "Corey send you here?"

Braddock chose his words carefully. Mulcahy and his men teetered on a sharp edge. Whether they'd be shoved over seemed to have everything to do with Corey. Association with him could save Braddock's life or get him killed.

"You couldn't say Sullivan sent me, but he told me how to get here."

"That little son of a bitch. I'm going to rip his heart out when I get my hands on him." Ricochet stomped around in a complete circle.

Mulcahy nodded and smiled. "In exchange for what? Corey doesn't do things for no reason."

Braddock hesitated, not liking Mulcahy's answer, because he recognized the truth in his words. Suddenly Braddock felt like a pawn.

"Protection. He had a deputy marshal on his ass, and he doesn't cover his trail too good. I took care of the law for him." The taste of the confession was unexpectedly bitter on his lips.

"Son of a bitch," repeated Ricochet, his eyes bulging to maximum capacity. He was literally slobbering. "If he gets himself strung up . . ."

Mulcahy held up his hand, a simple gesture that seemed to take all his strength, but was effective enough to silence his crony. "Where's Corey?"

"My guns," Braddock demanded in his steadiest, coldest voice.

Mulcahy closed his eyes while he rasped his next breath. He was fading fast. "Give the man his guns."

Cole complied while Ricochet burned a hole through his every move. Braddock meticulously checked the weapons for ammunition. "Saw him last near Arriba."

Braddock silently vowed never to let Lorelei go near the ranch again.

"He went back to his ranch. Jesus, that boy is stupid."

"Smart enough to fool you, Rowen," sneered Ricochet.

"He fooled us all, Ricochet. Even you," Cole spoke up. For the first time, Ricochet's withering glare didn't cower Cole.

"It's all right, Cole. I deserve it." Mulcahy turned to Braddock. "Got him off an orphan train a few years back. He's too loyal for his own good."

Mulcahy's admission of guilt effectively simmered the animosity boiling over from Ricochet. Braddock had to admit he seemed to be a good leader, even if he'd been on the wrong side. Not that Braddock knew what the right side was. The hatred he should feel for the sneaky trick that stole Jay's legs was suddenly hard to muster. Instead of an invalid wasting in a wheelchair, he pictured the laughing father of four with one on the way.

At the moment, Rowen Mulcahy appeared worse off than Jay. A slow death while holed up in a dirty shack couldn't have been more fitting. Maybe life had given him what he deserved without Braddock's needing to have a damn thing to do with it. But for some reason he felt sorry for Mulcahy. Maybe because he saw a glimpse of the end he himself had been heading for before he'd met Lorelei.

Unfortunately, now was not the time to lay down his guns and turn over a peace-loving leaf. He gripped the smooth handles of his Smith & Wessons and his confidence soared. This was the job he'd set out to do, and he planned to do it. Though he'd be bringing in a dead Mulcahy rather than a live one. Braddock would be surprised if the outlaw survived the night. Now the only problem was the gold.

"Why did you come here?" Mulcahy looked Braddock straight in the eye.

"Heard you were shorthanded. Figured you could afford to pay a fast gun."

All three men stared at him without expression. Finally a gasp escaped Mulcahy's throat. Braddock feared Mulcahy had drawn his last breath. But before Braddock could move toward him, a burst of laughter ripped from deep in Mulcahy's belly, halting Braddock's rescue attempt. Even the fit of coughing that followed, staining his lips with pink-tinged spittle, couldn't wipe away his smile.

"Corey tell you that?"

"Well . . ." Braddock was lost for the right answer. "Yeah."

This time even Ricochet grinned.

"You took care of the marshal for him, and then he sent you up here—wrong entrance, mind you—for your big reward?"

Braddock genuinely frowned. He didn't like the sound of this one bit. "Something like that."

Mulcahy shook his head. "Son, I guess you're right where you're supposed to be. Up here with the fools. What did I tell you about a fool and his money, Cole?"

"Soon parted." The boyish grin that tugged at the young man's lips showed he was still firmly in his teens.

Braddock didn't get the joke, but he was starting to figure out it was on him. "What are you trying to tell me?"

Mulcahy's grin faded into a defeated slump of his shoulders. "Sullivan's got the gold from the robbery. All of it."

With only the stars to guide him, Braddock wended his way down the dark canyon with more ease than when he had arrived. A singular thought lit his way: *Find Corey Sullivan.*

The night was moonless but clear, allowing the stars to blaze like a thousand blue suns. He didn't have to worry about guards this time. Ricochet's stare burned into his back as he watched Braddock go, but they thought him more fool than threat. Braddock had to agree.

After they had dropped their little mortar about Sullivan

having the gold, Braddock swore a blue streak that gave even Ricochet a few new words for his vocabulary. Of course, they all enjoyed his rage, laughing even harder. When Braddock vowed to find the little bastard, they believed him. He'd meant it, too. Never meant anything more in his life.

If Corey had pulled the wool over the eyes of Mulcahy and his gang, he had put a blindfold on Braddock and spun him around in a circle. Had he planned the whole thing, all the way down to Braddock getting Langston off his trail, then finding him a safe haven? Hell, Braddock had gone so far as to promise to convince the law Corey was dead so he could escape completely. *Son of a bitch.* All the while, the boy had had the gold. Braddock had made it so damn easy for him. And so Corey could sleep better at night, he'd rushed up Specter Canyon to get himself killed.

Braddock hugged the wall at the canyon's next turn, unconcerned with the pebbles that bounced off the smooth cliff, then fell soundlessly into the depths of the divide. Corey never would have gotten away with tricking Braddock if it weren't for Lorelei. Braddock sucked in his breath through his teeth. He didn't want to believe she was involved, but her intention from the first night she'd come to his hotel room had been clear.

All he had to do was see the look on her face when he returned alive, and he would know the truth. God, he must be a fool, because he wanted to believe her innocent. His sweet Lorelei wouldn't betray him. But he had seen people do worse for less, and Corey had a lot of gold on the line.

Why for a moment did Braddock think he could be like Jay?

The reins slipped in Braddock's hand when Lucky tossed his head, sensing his rider's unease. The sky had lightened to purple, and Braddock had to blink to orient himself. He couldn't recall getting down the canyon or even saddling Lucky. By the lay of the land and the position of the chain of mountains at his back, he had traveled a couple of miles from the canyon's entrance. He was heading back toward Jay's house, moving in the right direction on instinct alone.

Instinct served him better than his common sense. He longed for the time when his mind would go numb and that would be all he operated on. There were no messy feelings or moral dilemmas. He rode, ate, slept, and fornicated, all at his body's urging. Nothing else was involved. His life was about survival, pure and simple.

Braddock picked up Lucky's pace, following that rule of thumb. He wasn't sure when he had last slept, but resting was the farthest thing from his mind. His body tensed as if he were getting ready to ride into battle. And that was just what it would be if he found Corey at Jay's.

He realized he wouldn't. Corey would be long gone. Braddock started scanning the desert floor for tracks. But who did he want to see more, Corey or Lorelei? Braddock didn't like the answer. He wanted to see Lorelei. Something in him still believed in her. Some part of him that hung on like the needles of a cactus still believed she loved him—more than Corey, more than gold.

Lorelei could be believed in. She would probably be devastated to know that Corey had had the gold all this time. There was no way she could be a part of his scheme. Braddock started to breathe a little deeper, a little easier. The sun peeked across the dry horizon, lighting the red sand pink.

He would be at Jay's tomorrow, holding Lorelei, wondering how he could ever think she could betray him.

The trampled sage caught his attention first. He swung from his horse. Two sets of hoofprints led from the direction of Jay's house. He rubbed his eyes and looked again, sure he was overdue for sleep. The tracks were clear. Two sets of riders, and neither knew how to cover their tracks. His heart stopped and he hoped to God it would never beat again.

Chapter Sixteen

Braddock hunkered down and watched Corey from between the manzanita's dense branches. Sullivan sat on the ground, his knees curled to his chest. The smoke drifting over his head told Braddock he had just started a fire. Though the sun still hung high in the sky, he figured brother and sister would prepare an early dinner, then douse the fire once night hit. That was what he would have done if he were on the run.

After another glance around the clearing they had chosen for their camp, Braddock sucked a much-needed breath through his burning lungs. He would be spared Lorelei's presence for his confrontation with Corey. He'd rather face five armed men than one Lorelei Sullivan.

Braddock reholstered his pistol, unbuckled his scarred leather belt, and draped it over the thickest of the manzanita's branches. The sturdy round shrub sagged in the middle but held the gun's weight. Braddock rolled his shoulders and fisted his hands.

The risk involved in facing Corey unarmed was nothing in comparison to the satisfaction he'd gain in beating him with his fists.

Of course, Lorelei could show up cradling a rifle. This time, however, he welcomed it. He needed to witness her aiming a weapon at his heart. Then her betrayal would be brutal fact instead of a hard-to-swallow theory. Not that there was much room for doubt. She'd escaped with Corey the moment the boy left. And he had actually asked her to wait for him.

Prior to that, he hadn't exactly swept her off her feet with his gallant behavior. He'd given her plenty of reason to hate him for himself rather than the fact that he wanted to imprison her brother. Through it all, though, he had always tried to keep her safe. She, on the other hand, had let her brother set him up to die.

Braddock wiped his sweat-soaked palms on his soft wool pants, clenched and unclenched his fists, then closed the distance between himself and Corey at a full run. Corey didn't even have the chance to turn his head to see what barreled toward him. The impact of Braddock's full body weight against Corey's pliant form knocked them both at least a foot. The kid squirmed to get away, but Braddock held him fast with his knees. He reared his fist back and slammed it into Corey's face. The jolt that compacted his knuckles was pure pleasure.

Corey screamed, his lips and teeth smeared with blood. His desperate thrashing unhinged Braddock's grip with his knees, so Braddock grabbed the waist of Corey's pants with both hands to yank him back within reach.

"I know you have the gold, you little bastard."

Corey swung with both hands, squarely knocking Braddock on the side of the head. He heard the clank of metal at the same time stars burst in front of his eyes. He fell onto his right side and struggled to stay conscious. Through the haze of pain, Braddock watched Corey scoot away and awkwardly get to his feet.

Braddock pushed himself up to his hands and knees, desperate to gain his equilibrium. He'd never suspected the kid had such a hard swing. With great effort, Braddock focused his spinning gaze on Corey. Again with both hands, he wiped blood from his mouth. His reach appeared to be jerked short, and he had to lower his head to accomplish his task. Metal rattled again.

"You trying to kill me?"

Braddock staggered to his feet. Anger overrode the ringing ache in his head. "Like you tried to kill me when you sent me up to Specter Canyon. I'm going to see you swing, Sullivan. Your sister, too." Saying the words coated his tongue with the bitter taste of bile. He hadn't planned that far ahead, but he knew that if he wanted to save his soul, he'd have to go through with turning Lorelei over to the law. Get her out of his system once and for all. Treat her the way she deserved to be treated.

"Leave Lorelei out of it. She didn't know about the other entrance."

Braddock stumbled toward Corey. "You should have thought of that before you sent her to be my whore."

"You'd be dead right now if I weren't wearing these." Corey lifted both his hands, and Braddock finally recognized the source of the metallic jangle. Corey wore iron handcuffs. He'd knocked Braddock senseless with the solid steel of the cuffs. Corey's ankles were shackled too.

Braddock blinked. "What the hell?"

"Don't worry, I have some for you, too," said Wade Langston from somewhere behind him.

Braddock spun around, reaching for his guns that weren't there. The quick motion knocked him off balance, but he quickly caught himself.

"Looking for these?" Langston had a pistol in one hand, Braddock's gun belt in the other. "Turn around with your hands behind your back. And your little *wife* isn't around to save you this time, so you better just do it."

Out of habit, Braddock's first concern was for Lorelei. Hopefully she had escaped in the commotion and would head back to Jay's farm. The thought kicked him in the shin. He wanted her caught, didn't he?

The idea of Langston getting his hands on Lorelei disturbed Braddock enough to let Langston shackle his hands behind his back. He told himself it was because he wanted to bring her in himself, but wholly didn't believe it.

He lifted his head and met Corey's confused gaze. *What are you doing?* the boy mouthed silently.

Braddock kept his face expressionless. Having his hands full with both of them would keep Langston too busy to go after Lorelei. And when he was ready, Braddock would sort out exactly why that was so important to him.

Langston turned Braddock around, then directed him to the ground with a firm hand on his shoulder. He carefully secured his feet. Braddock didn't offer an ounce of resistance, though kicking Langston in the nose tempted him.

After Langston guided Corey to sit next to Braddock, he stood back and admired his handiwork. "I never liked you, Braddock, but I hate to see you come to this." He shook his head. "To think you finished West Point with honors. Now I know it was your father's influence that landed you your rank in the army. I came upon your horse first. Looks like he hasn't been properly tended to in days. I better not find Pegasus in that condition or I'm liable to string you up before the law gets a chance."

"I told you, your horse is fine. I took good care of him," pleaded Corey.

Langston waved his hand to dismiss them both. "You both can wait on your dinner while I groom that poor stallion."

"But I'm hungry," Corey called to Wade's back.

Langston wound his way through the overgrown sage and disappeared behind a small hill in the lumpy landscape, ignoring them both.

Corey kicked Braddock's boot. "Why in the hell did you let him capture you? Now we're both screwed."

Braddock strained against his bonds with the urge to have another swing at Corey. "You were screwed anyway. I didn't come to save your ass. I came to see you hang."

"I told Lorelei all you cared about was my bounty. I hope she didn't have to ride all the way to Specter Canyon to figure out you're a lying bastard."

"Quit the bull, kid. I know about the gold. I know what you two were up to."

Corey swallowed. "You didn't meet up with Lorelei before you made it to Specter Canyon?"

Braddock smiled. "Nope. Made it to Specter Canyon. Ricochet sends his regards."

"You don't get it. Lorelei went after you. She went to Specter Canyon."

Braddock studied Corey, looking for the con behind the kid's panicked expression. As painful as it was, Braddock could accept that Lorelei had used him. Her betrayal fit with his worldview better than the fact that she sincerely cared about him. He steeled himself against the thawing burn in his heart. Anything else was romantic nonsense.

Corey jangled the chains attached to his wrists with his attempts to tug himself free. "We have to see if she's still at the ranch. Hopefully Jay told her the idea was stupid."

"Why would she come after me?" As if from far away, Braddock watched Corey squirm around in the dirt. Lorelei hadn't turned against him?

Corey sagged against his bonds when he managed to do nothing but stir up a cloud of dust. "We've got to get out of here before she makes it to the dry creek bed. She won't stop there. I know her."

The idea of Lorelei stumbling into Mulcahy's camp sharpened Braddock's senses. He had no more time for the fuzzy circles his heart and head were spinning in.

"Tell me what you're talking about. Everything. What happened when I left the ranch?"

Corey hesitated. Finally he glanced away, defeated. "I never bought that load about you letting me go. I knew you'd be back to take me in."

"Because you knew you had the gold, and that's what I was really after."

Corey's jaw tightened. "Do you want to hear the story or not? Lorelei could be in a lot of danger because of you."

"I want to hear it." Braddock gritted his teeth against telling Corey who was the cause of all Lorelei's problems.

"I was going to take off the night you left. Lorelei caught me." Corey cast an accusing gaze at Braddock. "I wanted her to come with me, but she wanted to wait for you. I told her it was stupid, that you didn't care about her, but you had her all tied in knots."

Braddock stared at Corey, unblinking. He felt ripped in two, one part wanting desperately to believe Lorelei had given her loyalty to him over her brother, while his rational side warned he was an idiot even to listen. "Go on."

"I told her you weren't coming back. That you'd be killed. And still she wanted to stick around and wait. So she wouldn't waste her time, I told her about the canyon's second entrance."

"The one you forgot to tell me about."

"You deserved it. You had no right to ask Lorelei to wait for you. A real man would have made her his wife as soon as he did her wrong. It's not like I asked you to go to Specter Canyon. You're the one who wanted to go off and get yourself killed. I just made it easier for you."

"Then why the hell did she take off after me?"

"She wanted to warn you. But I told her not to go past the canyon entrance."

Braddock's eyes widened with the full impact of what Corey was telling him. "Why did you tell her how to get there at all?"

Corey's face reddened. "This isn't my fault. It's your fault. Besides, Jay wouldn't have let her go."

Knowing Jay, they had both gone. Braddock tugged hard on the metal clamped around his wrists, tearing open the rope-burn wounds from Specter Canyon. "We've got to get out of here."

"That's what I've been trying to tell you."

Braddock maneuvered himself until his back was facing Corey. He stuck out his wrists. "See if you can get these off."

"I can't. If I could, I would have my own off already. You never should have let him put you in handcuffs."

Braddock inched his way in the dirt in order to turn around. He'd trussed up more people than he could count, but he'd never been bound himself. If he knew how well it worked, he would have slept better when he was bringing in his prisoners. He had to think of something else to get them out of this.

Corey sighed. "She could just be at the ranch."

Braddock couldn't take that chance.

"Langston!"

"What are you going to do?"

"Langston," he yelled again.

Langston stomped over to them, a curry brush in his hand. "What the hell do you want? You're making the horses skittish."

"I've got a deal for you. We'll tell you where to find the gold if you take us to a ranch a few miles from here."

"No, we won't," said Corey before Braddock could finish.

Langston shook his head. "How stupid do you think I am?"

"Mulcahy doesn't have the gold. He does." Braddock gestured to Corey with a jerk of his head.

"Shut up, Braddock. He's too smart for us. Don't get him riled by lying to him," said Corey through gritted teeth.

"You're trying to tell me this half-pint outlaw with peach fuzz still on his face took the gold from Mulcahy? Tell me another one, Braddock. I haven't laughed this hard since West Point, when you and your buddies locked me out in the snow in my long johns."

Braddock inwardly cringed, forgetting the incident until Langston mentioned it, but apparently Langston hadn't. Braddock had to make him want to believe, and he knew how.

"He didn't take the gold on his own. I helped him. I planned the whole thing."

Langston took a few more steps toward them. "I'm listening."

"Picked Sullivan up on horse theft. Saw how I could use him."

"I never stole a horse in my life. Never." Corey protested so dramatically, even Braddock believed him.

Braddock continued, so far into his tale he didn't know or care about the truth anymore. "I hooked him up with Mulcahy and told Corey which stagecoach to hit. His sister showing up was just luck. I held on to her as insurance. I wanted to make sure the kid didn't double-cross me."

"I can't believe this. Not even from you. You're worse than I imagined." But Langston's unblinking fascination told Braddock he did believe the tale, and was enjoying every word of Braddock's downfall.

"We need to get back to the ranch. The kid won't tell me where he stashed the gold until he sees his sister." Braddock laughed, low and evil. "Thinks I did something to her."

"You better hope you didn't, Braddock. I knew from the beginning you were up to no good with that little lady."

"You wanted to take her to jail." Braddock couldn't stop the accusation. Though he intended to paint himself as an evil bastard, he resented Langston looking down his nose at him.

"In the name of the law, not to use her for my own sick scheme." Langston shook his head and the corners of his mouth tugged down in disgust. "Why did you do it? Can't be for the money. Your father has plenty."

Braddock looked him straight in the eye. "I did it because I could."

Langston fell silent for a moment, taking in the depths of Braddock's depravity. "I want a signed confession. I don't want it to be my word against yours, not with your daddy and your war buddies on your side. You won't be able to talk your way out of this one."

Braddock nodded. "You've got it."

"I didn't want to rob anybody, sir. He made me. Make sure he puts that in there."

Braddock cut his gaze to Corey. He looked just like the innocent boy he wasn't. Langston turned to rummage, presumably for paper, in his saddlebag.

Braddock lowered his voice for Corey's ears alone. "You'd better hope Lorelei's at the ranch 'cause if she's not I'm going to find a way to get out of these handcuffs. Now that I'm a wanted man, thanks to you, God knows what I'll do."

Corey lowered his angelic gaze.

Langston scrounged up a wanted poster and a coal pencil.

With his pistol in one hand, he unlocked Braddock's cuffs. He pushed the paper toward him with the toe of his boot.

"Start writing. And don't forget the part about stealing my horse. I want it all in your hand, 'cause no one's going to believe this."

Glad someone had, Braddock concentrated on resurrecting his lost penmanship, taking great care to make his usual scribble legible. Incriminating himself would be worth it if he found Lorelei at the ranch, and if he didn't, it wouldn't matter. He'd still be wanted, but for murder instead of stagecoach robbery. And Wade Langston would be his first victim.

Lorelei dismounted when the wash that had formed their path ended in a solid tangle of spiny catclaw and prickly sweetbush. Ahead, Specter Canyon yawned an invitation. The angle of the afternoon sun painted the rust-colored cliffs a deeper red but spilled cool shadows across the canyon. To Lorelei it looked like an open door. She glanced behind her to check on the state of her companions.

Jay watched her with serious eyes. He slumped in the saddle only slightly, but she'd seen the white lines of pain around his mouth often enough since they had entered the jarring, rocky terrain. Knowing that his pride would be hurt if she asked if he could stay in the saddle any longer was the only thing that held her silent.

Archie gulped water. His shirt was plastered to his thin chest, his pallor greenish. He mopped his brow once he lowered his metal canteen, a signal that he was having another bout.

Lorelei turned toward the canyon and began to pick her way through the brush on foot.

"Lorelei," Jay called her back. "We can't go any farther. I want to be well away from here before it turns dark."

Lorelei tugged at her skirt to free it from a branch. Jay's words hit her like a blow. In a violent yank, she ripped the thick brown wool of her only riding skirt. Frustrated tears stung her eyes as she poked her gloved finger through the hole. She'd let Christopher slip from her grasp like all her other dreams. She couldn't take one more loss, had no strength for any more grief. Though she had known Christopher for just a short time, loving him had used up the last of her hope. She had nothing left. Not even Corey, because she would never forgive him for this.

On wobbly legs that worked despite her desire to crumple, she led her horse to Jay and Archie.

"I'm going on."

Jay shook his head. "No, you're not."

Archie dismounted. "Please, Lorelei, don't even think about going into the canyon."

"It's partially my fault. I told him to believe Corey. Besides, he means everything to me."

Lorelei dropped her gaze to the rock-strew ground. Not partially—entirely her fault. She never should have stopped Christopher from arresting Corey in the first place. But the burning truth in her stomach told her she would do the same thing over again. Her brother would have surely hanged if she had not intervened. That she couldn't let happen. Nor would she let anything harm Christopher.

"He's going to be all right. I've seen Chris in worse scrapes than this, and he always comes out smelling like a rose."

Archie kept his face averted. His silence told her more than his words could. He thought Christopher already dead.

But she was in a desperate mood and would hear the worst. "What do you think, Archie? You know Mulcahy?"

He kicked at the dust with his toe. "Your going up there won't change anything."

Having a plan calmed her. She wasn't going back to the ranch without Christopher. No matter what. She gathered up her horse's reins.

"I still have to try."

Jay sighed. "Then I guess I'll have to go with you."

Archie sighed even louder, as if he exhaled his last breath. "I'll go. They know me. I'll see if he's there, but only if Lorelei stays behind."

"No, Archie, I've got to go."

Archie clamped his bloodless lips together. "I can't protect you. They'll do things to you we'd best not talk about."

Jay nudged his horse forward. "He's right. If Braddock is there, you'll just be a distraction. Archie can go in without suspicions and help him if he needs it."

While Jay spoke, he grabbed Lorelei's horse's bridle. She couldn't leave without breaking his grip. Besides, they were right. "All right," she finally said. "But we'll wait here."

"It's not safe." Jay urged his horse backward and hers forward, forcing Lorelei to relinquish the reins to hold her ground.

"Wait at the farm. I'll find you," said Archie.

"He might be hurt."

"He's not hurt." Jay picked up her horse's reins. "We'll make camp halfway between here and my property line. If Archie and Chris don't find us by noon tomorrow, we'll re-negotiate."

She glanced at Archie. He seemed to strengthen in the face of his mission. He had remounted and edged away from them as he closed the space to the canyon. His clear eyes spoke determination even in the fading light.

"Do you think you can help him, Archie?"

"I don't know, but I'll try."

She didn't like his answer, but she knew he was being honest. She didn't believe in promises anymore anyway.

"Good luck."

He nodded, then turned and rode toward the canyon. She watched until horse and rider disappeared, seemingly swallowed by the wall of solid rock.

She took her horse's reins from Jay and mounted. "Until tomorrow. If Archie doesn't find Christopher, I'm coming back here and I'm going to ride into the canyon."

Jay nodded, then turned his horse in the opposite direction without another word.

Chapter Seventeen

Braddock stretched his leg and winced. He must be getting old. Every joint ached. He rolled his shoulders and shifted again.

"Would you stop squirming? I'm trying to catch up on some sleep," complained Corey.

When Braddock finally settled into a more comfortable position, Corey relaxed against him. How could the kid even think about sleeping? Braddock had to keep moving just to assure himself his limbs still worked.

It was pretty damned clever of Langston to shackle them together. Back to back, handcuffs entwined, they were helpless—and if by some miracle they did escape, Braddock doubted his circulation would return in under an hour. Using a gun would be impossible.

By the position of the sun, Braddock gauged that Langston had been gone nearly half the day, though it felt more like a week. He could have easily reached the ranch and returned by now.

Braddock only hoped he didn't show up with Lorelei in handcuffs. He feared she would dispel his whole concocted story by pulling a rifle on Langston. Again. She was so easy to read.

In light of the situation, all three of them serving jail time seemed only a minor inconvenience. He just hoped she was at the ranch. If she wasn't . . . He couldn't think about that with his hands trussed behind his back.

"Hey, Braddock. What'd you plan to accomplish by having Langston ride out to Jay's while we sit here like stuffed pigs ready for the spit?"

"Shut up, Corey."

"Just checking," the boy said with a grin in his voice.

A metallic jangle followed the soft huff of a horse and alerted Braddock to the approach of a rider. Langston rode up as if in a dream. But it was a dream with sharp edges.

"Well . . ." He dismounted and put his hands on his hips. "She wasn't there."

Corey hissed a curse near Braddock's ear. Braddock forced the fear and desperation that oozed from his pores back inside. He had to stay focused on Langston. He had to think of something to do.

Langston pushed his hat back. "Nice lady at the ranch. She had a bunch of kids. Said her husband took Lorelei to town to catch the stage home." He scratched his forehead. "Can't figure it. So tell me, Braddock, what were you trying to pull over my eyes?"

Braddock stared at Langston while he tried to make sense of his words. He wanted to believe that Lorelei had packed up and went home, but he knew it wasn't true. Beth could charm a rattlesnake out of its hole; she probably had had no trouble convincing Langston of anything she wanted him to believe.

Langston shifted, folded his arms over his chest, and smirked at Braddock. "You might as well come clean instead of staring at me with that big, dumb look on your face. Obviously whatever you had up your sleeve fell out."

"I told him it wouldn't work," Corey spoke up. "He thought if we got you away, his friends would come rescue him."

Langston shook his head but his smirk rose a notch. He was pleased with Corey's answer. "When are you going to realize you're not the favorite anymore, Braddock? This isn't West Point. Daddy's money can't save your butt here."

Braddock's mind churned out a hundred different ways to overpower Langston. Unfortunately none seemed plausible. If only Langston would stop blabbering, Braddock might be able to come up with some options.

"I half expected you to be gone when I got back." Langston snorted, apparently unaware that Braddock wasn't comprehending a word he said. "Looks like your luck has finally run out. That's what happens when you go bad, Braddock. It catches up with you."

"Sir, I want to come clean. I don't want to be like him."

Langston skirted around Braddock to face Corey. "Go on. Let's hear what you have to say, and maybe I can put in a good word for you with the judge."

Corey took a deep breath, then let it out in a long, tortured sigh. "It's true what he said about making me get involved with Mulcahy and the robbery, but I made sure he sent my sister home, so I guess he held to that promise. I wasn't going to tell him where the gold was until I was sure I was in a safe place." Corey lowered his voice. "I was afraid he was going to kill me."

To get a glimpse of Langston's face, Braddock strained until his neck pulsed with tension. Langston's wide eyes and half-open mouth showed his total absorption in Corey's tale.

"You were right to be afraid, son. Go on."

"I'll tell you were the gold is. I don't want to carry this burden any longer. I'll have to take you there, because the place is hard to find."

Braddock closed his eyes. Corey had a plan. A damn good one.

"It's east of here, in a narrow canyon."

"Specter Canyon?" Langston's voice hovered above them. He had straightened.

"That's it," said Corey with too much enthusiasm.

Langston strolled around them to tower over Braddock

again. "And you got some real nice fellas keeping an eye on that gold for you. You two must take me for a real fool."

"I'm warning you, Langston. Let us go." Once Braddock finally found his voice, it was deadly calm. He'd have to kill Langston. Braddock didn't like the idea, but it wasn't going to stop him. There was no other way.

"It wouldn't do you any good if I did. You won't find refuge at Specter Canyon. A posse's headed that way. Your friend Douglas is in charge, no less. Can't wait to see the look on your old friend's face when I hand you over like a trussed calf."

"When will they reach the canyon?"

"Day or so." Langston smiled.

Braddock's breath of hope turned to lead as it soured and settled into the pit of his stomach. That wasn't soon enough for Lorelei.

"You can beat them and get the gold first," encouraged Corey.

"I'm no outlaw. I have respect for the law, unlike some people."

Braddock squinted as he looked up into the midafternoon sun that loomed over Langston's head. "Might get you that permanent marshal's job you're after."

Langston knelt between them and unlocked Corey's handcuffs, then pulled him to his feet.

"I'm just glad to serve my country. I don't need a fancy title or fame like you had, Braddock. I'm not trying to be a hero."

The deputy held his gun on Corey while the kid mounted the pinto at his urging. Once Corey was settled, Langston handcuffed his hands in front of him. Langston would have to unshackle Braddock long enough for him to mount, and that was all the help Braddock needed.

With one eye on his captives, Langston crept to his horse. He holstered his pistol, then unstrapped his rifle from his saddle. He braced the weapon's butt against his shoulder, taking careful aim directly at Braddock's head. For a moment Braddock thought Langston would shoot him right there and then. Luckily he felt only anger, no fear. His old self was seeping back. Langston was going to die, not him.

"I'll blow your head off if you even think of trying anything funny." With his finger still on the trigger, Langston tossed Braddock the key to the handcuffs. It landed with a soft puff of dust near his bound feet. Using both hands, Langston quickly reaimed the rifle.

Braddock stared at the key. "What am I supposed to do with that?"

"Unlock yourself."

"My hands are behind my back."

"Then I guess you're going to rot out here."

Braddock tried to melt Langston's determination with a serious glare, but the man was smarter and tougher than Braddock suspected. Finally he had no choice but to scoot around in the dirt and start the tedious process of freeing himself like a sideshow magician. His hands were already numb, making him drop the key more times than he could count. The image of strangling Langston urged him to paw through the dust until his fingers found metal. He steered his thoughts away from Lorelei. Fear for her made the intricate task impossible.

After what seemed like an hour, Braddock heard the lock click open. He flexed his fists and rubbed his arms. His circulation returned in needle-laced waves.

"That's enough. Unlock your ankles and get on the horse. Now."

Braddock leaned forward. Shards of pain shot through his arms but he barely noticed. Numbing instinct took over. His muscles bunched, ready to spring at Langston.

Before the hinge on the ankle shackles had time to fall open, Braddock pulled his legs under him and pushed off with his feet. His shoulder hit Langston in the knees. The rifle fired as Langston fell backward. Braddock didn't stop to consider if he had been hit by the stray shot. He tightened his grip on Langston's waist with no intention of letting go.

Langston squirmed, his arm outstretched for the fallen rifle. Braddock pinned Langston with his weight while he curled a fist in Langston's leather vest and yanked him away from the weapon. The pistols strapped to Langston's waist dug into Braddock's thighs, reminding him of their presence. As if Langston read his mind, he flopped and bucked for his life, forcing Braddock to hold on to him with both hands.

A large rock embedded in the sand a little to the right of Langston's head caught Braddock's attention. With a strength he didn't even know he possessed, Braddock crawled on his knees, dragging a writhing Langston across the dirt. Braddock positioned his old schoolmate's head over the rock. One hard knock would leave him unconscious; two or three would kill him.

When Langston realized Braddock intended to crush his skull, he fought with renewed strength. He wedged the base of his palm under Braddock's chin and pushed hard enough to force Braddock to loosen his grip or have his neck snapped. Langston flopped away, but Braddock yanked him back before he could crawl to the fallen rifle. Braddock flipped him over and punched him as hard as he could in the nose.

Langston went limp, making dragging him back to the rock a much simpler task.

"What are you doing?" called Corey from someplace far away. "Get the gun."

With his fists securely wrapped in Langston's vest, Braddock pulled Langston's upper body off the ground. The man's head fell back weakly. With no resistance to meet the rock, Langston would be harder to kill, but Braddock would make do.

"Stop it, you crazy son of a bitch. You're going to kill him," cried Corey.

"Shut up." Braddock couldn't think with all this screaming.

Apparently roused by the yelling, Langston wrapped a hand around the back of Braddock's neck.

Braddock easily disengaged his grip. "Sorry, Langston, but you're going to have to die. Since you won't—"

"You're not a killer."

Braddock paused. But he *was* a killer. Ever since the war he was a killer. Better to be honest about it than be called a hero.

He repositioned Langston, ready to slam his head against the rock, when the sound of galloping horses interrupted his momentum. Then he heard his name echoing in his mind. He knew his imagination tried to trick him because the voice belonged to Lorelei.

"Lori," yelled Corey. "Over here!"

Braddock froze, fearing that if he moved the dream would fade. In a cloud of dust, Lorelei barreled into the clearing, closely followed by Jay. Braddock watched her slide off her horse, then run to his side. She dropped to her knees and gently touched his shoulder. She glanced down at Langston, then back up to him.

"Let go of him," she said softly.

He glanced at Langston, whose face was swollen. Blood flowed steadily from the man's nose, soaking his shirt and dripping across Braddock's fists. Gently, as if he hadn't been the one about to bash Langston's head, Braddock laid him down so his head was cradled in the soft sand.

When he straightened, Lorelei vaulted into his arms.

He lowered his head, taking in her scent. Dreams didn't smell, and if he could smell her she must be real.

"I thought you were in Specter Canyon." His voice sounded strange to him, as if he had swallowed sand.

"I wanted to, but Jay wouldn't let me. I was so worried for you."

He crushed her to him. "I'm never letting you go again."

And he meant it. He wasn't going to fight it anymore. It was too late to escape.

Braddock watched Lorelei wipe Langston's blood off her hands with the hem of her tattered brown skirt. He wanted to look away, but he wouldn't let himself.

Jay laughed, and Braddock tore his gaze away long enough to see Corey stuff a whole biscuit in his mouth. How could he eat? Braddock's stomach had knotted itself up, but then again, Corey didn't almost kill a man with his bare hands.

Braddock returned his gaze to Langston. He leaned his head back, his face obscured by a wadded bandanna. Lorelei touched the back of his head and said something in a voice too low for him to hear.

"Lorelei, get over here," Braddock said too harshly.

Langston removed the blood-soaked bandanna from his face and glared. "You better do what he says. I don't want you getting hurt."

She laughed.

"Now," he said, cutting her off. He turned and walked away before she had time to argue. He needed to keep her from talking to Langston.

He stopped several yards away. A stunted pinyon bent over by the wind provided a place where they could speak privately. The gnarled tree reached no taller than his chin but would block Lorelei from Langston's view. If he thought she had something to fear from him, the more the better.

She caught up a few steps behind him. "You're angry."

He was sloshing through a dozen different emotions—relief to find her safe, disgust with his actions, fear of serious jail time—but curiously, anger wasn't present.

"I was sick when I found out what Corey did. I would have given my own life to save yours."

He gripped her shoulders and shook her. "Don't ever say that again."

Her eyes widened in shock; then tears blurred their shiny blue luster. "Please understand. Corey's my brother, but I wouldn't have let him lie to you. You believe that, don't you?"

He loosened his pinching grip and urged her more directly behind the hunched tree. Langston was watching their exchange with keen interest.

"I almost killed him, you know."

She jerked out of his grasp. "Corey?"

"No. Langston." He watched her cheeks redden, and she studied the ground instead of him. That her first thought was for her brother no longer surprised him. She could no more stop loving and protecting him than she could change the color of her eyes.

"You have every right to want to see him punished." She sighed. "I do understand."

He lifted her chin. "Lorelei, I'm in as much trouble as Corey right now. More. I almost killed a deputy marshal."

She shook her head.

"Yes. I was crazy with worry for you. I had to find you even if that meant killing Langston."

She touched his arm. "But you stopped."

"Because you showed up."

She briefly pressed her palm against her eyes as if trying to make the trouble they were in vanish. "What happened? Did you meet up with Archie?"

"I made it to Specter Canyon." He stopped himself. He couldn't tell her about the gold or anything else that had happened up there. The less she knew the safer she'd be. "Did Archie take off with Corey?"

She shook her head and clasped her hands together in a worried fist. "He went looking for you to keep me from going into the canyon. He should have been back by now."

He gripped her shoulders to calm her down. The furrowing of her brow warned that she was concocting another rescue scheme. "Archie can take care of himself," he said.

In fact, Braddock suspected Archie got one whiff of booze and went back to leading the life he had led before they found him—but that was just one more fact he'd have to keep from Lorelei. If Braddock had his way—and he planned to—she'd saved her last wounded dog.

"Langston's our biggest problem right now. When I found out that Corey tricked me I came looking for him, but I didn't expect Langston to have found him first. His nose is probably broken, and he's not going to forget how it happened."

"Now you're in even more trouble because of us. What are we going to do?"

Braddock let his breath out. If he only knew. He slid his hands down Lorelei's arms. They were too thin. He stopped at her hands, then turned her palms up as if he could read their future there.

He didn't like what he saw. The fine lines of her hands were encrusted with dried blood. He closed his eyes. If he loved her, truly loved her, he would get her as far away from here as possible.

He opened his eyes and forced himself to meet her soft gaze.

"*We* are not going to do anything. You should be out of the territory while—"

She jerked her hands from his. "You're not sending me away."

"Look, your brother is in more trouble than you know."

"And so are you, which you wouldn't be in if it weren't for me. I'm not going anywhere."

He gently gripped her shoulders. "Sweetheart—"

"No, Christopher."

"I can't marry you until I get this cleared up. I don't want you arrested."

"Marry? Did you say marry?"

"Uh." Spoken out loud, the proposition sounded bizarre, like volunteering to swallow live crickets. His stomach clenched, but he had crossed a line that he felt forced to step over. "I guess so."

"You guess so? You either want to marry me or you don't."

"Will you listen to me then?"

In answer to his question, she kissed him hard on the mouth.

He kissed her back, easily melting against the soft curves of her body, drinking in the taste of her. Not caring that it was completely inappropriate, his blood rushed to bring him to full arousal. After he'd almost lost her in a thousand different ways, the solid sensation of having her in his arms proved too enticing to resist. He cupped her bottom, urging her hips to melt into his. If he had a little more privacy, he'd be sorely tempted to take her here on the dusty ground, quick and fast. An urgent coupling to burn away the remnants of their separation.

He slid his hand across her rib cage to cup her breast. Her nipple strained through the worn fabric of her shirt. When he flicked his thumb across the awakened tip, her soft intake of breath shot down the length of his erection. What the hell was he doing?

He pulled his mouth away from hers and made instant eye contact with Langston's seething glare. Luckily their angle blocked him from Jay and Corey; and hopefully, blocked them from him.

"You're going back east until this is settled." Not only would sending her away keep her safe, but it would keep his head clear.

"Absolutely not."

"Lorelei—"

"What are you going to do?"

He dropped his hands from her, his arousal doused at the reality of their situation. "To begin with, your brother is a problem."

"I know."

"I don't know if I can keep him from jail."

"But he won't hang?"

Braddock couldn't look away from her blue stare. With the clarity of seeing Jay lying in mud created by his own blood, he saw Corey's limp body hanging from a rope and understood what that would do to Lorelei.

He pulled her against him. "I won't let anything happen to your brother."

"I don't have a right to ask you to help him. He doesn't deserve it."

"We can't help who we love." He understood what that meant for the first time. "He's your brother and you're going to be my wife. I'll make it right for all of us."

Braddock gazed over the top of her head at Langston and wondered if an ounce of those harsh stories he told about himself were true. To make things right, he'd have to keep Langston quiet any way he could.

* * *

Lorelei pried her bleary eyes open at the persistent shaking of her shoulder. Before she could draw breath, a hand slid across her mouth. In the same instant she was scooped from the bed she shared with Alice and Rachel as silently as a calm breeze. The girls didn't even shift their sleeping positions at the disturbance.

Instantly she knew Christopher's touch. Excitement curled in the apex of her thighs at the mere brush of his skin. He eased his hand from her mouth and wrapped his arm underneath her knees as he hauled her against his bare chest.

"Shh," He half whispered, half nuzzled into her ear as he carried her from the room on bare feet.

The moment they ducked into the boys' room, he closed the door behind them and slid her down the length of his body.

Before she could voice a halfhearted protest at being abducted from her bed, he gathered her against him by fisting his hands in her white cotton nightgown. As his mouth slanted over hers, he yanked the gown to her waist and sank his hands into her fleshy backside. He worked wicked magic with a thrust of his tongue while he kneaded her with powerful determination.

His arousal burned through his carelessly buttoned trousers. He dipped his knees and pulled her closer as he fiercely raked himself against her.

Panting for breath, he tore his mouth away from hers. "Why didn't you come to me?"

She had to grasp his taut upper arms to stay on her feet. "You said you wanted to get a couple of hours' sleep before you left to find the posse."

He covered her neck with wet, openmouthed kisses. "That meant that I wanted to take you to bed. Didn't you see me look at you when I said it? I've been lying awake in petrified agony waiting for you."

His words tempted her to touch him to see for herself. She slipped her hand inside his partially unbuttoned waistband. As soon as her fingers closed around him, he thrust into her hand. Warm liquid coated the head on his second push.

"You're starting without me," she teased, then kissed the center of his chest.

"Sweetheart, my mind's already made love to you five times in the last hour. My body has some serious catching up to do."

He lifted her and she wrapped her legs around his waist. With two long strides he erased the space to the bed, then whirled around to land on his back with her straddling him. He yanked at the buttons of her nightgown, tearing the flimsy cotton in the process. The same urgency had her attacking the fastenings of his trousers. She lifted her hips and he guided his length inside her. He grasped her bottom and arched off the bed while she came down on a long sigh.

They ground into each other, their movements slight. The sheer heat of him, filling her in a way he hadn't before, left her lightheaded. She gripped his shoulders and hung her head, her hair spilling across his chest and leaving her in a hazy, ecstasy-filled world of her own making.

He dug his fingers into her hips, pulling her down as he surged up, though there was no more room to maneuver.

"Lorelei, you feel so damned good."

His husky voice drifted around her. Even his slight movement sent unbearable pleasure cascading through her. She gasped for breath, sure she was floating above herself in a whirl of heady lust too powerful to contain.

He rocked beneath her, and she could do little more than hang on. Her climax descended on her like a thunderclap, ear-ringing and powerful. She tossed her head, shaking her hair away from her face to gasp for breath.

Christopher murmured her name in deep, reverberating waves. She knew only the rapture of her own body, unable to discern anything but his hard flesh clamped in the center of her inwardly spiraling pleasure.

When the stars that clouded her vision started to fade, she cupped his rough cheek, feeling a little guilty for getting so carried away. He muffled an angry curse, gripped her by the hips, and lifted her off him. He groaned deathly low in his throat. Hot liquid spewed between them, splattering her and dousing the hair of his chest.

Her fog of pleasure conceded to the sharp clarity that he chose not to risk creating a child. They hadn't spoken of children, but that was what marriage meant, didn't it?

He laid his head on the bed, his eyes closed. His chest rose and fell raggedly.

She stared at him, the man she would marry, and suddenly she was unsure of herself and him. The idea of being a wife to a man she desperately loved had thrilled her like a dream come true. But theirs was no ordinary relationship, and Christopher no ordinary man.

He lazily opened his eyes. "Christ, you came so hard you about took my head off." His satisfied grin turned down at the corners. "What's wrong?"

Instead of blurting out her fears, something she instinctively knew would change the mood irrevocably, she softened her stance. She toyed with the soft smattered hair in the center of his chest.

"Why did you pull out? I didn't like it."

He gripped her wrist and brought her hand to his mouth to kiss her knuckles. "I hated it."

"Then why?" She bit her lip to keep her question inside her head, but her tongue pushed against her teeth anyway. "Don't you want children?"

He stiffened beneath her and let out his breath. "I don't know."

He must have seen the look of sheer horror on her face.

"I mean, can't we get married first?"

It was hard to become indignant with your legs spread across a man's hips, but she managed. "I want children, Christopher. Surely that's no surprise."

He tugged at her wrist and rolled her over so he lay on top of her, taking control physically, apparently the only way he felt comfortable.

"I want to give you everything you want. Including children. But I have to straighten things out first."

She relaxed beneath him, somewhat mollified by his answer, but not completely.

"You're not going to get bossy and try to run the show again, are you?"

He smiled and tweaked her nose. "Yes. That's what a husband gets to do."

She slid her hands around his waist and cupped his lean flanks beneath his hastily opened trousers. "Not my husband. I want to be in charge sometimes."

He sucked air through his teeth. "I like the sound of that." He was already stirring back to life against her thigh. "I'm your humble servant, ma'am."

She pressed her leg against him. "This time don't pull out."

He pulled away from her, bracing his weight on his hands and knees. "Lorelei. Be reasonable."

Oh, but she didn't like the ring of his words. He only thought her unreasonable because she wasn't giving in to his demands. "We'll be married before I even start to show."

"I'm not some prize stud."

She nipped at his braced arm. "I disagree."

He laughed low in his throat, gathered her up in his arms, and kissed her long and hard on the mouth. "You tempt me, woman, but let me do what I have to. I don't want to have to worry about you carrying our child until I can devote my full attention to it."

She traced his cheek and saw the earnestness in his eyes. She suddenly felt guilty for demanding so much of him when the problems he faced were created by her and her brother. "I'm a lot of trouble, huh?"

"You're worth it."

"So you think the marshal will listen to you over his deputy?"

He nibbled her shoulder. "I think so. Let's change the subject. Tell me a place I haven't kissed you yet."

She squirmed beneath him, enjoying the attention but also realizing he was purposely covert. "What are you not telling me?"

He lifted his head and looked at her seriously. "The less

you know, the better. I don't know exactly how it's all going to work out, but you have to trust me."

"I do," she said, shocked that he would insinuate she didn't. "Haven't I trusted you from the beginning?" She stopped herself, glad it was too dark for him to see her gaze falter. "With only a couple of exceptions."

"Those exceptions are what's got me worried."

"On the way back I promised you I was going to stay here with Jay no matter what, and I intend to keep that promise."

"Good. Because if you run off, Jay will come too. I need you both to keep an eye out for each other. I don't want Jay and his family to be dragged into this any more than I want you to get into trouble with the law. I'm going to have trouble enough keeping your brother and myself from swinging."

"Don't say that." She kept the tears from her eyes, but obviously not the anguish from her voice.

He gently kissed her forehead. "It would kill me if you had to face prosecution. Promise me you won't say a word about our relationship to anyone who might come around here asking questions."

"We're going to be married. I'm not going to keep that a secret."

He squeezed her shoulders roughly. "You have to, or it could look bad for you if I can't clear my name."

"No, Christopher." A cold, familiar fear snaked up her spine. Berkley had forced her to keep their marriage plans a secret until he could fix things. Only later did she realize that that was because he had no intention of marrying her at all.

"Promise me, Lorelei. You'll do nothing but stay on this farm and act the innocent bystander that you are."

She hesitated. This was nothing like with Berkley. She and her brother had dragged Christopher into this situation. All he was doing was trying to arrange it so they could all live happily ever after. Of course, she knew that happily ever after didn't really happen, but she felt like she was close . . . so close.

She lifted her head and tagged him with a kiss on the mouth. "I promise."

He relaxed against her. "Good. Now be quiet so I can spend my last hour making love to you."

She let him kiss away any objections. She wanted to remind him that he'd have the rest of his life to make love to her, but she didn't want to jinx them.

Chapter Eighteen

The encroaching dawn turned the desert light blue. Rocks and cactus lost their menacing shapes. Shadows transformed from hidden threats to ordinary scenery. Braddock shifted in his saddle, relieved and distraught at the same thought: he couldn't kill Langston in cold blood. Hell, he didn't even think he could kill him in a fair fight.

Knowing that Lorelei lay wrapped in a warm bed still sated from their parting melted the desperate fury that, less than twenty-four hours ago, had urged him to bash Langston's head against a rock. A patch of crisp air left over from the frosty night curled around Braddock like a choking vine. Braddock shivered and pulled the thin coat he should have exchanged for his sheepskin jacket tighter around him. Cold, tired, and hungry, he didn't feel like half the badass he'd once thought he was.

Looking for a reason to turn back, Braddock studied Langston and Corey. Corey's head was down, watching the clip-clop of the horse's hooves in front of him. He looked asleep in the saddle. Langston, on the other hand, was wide-awake, glaring poisoned arrows at Braddock.

Unfortunately, killing Langston would be wrong. Taking an innocent man's life went against everything Braddock had been taught and—damn his honorable soul—everything he still believed in. After all the men he had killed, after all the men who had tried to kill him, how Braddock could still feel honor played a part in this world was beyond him. But like it or not, Christopher Braddock was an honorable man. At his ripe old age, he'd better just accept that about himself and get on with it.

Braddock slowed his mount to walk beside Langston's. "Won't be long until we pick up the posse's trail."

Langston stared straight ahead, his chin raised. "Won't be soon enough for me."

The skin under both Langston's eyes had started to blacken. His nose swelled a painful shade of purple. Braddock scoured the horizon. He couldn't exactly blame Langston for wanting a piece of his hide.

"Do you really think Douglas is going to believe I'm an outlaw? Especially when I'm riding out to meet the posse?"

"I have your signed confession."

Braddock shrugged. "No one will believe it. I wanted you to believe I was on the wrong side. I was trying to get in with the gang so I could find the gold."

"You planned it. You said you did."

"I was worried about Lorelei Sullivan. I would have said anything to find her."

Langston brought his horse to a halt, and Braddock was forced to look at him.

"Why couldn't you just tell me that? I never wanted to see an innocent woman dragged into this."

Braddock raised an eyebrow. "That's why you held her at gunpoint in her nightgown?"

"I was just doing my job." Langston slumped slightly in his saddle, giving Braddock hope that he was getting to him.

"You know, Langston, this is your chance to get on Douglas's good side. We'll tell him you tracked down Sullivan. The kid was scared and wanted to help you get Mulcahy. I was tracking Sullivan too, and when I caught up with you, you let me come along."

Langston clamped his lips together. "You broke the law."

"None that anyone's going to pay any attention to. Especially not out here in New Mexico territory. All they want are gangs like Mulcahy's wiped out and the railroad's gold back. And we'll give them both. Right, Corey?"

Corey had stilled his mount and watched them like a dazed spectator. The dark smudges under his eyes emphasized the pale smoothness of his skin. Braddock doubted if the kid was even eighteen. "You're the boss, Braddock. Lorelei said so."

Braddock unlocked Langston's handcuffs. "Do yourself a favor. Don't fight me on this. You can't win. You want to be a hero, maybe even become a U.S. marshal? Stick with my story. The truth isn't going to do anyone any good."

Langston rubbed his wrists. "You're not fooling me, Braddock. You might think you're above the law, but you're not. And you're not going to do any good by that woman. A leopard doesn't change its spots."

A flash of fury surged through Braddock's limbs. He snaked out his arm and gripped Langston's vest. A told-you-so smile curled Langston's thin lips.

Braddock released him and scanned the horizon one more time. The landscape blurred in chunks of gray-green shrubbery and miles and miles of dirt. A hot blue sky burned out the last inch of night, then stretched over them in unrelenting dominance—and the sun hadn't even made a full appearance yet. Braddock tugged his hat brim over his face, wishing the day could as effectively whisk away the dark shadows in his heart. He could be good for Lorelei. He wanted to be good for her. Sure as hell more than he wanted to ride back up to Specter Canyon.

A plume of smoke rose above a distant clump of brush. It was too late to turn back. He nodded to the gray streak across the cerulean backdrop. "It's the posse. If we ride hard, we might be able to catch up to them before they finish their breakfast. Are you with me, Langston?"

Instead of answering his question, Langston slapped his reins against his horse's hide and took off toward the column of smoke.

"I hope that's the posse and not Apaches," yelled Braddock at his back.

Langston slowed his mount. Braddock rode ahead, knowing that at least for the time being, Wade Langston was at his mercy. But for how long was a real question.

Braddock hung back while members of the posse crept through Mulcahy's abandoned hideout. The place was a ghost town. Literally. Perhaps a few of the outlaws that hadn't been wounded in the bungled robbery had moved on, but before they had, they'd slaughtered the ones they left behind. Considering the state of things on his last visit, Braddock wasn't too surprised. Though that and the culprits' obvious desertion didn't stop the sensation of danger crawling over the back of his neck.

Douglas kept his rifle poised to fire as he nudged the leg of one of the several lifeless bodies sprawled in the trampled dirt. "Jesus, looks more like an execution than a fight. What kind of animals would do this to their own men?"

Despite the gore surrounding them, others in the posse had let their weapons go slack. Langston moved cautiously to the side, fanning out to the perimeter of the camp as Douglas had instructed. Braddock couldn't afford to speculate on the answer to the marshal's question. He kept his finger on the trigger of his gun, waiting—for what he didn't know.

He glanced to where Corey stood with the horses. Without a weapon, the boy presented an easy target. For once he did as he was told and stayed back. His gaze darted from the dark opening of a tent to a thatch of giant sage that caught a lone breeze. Fear shone on his pale face. He didn't want to be up here, but he'd given little argument when Douglas had told them the plan.

When Braddock, Corey and Langston had caught up with Douglas and the posse of twenty-odd men, Douglas hadn't seemed to give a damn about how they arrived or where they'd been. He was just glad Braddock was there. And he was downright thrilled to have someone who had ridden with the gang to fill them in on the layout of Mulcahy's refuge.

Of course, Langston hadn't said more than a few words. He'd almost swallowed his tongue when Douglas had jumped down from his horse and embraced Braddock. Though Braddock hadn't seen Douglas more than a handful of times in the last ten years, his college friend didn't seem to hold it against him.

The last time he and Douglas had exchanged more than a few brief words had been the night after their graduation from West Point. A group of them had laid bets on who could get the drunkest and remain standing. He and Douglas had tied. And, like that night, now only he and Douglas were still standing. All the others from their class had been killed in the war.

He moved into the camp. After finding its only occupant shot through the head, Braddock let a tent flap fall back into place. He didn't want to know who would finally win this contest and stay on his feet the longest, he or Douglas. A few of the dead men littering the compound cradled weapons in their stiff hands; some were surrounded by empty bottles of liquor.

Braddock rolled a man over to find a bullet hole clean through the throat. Another man's shirtfront was thick with blood. Braddock removed the dusty hat that fell across the man's eyes to study the bearded face. As he examined the frozen features of the fourth corpse, he realized he was looking for someone besides Archie. He picked his way to another group of fallen men. He flipped one over and discovered the man was lying on a pile of cards. None of the four in this group had guns. It looked like they'd been playing cards when someone shot them all to hell. It wasn't hard to guess who could do something like that.

Braddock turned abruptly. The old familiar instinct for survival had just given him a hard shove. Douglas brushed back an old blanket that had been used for a door on a dilapidated shack.

"Get back," yelled Braddock.

Douglas's quick reflexes had him flattened against the planked wall before the cloth fell back into place.

Braddock counted every breath as he watched the moth-eaten wool sway with each slight breeze. A rifle's nose peeked around the Union-blue blanket before Mulcahy stepped out. Against the pale full moon of his face, his mouth and red hair stood out like paint. He looked more dead than alive, except for the rifles he held with each hand, their butts braced against his side. He started firing at anything that moved.

One of Douglas's men yelped and rolled away.

"Hold your fire!" yelled Douglas above the roar of his posse's return fire, though no one seemed to hear.

Braddock had already hit Mulcahy's bad shoulder, and someone else's shot had grazed his neck, yet still the outlaw stood. That was, until Douglas eased up behind him and hit him on the back of the head with the butt of his rifle. Mulcahy toppled face-forward.

Douglas kneeled to turn the man over. "Shit. I wanted him alive."

Braddock sprinted to Mulcahy's shack with more urgency than caution. He ripped the blanket from the doorway, then stepped in with both pistols cocked. The room was empty. An overturned chair and a cot covered in tangled blankets served as the room's furnishings. Empty whiskey bottles littered the floor, but the liquor's strong scent couldn't overpower the stench of death.

In need of fresh air, Braddock abandoned the dank enclosure. Several men crowded around Douglas and Mulcahy. Braddock shouldered his way past.

Douglas slapped Mulcahy on the cheek. "Where's the gold?"

Miraculously, Mulcahy's features tightened in response.

Douglas laid his ear against Mulcahy's chest. "Somebody get me some water."

Corey squeezed through the circle of men. "Is he dead?"

At the sound of Corey's voice, Mulcahy's eyes struggled open. "Sullivan, you little son of a . . ."

Mulcahy's voice was weak, but the hatred forcing him to speak was strong. Corey backed away.

Douglas motioned Corey forward. "Get over here, Sullivan. Talk to him."

One of the men pulled Corey forward by the collar. Corey jerked away, but had no choice but to stand awkwardly over Mulcahy.

Braddock laid a firm grip on Corey's shoulder. If Mulcahy accused Corey of having the gold, Braddock's plans would be ruined. Why didn't that bastard Mulcahy die?

Mulcahy obviously struggled to keep his weighted eyelids from closing. "Somebody's after you, you little traitor. He's gonna skin you alive."

Douglas turned Mulcahy's head toward him. "Where's the gold?"

Mulcahy spit in the marshal's face, forcing Douglas to jump to his feet cursing. Braddock quickly took the opening at Mulcahy's side and knelt to block the others' view. Mulcahy was going to die even if he had to wring his neck. But first he needed to know something that was a hell of a lot more important than the location of the gold.

"Where's Ricochet?"

Mulcahy had lost the strength to turn his head, but he strained to gaze in Braddock's direction. He grinned a lopsided sneer. "Captain Braddock. I 'member you now. You like the presents I left you in that field?"

"You like the idea of being propped up outside the Santa Fe courthouse? That's what we're going to do with you. All the folks will want to make sure they get a picture with you and all your bullet wounds."

Douglas grabbed a handful of Braddock's shirt and tried to yank him away. "Not if you tell us about the gold. You tell us about the gold, and we'll give you a proper burial. A Christian one."

Mulcahy's eyes drifted closed, but a smile still curled his

pale lips. "We know all about you, Braddock . . . and . . . the sister."

Braddock bolted to his feet and sprinted to his horse before Douglas could call him back. He suddenly knew what the tickling at the back of his neck meant. Someone was going to die, and, as usual, it wasn't going to be him.

Chapter Nineteen

Lorelei stepped into the wash of late-morning sunshine, only slightly surprised by the return of the heat. Last night the cold had crept through the walls, forcing her to sleep with an extra quilt, but the days remained hotter than ever. She doubted she'd ever get used to the extremes of the West. Never had she been so happy or so afraid. Jay had tried to reassure her, but she couldn't shake the feeling she might never see Christopher again.

She strode to the well, swinging a wooden pail and convincing herself she was being silly. She didn't have time to waste worrying about things that might never happen. The breakfast dishes needed to be cleared, and if she didn't start supper soon, she wouldn't have the bread baked by the time Jay and the kids returned from the field. Beth's nap with little Rachel would be her last, and the woman would be working until her baby dropped if Lorelei couldn't prove she could at least handle the meals on her own.

Lorelei hung the bucket under the spout and primed the pump. After the fifth hard crank, she had to stop and wipe away the perspiration that threatened to drip into her eyes.

How did Beth do it on her own? Lorelei would be lucky to have supper on the table, and that was without a baby tugging on her apron strings or a pile of mending to finish!

Lorelei attacked the pump again with a smile. She couldn't think of anything that would make her happier than caring for her own family. After several more pumps, a stream of water splashed into the bucket.

The clean and pure gurgle spat sunlight as it cascaded forth. Lorelei laughed at the sheer pleasure of the sound. She stuck her fingers in the stream and patted her face with the icy wetness. Everything would be fine. How could it not be?

She heard her name on the wind, but she was so lost in the moment, she didn't react until she heard the call a second time. When she turned, she found Archie standing at the edge of the barn. A prayer had been instantly answered. Everything was going to be all right. She picked up her skirts and ran toward Archie, but at her sudden burst of motion, he disappeared around the barn's side.

"Archie!" She slowed her pace. "What's wrong?"

He peeked his head around the corner. "Shh. Come here." With a limp flap of his hand, he waved her over, but the motion sent him stumbling back a step before he could right himself.

The realization that Archie was falling-down drunk hit her at the same time as the stench of liquor.

She stepped around the side of the barn, and instantly forgave him his lapse. His face was swollen with purple bruises, his lip split. His dirty and rumpled clothes attested to the fact that he'd been dragged through hell. She couldn't blame him for falling off the wagon. By the looks of him, he'd been shoved off. And she had had a hand in giving him that shove. If it weren't for her, he'd never have had to return to Specter Canyon.

She reached for his chin, intending to angle his head for a better a look at the damage. A bleeding cut above his right eye looked like it might need stitches.

Archie jerked away. "I'm sorry you had to see me like this. I'm just plain sorry," he said, his voice breaking.

"No." The awful thought was there before she could stamp it out. "Please don't tell me something has happened to Christopher."

He tilted his head, his face almost comical in his drunken confusion. "Who's Christopher?"

She placed her hand on her chest and tried to cushion the pounding of her heart, unable to find anything amusing under the circumstances.

"Christopher Braddock. The man I was with when we met. He and Corey joined the posse heading for Specter Canyon. Didn't they rescue you?"

Archie snorted. "Do I look rescued?"

Lorelei searched him with her gaze. She wanted to shake him, but communicating with him in his condition was useless. Instead she scoured the compound, looking for the others, or any clue as to how Archie got there.

She turned to go back to the house, but Archie grabbed her arm to stop her. "Whoa, don't go anywhere. I don't want the others to hear you."

Her eyes widened at the force he used to restrain her. His grip hurt. She shook him off and he released her, shamefaced.

He lowered his gaze to the ground. "I'm sorry, Miss Lori. I don't want anyone else to see me like this." He rubbed his forehead. "I didn't see that man of yours or the Sullivan kid."

Despite the fact that he swayed on his feet, he suddenly sounded reasonably sober.

"How did you get away from Mulcahy? We worried when you didn't come back sooner."

His complexion paled under his bruises. "I need a drink." He grabbed her arm, yanking her behind him as he walked away from the house. "You've got to come with me down to the spring. You know, the one you took me to that day."

She planted her feet and tugged against his force. "I don't think so, Archie."

Instead of the battle for strength she expected, she stumbled when he released her abruptly.

"Please, Miss Lori. I don't want those kids to get involved. I don't want them to see me like this. You have to take me to that spring like you did before and clean me up."

At least she agreed with that. The only way she'd pry any coherent information from him was to sober him up. "Let's go back to the house and get you something to eat. That will clear your head faster than anything."

"No, no, no." He shook his head. "I don't want that pregnant lady to get hurt. You have to come with me. They can't see me."

Lorelei glanced back at the house, looking for divine intervention in the form of Jay and the kids returning early from the field. When that didn't happen, she resigned herself to the situation. She knew from her father's binges that there would be no reasoning with him until he sobered.

"All right." She hooked her arm through his and steered him in the direction of the spring. Archie was harmless, she assured herself—all the while knowing that what she was doing was a mistake.

The closer they got to the creek, the shakier Archie's steps became. By the end of the trail she was practically dragging him.

When they heard the gurgle of the small stream, he struggled out of her gasp. "I changed my mind. Let's go back to the house."

In his condition, he'd fall flat on his face before she could guide him back to the house. The blood had drained from his face, leaving his bruises blackish and his lips looking a sickly shade of white. He was either going to pass out or be sick. The small stream provided the nearest shelter. Small scrub trees grew along its bank and would shade Archie from the blazing sun.

She recaptured his arm and tugged him down the slope that led to the creek. "Come on, Archie. Just a little farther."

He yanked out of her grasp again. Once he righted himself, he wiped his mouth with the back of his hand. "You know that brother of yours did some bad things. I don't want you doing anything silly just to protect him. You've got to protect yourself. That's what I had to do."

"That's why they beat you. For knowing Corey. For helping us escape Coyote Pass. Oh, Archie . . ." She dropped her gaze, her words stuck in her throat, squeezed by guilt. "It's a miracle they didn't kill you."

He rubbed his temples with shaking hands, his eyes closed. "I wish they would have killed me." When he opened his eyes, they watered with pain. "I need a drink, Miss Lori. I need a drink real bad."

Lorelei hated that he would have to go through the awful withdrawal all over again. She knew from her father's experience that the second time would be worse. She didn't doubt he would wish himself dead once the visions started. "Let's go to the stream. The cool water will help your headache."

Archie let her guide him. He kept his hands on his temples as they walked. He winced with each step. "Just remember what I told you. You cooperate, and you won't get hurt. I've been promised."

She followed without comment. He was starting to babble again.

When they'd cleared the stunted desert willows lining the stream, she saw two saddled horses grazing the sweet grass along the bank. "Is someone with you?"

Archie didn't open his eyes. Talking seemed to be a struggle. "I'm sorry, Miss Lori."

A man straightened from the shrub, a gun in one hand, a bottle in the other. "Good job, Archie."

He tossed the bottle at Archie, who used all the strength he had left to catch it. Ignoring her, he pulled out the cork and greedily drank.

The man kept the gun aimed in her direction. "Get over here. And if you scream, that mama and her baby ain't going to live. I don't need them, but I need you."

Lorelei glanced to Archie, desperate for him to do something. He lowered the bottle, then wiped his wet chin with his sleeve. His breath came in hard pants. "You should have left me for dead back at Coyote Pass."

Archie had brought her here intentionally! Her heart seemed to pump ice as numbing shock swept through her.

She forced her attention back to the gunman. "What do you want?"

The man crossed the stream in a few short strides. He grabbed her arm and yanked her toward the horses. She opened her mouth to argue, but he squeezed her hard in warning.

"Like I said, you don't want that lady in the house to come down here and find out what all the commotion is about. You just come along with me and mind yourself, and we won't have any trouble. All I want is the gold."

Water weighed down the hem of her skirt and soaked her shoes as he dragged her across the stream. But it felt no different than hot sand. She seemed weightless, floating above herself, acting out her part in a very bad dream.

The man shoved her toward the smaller of the two horses, a gray mare that looked as skittish as she felt. She hesitated, knowing that if she mounted, it would be the last anyone would ever see of her.

"I don't have any gold. Please—"

"That's enough talk. One more word and I'll gag you." He strode around to the big sorrel with fiercely flared nostrils.

Archie staggered across the stream to join them. He shoved the cork back in the bottle and stuck it in the gray mare's saddlebag. He calmed the skittish animal with a long stroke down its neck.

The other man had already mounted. "You ain't going. You stay here and tell Sullivan I got his sister. Tell him he can have her back when he brings me the gold."

"He doesn't have the gold," cried Lorelei. Arguing with the gunman probably wouldn't do any good, but she was beyond reason. "Really, he doesn't have any gold."

The man stared at her, his jaw clamped tight. "What did I tell you?" Without warning, he swung off his mount and stalked toward her, fury in every short jerk of his body. He looked as though he planned on strangling her right then and there. "I already killed more men than I can count for this gold. You want to join them, you keep on sassing me."

She backed into the mare, making the animal paw at the

ground and toss its head. She wanted to turn and calm the frightened horse before it whinnied, but to do so meant she had to turn her back on the madman. Fear froze her muscles, forcing her to watch his every move. She prayed Beth and Rachel would stay asleep.

The man untied the bandanna from around his neck and balled it in his fist. Archie moved to block his path. "You said you weren't going to hurt her. I'm going with you to make sure you keep that promise."

The man grabbed Archie by the shirtfront and shoved him hard. "You're lucky I didn't shoot you the moment I saw you."

Archie landed on his backside in the stream.

The gunman turned back to Lorelei, apparently not giving Archie a second thought. "Open your mouth."

Lorelei clamped her lips together, her jaw clenched.

She didn't even have time to consider how he would take her defiance before he slapped her hard across the face with his open palm. She stumbled back, but somehow caught herself from dropping to her knees. Never had she been struck before, not even by her parents for punishment or her brothers in play. And this man was definitely not playing. Stars danced before her eyes. Pain and shock squeezed her throat. She righted herself and opened her mouth obediently.

He placed the front of the bandanna across her open mouth and tied the ends behind her head. Before he could secure the knot, a moving blur caught her wide gaze. Archie lunged at the man, using all his body weight to shove him away from her. They landed on the ground in a shower of dust. Archie reared back to hit the other man, but was easily thrown off. The man quickly got to his feet, a knife in his hand.

Archie struggled to regain his balance, but his own equilibrium swayed him like a slowing top.

The stranger gripped and ungripped the knife in his right hand. His face shone with a combination of hatred and pleasure. Archie didn't have a chance, and neither did Lorelei if she didn't do something fast.

She thought to run, but the two men were blocking her path to the house. If she headed toward the desert, he would surely find her.

The man stalked to Archie, a smile on his face. "I'm going to enjoy killing you, you two-faced drunk. You're the one who hooked us up with Sullivan in the first place."

Archie backed up no more that a few feet, then apparently braced himself for his assailant's attack empty-handed. He never glanced her way, but she noticed he had left her room to dart past once the other man was close enough to attack. Archie had said she should save herself. Though she hated to leave him, she saw no other choice.

Once the other man had his back to her, she inched her way forward. She searched the ground and found a good-sized rock. Maybe she could hit their assailant on the back of the head. He wasn't tall for a man, but he was still taller than she.

The outlaw laughed when he came in striking range of Archie. The fact that Archie held his ground seemed to amuse him. "You gonna dance for me?"

He jabbed at Archie's head, forcing him to duck to miss the blow. The madman then thrust to Archie's left side, then stabbed at his right shoulder. He pulled back the blade at the last minute. His soft laughter echoed with each twist and jerk Archie made.

The man's perverse game cemented Lorelei's resolve not to let Archie be cut down. She came up behind the knife-wielding lunatic, the rock she had spotted earlier lifted above her head. She hoped using both hands would give her the strength she needed.

Just as she rose up on her toes, the man dipped his right shoulder and jabbed the knife into Archie's midsection. He arched the blade upward, practically lifting Archie off the ground.

Lorelei brought the rock down on the man's head as hard as she could. As soon as it connected with a sickening thud, she dropped the stone and ran.

In a brief burst of hope, she thought she had escaped.

When the hem of her dress caught, she tugged as hard as she could, not caring if she tore the garment. She didn't dare turn around.

When she couldn't free the dress dragging her backward, she knew she hadn't come close to escaping.

Finally she twisted to face her opponent. He lay on the ground with his hands securely wrapped in the end of her skirt. She kicked at his face in an attempt to dislodge him. The movement was a mistake. He easily caught her ankle and brought her to the ground hard on her rump. He dragged her to him and yanked her up by her neck as he got to his feet. He held her tightly, cutting off her breath.

Before she could worry about being choked to death, he slapped her hard across the face with his palm, then with the back of his hand. She sagged, the grip he had on her neck the only thing keeping her upright. The permanent sneer on his face, the deep green shrub behind his right shoulder, blurred. Darkness crept around the edges of her vision. Just as she thought she had taken her last breath, he released his stranglehold.

He prevented her collapse to the ground by gripping her shoulders and shaking her hard. She was too stunned to keep her head from snapping back.

"You do something like that again and you'll be sorry, you little bitch. I'll work you over good."

His angry red face invaded her senses and sharpened her return to reality. She closed her eyes, not wanting to see him. Not wanting to be conscious at all. He slapped her again lightly, not to hurt her, but to get her attention.

"You listen to me when I'm talking. You know how to write?"

She couldn't answer. His words didn't make sense. Nothing made sense.

He squeezed her arms. "You know how to write?"

She blinked. "Yes," she said, relieved she could answer in the affirmative. He might kill her if she said no.

He whipped her around. "Good. 'Cause we're going to leave your brother a message before we go."

With a bone-crunching grip on her forearm he dragged her to Archie's body, which lay sprawled, flat on its back, a knife sticking from the center of the chest. Blood stained his shirtfront a slick, shiny red. A pink cloud swirled, then dispersed as Archie's life drained down the shallow stream.

The man held her as he leaned forward to retrieve the knife. She unconsciously tugged away, unable to look any closer. He yanked her with greater force, sending her to her knees beside Archie.

"You get a good look, girl. You give me a second of trouble and that's what you'll look like." He came down behind her; a firm grip on her shoulder kept her on her knees.

"Let's see here." He swayed to grab something on his left. "This will do."

He handed her a twisted twig less than six inches long. "Just dip that into his blood and we'll leave your brother a message that will tell him we mean business."

She held the stick in her right hand, unable to follow his request. Hot tears stung her cheeks before she realized she was crying. She was afraid to refuse him, yet feared she couldn't comply with his request no matter how grave the consequences.

"Oh, come on. He's dead already. It ain't going to hurt him." He grabbed her wrist that held the twig and forced her to stick the end in the puckered wound in Archie's chest. She turned her head away and closed her eyes.

"Now get it good and bloody. I want my message to be real clear."

He jerked her in another direction. "Come on. Open your eyes. You got to write."

She did and was grateful she was staring at a patch of dirt. If she kept her gaze averted, she couldn't even see Archie.

"W-what should I write?" she asked, surprised that she still had a voice at all.

"Ricochet. That's all. He'll know what that means."

Braddock rode into Jay's silent homestead with the devil on his heels. Both pistols were drawn before his feet hit the ground. Keeping low, he made his way to the side of the house, flattened himself against a spot free from the window's view, and waited and listened. He should have left Lucky far from the house and approached on foot. Thinking clearly hadn't been an option. Getting to Lorelei had been driving him ever since he left Specter Canyon.

Braddock's heavy breathing was the only sound that filled the yard. Maybe he had beaten Ricochet here. Or maybe he was too late and they were all already dead. Ricochet had already murdered a dozen or so hardened criminals, his own friends. Killing women and children and a man who'd lost a leg would hardly make him break a sweat.

He should have known Archie would return with trouble. Either he'd brought Ricochet here in a drunken stupor or the outlaw had just followed him. Archie would have started drinking once he arrived at Mulcahy's hideout, if only to show the gang he was still a harmless drunk. And once the alcohol touched his lips, it would be all over—Archie was a talkative drunk.

Braddock slid along the planked wall and peeked in the kitchen window. The sight of plates still on the table, food left unwrapped to spoil, scared him more than if he had seen Ricochet holding a knife to Lorelei's throat. That, he could fight. The sense that he was too late, that the curse had won its biggest victory yet, squeezed the breath from his throat.

And Braddock had played right into the curse's hands. He had ordered Lorelei to stay at the ranch. All the while, death and destiny had been rushing forward to meet her. Braddock pushed away from the house. He should have known.

He *had* known. He had killed Lorelei as surely as if he had done it with his bare hands. How many had to die before he figured it out? The curse would always be with him. He lived by sucking the life out of everyone around him.

He strode to the barn, no longer making any attempt at stealth. He wanted to be seen. Needed something to fight. He stopped suddenly, a step away from obliterating a trail of footprints. A churned patch of dirt narrowed into the shape of boots and the smaller prints of a woman as it wound around the barn. Lorelei.

By the size of the booted feet, he guessed the man to be close to his own height. Not Ricochet, but probably Archie. Braddock fought the urge to follow the prints in a mad dash. The trail was still distinct. But the dry, windless day made placing an accurate time on them impossible.

One last glance around the yard drew his attention to the pump. A full bucket rested underneath the spout. It flowed over with each new drip. A deep well didn't stay primed long. Each splash that fell from the spout said that someone had been there. Recently.

He turned and followed the path, his pistols gripped with renewed fierceness. He sprinted, careful to keep his heavy footfalls off the trail. The prints blended together, then veered drunkenly. Lorelei and her companion walked close together. Either she guided and supported the other man or he dragged her. Braddock didn't have time to figure out which.

He pushed his way through the heavy brush choking the stream's bank. The top of Ricochet's head appeared above a giant sage as he swung up on his horse. Braddock kept moving while he took aim.

His boot hit something solid. Glancing down, he saw Archie lying in the stream. He stepped over him without another thought. His peripheral vision told him Lorelei sat on the horse next to Ricochet. It took all Braddock's effort not to let his gaze stray to her.

Ricochet didn't appear to notice the gun pointed at him. He tugged on the reins of his horse, ready to ride off in the other direction.

Without the slightest qualm about shooting a man in the back, Braddock pulled the trigger.

He missed.

The horse screamed and went down as Ricochet tried to whirl the animal in the shot's direction. Lorelei turned to see what had happened. She quickly took control of her own panicked mount and spurred the animal toward Braddock.

Though she blocked his line of fire, he couldn't stop the smile that broke across his face, his relief at seeing her alive and well a tangible thing.

"Go. Head back to the house," he yelled at her.

In the same instant Ricochet untangled himself from his fallen horse. He walked toward Braddock with a rifle propped against his shoulder.

Braddock reaimed but staggered back at the sound of the rifle's discharge, dropping his gun.

"No!" Lorelei screamed. Her voice sounded muffled and farther away than he knew she was.

He tried to right himself and grab his other gun. Ricochet didn't seem to notice that he hadn't killed him. He trained his rifle on Lorelei's retreating form.

"Run," Braddock wanted to yell, but instead he fell to his knees. His left arm didn't seem to work, so he grabbed the gun from his useless grip with his other hand. Pain burst over him like a mortar shell, stealing the breath from his lungs, but he wasn't exactly sure of its origin. He knew he'd been hit but didn't dare look to see where or how bad.

For some reason, Ricochet fired a shot that purposely missed Lorelei. "Get back here, you little bitch. You make me chase you to the house, there're going be some dead kids."

Braddock realized Ricochet wanted her alive. Not caring why, he used all his strength to get to his feet. If his aim had been off before, it was now hopeless. He might as well shoot with his eyes closed. He fired, but with his eyes open.

He didn't hit Ricochet but forced the man to aim the rifle at him and away from Lorelei. Ricochet moved forward in long strides. He positioned the rifle to shoot Braddock in the forehead. Braddock's pistol slipped from his limp fingers. He could feel the life draining from him with his blood. He heard the sounds of horses' hooves beating the ground behind him. They sounded closer, not farther away. Jesus, why wasn't Lorelei heading toward the house? Braddock fell to his hands and knees, desperate to retrieve his gun.

Ricochet kicked the only pistol within Braddock's line of vision away, then touched the muzzle of the rifle to Braddock's forehead. The hot steel burned his skin.

He heard the rifle blast but felt nothing. Maybe he no longer had a head. He slumped to the ground and waited. A wound in his midsection throbbed, sending streaks of pain through every nerve. Gunshot wounds hurt more than he had imagined. The experience definitely rivaled any guilt he had incurred watching his men die during the war. He didn't let his heavy lids close, though all he could see was dirt. He wanted to greet death with his eyes open. They'd both been waiting a long time for this meeting.

He heard Lorelei's voice in the distance, then another voice telling her to stay back. He wanted to push up, to turn to see what was happening, but his limbs didn't respond. He strained his gaze until he saw the worn soles of a pair of boots. The right one had a hole on the ball of the foot, and the owner wore fuzzy red socks the color of overripe apples. Braddock closed his eyes, unable to see anything else.

Hands on his shoulders tugged at him, making him cry out when he didn't want to. He was rolled over onto his back, and the movement sliced through his entire body. The whole dying business was much more unpleasant at this end. He wouldn't forget that again.

Lorelei's face loomed above his. He wanted to smile but doubted those muscles worked either.

"Oh, my God, Christopher. My God."

She fumbled with his clothes, expanding the pain in sharp jolts. He weakly tried to push her hands away, but she easily overpowered him.

"Please be still. We have to stop the bleeding."

She probed around the wound, and then he felt pressure as she pushed down hard with both hands. He moaned softly, glad he didn't have the energy to scream, as he intended. Miraculously the pressure she applied eased the fist that had been squeezing his lungs, and he was able to draw a steady, calming breath. Lorelei's presence made it all all right. She was alive. Ricochet hadn't killed her.

Relief flooded his tight muscles. Maybe he would close his eyes for a while.

"Is he dead?" Braddock heard her ask softly.

"Yeah, he is. I never killed anyone before, Lori."

Braddock pried his eyes open. He wasn't dead yet, but he didn't have the strength to tell them so. Corey knelt in front of him, a shotgun clutched in his right hand. He looked pale, as if he had been hit too. But Braddock didn't see any blood. The kid had obviously never killed anyone before. At least he had been telling the truth about that. Since Braddock knew Corey didn't shoot him, he gladly assumed they were talking about Ricochet.

"Thank you. You saved Christopher's life."

Braddock watched the expression on Corey's face as the boy gazed at his wound. He didn't seem to think he had saved Braddock's life at all.

Corey's gaze darted back to his sister. He gently touched her taut arm.

"Lori," he said softly.

"Go to the barn and gather up some cobwebs. We need to get the bleeding stopped. The bullet passed through his back. I saw the wound. He has a chance."

Corey studied Braddock's chest again. He chewed his bottom lip, his eyebrows drawn together. If his expression weren't enough, Braddock noticed he was in no hurry to follow his sister's orders. "Lori," he said again softly.

"Dear Lord!"

Braddock recognized Beth's voice. Through hooded eyes he watched her stop in front of him. She held little Rachel to her chest, cradling her head in her palm, keeping her face buried in her shoulder. He closed his eyes, not wanting Beth to see him like this but unable to do a thing about it. For the first time in his life he was completely and totally helpless.

"What happened?" asked Beth.

"It's a long story. Could you bring some hot water and bandages? And hurry, please," pleaded Lorelei. Her voice sounded rough with unshed tears.

"Where are Jay and the kids?" Beth's voice shook with fear instead of sorrow.

Before Braddock could think what he was doing, he pushed up on his elbows. He assumed Jay was in the field. Lorelei, Beth, Rachel, even Corey were all safe. Nobody had died except Archie, whom Braddock didn't grieve for too much, since he had led Ricochet to Lorelei. Apparently Ricochet had died —but that was justice at work, not the Braddock curse.

Corey forced Braddock's shoulders back to the ground. The silent tension left in the wake of Beth's unanswered question forced Braddock to lift his head. He couldn't rest until he knew what had happened to Jay and his kids.

Lorelei's face was red when she leaned over him. Her tensed arms strained to keep his blood from leaving his body. "Keep him down, Corey."

Corey pushed on his forehead, forcing his head back, but not before Braddock saw the blood coating Lorelei's hands and wrists.

"Ma! Ma!"

Jason stopped next to his mother, his chest heaving from running hard. "We heard the gunshots." His gaze fell to Braddock. And, as if he didn't already know, the boy's wide-eyed look of horror proved to Braddock that he was a goner.

Beth grabbed the boy's shirt with her free hand and tried to pull him away. "Where are the others?"

"They're coming."

"All of them?"

The boy nodded, unable to tear his gaze away from the sight of a dying man.

Braddock let his eyes drift shut. His breath came in ragged gasps despite Lorelei's best efforts to hold him together. Each rise and fall of his chest hurt like hell. He didn't even want to keep on breathing. Not that he wanted to die. He couldn't actually believe that he was. But the timing seemed appropriate. He had cheated death so many times; finally his time had come. Saving Lorelei was worth it. Braddock could live with that. Actually, he was going to die with that. His curse had been broken.

"Jesus Christ!" He heard Jay above him. He took Corey's

place and cradled Braddock's head in his big palms.

He heard a girl's gasp. "What happened, Ma?"

"Let me see. I want to see," cried a little voice much too young to see so much blood.

"Keep him back, Alice," said Beth.

They were all safe. All accounted for. Nobody he cared about was going to die today, except himself, of course. He had prayed for death during the war. Each day, each night, he'd prayed not to have to do it one more day. Not to have to watch his men die. And then he didn't pray at all.

He forced his eyes open. Keeping Lorelei safe had been his first prayer in a long time, and the first one God had ever answered. He tried to smile at her. Her blue eyes shone bright with tears. They were bluer than the sky haloed around her head. *Ah, Lori, don't cry,* he wanted to say, but all he managed to do was lick his dry lips and sigh. But she was safe. She would have a life safe from him.

He let his eyes drift shut, let the darkness in, let the pain overwhelm him until there was no pain at all. His luck had finally changed.

Chapter Twenty

Lorelei wished they wouldn't stop. A doctor should have been brought to the wounded man, not the other way around. The dust the posse kicked up was enough to choke Lorelei. She hated to think of what the red cloud did to Christopher.

She wiped the mixture of sweat and grit from his brow, then checked the bandage. Blood dotted the white cotton strip in a faint red oval, but didn't soak through the first layer. Though his bleeding had slowed, it was still a miracle he hung on to life at all. He'd lost more blood than she considered humanly possible. Moving him to Arriba was insanity.

Yet since Garrett Douglas, the federally appointed United States marshal of the New Mexico territory, had ridden onto Jay's farm with his posse of men, his word had become all-powerful. Her twenty-four-hour vigilance at Christopher's bedside, her efforts to keep him alive using every means at her disposal including sheer force of will, mattered not. Marshal Douglas had decided Christopher needed a good doctor. An eastern doctor.

After a one-way argument, Douglas only pretending to

consider Lorelei's opinion, Arriba became their destination. Though there were no doctors in Arriba, Douglas reasoned they could telegraph a decent doctor in Santa Fe.

"How's he doing?" Douglas stood at the back of the wagon.

"His fever won't break. The water from Jay's well might have cooled him off," she said more rudely than she meant.

Unfortunately, Marshal Douglas didn't appear put off. He climbed into the wagon's bed and crawled across the planks, ducking his head beneath the canvas they'd stretched across the buckboard's sides. He paused to check the thickness of the mattress that swallowed most of the wagon's space.

"Do you think he's comfortable enough?"

The fear in the man's voice deepened it. That he was uncomfortable seeing Christopher so helpless showed in the nervous dart of his gaze. They had been friends since they were boys, she had heard him say. She didn't have an exclusive on loving Christopher Braddock.

"The traveling is taking its toll. I'll just be glad to get him to Arriba."

"And into the hands of a qualified physician."

Lorelei stiffened but dropped her gaze and said nothing. Didn't they know she would walk across fire to see Christopher recover? Even give her own life. She didn't see how a doctor could do more.

"I'm sorry, Miss . . ." He hesitated.

"Sullivan." She glanced up. He didn't even know who she was, much less that she would be Christopher's wife. Nor could she tell him. The promise she'd made to Christopher the last night they had been together prevented that.

"You're Corey Sullivan's sister." He studied her with cool brown eyes.

She wondered if he had truly forgotten her name or had just been trying to trick her. Suddenly she felt like she was being questioned.

"Yes. That's right."

His sharp features softened. The look of suspicion eased. "Sorry again. I can't remember the last time I slept. I'm too used to interrogating people."

He ran his hand over his stubbled chin. "I'm grateful for all you've done for Chris. His parents will be grateful, too. They're very wealthy."

"I don't want a reward," she said too sharply. She hadn't known Christopher's parents were wealthy. Discovering that his father was a United States senator had been even more of a shock. Why hadn't Christopher mentioned any of this to her? For some reason she had assumed his parents were dead. That he was as alone as she.

"You deserve a reward. You have to be exhausted. Why don't you climb down and stretch your legs?"

"I don't want to leave him." The sensation of Douglas's piercing stare forced her to lift her gaze.

He smiled. "I see. Chris has quite a way with women, the lucky bastard."

Lorelei didn't return his smile. She burned to tell him that Christopher loved her, wanted to marry her, but the quirk of Douglas's lips told her he would only find that amusing. She had nothing to be embarrassed about. But she did feel ashamed, as if she weren't good enough to be anything other than a passing fling to Christopher Braddock, son of a U.S. senator.

Douglas cleared his throat. "I didn't mean anything by that. You know, I'm going to put in a good word for you with the judge."

"Am I in trouble?"

"No, but your brother is. Surely you know that."

She had the distinct impression he was studying her reaction, hoping she'd reveal something.

"I know Corey made a mistake."

"A big mistake. Jay said he shot the man who tried to kill Braddock, but that doesn't change the fact that he was part of the robbery."

Lorelei had vowed to quit defending her brother, but she couldn't stop herself. "Corey was afraid of those men. He got away from them the first chance he could."

She plucked the damp cloth off of Braddock's head, avoiding Douglas's harsh gaze. He made her feel as if she should confess something.

"If he told us where the gold is hidden, it would help his story."

"I thought the gold was at Specter Canyon?" Something Ricochet had said popped into her mind. She hadn't had time to think about the awful moments before Christopher was shot. Ricochet had thought Corey had the gold.

"We searched every crevice of that hellhole. Most of the gang's dead, including Mulcahy. But the owners of the Rio Grande Railroad want their gold. And powerful men in Santa Fe want the railroad. Heads are going to roll, starting with mine."

Lorelei rested her palm against Christopher's cheek. Fever still burned through him. She couldn't think about the gold, didn't dare think about what Corey knew of it. She let her hand stray to Christopher's heart. The wound had missed it by barely an inch. She slid her hand back up to his throat, checking his pulse. The faint beat barely reached her fingertips.

"We should be on our way. He needs to be in a bed."

Douglas nodded. "You're right. He wouldn't have made it this far if it weren't for you, Miss Sullivan."

He smiled sadly, and she wondered if it was because he thought Christopher wouldn't survive in the end, or because he could tell she was in love with him.

"Thank you. Call me Lorelei."

"Thank you, Lorelei." He crawled out of the wagon. When he was again on solid ground, he turned to face her. "You'll be staying in Arriba, won't you?"

"Of course."

Douglas retrieved his hat from the edge of the wagon. He put it on, angling it over his eyes. "I'll need to question you once we get him into a doctor's hands. None of this makes sense, Lorelei."

She nodded, then sagged in relief when he finally sauntered away. Reminding herself she hadn't done anything wrong didn't stop the swirl of dread that squeezed her chest.

She stretched out next to Christopher, praying for him to wake up. But her fear wasn't for him, nor even for Corey. This fear was for herself.

Lorelei marched down the steps of the clapboard house Douglas had commandeered. He had no right to keep her from Christopher. Though the doctor from Santa Fe slipped past the bedroom door to assure her Chris was still alive, he was under instructions not to allow him visitors. The only thing that kept her from barging past him, besides the fact that he outweighed her by at least a hundred and fifty pounds, was that she didn't want to disturb Christopher's rest.

She dragged herself down the dusty street, not daring to think Christopher didn't want her there. It was all Douglas's doing, and as soon as Christopher awoke he'd set everything right.

Wade Langston separated himself from the shade cast by the house's sloping roof and fell in by her side. She hadn't spoken to him since he had sat tied to his horse on Jay's farm. Tinges of yellow replaced the ugly purple bruises left by Christopher's beating. Lorelei thought to apologize, but feared incriminating herself further.

"You don't have to follow me to my hotel, Mr. Langston. I'm not going to run away. I have nowhere to go."

"You can call me Wade. And you don't have to worry, Lorelei. I don't blame you for things you had no control over."

Lorelei sleepwalked in the direction of her hotel, letting Wade follow her if he liked. She had assumed the deputy would want retribution and that the others would be on her side.

"They're going to get what's coming to them, Lorelei. I'm going to see to that."

She didn't know who "they" were, nor did she care. She was tired of fighting. Tired of pleading her case to anyone who would listen. "They're not worth it, Wade. The only person you can prove anything to is yourself."

She didn't know from where the sudden insight came, but it was true. She was good for Christopher. She knew she'd make him a good wife. That was all she needed to know. It didn't matter who Christopher Braddock's parents were.

"I have to see that justice is served. It's not right for him to get away with wrongdoing just because his daddy's a senator."

Lorelei halted in the middle of the deserted street, suddenly caring a great deal about who "they" were. "What do you mean?"

Langston pushed his hat back, leaning closer so as not to be overheard. "I'll hold my tongue while he's recuperating, but I can't stay silent forever. Withholding evidence is against the law."

Her dawning horror must have shown on her face, because Wade gently touched her shoulder to steady her. "Don't be afraid, Lorelei. I know you were his pawn just like your brother. I have it all in writing. Braddock's writing."

"You must be mistaken."

"He confessed that he planned the stagecoach robbery. He forced your brother to persuade Mulcahy into doing the dirty work. Says he held you hostage to make sure your brother gave him the gold. Braddock's the reason we didn't find the gold at Specter Canyon. He knows where it is."

"None of that's true."

The pitying look he'd given her earlier returned. "I know you're in love with him. He's a strong man in his own right. He'd be something to reckon with even without his father's influence. I'll give him that."

"Wade, you know him. You know he wouldn't do any of those things."

"He stole my horse. Saw it with my own eyes. I don't want the Hartmans to come to any harm, seeing as Jay's crippled and all, but he should have considered that before he hid a stolen horse. If Jay didn't know what Braddock was doing, he can say so in court. For once Braddock's going to have to own up to his actions."

Dear God, Christopher had taken Wade's horse, and he'd willingly go to jail to keep Jay out of trouble.

Lorelei paused to lay a hand on Wade's arm. "I'm sorry about your horse. We just borrowed it. We took the best of care with him. Christopher was desperate to find Mulcahy, but he had nothing to do with the robbery."

Wade shook his head. "I was as shocked as you when he told me his tale. . . ."

"Because it's nothing but a tale. He made it up."

"They haven't found the gold, Lorelei. There *is* something to it. Besides, I'm not a judge. I'm a lawman, and honor-bound to turn in any evidence I have. And let me tell you, Christopher Braddock's signed confession is pretty strong evidence."

"No one will believe it."

"Douglas said there are men in Washington who have staked their whole fortune on the Rio Grande Railroad making it to Santa Fe. They need that gold. They'll want to believe it."

"But it's not true," she argued, knowing she was going in circles.

He held up his hand to stop her plea. "The truth will come out in the trial."

"A trial? Christopher's name would be dragged through the mud." And God knew what would come out about her and Corey and their unscrupulous father. If Jay was implicated too, Lorelei would never forgive herself. And she feared that neither would Christopher.

"Corey can clear this up." Lorelei gathered her skirts and strode in the direction of the hotel.

Wade hurried to keep pace with her. "I'm sorry, Lorelei. I'm a man of the law, and it's my duty to turn over the confession as evidence. I'd be breaking the law if I didn't."

The Crystal Palace, Arriba's only hotel that didn't also serve as a bordello, looked more like a prison than it had before. The squat, two-story adobe's peeling plaster and cock-eyed sign heightened Lorelei's sense of desperation. She turned her back on the gloomy reminder of her situation.

"Give the confession to Douglas. Let him handle it. He's your boss, isn't he?"

Wade glanced past the end of Arriba's one street and out into the empty miles of dry desert brush. If Lorelei suspected that his desire to see the confession exposed to public scrutiny was more than following the letter of the law, his evasiveness confirmed it.

"You know how you felt when Douglas wouldn't let you in to see Braddock? That's how those boys made me feel since I was a young man. I had a chance being accepted into West Point. I had a chance to be a great man. My parents broke their backs so I could have that chance, and those boys tried to take it away from me at every turn." He straightened. "Justice will finally have its day. You can count on that."

He tipped his hat, then turned and picked his way across the rutted dirt street. Lorelei had little time to waste. She sprinted through the hotel lobby, purposely ignoring the guard, who stood as soon as soon as he spotted her. At the moment she didn't have the patience to pretend his presence was for her protection.

By the time she reached the battered door of the hotel room she shared with Corey, she had to pause to catch her breath. She turned the knob, finding the door unlocked, and rushed in without first announcing her presence. The empty room stared back at her with an air of doom. The bed she'd made this morning looked as if it hadn't even been sat upon. Perhaps Corey had stayed in town after she'd ordered him from the room so she could dress.

She collapsed onto the natty cotton bedspread and stared up at the smooth adobe ceiling with its rounded edges, no longer comforted by the fact that she had first confronted Christopher in a similar room down the hall. When she had so long ago asked him to help Corey, she had never expected it to cost him so much. Maybe she wasn't good for him after all. The thought forced her off the bed.

She couldn't let Wade use that signed confession against him, though. She didn't know why he had done it, admitted to things she knew he had nothing to do with, but she guessed it had something to do with protecting Corey or herself. Either way, he had sacrificed his own interests for her.

She dragged herself over to the cracked mirror that hovered above the washstand and rearranged the pins in her wilted hair. Corey was probably lingering at the saloon. Once she found him, she'd have Corey explain it all to Douglas, and maybe he could head off any damage Wade Langston would do.

Corey had been unusually thoughtful since they'd arrived in Arriba. When he had insisted on sneaking away from Douglas's watchful eye to check on his ranch, she had been a little surprised to see him return as he promised. She'd been even more surprised that he had not only brought her clean clothes, but a brush set. Perhaps he would be just as eager to discredit Wade's story as she.

When she reached to splash the water she'd left in the basin on her face, she saw the note tucked under the rim. Her fingers shook as she lifted the torn scrap.

Dear Lori. Bratak is gettn better.
He will take care of you. But if he dosnt I
left somen for you in the picture. Luv Corey.

Lorelei glanced around the room. The walls held signs of water damage, but nothing else. She quickly reread the note. *Damn it!* She should have known he would do something like this. Corey had never taken responsibility for his actions a day in his life.

She resisted the urge to crumple the note in her fist and scanned it one more time, hoping she had read it wrong. When she glanced up, she noticed the porcelain pitcher next to the basin. He meant pitcher, not picture. She tossed the note on the washstand, not caring if it fluttered to the floor instead. She grabbed the pitcher's handle, but when she tried to lift it, the pitcher stayed firmly planted. With both hands wrapped around the base, she heaved it off the table. A quick glance down the pitcher's slim dark mouth didn't give her a hint as to what lay inside. Whatever it was jangled against the porcelain. Once she reached the bed, she dumped the pitcher upside down.

A shower of gold coins covered the off-white bedcover. She blinked. Never had she seen so much money; she couldn't even guess how much it might be. She reached down and picked up a handful of the cool gold. Where had Corey gotten this kind of money?

She dropped the coins on top of the others and backed away. First she covered her mouth to keep from crying out the most obvious and only answer; then she covered her eyes. She couldn't have been so stupid. There had to be another explanation. Maybe it wasn't really as much gold as she thought. Maybe Corey had just sold the ranch. She slowly took her hands from her eyes, almost believing the gold would be gone. It wasn't. Its dull sheen told her a truth she hadn't wanted to see since Corey was first accused of cheating at cards back in Louisville.

She darted her gaze to the door, half expecting Douglas and a group of armed men to burst through and lead her away in chains. She couldn't say she didn't deserve it. Being this big a fool seemed to call for such drastic measures. She glanced back to the gold on the bed without wanting to. Corey had had the gold the entire time. From the moment he'd sent her out to confront Christopher, her brother had forced her to be a party to his lie. He'd put them all at risk for his own selfish ends.

She scooped the gold back into the pitcher as quickly as she could. Despite the guard downstairs, Corey's escape would have been a simple matter. And he didn't have to worry about coming back this time. She wasn't sure what hurt the most: the fact that he could betray her so thoroughly or that he could leave without so much as a good-bye.

She rearranged the pitcher next to the basin, then retrieved the note from the floor and crammed it into her drawstring bag. After a quick glance around the room, she went back and straightened the bedcovers, wiped off the dust that had been left by the coins, and refluffed the pillow for good measure. The room looked as dreary as when she'd found it.

She returned to the pitcher and eased her small hand through its mouth to grab a handful of coins. She knew what she had to do.

By the time she reached the stables on the edge of town, Ivar, the stables' owner who sat in the shade outside, assured her that her search was over.

Lorelei took a bracing breath. Maybe all her efforts would be futile and she could never have the life she longed for, but she *would* do the right thing. The thing she should have done when Corey asked her to face an armed man and lie to him.

With renewed conviction, she trudged into the darkened stable and called Wade's name.

He stepped from a stall. "Over here. Is something wrong?"

She crept forward, blinking until she could clearly identify Langston's face. A quick glance around the darkened stable assured her that nickering horses were their only company. A sleek gray head peeked from the stall, then nosed Wade's shoulder in a demand for attention. The brush Wade held in his right hand confirmed that Lorelei had interrupted a grooming.

Lorelei didn't speak until she was close enough for Wade to read her earnest expression. "Yes, Wade, something is very wrong."

He studied her face. "Is it Braddock?"

"No." She cleared her throat and forced herself to continue before she changed her mind. "I know where the gold is. I'll trade you Christopher's signed confession for the information."

"You told Douglas about this?"

"No. I want you to find the gold." To her surprise, her words were true. Of course, her reason for coming to him was to obtain the confession, but the idea of Wade finally receiving recognition, being accepted, made her feel that all this pain might be worth something. And it gave her hope for herself.

He shook his head. "Pardon me for saying so, Lorelei, but I don't believe a word of it. If you'll excuse me, I need to get back to Smoky. Douglas should take a stick to his men for not taking better care of their mounts." He turned back to the eager horse.

"Wait. I can prove it."

When he swung his glance back to her, she didn't bother with words. Instead she fished in her bag, then pushed her palmful of gold under his nose.

He stared, his eyes wide.

"May I?" he asked, nodding toward the gold.

"That's why I brought it."

He picked up one of the coins and examined it.

"Do we have a deal?" she asked.

"Did you have a hand in this, Lorelei?"

"No. I just found out who did, though."

"Was it Braddock?"

"No. It was Corey. My brother."

Wade's calculating stare told her she had said too much. Wade had been to the ranch. He could find Corey as easily as anybody. She had given herself away prematurely.

He dropped the coins in his trouser pocket, then reached inside his soft leather vest and retrieved a folded piece of dirty paper covered with printing. "I don't think you'd make a very good criminal, Lorelei," he said as he handed her the paper.

She quickly unfolded the square and briefly scanned the wanted poster before she found Christopher's confession on the other side. Even if his full name had not been scrawled on the bottom, she would have known to whom the forceful script belonged.

She pressed the paper to her chest. "Thank you, Wade."

"I'd better head out if I want to catch up with Corey. Do you know where he went?"

"Not for sure, but I'd try the ranch. He'd gone there to fetch clothes and brought back part of the gold. I'm assuming he has the rest hidden near the ranch, though I've never seen any of it."

"He should be easy enough to find."

Wade strode to a stall near the rear of the barn. Lorelei waited as he saddled his horse. When he led the palomino out a few moments later, a rifle strapped to the saddle captured her attention. The implications of what she'd done finally sank in. Her throat tightened, making it hard to swallow her sudden rush of fear.

"Don't hurt him. I know he's done a lot of bad things, but truly, he never meant to hurt anyone. He'd never killed a man before Ricochet, and he only did that to save Christopher's life. He had nightmares all week, though he made me swear I wouldn't tell anyone."

Wade nodded. "I don't like unnecessary violence. All I want is to return the gold and let your brother have his day in court. If he doesn't give me any trouble, there won't be any."

She clasped her hands together to keep them from shaking. Turning Corey in was the right thing to do, but she also knew she couldn't live with herself if Corey was killed in his capture. She dropped her gaze to the hay-strewn floor to keep from pleading with Wade.

"If it makes you feel any better, I'll tell you a secret. I've never killed anyone either, and I don't plan to start with a boy still wet behind the ears."

She returned his smile. "Your secret's safe with me."

Wade tipped his hat good-bye. "Once Braddock wakes up, I hope he realizes how lucky he is."

Lorelei watched Wade ride past the open stable door, no longer believing Christopher would ever consider himself lucky to have her in his life.

Chapter Twenty-one

Braddock batted at the hand that pawed his face. The effort it took to shove the thick fingers aside strained his muscles until a fine sheen of sweat coated his body. He felt as if he had been wrapped tightly in an unbreakable spiderweb.

"Lorelei." He pushed the word through his heavy lips, unsure if he could be understood at all.

Forceful hands pressed him down into the bed. "Calm yourself or you'll tear my handiwork."

Braddock thrashed, trying to wake himself from the nightmare. The Scottish burr haunted him as he tried to place the last time he had heard the accent. A heady sense of danger had him swimming toward consciousness despite the pain in his body.

"Lorelei," he called again. If he could hear her voice, maybe he could go back to sleep.

The silence that greeted him forced him to open his eyes. A gray-haired man with wild eyebrows stared down at him from a furrowed face. Braddock squinted. The light pierced his eyes like a thousand cactus needles.

He gathered all his strength and pushed the man back. He had to get out of here and find Lorelei.

Braddock tried to sit up but found he couldn't lift his head off the pillow. The force it took to send the old man stumbling left him panting. He swallowed, finding nothing but sand in his throat. His mouth tasted like he'd licked the underside of a saddle. But he was alive. He fumbled his way to the bandages stretched around his midsection. The tender wound underneath screamed in protest.

"That's a fine thank-you," said the man from a safe distance. He strode out of Braddock's line of vision. "Send for Marshal Douglas. He's awake," he said to someone, and then Braddock heard the closing of a door.

Marshal Douglas? Last time Braddock had heard, Douglas had reached the rank of lieutenant colonel.

Once Braddock settled back against the bank of pillows, he noted that he was alone in an ordinary bedroom, not in a makeshift hospital surrounded by other wounded. It was as hot as hell.

He stared at the plastered ceiling. A sudden chill swept through him, numbing his discomfort. He didn't know Lorelei during the war.

He rubbed his forehead, forcing himself to think, to remember. He reordered the pieces of his memory. She was safe. He recalled bits of the trip in the back of the wagon and her constant presence. She had been the sweet reassurance that had allowed him to sleep in peace.

He dropped his hand and gazed over at the doctor suspiciously. "Where's Lorelei?"

The man took a backward step toward the door. "Marshal Douglas will explain everything to you. I'm just the doctor."

He glared at the physician while he placed a hand on his chest. The accelerated beat of his heart throbbed in his wound, but he had no choice but to get out of bed and find Lorelei. He took a deep breath and struggled to a sitting position. The room spun, then settled.

When Douglas strode through the door, Braddock rested against the bedframe, relieved that he wouldn't be forced to stand.

A smile broke across Douglas's face. "How you feeling, old friend?"

Braddock scowled. "Like hell. Where's Lorelei?"

Douglas laughed. "She's at the hotel. I've got a guard on her. She's not going anywhere."

A nerve jumped in his Braddock's jaw. "Douglas, you son of a bitch."

Through sheer force of will he yanked back the covers and swung his legs over the side of the bed. A wave of nausea battled with the pain that shot through every nerve ending. Braddock wasn't sure if he was going to pass out or throw up.

Despite his obvious weakness, Douglas stepped back as if he expected Braddock to leap off the bed and do him serious bodily harm. "I've treated her with nothing but respect, Chris."

"You'd better have. She's going to be my wife."

The burly doctor trudged to Braddock's side and eased him back onto the bed. "You lose any more blood, Mr. Braddock, and there will be nothing anyone can do for you."

Douglas ran his hands through his hair. He looked as dazed as if Braddock had given him the blow he so dearly deserved. "Is that really necessary? True, she nursed you back to health, but—"

"But what?" Threat remained in Braddock's voice, though with the help of the doctor, his head again rested firmly on a feather-stuffed pillow.

"But nothing." Douglas seemed to search for something to say. "She just never mentioned you two had that kind of relationship."

"Would you have believed her if she did?"

"The circumstances of your shooting were strange. You never miss. There was the chance you had a lover's quarrel. Or Lorelei was in on it with her brother and needed to get rid of you."

Braddock swung his heated gaze to the doctor, who watched with open interest.

"Get out. I need to talk to Douglas in private."

The doctor stiffened. "You, sir, are the most ungrateful patient I have ever had the misfortune to treat." He left the room without a backward glance.

Douglas watched the doctor's exit, looking as if he longed to join him. He rested his hand on his pistol before he faced Braddock again. "I was just doing my job. Lorelei and her brother are in trouble. Trouble I didn't create."

"I know you, Douglas. You'd interrogate your grandmother if you thought she had something to hide."

"And what does Lorelei have to hide?"

"She'd do anything to protect her brother. Or me." And for the first time, Braddock knew that to be true.

"Unfortunately, when your brother's a criminal that's against the law." Douglas rubbed the back of his neck. "They're turning up the heat in Washington. If the Rio Grande Railroad goes belly-up over this, important men will lose their fortunes. They want the gold, but if they can't have it, they'll take blood."

"Fine. But it's not going to be Lorelei's or her brother's."

Douglas shook his head. "I have no other leads. Mulcahy and his gang are done, but the gold wasn't at their camp." Douglas studied him, and Braddock was too weak to put on a good poker face. "What do you know? You used to be able to tell me anything."

"I'll find the gold. You know I'm a better tracker than you."

"Why did you leave in such a hurry, anyway?"

"I had that feeling. When I didn't find Ricochet at the camp, I knew Lorelei was in danger."

Douglas laughed. "Yeah. That feeling used to save your butt."

Braddock's dried lips cracked, but it didn't stop the smile that crept across his face. "It did this time, too. If something had happened to Lorelei, it would have done me in."

Douglas sank into the chair next to the bed. "I can't believe this. That bullet did more damage than you realize. You've gone soft on me. You of all people."

In spite of the ache in every part of his body, Braddock laughed. "It's really not that bad."

Douglas leaned back in the chair. "Is she pregnant? Is that what all this marriage talk is about?"

"Nah, I'm just in love."

Douglas made a wounded sound. "Better you than me, pal. Better you than me. I'd rather take a shot to the chest."

Braddock pressed a hand against the bandages binding his wound. "A shot to the chest hurts worse. Believe me."

Lorelei flinched when a firm knock sounded at the door. She jumped from the chair she had dragged next to the washstand and paced a semicircle around the bed, looking for a better place to hide the rest of the gold. The hotel's plastered walls collapsed to the stark perimeters of a jail cell.

She glanced at the pitcher. The gold seemed to radiate through the porcelain like the guilt shining off her skin. She feared everyone would know by one simple glance.

"Lorelei? Are you all right?" called Douglas. The slight panic in his voice forced her to forget that the marshal was the last person in the world she wanted to see.

She rushed to the door and flung it open. "Is Christopher all right?"

"He's fine. He's up and talking." Douglas paused. "And yelling."

Lorelei gripped the knob as Douglas studied her in a way he hadn't before. She prayed she didn't visibly tremble. No one would believe she wasn't in cahoots with Corey, especially since she was hiding a king's ransom in gold. She would be condemned by association, only this time she couldn't say she didn't deserve it. If not for her blind loyalty to her brother, Christopher wouldn't have been hurt.

She narrowed the gap between the door and frame to merely a sliver. "Thank you for word of Christopher." She lowered her voice. "But Corey is sleeping."

He placed his hand on the door, stopping her from closing it completely.

"Don't you want to see him?" he asked, confusion, not suspicion, in his voice.

She'd thought of little else since she'd been driven away

from his bedside. After finding out about the gold and Corey, she couldn't help but feel Douglas was justified in his treatment of her.

"I don't want to upset him."

Douglas increased his pressure on the other side of the door. "He's already upset. If I don't come back with you, he'll take my head off."

She slipped out into the hall and managed to close the door behind her. She had to face Christopher sometime. She didn't have any illusions that he would be able to forgive her for all this. Why should he? She could hardly forgive herself.

"Let's go."

They silently walked out of the hotel and onto the baked-dirt street. Douglas's sideways glances brought a film to her palms. He suspected. He'd probably be quick to officially arrest her once he learned the truth. And the truth was, she was acting as Corey's accomplice. Though she'd turned him in to Wade, she didn't want Douglas to know of her brother's escape. Douglas would track down Corey and the gold, not caring whether he returned his prisoner dead or alive.

"You don't look very happy," he finally said.

She shrugged. "Can you blame me? You've treated me like a criminal, and I haven't forgotten I might be facing serious charges."

Douglas stopped, then stepped in front of her, blocking her path. "Hold on a second. I didn't say for sure. I just said I needed to sort things out." He took off his hat and brushed back his thick hair before replacing it. "I can't help my suspicions. I see only the worst in people. Forgive me?"

His unexpected request stirred the cauldron of guilt roiling in her stomach. She sidestepped him and continued down the street, fearing he'd read her expression too clearly.

"There's nothing to forgive."

He fell in beside her. "Make sure you tell Braddock that."

She couldn't help but grin at the tone of his voice. "You're afraid of him, aren't you?"

"He already told me that if I did anything to upset you,

he's going to beat me. I know him. He'll keep his promise the minute he's on his feet."

She followed Douglas in a daze. His words should thrill her, but Christopher didn't know the truth yet. Would he hate her once he learned that her blind loyalty to her brother had almost cost him his life?

Douglas tightened his grip on her arm. "Lorelei, you'd better snap out of it before I take you to Braddock, or I'm going to get that beating."

She nodded but would have tripped on the clapboard house's first planked step if Douglas hadn't been there to guide her.

The marshal pushed open the door and practically shoved her through the front room and into the one bedroom.

Christopher sat up in bed. His eyes were red-rimmed and puffy. His hair stood at awkward angles and his pallor rivaled the white walls, but he was alive and awake. To Lorelei, he'd never looked better.

"Christopher." She forgot all the things that would keep them apart and rushed to his side. His recovery was miracle enough. If she had to choose, she'd gladly choose Christopher's health over her happily-ever-after.

Ignoring the chair, she nestled beside him on the bed. She gently placed her hands on his bare shoulders and leaned forward to kiss his cheek.

His arm snaked around her waist, pulling her forward as he turned his head to capture her mouth.

She braced her hands on his shoulders to keep him from crushing her against him. "Your wound."

"Yes, I was about to mention that," said Dr. Gavin from behind her.

She glanced over her shoulder, then delicately tried to free herself from Christopher's hold, but he restrained her with surprising strength.

"The doctor was just leaving."

Dr. Gavin buckled his leather medical bag. "I'll leave it to Miss Sullivan to remind our patient that he hasn't yet fully recovered. Mr. Braddock seems to think he's stubbed his toe rather than survived a wound that would have been fatal to another man."

She angled herself so that she sat next to Christopher instead of sprawled on top of him.

"I'll make sure to remind him if he forgets again, Dr. Gavin."

As soon as the doctor left the room, Christopher hauled her back into his arms. "Are you all right?"

She tried to resist, but he was stronger than she thought. Fighting him might cause more strain than letting him have his way. Avoiding his wound as best she could, she pressed against him as he dipped his head for a deep, wet kiss. The pain of almost losing him burst in her chest like a flowering ball of fire, and tears unexpectedly stung her eyes.

He finally broke the kiss but held her face in his hands. "I've been worried. Tell me what happened. Are you all right?"

She gripped his wrists. "I'm fine. You're the one who was almost killed."

The tightness around his eyes eased, and he grinned. "I was, wasn't I? I'm just like everybody else."

His rude reminder forced her to pull out of his grasp. What she had to tell him would be hard enough without pretending they could actually have a future together. "You're not like everybody else, and you wouldn't have been hurt if it weren't for me."

"Did Douglas tell you that?" The fierce man who had first come to her door, pistol in hand, returned in his scowl.

"He didn't have to. It's true." She clasped his hand to keep from touching his face.

She swallowed the thick emotion that coated her throat. Letting him go was the right thing, no matter how much it hurt. His earnest hazel eyes showed he'd finally defeated his ghosts. He'd seen Jay's happiness, and even learned to love again.

Unfortunately, her past continued to haunt her. In fact, one of her demons was on his way back to Arriba in handcuffs. She would be involved in the trial of the year rather than the wedding of the year. Christopher was healed. Now that he could, he'd find another woman to love.

When she returned her gaze to his, he studied her as if he had read each of her desperate thoughts. "You're going to still marry me. I don't care what Douglas said—"

"Not Douglas." She dropped her eyes, unable to look at him while she told him why they couldn't marry. "My brother."

"Lorelei, no." The note of desperation in his voice jolted her gaze back to his. He'd laid his head back on the pillow as if he were too weak to fight any longer. "Don't let him do this to us."

She couldn't stand the defeated pull on his eyes. He was hurting. The fact that he really did love her gave her no joy.

"He had the gold, Christopher. He had it the whole time. He had it when you came to the ranch the first time, when we were at Jay's, even when he sent you to Specter Canyon."

He rubbed his forehead. "Damn. I didn't want you to find out."

"You knew?" She blinked back her shock. "How long have you known?"

"Since the first time I rode to Specter Canyon."

Lorelei studied his serious gaze. "I don't understand. Why didn't you tell me?"

He clasped her right hand in his. The contrasts in their skin and size seemed to hold his attention. "I . . ."

His uncharacteristic hesitation caused dread to surge into her throat. She placed her other hand on top of his, stopping the glide of his thumb across her skin. "Please, Christopher. Just tell me."

"I was afraid you'd get yourself in more trouble trying to protect him. I didn't want to lose you."

She couldn't continue to meet his sincere gaze because she couldn't deny his words. "And in trying to protect Corey, I almost got you killed."

She pulled away from his grasp and stood on shaky legs. In all the bad things that happened in her life, there had been one common theme: Lorelei Sullivan. She was the cause of all her own troubles. She had believed Corey's elaborate fabrications because she wanted to.

Her gaze fell to the hollows under Christopher's cheeks, then slid to the white bandage wound around his chest. His tanned skin had started to fade and his collarbone stood out in strong relief. He'd lost weight, but he'd recover. Especially if he no longer had her to drag him down.

"Lorelei, if you don't want me to get out of this bed, you'd better sit down and talk to me."

She fumbled for a chair and forced herself to sink into it. "I can't marry you, Christopher. There's going to be a trial, and Corey—"

"We're going to marry."

She shook her head. "I told Wade Langston about the gold and Corey."

Even under his week-old beard, his jaw perceptively tightened, a sure sign he was furious. "Why did you do a fool thing like that?"

She stiffened. Expecting his censure didn't ease its sting. "I'm tired of hiding from the truth. I'm ready to accept the consequences, whatever they may be."

He raked his hand through his sleep-spiked hair. "I could have kept him out of trouble. With Corey's help I could pretend to track down the gold and everyone would have been happy."

"Except Corey. And Wade Langston. I traded your confession for the information about Corey."

Christopher stared at her blankly, his eyebrows drawn in confusion. After a moment he laid back against the pillows, apparently waylaid by the return of his memory. "I forgot about that. I had to do something to get Langston to look for you."

A grin tugged at her tight features, though how she could smile she didn't know. "I imagined I was the reason you confessed to something you didn't do."

"Is that why you sold your brother out—to save me?"

"I wish you wouldn't put it like that, but yes. I love you. I couldn't bear for you to be hurt any more by my mistakes."

He grinned, and his teeth shone a healthy white against his dark beard, challenging the shadow of illness that clung to his skin. "I always thought you'd choose him over me."

"Well, I didn't. And now I have to live with it."

His obvious pleasure at her devotion cast a flicker of hope in her tight chest, but remembering what that happiness would cost her brother quickly snuffed it out.

He covered her hand with his. "We'll live with it."

"There will be a trial. Even though I turned him in, I'm going to see Corey through it."

"We'll see it through together." He squeezed her hand. "I get it now, Lorelei. I understand how Jay could pick himself up again and why he works himself to death on a patch of desert. Well, maybe I don't exactly understand that, but I do know what makes all the sweat and tears worth it. Marry me. I can face anything if I know it's with you."

She couldn't stop the tears that formed in her eyes. "I do love you. But what about Corey?"

Christopher sighed. "He's going to jail, sweetheart."

She looked into Christopher's sincere face and saw what could be her future. A future that still existed no matter how much life had thrown their way. It was as eternal as the sun, as reliable as the moon. She was still breathing. She was still able to love and take love's hand when it reached out to her. For once she let fortune smile on her and let the pieces fall where they might. She squared her shoulders.

"All right."

Epilogue

The carriage's roll to a stop reignited Lorelei's doubts. Though she'd written Corey daily, she hadn't received word from her brother since his arrival at New Mexico's territorial prison.

Christopher tightened his grip on her hand. "We're here."

Her jerky nod tugged at the pins securing her new hat. The silk concoction had been dyed to match her mother's gown, but the excessive use of Spanish lace seemed inappropriate when she tried them on together. Her new expensive hat and her mother's old dress seemed to clash despite her efforts to piece them together. Even with alterations, Lorelei's mother's wedding gown didn't fit as well as she'd hoped. Part of her felt like she didn't have a right to wear the heirloom. After all, she'd betrayed her family. Would her mother have forgiven her? Would Corey?

Christopher lifted the veil and leaned forward to press a hard kiss on her mouth. "You'd better not have changed your mind about becoming my wife. Again."

She touched his face. "I haven't changed my mind. I just hope Corey isn't upset with our surprise."

"You know how I feel about your brother, Lorelei, but I do believe he wants your happiness."

She stared down at her gloved hands. "I wonder if he's forgiven me."

Christopher stepped out of the carriage, only slightly favoring his good side, and held his hand up to her. "One way to find out."

The prison, which looked more like a fort, immediately captured her attention. Logs honed into wicked-looking spikes stabbed the clear blue sky. Not even the tip of a chimney could be viewed past the sturdy fence.

Christopher placed a comforting hand on the small of her back and nudged Lorelei forward. "I'm told it's not as bad as it looks."

She tried to shake off the guilt that pressed on her shoulders and made it even more painful to walk in her new high-heeled slippers. Thanks to both Douglas's and Christopher's testimony, Corey had escaped hanging, she reminded herself.

The big wooden gates slowly creaked open at the force of two burly guards, and Christopher guided her into the prison's stark interior. Not even cactus dotted the yard. The compound consisted of dirt, tall fences, and a long adobe structure with tiny slits high in the walls that served as windows.

She remembered the look on Corey's face when his sentence was read. His relief at escaping death was short-lived. Ten years must have seemed like a lifetime when he came face-to-face with his new home. Even the fact that five years could be sliced off his sentence for good behavior was probably little comfort.

She turned to escape the fence's oppressive arms, but Christopher blocked her exit.

"You're not going anywhere."

"This is a mistake."

Something over her shoulder caught Christopher's attention. He lifted his hand and waved. "How you doing, Wade? Come over here and assure Lorelei you're not keeping her brother in a dungeon."

Wade Langston strode toward them wearing a dark blue uniform. When he reached them, he nodded to her first. "Miss Lorelei." He turned to Christopher and grasped his hand in a firm shake. "Chris."

Lorelei's gaze darted between the two men. She wondered when they'd switched to using each other's first names, and, even more surprising, with such warm regard in their voices. Of course, she hadn't seen Wade since the fateful day she'd traded her brother for Christopher's confession, except on the witness stand. She'd heard Wade called a hero for recovering the gold. Still, she owed him a debt of thanks for all the things he didn't do or say.

"I never had the chance to thank you, Miss Lorelei."

She studied the trampled dirt. "Please don't. I can't say I'm proud of turning my brother in."

"No, not for that. For having faith in me."

She gazed up at him. "Well, thank you for bringing Corey back in one piece."

He grinned. "Glad to do it. Your brother is one fine horseman."

Lorelei couldn't return his smile. "Yes, he was. If he'd just stuck with what he knew, he'd never have gotten in so much trouble."

Christopher wrapped his arm around her shoulders. "We'd better show her, Wade. A bride isn't supposed to look so miserable on her wedding day."

"I think we can put a smile on that face. This way."

Instead of heading toward the iron bars that fronted the adobe's entrance, he skirted the side of the building. Christopher gently shoved her along her as they followed Wade's lead.

"It's going to be all right. I wouldn't have brought you here if I thought your brother was suffering."

Wade led them past a large stable. She could hear the whinnies of a barnful of horses. Before she could ask why the prison had so many, the corral came into view. There in the middle, working with a skittish horse, was Corey.

As they came closer, she could see her brother held a

coiled rope in his hand. Horse and man were on a stand-off. Corey remained completely still while the horse bobbed his head up and down. Slowly Corey stretched out his hand and the horse sniffed him, then turned and ran to the other side of the corral.

"You'll have that one saddled by tomorrow," yelled Wade.

Corey turned, a huge grin splitting his face. "The end of the day, I'd wager."

When Lorelei caught her brother's eye, the grin slid away.

"You have other plans today, Mr. Sullivan," said Wade.

Corey warily held Lorelei's gaze, but didn't make any attempt to approach them. When she glanced to Christopher for support, she found both he and Wade had discreetly abandoned her.

Before the trial she'd been under strict orders not to discuss anything pertaining to the case with Corey. She couldn't even ask him why he took off, nor explain why she'd turned him in. But she'd told him that she loved him, and his silent response broke her heart. After the trial he'd been immediately shipped off to the territorial prison. She'd have come sooner, but Christopher had talked her into giving him a couple of weeks to adjust. He'd convinced her that her presence might only make things worse.

She gripped the corral railing that restrained her from going to her brother. He had to come to her.

He slapped the end of the rope he held against his leg, staring at the dust. Finally he strode toward her. He stopped short of the fence, seeming to use the space as a barrier.

"Why are you here?" He kept his attention on the rope he twirled between his fingers.

"I wanted to see if you were all right and . . ." She let her words drift off. What would she do if he refused her request? Christopher had been so patient. Though being married in a prison was probably not his first choice, he didn't raise the slightest protest when she'd suggested it.

Corey glanced at her from the corners of his eyes. "You don't hate me?"

"No. You should hate me. I'm the one who turned you in."

He shrugged. "I figured you would. I just was hoping I'd be in Mexico by then. I don't suppose they let you keep any of the gold I left you."

"I gave it all back. You must have been pretty upset with me when Wade caught up with you."

"No. I didn't really want to go to Mexico."

Corey fashioned the rope into a lasso and danced it around his feet. He let the swirling loop go limp, then dropped it to the ground. "I couldn't stand not ever seeing you again, even if you probably wished I weren't your brother."

She pressed herself against the fence. "I never wished that. I hated turning you in but I had to. Wade had Christopher's confession, and besides, someone would have caught up with you eventually. I didn't want you to get hurt."

He took a step toward her. "You don't have to explain yourself to me. You were just doing what was right."

He dropped his gaze again. "I didn't want to run." He shrugged. "I guess I thought you'd be better off without me. Figured Braddock would tell you how rotten I was once he woke up."

"You're my brother. I love you. I don't like some of the things you've done, Corey O'Sullivan, but you're family. And you know how the Sullivans feel about family."

He stared past her. "Braddock's your family now."

She stuck her hand over the fence and reached out to him. "No, not without your blessing."

He didn't take her hand. "After all I've done, after all I've put you both through, why would you care what I think?"

Lorelei kept her hand extended to him. "Because you're my brother. You know what I've been through. We survived it together. You share my memories and keep them alive."

He grabbed her hand. "I'm sorry for being so much trouble."

Lorelei pulled him into a hug, heedless of the fence. "I wouldn't know you if you weren't."

He eased out of her grasp, a mischievous grin on his face.

"I haven't given my approval yet. If I said no, would you not marry Braddock?"

She matched his grin with a wicked one of her own. "Let's say I'd let him change your mind."

"Does all this hugging mean we're going to have a wedding today?" Christopher strode up behind her.

Corey glared at him, but his grin took away the bite. "You bet your ass, Braddock. And I say it's overdue as it is."

Christopher raised his hands in surrender. "You won't get any argument from me."

"So you won't mind giving me away?" asked Lorelei.

Corey nodded, the conspicuous jump of his Adam's apple revealing what he didn't say in words.

Christopher studied the pony dancing around the far perimeter of the corral. "I'm impressed with the way you handled that horse. Wade says you're getting a reputation in the short time you've been here."

Corey seemed eager to shift to a less emotional subject. "The cavalry needs as many horses as I can tame. There's a whole mess of wild ones in a corral on the other side. If Wade hadn't come up with this idea, I'd be working on the railroad with the other prisoners."

"We're keeping up your ranch for you. When you get out, you'll be able to raise horses just like you planned," said Lorelei.

Braddock wrapped his arm around her shoulder and gathered her against his side. "I hate to tell you, but she's planted rosebushes and I'm afraid they're actually going to bloom."

Corey smiled. "I like roses. You two don't have to worry. I'm going to be as straight as an arrow when I get out."

Braddock slapped Corey on the shoulder and squeezed. "We're not worried about that, brother. I bought a spread near yours, and I'll be keeping a watchful eye."

Corey shrugged off Braddock's grip but didn't lose his smile. "Doing what? Jay said you didn't know one end of a plow from another. He said you tried to help him when he first moved west and about killed yourself and a good plowhorse."

"True. That's why I'm going to stick with cattle and hire a foreman. That'll give me time to get involved in the territorial government. Think I'd make a good sheriff, little brother?"

"I think I liked it better when you called me 'kid.' "

Lorelei glanced between the two men, unable to contain the happiness that swelled in her heart and spilled over to dampen her eyes. Working with horses had always been Corey's dream; hers had been having a family again. Of course, neither of them ever expected their dreams to come true like this. She studied the grinning face of her future husband and guessed that dreams had a mind of their own.

SWEET RELEASE
PAMELA CLARE

Though Cassie hates the slave trade, her Virginia plantation demands the labor, and she knows this fevered convict will surely die if she leaves him. But Cassie realizes Cole Braden is far more dangerous than his papers have indicated—for he can steal her breath with a glance or lay siege to her senses with a touch.

Abducted and beaten, Cole goes from master of an English shipbuilding empire to years of indentured servitude in the American colonies. And while he longs to ravish the beauty who owns him, his one hope of earning her love—and his freedom—is to prove his true identity. Only then can he turn the tables and attain his sweet release.

BROKEN BLOSSOMS
PAM CROOKS

Trig Mathison knows the danger of opium's spell—his brother died from it. And though he vows vengeance, the undercover agent wonders if a forbidden yearning will destroy him as well. The beauty he pursues—one whose very blood marks her his enemy—arouses in Trig not a desire for justice, but a hunger for love.

The flower of her innocence crushed by her father's lies, Carleigh Chandler is on the run. Chased by a handsome bounty hunter, she succumbs to temptation in his arms. But will their passion be strong enough to untangle the web of deceit that ensnares them?
